"A rising star on the horror scene!"
—FearNet.com

"Joe McKinney's first zombie novel, *Dead City,* is one of my all-time favorites of the genre. It hits the ground running and never lets up. *Apocalypse of the Dead* proves that Joe is far from being a one-hit wonder. This book is meatier, juicier, bloodier, and even more compelling . . . and it also NEVER LETS UP. From page one to the stunning climax this book is a rollercoaster ride of action, violence, and zombie horror. McKinney understands the genre and relies on its strongest conventions while at the same time adding new twists that make this book a thoroughly enjoyable read. That's a defining characteristic of Joe's work: the pace is so relentless that you feel like it's you, and not the character, who is running for his life from a horde of flesh-hungry monsters.

"And, even with that lightning-fast pace, McKinney manages to flesh the characters out so that they're real, and infuse the book with compassion and heartbreak over this vast, shared catastrophe.

"This book earns its place in any serious library of living-dead fiction."
—Jonathan Maberry, *New York Times* best-selling author of *The Wolfman*

"*Dead City* is much more than just another zombie novel. It's got heart and humanity—a merciless, fast-paced, and genuinely scary read that will leave you absolutely breathless. Highly recommended!"
—Brian Keene

PLAGUE
of the
UNDEAD

JOE
McKINNEY

PINNACLE BOOKS
Kensington Publishing Corp.
www.kensingtonbooks.com

PINNACLE BOOKS are published by

Kensington Publishing Corp.
119 West 40th Street
New York, NY 10018

All Kensington titles, imprints, and distributed lines are available at special quantity discounts for bulk purchases for sales promotions, premiums, fund-raising, educational, or institutional use. Special book excerpts or customized printings can also be created to fit specific needs. For details, write or phone the office of the Kensington special sales manager: Kensington Publishing Corp., 119 West 40th Street, New York, NY 10018, attn: Special Sales Department; phone 1-800-221-2647.

This book is a work of fiction. Names, characters, businesses, organizations, places, events, and incidents either are the product of the author's imagination or are used fictitiously. Any resemblance to actual persons, living or dead, events, or locales is entirely coincidental.

ISBN-13: 978-0-7860-3397-3
ISBN-10: 0-7860-3397-5

First printing: October 2014

10 9 8 7 6 5 4 3 2 1

Printed in the United States of America

First electronic edition: October 2014

ISBN-13: 978-0-7860-3398-0
ISBN-10: 0-7860-3398-3

CONTENTS

PUBLISHER'S NOTE

ACKNOWLEDGMENTS

A lot goes into taking a book from a nascent idea to a finished product in the reader's hands. The famous writer's adage of put butt in chair is certainly a major part of that process, if not the most important part. Along the way, though, there are countless encounters, countless accidental readings, conversations, observations, whatever, that eventually shape the final form of a book. The volume you hold in your hand is no different. It is the result of many hours of butt in chair, but also many more accidental moments of inspiration than I can possibly remember or acknowledge here.

But I'll try.

These are just a few of the people who helped me put this book in your hand. Ethan Humble, Steven Grover, Anastacio Hernandez, Steve Almanza, and Genaro Villarreal for minding the store at West Patrol so I could take the time off to write this book. And a special second thank-you to Ethan Humble and Steve Almanza, for sharing their gun expertise. What I got right here I owe to them. What I messed up, well, that's on me. I owe a huge debt of gratitude to the members of Candlelight—David Liss, Robert Jackson Bennett, Hank Schwaeble, and Rhodi Hawk—for their wisdom as story doctors and for the hours of great conversation. I'm also fortunate enough to be a member of Drafthouse, along with my very good friends Sanford Allen, Beckie Ugolini, Thomas McAuley, and Brian Allen, fantastic writers all who shared their time and storytelling skills again and again. I also want to thank my editor at Kensington, Gary Goldstein, for his sage counsel in my hour of need, and my agent, Jim Donovan, for going the extra mile on my behalf. And, most of all, thanks and gratitude and love go out to my wife, Kristina, and our two girls, Elena and Brenna, for putting up with the epic amount of crazy that went into writing this book.

PLAGUE
of the
UNDEAD

While walking in the tall grass that has sprung up around the city of Troy, Balso Snell came upon the famous wooden horse of the Greeks. A poet, he remembered Homer's ancient song and decided to find a way in.

—Nathanael West,
The Dream Life of Balso Snell

part one
KILLING JERRY

1

As Jacob Carlton crossed Main Plaza, his boots crunching on the frozen grass, he was thankful the woman had finally stopped screaming.

For the last two weeks, ever since her husband's sentence was handed down, Amanda Grieder had been living in the street outside her husband's cell, crying for someone to come to their senses and show a little mercy. It was February, and it was cold, and most mornings found her hair and clothes crusted with ice. She'd stopped eating, stopped taking care of herself. She couldn't be consoled. Her friends tried to get her to go home, even tried to pick her up and carry her home at one point, but she would have none of it. After that, whenever they tried to touch her, she fought them, and then the screaming and wailing would start up again and it would carry through the whole town like a sickness, laying everybody low. There was talk that the law should make her leave, do something with her, for her own good, for everybody's peace of mind, but so far Sheriff Taylor had held off doing that. Jacob didn't understand the old man's reticence, but he knew Sheriff Taylor had his reasons. He always did.

Jacob braced himself as he turned the corner onto Jackson Avenue, where Amanda had set up her temporary residence. He said a silent prayer that he wouldn't have to deal with her again today. Every morning he had to pass the little makeshift shelter where she kept watch. He'd try to walk by unobserved, but then she'd see him, and no matter how cold or hungry she was, no matter how shredded her voice was from howling all the day before, she always seemed to have a little extra just for him. She'd get up from the sidewalk and rush at him, screaming that he'd made a mistake, that he was wrong about her husband. As sick as her accusations made him feel, he knew he wasn't up for enduring that gauntlet today. Not today, not the day of the execution. He just didn't have it in him.

But to his surprise—and this shamed him, for he was relieved—she wasn't there. The blankets and baskets of food well-meaning folks had brought for her were still there, but she was gone.

He let out the breath he'd been holding and tried to collect himself, but his nerves were a jangled mess. His skin felt hot one moment, cold the next. His stomach was twisting into knots. He had the jitters, like he'd drunk too much coffee on an empty stomach. For two weeks he'd felt this way, and he suspected it was making him sick. Not only heartsick, but actually physically ill.

But sick as he was, he had to keep moving. If he stopped, he'd lose his nerve. Looking into himself, he knew that. The way things were piling up inside his head, all it would take would be to stop moving. If that happened, he'd likely as not turn tail, run home, and hide his head in the toilet as he vomited away his jitters. If, indeed, that was even possible. So he ducked his head against the cold February wind and shoved his hands into his pockets and slipped into the constabulary office like a villain.

It was early, and Steve Harrigan was the only one in the

office. He was standing over by the filing cabinets, and when he heard the door and saw Jacob standing there he looked genuinely surprised. "Wasn't expecting to see you this morning," he said.

Jacob nodded. "Where's the bike checkout log?"

Harrigan studied the younger man for a long moment. He closed a metal drawer and it shoved in place with a heavy clank. Harrigan gestured toward the back wall with his chin. "Should be over there on the shelf, behind Harris's desk."

Jacob crossed to the shelf the older deputy had indicated. The bike log was a red, hardbound memo book that was almost as old as Jacob was. There were entries going back as far as his school days, when he was taking his first lessons in the Code he now enforced. He turned to the back and quickly scribbled his name on the next open line.

"Gonna try to clear your head?" Harrigan said.

"I was thinking of going for a ride, yeah. I thought I'd go check on the new construction over on the east wall."

"Still draining the wetlands, from what I hear."

Jacob nodded. "Where's Taylor? I noticed Amanda's gone."

"He's with her in his office."

"Oh, God, really?"

"Yeah. They've been in there for about an hour now. She finally stopped crying just a bit ago. Poor woman, she's coming apart at the seams."

"Is he gonna let her be in the Square today?"

"Can't tell her no. It's her right under the Code."

Jacob could tell the older deputy was sizing him up. Harrigan was a real cop, trained in the old ways, from before the world fell apart. Not like Jacob, who had sort of stumbled into the role of chief deputy, a kid trying to figure it out as he went along.

Harrigan was an affable, lanky man with pale skin and thin gray hair and liver spots on his face, always quick with a smile. But of course that smile was gone now. He put the file he was holding on his desk, lit a candle, and shook the match out. "We're almost out of these," he said, and dropped it into an ashtray. "The ones they make over at the school don't hardly ever work. We go through 'em so fast."

"I'll tell Frank Hartwell to get some more next time he's outside the walls."

Jacob put the ledger back on the shelf and turned to leave. He was almost to the door when Harrigan called after him. "Hey, Jacob, a moment."

Jacob stopped in the doorway, looking back at him over his shoulder. "I'm not much in the mood for a speech, Steve, if you don't mind."

"No, I bet not. But I know this is tearing you up inside. You wouldn't be half the man I know you to be if it wasn't."

"I don't feel like a good man right now, Steve. All I want to do is go stick my head in a hole and hide."

"Same thing Arthur went through when he had to do it."

"And how did Arthur handle it?"

"Spent the whole morning throwing up."

Jacob nodded. "Sounds about right."

"Nobody said it was easy."

"Easy," Jacob said, and laughed in disgust.

"This is the right thing to do, Jacob. I believe that. I believe in the Code. It's us against the world. We have to trust each other. Any man who steals from his brother breaks that trust. And that man has to die."

"That's the same thing you told me when you were teaching my Code class back in school. You need to get a new line."

"It's not a line, Jacob. It's what I believe in. It's what everybody in this town believes in. The Code is hard sometimes, but it's what keeps us alive. Think on that while you're riding."

The older deputy didn't cow Jacob, not these days. In his youth, all the First Generation had seemed hard and determined, like iron, but he was thirty-five-years old, and he'd faced most of them in council meetings and in the living rooms of their homes when things went wrong. So Harrigan's words didn't rattle him. They only made him tired. He'd heard the same thing every day of his life since the time he was old enough to understand what was being said to him. And he'd always thought he believed it. But now that he was going to have to kill a man he'd known since they were kids, belief came a lot harder.

"I'll be riding the east wall," he said.

2

Jacob got one of the bicycles from the shed and headed east, into the sunrise.

During the summer, Arbella felt crowded. Nearly ten thousand people, all of them crammed together in a town that had once housed barely four thousand before the First Days. Many of the First Generation families still had their own residences, but elsewhere in the town, as many as three families shared a single three-bedroom home. To meet the rising demand for food, nearly every lawn had long since been turned into a vegetable garden. The stoplights had come down because there weren't any more cars to stop, just young children with sticks and dogs by their sides driving herds of goats or sheep into the markets in the center of town. The Pecan Valley Golf Course out on Southton Road was now a dairy farm. The peach orchards out on Interstate 55 were now home to thousands of pigs and turkeys and chickens. And even the wetlands that stood between the town and the river to the east were being turned into cropland. But with the coldest days of winter upon the town, there wasn't much going on. Most of the shops were still dark. Jacob saw lamplight in a few windows, but only a few. Save for the horse-drawn milk wagons coming up from the dairy, he had the town of Arbella pretty much to himself. Just his thoughts for company.

Steve Harrigan was right of course about the Code. Jacob hated how simply he'd put it, because it made the Code sound like a platitude, but for all that, he *was* right. The Code really did keep them alive. It was their moral core, the center around which their entire society orbited. Arbella was an island in a world that quite literally wanted to devour them, and the Code they lived by helped them to not only survive, but thrive in that world. They worked for each other, giving freely of their skills and their goods, so that all had a chance to survive. You had to trust your fellow citizens. You had to believe that, together, you were greater than the dangers of the wasteland. You had to believe it, because anything else meant surrendering to the fear and pain and death that lurked beyond the walls. Jacob's thoughts turned to Jerry Grieder, Amanda's husband. It wasn't just some stolen jewelry, he told himself, thinking of Amanda's pleas for mercy for her husband. Jerry hadn't just stolen some young girl's beloved locket, but rather the trust from the entire community. Jerry Grieder wasn't just guilty of burglary; he was guilty of contaminating everything the people of Arbella stood for, what kept them alive.

Jacob pedaled faster, the biting wind on his face the only thing that kept his tears from bursting loose. He was almost grateful for the sting on his cheeks. It felt good to hurt, because it was the only thing he could think of to convince him that he was still human. He'd known Jerry Grieder since they were children. How in the hell was he going to put a gun to the man's head and pull the trigger? He just didn't think he was going to be strong enough.

Gradually he tired of the hard pedaling and coasted, letting the bike carry him along. His face and knuckles were raw with the cold, but he didn't care. He kept going, watching the sleeping buildings, thinking about his home.

Thirty years ago, before the First Days, Arbella was a little town nestled comfortably on a bend of the Mississippi River known as New Madrid, Missouri. Sheriff Taylor led the First Generation, a little over a thousand of them, out of Arkansas and into Missouri, fighting and dodging the undead the whole way. They happened upon New Madrid and found the place deserted. They put makeshift barricades up around the town, and over the course of four months fought the zombie hordes to a standstill.

In honor of their victory they renamed the town Arbella, after the flagship of Governor John Winthrop's Puritan fleet that had settled the Commonwealth of Massachusetts. It was from the deck of that ship that Winthrop delivered his famous "City Upon a Hill" sermon, and it was in that same spirit of shining a light on a cold and hostile world that Jacob's mother, and the other members of the First Generation, turned an abandoned hamlet into a home.

The barricades became sturdy twenty-foot walls of wood and razor wire, wide enough for the lookouts and the sharpshooters who continued to guard against the zombies that sometimes wandered too close. The empty churches were turned into grain silos. Dairy cows took over the golf course. Babies were born. Lives were lived. And very quickly, Arbella turned into a self-sufficient island of peace in the wasteland.

Jacob was three when that happened.

He didn't remember the time before the First Days. All his life had been spent in and around Arbella, watching it grow, watching it prosper, watching it swell at the seams from the bounty the town made. The original thousand members of the First Generation had since had children, and taken in those healthy few who now and then happened upon the town and were willing to work hard. In the blink of an eye one thousand became ten thousand, and more were being born every day.

Jacob watched daylight spread over the rooftops of the town and over the gardens. It dappled the metal roofs of the water purification stations like molten copper, and in that moment, Jacob swelled with pride for his town. True, he wasn't there at the fight that ended the First Days, but he'd helped to build Arbella. He'd served it as a citizen, and as a member of the salvage teams sent out into the wasteland to gather the things the town needed, and most recently, as the chief deputy of its constabulary. He was thirty-five years old, and in line to take over the leadership of Arbella when the First Generation was ready to pass that baton along. In that moment, proud of his town and of himself, he found it easy to believe in the Code again. Its values were his values, and the town it protected his home.

But the quiet didn't last. A raid siren filled the cold morning air, sudden and shrill.

Jacob was on Oberlin Street at the time, near the intersection with Yale, the east wall still about three blocks away. Within seconds of the siren going off the streets filled with people. Men and women came down from their porches to the edges of their gardens and looked at one another. The raid sirens were hardly used anymore, for there hadn't been a sizeable zombie horde at the gates for more than twelve years.

"Jacob, what is it?"

He turned and saw Linda Moffett standing by her front gate, a dishtowel in her hands.

He was about to tell her he had no idea, when the hue and cry came down the street: "It's Jim Laymon up on the wall!"

A woman ran into her yard. "Somebody make him kill that noise!"

"He's lost his mind," somebody yelled back at her.

Jacob stood up on his pedals and rode hard for the wall. A crowd had gathered in the street beneath Jim's lookout station, and it was getting bigger by the moment. Some were yelling questions at him, others frantically trying to get him to cut out the noise. Nobody seemed to be getting his attention.

Jacob saw a ladder leaning against the fence and scaled it.

Jim was the very model of the Code. At eighty-four, he was one of the oldest citizens of Arbella, yet he manned a lookout post on the wall three days a week. *Everybody works; everybody pulls their weight.* That was the essence of the Code, and Jim lived it.

He had set up a comfortable workstation for his day. There were jugs of water at his side, a basket of food a little ways off. His binoculars hung from a nail on the railing. There was even an umbrella, for later in the day, when the sun came out. He had heavy blankets over his shoulders and across his lap, though now the blankets were coming off as he leaned over the raid siren, working the hand crank with everything he had.

Jacob ran over to him and put a hand on the crank to stop it.

"What are you doing, Jim? Stop it."

"Look!" he shouted toward the river.

It was a few hundred yards away. Jacob could smell the warm, sweet decay of its muddy banks and the upturned earth where the dredging teams were draining the wetlands just outside the wall. The clatter coming up from their pumper trucks was tremendous. But he didn't see what Jim wanted him to see.

Not at first.

And then he saw movement in the darkness down by the river.

Jacob squinted, straining his eyes to see into the shadows. "Oh, no," he said.

From below, someone shouted, "Hey, Jacob, what's wrong?"

He leaned over the railing and yelled at the crowd, "Zombies on the wall! I need sharpshooters up here now!"

Nobody moved; nobody spoke. They just stared up at him in shock.

"Sharpshooters!" he said. "Send up the alarm."

It took a moment, but once a few members of the crowd scurried off, the others followed suit. Jacob turned back to Laymon.

"Where's their sentry? Why aren't you using your mirror to signal them?"

"They ain't got one."

"What?"

"They ain't got a sentry."

"What do you mean? Where is he?"

"They ain't got one. Just workers."

That was a huge violation of protocol. Nobody but salvage teams ever went beyond the wall without sentries to cover their backs. That was never supposed to happen.

"I need to get down there," Jacob said.

He pulled the ladder over the wall and hurried down it. When he was on the ground again, he pushed the ladder into the grass and ran for the workers.

The noise from their pumper trucks was deafening, and all the men wore ear protection. It was no wonder they'd failed to hear the warning siren. Their foreman was leaning over a table, looking at a map scroll. Jacob grabbed him by the shoulder and spun him around.

"Shut off those machines!" he yelled. "Shut 'em down!"

He heard Jacob, Jacob knew he did, but he didn't understand. Jacob pointed at the machines and drew his hand across his throat. "Shut 'em down! Right now!"

He still didn't understand.

Jacob grabbed him by the shoulder, shoved him toward the front of one of the trucks, and pointed toward the river.

A herd of zombies was coming up from the water's edge pulling themselves along through thick mud.

"Shut off your machines!" Jacob yelled.

Now he understood. The foreman jumped into the cab of the nearest pumper truck and hit the kill switch. As the pumps wound down, workers looked up from their hoses in confusion. The foreman made frantic X's with his arms across his chest, and within seconds, the other three trucks went silent.

Men turned from their work, pulling the earplugs from their ears.

"Go to the wall," Jacob shouted. He pulled his pistol "Go, I'll cover you."

They seemed as confused as the foreman had been until Jacob leveled his weapon at the approaching forms materializing out of the fog that clung to the river's edge.

Once the moaning started, they all ran.

The trucks had big floodlights mounted on top of their cabs. They threw a blinding ring of light on the area the pumpers had been draining, and it kept Jacob from seeing anything beyond the light with any sort of clarity.

A figure staggered into view less than twenty yards away. More stepped out of the fog on either side of him.

Jacob raised his pistol at the first zombie and, for a moment, locked up in fear. He'd seen zombies before. More than most, in fact. During his time with the salvage teams he'd seen at least a hundred. He'd even put down a few. But he'd never seen one like the undead thing facing him now. It was covered in river scum, mud dripping off its frame. Jacob couldn't tell if it was man or woman, much less what color the thing's skin had been. Black, white, Hispanic, Asian . . . he had no clue. When they decay that badly, they all looked the same. All Jacob saw was river gunk dripping off a skeleton wrapped in a wrinkled leather sheet. The thing could barely walk. With every step, it looked like it might collapse.

But walk it did, and it closed the distance between it and Jacob soon enough.

The zombie raised its hands to claw at Jacob's face and in that moment he got a glimpse of mud-covered bone showing through the decayed skin of its arm.

Jacob raised the pistol to its face and fired.

The thing's head snapped back, and the next instant it folded to the ground in a heap.

"Whoa!" he said, and clawed backwards toward the lit work area.

More zombies staggered into the ring of light on rickety legs, all of them covered in river scum, all of them badly decayed. Jacob scrambled to his feet and was about to turn toward the wall when he heard someone yelling for help.

It was an eighteen-year-old kid named Winston Roberts that he had arrested at least half a dozen times for fighting and public intoxication. Roberts was tangled in a nest of heavy hoses and wires, like a man wrestling with a giant snake.

Jacob ran over to him and helped him climb loose of the hoses. "Go that way," he said, pointing with his gun toward the wall.

"What the hell, man? What is this shit?"

"Go!" Jacob said. "Get moving!"

Some people, even when it's for their own good, just won't take orders. Jacob had just pulled him from a muddy pit of hoses. He could see the zombies closing in around him. But all the kid heard was a cop telling him what to do. It was like his mind switched off. He bowed up like he wanted to fight him. Jacob turned and shot two of the things in the head, felling them at his feet. That was what it took to knock some sense into Roberts. He scrambled out of the mass of the hoses, the horror plain on his face.

"Go!" Jacob yelled. "Get to the wall!"

In the mud were the two zombies he'd just put down.

The others moaned as they closed in around him. But Jacob didn't move. He was still staring at the two zombies he'd put down. He'd never seen any so badly decomposed before. There barely seemed to be enough muscle tissue remaining to haul the things around.

A muddy hand fell on his back, grabbing at his shirt.

Jacob yelled and spun away from it, breaking the zombie's fingers as he twisted.

He tripped over a hose and nearly fell. His right foot came down hard in the mud and he sank up to his calf. From the wall he heard people screaming, and all around him, the bloodcurdling moans of the dead.

Mired in the freshly turned river soil, Jacob pulled on his leg with everything he had. "Come on, come on!" he muttered.

One more pull and he was free, his foot coming loose without his boot. But there was no time to go back for it. The workers were gathering at the base of the wall, pushing the ladder back into place. Most of the zombie herd was closing in on Jacob's position, but a few were making their way toward the panicked group of workers. He had to cover them.

Jacob ran for the wall. The workers were shoving each other and yelling.

"One at a time," Jacob said. "Move quickly. I'll cover you."

He stepped away from the crowd, putting himself between the wall and the approaching zombies. There were more than he'd first thought, sixty or seventy at least. Most were still recognizable as men or women, but some were barely more than skeletons, with only scraps of muddy cloth left of their clothes.

Jacob looked down at the pistol in his hand and tried to remember how many shots he had left. There hadn't been enough ammunition for him to top off his magazine before he went in to work, and he'd fired four rounds already.

"You guys need to hurry up!" he yelled over his shoulder at the workers.

They were climbing the ladder three at a time now, and Jacob could see it shaking and bowing under their weight.

He turned back to the approaching zombies, took a deep breath, and shot the two nearest him. A third put on a sudden burst of speed and charged out of the herd. Startled, Jacob wheeled on the woman and fired without aiming. The bullet hit the top of her head and made it snap back, so that she was looking up at the sky. A wet chunk of her scalp flew out behind her. She stopped in her tracks, and then slowly lowered her gaze on Jacob again.

For the second time that morning, he froze.

Her eyes were dead and empty, yet somehow lit with an insane and insatiable rage. Or was it hunger? He couldn't say for sure. He only knew that her eyes held him transfixed, like a rabbit caught by a snake's stare.

Shouting from above shook him loose of the thing's stare.

He glanced up and back. The last of the workers were on the ladder now, and Jim Laymon was motioning for him to come up.

"We got sharpshooters on the way," he said.

Jacob didn't need to be told twice. He turned back to the woman he'd just shot, aimed carefully at her nose, and put her down. Then he turned and ran for the wall.

He went up the ladder in a daze. Somebody grabbed him and pulled him out of the way while someone else lifted the ladder over the wall.

Dale and Barry Givens, two of Arbella's best snipers, were standing there, rifles at the ready.

"Can we take 'em down now, boss?" Dale said.

Jacob stared at him for a moment, confused. Then he remembered they needed the approval of the constabulary to fire outside the walls. The noise was the big issue. The town had learned over the years that noise was the enemy when dealing with the undead. It brought them out of the wood-work.

Jacob didn't feel much like a cop. His chest was heaving. He was rattled through and through. He was covered in mud and only wearing one boot. He holstered his weapon and tried to calm the wild bird beating against the inside of his rib cage.

But when he spoke, the definitive note of command was back in his voice.

"Yeah, take 'em down."

3

An hour later, Jacob was back at the office, sitting in front of a blank sheet of paper, trying to figure out what to say in his report.

The workers should have had a sentry in place. At least one. Protocol called for one armed guard for every ten men working on a project outside the wall, and not following that protocol was just a stupid error. There was no other way to describe it. Even if they hadn't been able to find a sharp-shooter to do the job, the foreman should have at least used one of his crew. After all, every man and woman in Arbella knew how to handle a gun. They learned as children, as part of their schooling. It wasn't worth risking everybody's life just to finish a job quicker. Somebody was going to get it over this, and Jacob had his money on the foreman.

But it wasn't the lack of leadership that really bothered him. It was the zombies that he'd shot. The amount of decay he'd seen was way beyond anything he'd ever seen before. Back when he was training to go outside the walls with the salvage teams, he'd been shown pictures of zombies, and told what to look for. Some of the old ones could look like moldering corpses rotting away in doorways, their skin so cracked and dry, their muscles so atrophied, they looked more like hunks of beef jerky than zombies. But they could get up. They could go from dormant to attack mode in the time it took you to turn your back on them. And they were every bit as lethal as the freshly turned ones.

Somebody had asked the trainer how old a zombie could get before they finally rotted away, and the trainer had said she didn't know. Nobody knew for sure. Six years maybe, maybe even eight, if they lived in the right climate and didn't tear themselves apart while hunting their prey.

Flesh could only last so long, after all, even with the help of CDHLs.

Back in school he'd learned about the First Days. The zombies weren't the product of terrorism or a rogue virus or junk DNA, but the entrepreneurial desire to make vegetables last longer on the shelves.

China, his teachers said, had experimented with pesticides and preservatives, looking for a way to make their domestically grown foodstuffs stay fresher longer. Their efforts culminated in a family of chemical compounds known as carbon dioxide blocking hydrolyzed lignin, or CDHLs. The Chinese tested it, claimed it was safe, and spread it over everything that grew.

The compounds were tested, and eventually vetted by the FDA. Once the Food and Drug Administration declared CDHLs safe for human consumption, they spread across the globe. Suddenly plums could stay purple and juicy for months at a time. Roses never wilted. Celery, carrots, even lettuce could sit on a grocery store shelf for weeks and still look as fresh as the day they were harvested. Even bananas could stay traffic light yellow for three months.

The blood banks were the first to report signs of trouble. CDHLs didn't appear to break down in the human bloodstream the way they did in plants. There was no cause for immediate worry, except that blood supersaturated with CDHLs seemed to stay unnaturally healthy and vital well beyond any sort of conventional measure.

In hindsight, Jacob's teachers had said, it should have been obvious.

CDHLs were linked through study after study to hyperactive behavior in children.

Unfocused aggression was a common symptom of adults of middle age. Housewives killing their children and waiting at the kitchen table with a butcher's knife for their husband's return from work shouldn't have seemed like business as usual.

And yet it was.

The First Days had crept up on them like a thief in the night, even though it should have been obvious what the CDHLs were doing to them.

The trouble started in China. The central cities of Weishan and Qinghai were the first to erupt in anarchy. The Chinese, much to their credit, made no attempt to cover up what was going on. Video streamed out to every news service and website, and those first glimpses of the dead crowding the streets were terrifying beyond all reckoning.

From Central China the zombie hordes spread to the more densely populated coastal cities, and by that point there was no saving mainland Asia. Everyone who could evacuate did. They fled to Japan and Australia, some even to the United States, but many millions were left behind to be devoured. There were simply too many to save.

The rest of the world watched it happen, believing that their quarantine efforts had worked. But of course the quarantine effort was merely shutting the barn door after the cow was already out. The culprit, the CDHLs were already in the ground, already in the food, already in the bodies of everyone who had ever eaten something bought from the grocery store. All that was needed was for the body to reach a point of super saturation. Once that happened, zombification spread.

Eight months after the first incidents in China, more were reported in Japan, and Mexico, and the United States. Living through the First Days was like being caught up in a wildfire. No sooner had you smelled smoke than the flames erupted all around you. Every night the televisions had shown maps, and on those maps, red circles spread like bloodstains.

But the real terror, and it was a terror that every man, woman, and child still lived with, was the fact that the CDHLs were already in their bodies. You didn't become a zombie by being bit, or scratched, or accidentally ingesting any of their bodily fluids. You didn't have to, because you were already a zombie waiting to happen. They were all, to a body, carriers of the zombie plague.

And once they died, they came back.

There was some hope, though. The belief of those who claimed to know such things was that the levels of CDHLs in the soil and in the crops were starting to go down. In Jacob's salvage days, the botanists had asked him to take soil samples. Those results, they said, were encouraging. So, too, was the fact that fewer and fewer zombies seemed to be lasting more than a year or two. The more a zombie fed, the more CDHL it ingested, thereby keeping it viable longer, preserving it. The zombies from the First Days had lasted more than a decade, Jacob had been told. That wasn't thought to be happening anymore.

And that was what troubled him.

The ones he'd shot down by the river were far older than anything he remembered seeing in those training pictures. It made him wonder if they really knew half of what they thought they knew about the outside world.

But of course that was a whole other issue. And a bitter one.

With a heavy sigh, he started writing again. He had only put a few words on the page when Steve Harrigan appeared in the doorway behind him.

"Jacob, it's time."

Jacob's blood went cold. He put his pen down and felt his face flush with heat. Had he really forgotten what he was about to do? It seemed impossible, but that's what he'd done.

He put both hands on the table and tried to steady himself, but it was no good. All over again he was a jangled mess.

Steve put a hand on his shoulder and said, "Come on."

Slowly, as if he were going to his own execution—and maybe, in a way, he was—he rose to his feet. "I think I'm gonna be sick," he said.

"You're gonna do just fine." Steve held out his hand. "Here, take these. I didn't know if you had any left after this morning."

Jacob held his hand out. The older man dropped four rounds into his palm.

"Oh. Thanks."

With trembling hands, Jacob used the bullets to top off his magazine. "How do you know I'll do fine?" he asked, and seated the magazine into the receiver.

"You remember the words you're supposed to say?"

"Yeah."

"Then you'll do fine. Just point the weapon at his forehead and fire. Don't look away. Just say the words and fire."

"Do I look him in the face? I don't know if I can do that."

"You have to. If you don't, your hands will shake. You might miss, or worse, hit him with a glancing blow that doesn't kill him. Nobody wants that." Steve put a hand on Jacob's shoulder and guided him toward the cells. "Come on, it's time."

They walked back to the cells in silence, just the echo of their boots on the tile floor. Jerry Grieder was in Cell Two, sitting on the cot, his face in his hands. Like Amanda, he'd stopped caring for himself. He hadn't eaten a full meal since they'd locked him up. His clothes were dark with sweat and grime and he hadn't shaved in a week. Sheriff Taylor had at first refused to let Amanda in the cell with him, but in the end had relented. She'd spent most of the morning with him. She wasn't there now, but there were flowers on the bed next to him.

Steve said, "Jerry, time to get up."

Jerry said nothing. He didn't resist either. He let out a sigh, and then slowly pulled himself to his feet. He was a tall, flat-footed man with long, stringy brown hair. Jacob moved in close to handcuff Jerry and caught a whiff that made him flinch. He steadied himself and took Jerry by the wrist. He pulled back the man's sleeves and was surprised to see a bright pink lacy cloth bracelet there. Except for the fabric, it looked like the bracelets the children over at the school made. At first Jacob was confused, until he remembered that Amanda was a schoolteacher. Technically, he should have removed it, but he put the handcuffs on like he hadn't seen it.

He stepped to one side of Jerry and Steve went to the other.

"All right, let's go," Steve said.

The three men left the cell and walked in silence out the front door. The sunlight was bright and Jerry recoiled against it. Jacob and Steve gave him a moment to recover, and then they rounded the corner that led on to Main Plaza.

There were perhaps forty people gathered near the old stone fountain, among them Sheriff Taylor, all but two members of the town council, and of course, Amanda Grieder. Jacob was surprised, and grateful, too, to see his friends Kelly Banis and Nick Carroll. Kelly's husband, Barry, put his arm around her and she melted into him. She was crying, but trying not to. Beside them, Nick had his hands thrust into the pockets of his jeans. He nodded to Jacob in quiet support.

Amanda began to cry as soon as Jerry came into view, her moans the only sound as a cold wind swept through the square.

Jacob put a hand on Jerry's elbow and led him forward.

"You can't do this," Amanda shouted. "He's innocent."

Nobody else spoke.

Jacob and the others continued on to the fountain, and as they walked, Jacob couldn't shake the thought that the others had chosen the fountain, the centerpiece of which was the Blind Lady of Justice, not out of tradition, or a sense of symbolism, but out of fear that the executioner might lose his nerve and miss.

They wanted a backstop.

"You didn't even find the jewelry," Amanda yelled. "How can you say he's guilty?"

That much was true, Jacob thought, They hadn't found the locket. But Jerry Grieder was guilty of burglary, that he knew beyond a shadow of a doubt.

Seventeen-year-old Jasmine Simmons had awakened in the middle of the night to see a man standing in a dark corner of her room, watching her. She'd screamed to holy hell, and the man had bolted from her room, shattered a window in a spare bedroom, and jumped through to the lawn below. She'd gone on screaming until the neighbors woke and raised the cry of thief.

A crowd gathered. Jacob and Deputy Ted Harris happened to be riding by and descended on Jasmine's house. They found Jerry Grieder standing near the broken window, his clothes torn and his arms sliced up and bloody. He was even holding a shard of broken glass.

When asked what he was doing there, he'd muttered a half-baked excuse. When questioned further, he'd gone into a shell.

Jasmine, still a girl but living on her own for three years now, had claimed that he'd stolen her mother's locket. A silver heart containing a cameo of her mother.

Jacob searched Jerry, but didn't find the locket. The crowd searched the area, but they didn't find it either.

Attempts to question Jerry further led to nothing. His rambling story was so full of holes and inconsistencies that it became obvious to everyone he was lying.

That certainty propelled Jacob forward. Feeling numb down to his toes, he led Jerry to the base of the fountain, turned him around so that the man's back was to the Blind Lady of Justice, and backed away.

"Please don't do this," Amanda begged from somewhere off to his right. "Please, somebody make it stop. They didn't even find the locket."

Jacob pulled his weapon. It felt impossibly heavy in his hand, as if he could never lift it.

He looked around at the assembled faces, and saw nothing but stone statues staring back at him. The wind picked up, carrying the wood smoke smell of a nearby cooking fire. Somewhere far off, a dog barked. This was his town, his people. And they were about to compel him to do something truly awful.

"But no man can make you do something you don't want to do," Sheriff Taylor had said to him on the day he proclaimed him chief deputy. "You've been given this position because you're capable of knowing your own mind, and being a man of conscience. Sometimes you will have to do that which nobody wants you to do. Sometimes, you will have to refuse that which everybody wants of you. It'll be up to you to know what is right. And you will know, so long as you let the Code be your guide."

The Code, thought Jacob. He cleared his throat and began to speak. His voice was loud and sounded remarkably clear and steady, free of the fear tearing him up inside.

"The Code speaks clearly on our role here today. Jerry Grieder, you have been found guilty of the crime of burglary. You have broken into the home of a fellow citizen with the intent to commit theft or assault. You are a thief, and a thief is a threat to the trust that protects and preserves us all.

"You have harmed our community by your actions. Our survival is always in doubt, and we must protect one another as neighbors, as friends, and as family. We must believe in each other. We must trust one another. And Jerry Grieder, we no longer trust you. To whatever god you worship, or code you follow, may it preserve you and offer safe passage for your soul. The sentence of death by firing squad will now be carried out. Is there anything you want to say?"

Jacob waited.

Jerry lifted his gaze to Jacob. There was no recognition in his bloodshot eyes, just panic and fear and misery. Then he looked past Jacob and scanned the assembled crowd until he found Amanda.

Then, much to Jacob's surprise, Jerry managed a faint smile. "I love you, baby," he said. "With all my heart."

Several people were crying.

Amanda shouted, "You can't do this to him. It isn't right!"

A few people agreed with her and they yelled for mercy. But nobody else picked up the cry, and soon the square fell silent again.

Jacob stepped closer to Jerry, barely more than an arm's length away. He thought again how horrible it was that Jerry wasn't blindfolded. It certainly would have been easier on him to fire if he didn't have to look the man in the eyes while he pulled the trigger. But that was the point, wasn't it? The law was cold and absolute, but men mustn't be. Men make laws to live by, and they should be man enough to face the consequences of those laws when the hard choices have to be made. It was an awful act, and an incredibly tragic one, which was why, Jacob figured, that more of the town hadn't turned out for the execution.

Jacob raised his pistol and adjusted his grip.

From somewhere behind him Amanda screamed, "Oh, God, Jerry, I love you!"

Jacob told himself to do it. Wait any longer and he'd lose his nerve completely. His hands were slippery with sweat, and he had to adjust his grip on the weapon yet again. Then he squeezed the trigger, and the gun jumped in his hand.

He saw the flash. Jerry's head snapped back, and he crumpled to the wet grass, his face turned to the sky, a nasty red hole where his right eye had been. Jacob swore silently. He'd been aiming for Jerry's forehead. He'd intended something clean and quick. Not a horror show.

There was a sudden stench as Jerry's bowels and bladder released. The grass beneath Jerry's head turned dark.

A few people moaned, but the sound of their grief soon died away and the quiet crowd was left with nothing but the echo of the shot and the ragged sobbing of Amanda Grieder, now a widow.

Steve put a hand on his shoulder. "Lower your weapon," he whispered.

Jacob did as the older deputy instructed, then holstered the gun. Dr. Gary Williams, the town's only remaining properly trained doctor from the First Generation, stepped from the crowd and knelt next to the body. He checked for a pulse, and then pried open Jerry's one remaining eye so he could study the pupil for any signs of dilation. If Jerry were going to rise, the first sign of it would be there, in the pupils.

To Jacob's great relief, the doctor motioned for two of his apprentices to bring a blanket. They draped it over Jerry's ruined face and then Dr. Williams went over to talk with Sheriff Taylor. As the two men conferred in low tones, somebody led Amanda Grieder away.

They had two men and a horse-drawn cart standing by to remove the body to the crematorium, but Jacob didn't stick around to watch that part of the process. He walked back to the constabulary office with his head wrapped in a haze. He was barely aware of his steps, and saw nothing but the scrap of ground directly in front of his feet. He went straight to the bathroom, collapsed to his knees in front of the toilet, and vomited.

4

It was almost dark when Sheriff Taylor finally came for him.

Randall Taylor was a legend around town. He had led the First Generation out of Arkansas and into Arbella, had rallied them at the barricades, and fought like a lion to beat back the tide of the dead. He was one of the authors of the Code, and the sentinel on the wall that kept the rest of the world at bay. Like his old friend Steve Harrigan, Taylor was a tall, slender man. But where Harrigan was known for his affable smile and endless parade of jokes, Taylor was a far more serious man. He said little when he didn't have to, and looked on everything and everyone with a quiet intensity.

He had been, according to Jacob's mother, quite good looking back in the day. Gray hair, wrinkles, and liver spots had erased some of that former glory, and his sharp, handsome features seemed more gaunt than rugged these days, but he was still obviously a powerful man, one who carried himself with a confidence that was immediately apparent to all who met him.

He leaned against the doorway of the bathroom, a matchstick tucked into the corner of his mouth. He pulled it out and held it up for Jacob to see. "Steve said you promised to talk to Frank Hartwell about getting more of these next time he's outside the walls."

Jacob looked at him, confused. The words made no sense to him.

He was still hugging the toilet, though he hadn't thrown up again after that first time hours earlier. He stood up, lowered the lid, and sat down.

Taylor pointed to the sink. "Wash your face off first. I want to talk with you."

Jacob ran water into his hands and splashed it into his face, scrubbing his mouth and cheeks with the heels of his hands. He took the towel down from the ring and dried his face. Then he put the towel back and looked at his reflection in the mirror. He didn't recognize the face staring back at him.

"You did well today."

Jacob turned to face his boss. "I killed a man."

"And you saved twenty more." Taylor put the matchstick back in his mouth and rolled it over to one corner. "I'm proud of you."

"I feel sick."

"Yep. Just pray you feel that way every time you have to do it."

"I never want to do that again."

"I can't promise you that."

Jacob nodded. "Yeah, I know."

"You know, I'm not the only one you impressed today. I've been talking for the last few hours with the town council about you."

Jacob didn't say anything to that. All he wanted to do was drown himself in some of Kelly Banis's infamous bathtub gin.

"Folks have got questions, though."

"What kind of questions?"

"What you did today, out there in the square, was reaffirm the Code that's kept us alive all these years."

"I know that," Jacob said. He sighed. The Code had been on his mind all day, and he'd already covered this ground many times. The whole sound of it was turning sour.

"Now hold on. Give me a chance to speak. People want to know why a man who so ably filled the Code's hardest task is so keen on leaving."

"Leaving? What . . . who said anything about leaving?"

"Well, ain't that what you and some of the others been talking about the last ten years? You and Kelly Banis and Nick Carroll."

"You mean the Expansionists? What . . . I don't understand. You want to talk about this now?"

"Why not?"

Jacob started to speak, but he didn't know what to say. He felt blindsided. "Sheriff, with all due respect, sir, I don't really feel like a political discussion right now."

"And why is that?"

Jacob stared at his boss. Where to begin? "Oh, I don't know. Because I just put a man to death. Talking politics with that hanging over my head, it feels obscene somehow."

Taylor chewed on his matchstick a moment before taking it out and looking at it like a bad habit he couldn't shake. He flicked it into the waste can with a practiced motion. Why he even bothered to throw them away anymore Jacob could hardly say. There'd be another in his mouth five minutes from now. Was it any wonder they were running out? Again?

So he wanted to talk politics. Jacob shook his head. Fine. So be it. The expansionist question was endlessly complex, but really it boiled down to one simple truth. Arbella had survived the zombie apocalypse. They'd done well for themselves. They'd turned a deserted town into a new home, and there, they'd not only survived, but thrived. They'd walled up the town and turned every available resource toward the maintenance and the prosperity of their community. The Code was the formal statement of that purpose, its manifesto and its constitution, for lack of a better analogy. And the program had worked.

Now, thirty years later, they had become so successful that Arbella's old walls couldn't hold them anymore. Jacob and quite a few of his friends, nearly all of them of the younger generation, now of age, believed that the answer to the problem was expansion. They were living in a Malthusian pressure cooker. It hadn't exploded yet, but it was only a matter of time. The First Generation had already admitted the necessity of expansion. Jacob's fight down by the river that very morning was the result of a small expansionist program organized by the town council, though of course you'd never hear any of them saying that the purpose of the work had been to expand Arbella's borders. The work was an improvement, they'd say, nothing more.

The First Generation, Jacob's mother included, invariably came back with some version of the same tired old truism. *Our strategy saved our lives, and it has worked brilliantly since then. The world out there wants to kill us. No good can come from pushing into that world. You are safe here. You have a good and a happy home here. Outside those walls you'll find only death.*

Jacob and his friends had argued till they were blue in the face, but the First Generation refused to budge.

"You get mad real easy, Jacob," Taylor said. "I want you to work on that. Being quick to anger never did a cop a bit of good, believe me. I've seen plenty of good cops throw their jobs on the old compost heap because they couldn't control their temper."

"Look, Randall—"

"Are we on a first-name basis now?"

Jacob stared at him, trying to gauge the man's motives. Jacob had once heard Bill Christie boast at a Christmas party that he had fought next to Randall Taylor during the Battle of the Gates. He'd stood there shoulder to shoulder with Sheriff Taylor, gunning down zombies as they climbed over the barricades in an endless wave. "Me and him," Christie had boasted, thumping his chest, "we're tight."

"Then go and slap him on the back," someone from the crowd had challenged.

"Yeah, do it!" someone else said.

Like a drunken blimp on a crooked course, Christie had wandered over to where Taylor was talking with a few of the town leaders and slapped the sheriff merrily on the back, nearly causing Taylor to spill his tea all over Wanda Shane, head nurse of Arbella's hospital.

Taylor had turned on the man and leveled such a withering stare at him that Christie immediately dropped his hand. He muttered some sort of incoherent apology and then shrank away, utterly embarrassed.

But Jacob wasn't a drunk, and he wasn't some minor hero of the First Generation.

He said, "If this is an on-the-job talk, forgive me, it'll be Sheriff Taylor from here on out. But if you're going to come in here while I'm feeling like a warmed-over dog turd and ambush me with questions about Expansionism, then, yeah, it's gonna be on a first-name basis. So you tell me, sir, what's it gonna be?"

Randall Taylor looked at him for a long moment. When Jacob didn't crack, he nodded, pulled another matchstick from his shirt pocket, and jammed it into his mouth.

"Do you know why I had you handle the execution today?"

"Because I'm chief deputy. It's the job of the chief deputy to do all executions."

"Is it?"

Jacob felt lost again. What, exactly, was he being asked?

"It's part of the Code," Jacob offered hesitantly.

"Is it? Where is that written?"

"It isn't. It's just always been that way."

"Has it? I did the first three executions myself. Men that fought with me at the Battle of the Gates. Men I thought I trusted."

"Yes, sir, I know that."

"Then how can it be tradition?"

Jacob desperately searched his memory for some explanation, some light he could turn on this issue, but all he could manage was a shrug.

"I don't know," he said.

"Did they teach you about John Adams when you were in school?"

"The American president?"

Taylor nodded. "Second president of the United States, yes." He pulled the matchstick from his mouth and flicked it into the waste can. "Adams lived through the American Revolution, and then helped build a country out of what was left over, and when he reflected back on that, he gave what I think to be one of the most balanced takes on the importance of politics in everyday life ever put to paper. He said: 'I must study politics and war that my sons may have the liberty to study mathematics and philosophy, geography, natural history, and naval architecture, navigation, commerce, and agriculture, in order to give their children a right to study painting, poetry, music, architecture, statuary, tapestry and porcelain.' It all comes down to politics, son. Get that wrong, and the best of intentions ain't worth nothing."

He pulled out the little box where he kept his matchsticks from his shirt pocket, opened it, looked at the contents ruefully, then slid it closed and put the box back.

"Jacob, I'm taking the long way around to say this, and that ain't my style, but I don't know any other way. I had you take care of Jerry Grieder because I needed to see for myself that you were ready. That you were prepared to be that second generation of leaders John Adams talked about. You proved today that the Code will survive to the next generation, which is why the town council approved my decision to name you as my successor."

Jacob's mouth opened. He said, "What?"

"You heard me right. You're the obvious man for the job, and after all you did today, ain't nobody gonna doubt the logic of it."

"I . . . I don't know what to say. You're not ready to retire. You're still—"

"I'm ready to retire, Jacob. I'll be seventy come October. I've worn a badge nearly fifty years now. Trust me, that's a long time."

Jacob let out a long breath. "Craziest day ever," he said.

"Well, not so fast. We still got this question about expansion that needs answering first. The town council all agreed you're the man for the job, but they're troubled by the fact that you want to leave so bad."

"You said that before. Where's that coming from? I don't want to leave. Nobody said anything about leaving. All we want to do is explore what's out there. It's been thirty years. We don't know anything about the world we live in. An expedition is all we want, a chance to look around and see how far we can expand our town."

Taylor took the matchstick box out again and jammed one into his mouth. It was a practiced motion so casually done that Jacob wondered if the man even realized he was doing it.

"I saw those zombies you shot today, the really old ones. They had to be twelve or thirteen years old at least. The zombies are lasting a lot longer than we thought. Isn't that proof enough that we don't want to go beyond the walls?"

"No, exactly the opposite. Don't you see? We have no idea what's out there. Maybe it's still as bad as it was. But maybe it isn't. Either way, we have to know. We're going to have to do it soon, too. The resources we've got won't support our population for more than another few years. We could end up starving here. Or worse."

Taylor nodded. "I know all that's true. That may sound funny coming from me, but I do know it's true. I suspect I've known it for years now, just haven't wanted to admit it to myself. That's why I learned that John Adams quote, so I could use it on the town council. Me, and all the others on the council, we studied politics and war so that we could give you the Code and this town. Now it's your turn to study geography and navigation and all the rest of it. You get to be our Lewis and Clark, Jacob. We're a long way from tapestry and porcelain still, but with you at the helm, I think we'll get there."

"I don't understand. What are you saying?"

"I'm saying I got the council to agree to your expedition."

"What? Are you kidding?"

"Nope."

"Oh, my God." Jacob laughed. He wanted to grab Taylor by the shoulders and shake him. Or hug him. God help him, even kiss him. He was suddenly so excited he could barely stay in his skin.

"Well, don't go running off the reservation just yet," Taylor said. "Council's asked for a full report on what you expect to achieve, what resources you'll need to make it happen, and who all will be going with you, and they want it to be delivered in session tomorrow morning."

"Tomorrow?" That wiped the smile from Jacob's face. "But how can I prepare a full report by tomorrow morning? I need time for that."

"All you've done for the last ten years is talk about this, Jacob. How much more time do you need?"

"Yeah, but . . ." Jacob's mind was racing. He was stunned,

still unable to process his good fortune. There was so much to do, so many people to talk to. He laughed. "I can't believe I'm finally gonna get to lead this expedition."

"Well, not so fast on that, either."

Jacob's smile drained away. "What do you mean? You're gonna let me go, aren't you?"

"Of course. But you're gonna be coleader."

"Co . . . ?"

"Yep," Taylor said. "I'm going with you."

5

Word traveled fast about the council's change of heart. Kelly Banis and her husband, Barry, offered up their house for a party, and promised to provide as much of Kelly's famous—or infamous, depending on who you asked—bathtub gin as the group could drink. It was a nice night, clear and crisp but not too cold, and by eight o'clock there were already enough people to force the party out onto the front porch and into the street, and a good many of them were already drunk.

Jacob didn't go straight over to the party. He went home first and ate a small dinner of bacon and pickled vegetables from his mother's garden. Then he changed out of his uniform and into clean jeans, a sweatshirt, and a light jacket, and headed over to Nick Carroll's place on Lester Street, over by the north wall. Nick had promised to wait on him so they could go over together.

Nick was sitting on his front steps drawing in a sketchbook when Jacob walked up.

"You ready?" Jacob said as he came up the front walk.

"Yep, just about."

Jacob climbed the steps so he could see what Nick was drawing. On the page, rendered in pencil, was an amazing likeness of a pretty young girl, nude from the waist up, her fingers running through her hair.

"What do you think?" Nick asked.

"Uh, nice tits."

"You recognize her?"

Jacob squinted at the picture. He knew the face. He'd seen her around.

On the name, though, he was drawing a blank. "Well, I . . ."

"That's Gina Houser."

Jacob looked again. Nick was a talented artist, and now that he had a name to put to the picture, he could totally see it. He'd just never given Gina much of a look before. She was still a kid.

"Gina's kind of young, isn't she?"

"She's nineteen."

"Well, yeah. Did she . . . pose for that?"

"Damn straight she did," Nick said, and shot him a wicked grin. "She does a whole lot more, too."

"But isn't she dating that kid from, uh, what's his name?"

"Ted Roth, over at the Howth Farm. Yeah, they're dating. But a girl her age, you know, likes a little fun now and then. And what her boyfriend don't know won't hurt him."

"Really? Nick, what are you doing?"

"Don't be jealous."

"Whatever," Jacob said. "Come on, let's go."

"Okay." Nick closed the sketchbook. "Let me put this up."

Jacob watched his friend enter his house. Nick was a blowhard, always had been. He was only five-nine, and his forehead was scarred with acne from his teenage years, but he talked loud and he talked well and for some reason the girls seemed to like him. He had no doubt that young Miss Gina Houser had soaked up his attention, loving every second of it. She wouldn't have been the first. Not by a long shot.

As he stared into the darkened recesses of Nick Carroll's living room, a memory rose up in Jacob's mind. They'd gotten into a fight when they were sixteen and Jacob had come away with a black eye, a bleeding ear, and a mouth that looked like a tomato somebody had crushed beneath their heel. Nick had barely had a scratch on him. Jacob couldn't even remember now exactly what was said to start the fight. They'd just been hanging out with a group of boys, waiting for a baseball game to start, and some of the other guys started kidding Nick about his last name, calling it a girl's name. Nick seemed to take the ribbing pretty well, but when Jacob joined in it had sent Nick over the edge. Next thing Jacob knew they were circling each other inside a ring of boys all yelling, "Fight, fight!" Then the ass beating started.

That'd been a long time ago, twenty years now, and they'd been through a lot together since then. They'd dated some of the same girls, fought again over some of the same girls, only to come together again and again, always the two of them. They'd worked in salvage together, gone outside the walls together. They were tight.

Still, for Jacob at least, and maybe for Nick, too, there was always that fight. It lurked there in the past, in the back of his mind, the way failures sometimes do. It had cast a long but subtle shadow over their relationship, one that made their friendship one of always seeking dominance over the other, rather than understanding, and Jacob couldn't help but feel that this latest conquest of Nick's, this teenage girl with the nice pair and the pretty face, was just another way of Nick's to show he was more of a man than Jacob.

And then Nick was standing in the doorway.

"Hey, man, you all right? You look like you're someplace else."

Jacob forced a smile. "I'm good. You ready?"

"Let's go party."

The walk over to Kelly's place was short, the talk small. They rounded the corner and were hit with a wall of drunken voices. A cheer went up when they arrived. As they walked into Kelly and Barry's front yard, friends ran up to shake Jacob's hand and clap him on the back. Memories of his lost fight with Nick started to fade, and despite all he'd been through that day, Jacob felt kind of loose, ready for a good time.

"Hey, Jacob," Nick said, a hand on his shoulder. He pointed to the north. "Look up there."

Jacob followed the line of Nick's finger. Kelly and Barry lived about four hundred yards from the north wall. A good portion of it could be seen from her front yard. And on the wall, a rifle slung over his shoulder, was Sheriff Taylor, making his rounds. His nightly tour along the town's walls was a fixture of life in Arbella.

"You ready for that?" Nick said.

"You mean walking the wall every night? You think that's something I should keep doing?"

"Don't you?"

"You know," he said, "I remember as a kid watching him walk that wall before bedtime. I remember my mom used to say, 'Look up there. Sheriff Taylor's on the wall. I think we're gonna be okay.' "

"Everybody's mother used to tell them that," Nick said.

"Yeah."

"I think you're gonna have to do it," Nick said. "At least for a little while. People see that, and they feel a little better closing their eyes at night. Is he really coming with us?"

"Yeah, I think he's serious."

"Why?"

"Well, he's got his own reasons, I suppose."

"You didn't ask him."

"Oh, I asked him," Jacob said. Taylor had told him it was a political move, that if people saw them co-leading the expedition, it'd be a sign that Jacob had Taylor's blessing as sheriff. He said it would help with transition, which Taylor wanted to happen when they returned from the expedition.

He said, "He just said he was craving a little adventure."

Someone spoke behind them. "What are you two looking at?"

Jacob turned around. Kelly Banis was standing there, a pair of mason jars in her hands. She held them out to Jacob and Nick. "Gin and tonics, to get you boys started?"

"Hell, yeah," Nick said, and took his.

"Thanks," Jacob said.

"I'm sorry about today," she said. "I really am. That must have been so hard."

Nick took a big gulp of his drink, smacked his lips loudly, and slapped Jacob on the shoulder. "Hard, my ass. Old Jake here was steady as a rock up there."

Jacob held his smile, but inside he was fuming. He wanted to tell Nick to shut the hell up. The man had no idea.

But he held himself in check.

Jacob kept his gaze on Kelly. "Thanks," he said. "It meant a lot that you guys were there today. There was a moment there that I almost locked up. Seeing you guys really helped."

Kelly put a hand on his shoulder.

Nick took another drink of his gin and tonic and scanned the party for a pretty face.

It was only then that Jacob noticed Kelly was wearing the necklace he'd made for her after his first salvage mission. A cluster of buttons he'd found at a mall and knotted together with a silver chain. It never even occurred to him that she still had it.

Kelly caught him looking at the necklace and she put a hand over it, a hint of a guilty smile on her face.

Had he really seen it, that smile, or was he just wishing? Either way, the thought broke off clean as Barry Banis, Kelly's husband, materialized out of the crowd and put his arm around her. Barry was drunk, as usual, and grinning ear to ear.

"It's finally gonna happen," he said, raising his glass. "Thank you, Jacob. Here's to you."

"Thanks, Barry."

Jacob found it hard to be jealous. Barry was head of the Agricultural Sciences Center over at Landry's Farm. He pretty much decided which vegetable crops got planted within Arbella's borders, and for the last twelve years, his right-hand woman had been his wife, Kelly Banis.

Jacob was proud of Kelly. She was, almost certainly, the smartest person he'd ever met. She was an authority when it came to plants, to be sure. His own mother quoted her articles in the town's paper. But Jacob's mind kept turning back to that summer they'd shared together, back when they were seventeen and young enough to ignore the future and revel in each other. They'd been joined at the hip all summer, sharing shrimp and catfish and beer. Lots of beer and lots of sex. There wasn't much to do in Arbella when you were a teenager. You drank and had sex, that was about it. And afterward, if you really thought there was a future with this girl, you propped yourself up on your elbow and you listened to what she had to say. Kelly's conversation had ranged from botany to making moonshine to Tennessee Williams to physics. Meanwhile, he'd been unable to think of little more than climbing back between her legs.

But so much for memories.

Now she was with a man ten years her senior, and one who was, arguably, the smartest man in Arbella. In another ten years, Barry Banis would undoubtedly be on the town council.

And all the while, Jacob had been nothing but a cop.

Still, nearly twenty years had gone by, and she still wore the necklace he'd made for her. Maybe she still held an ember of the fire they'd lit that summer.

And maybe Nick was right. Maybe every girl deserves her little secrets.

"So what's the plan?" Kelly said. "Have you figured out what you're going to tell them tomorrow?"

"Just what we've always talked about. Twelve people, picked for a variety of skills. Nick here as cartographer. You and Barry as botanists. Me for salvage. A few others. I figured we'd head north up Interstate 55 to St. Louis, then zigzag back south all the way to Little Rock, then come back here. If we take our time and do it right it should take us about five months."

Barry pushed his glasses high up on his nose with his thumb. "I like that plan." He turned to Kelly. "It'd give us a chance to test . . ."

There was a commotion out in the street. Jacob and the others turned that way just as people started screaming and backing away from a dirty figure, dressed in rags, long stringy hair forming a curtain in front of her face.

And she held a pistol in her hand.

"Oh, Christ," said Kelly. "It's Amanda Grieder."

Jacob drew his weapon and advanced into the street. He held the weapon at low ready, not pointing it at Amanda, but afraid he was going to have to.

He said, "Amanda, stop, please."

She turned toward him and the hair parted from her face. She'd been crying. Dirt and grime were tracked all over her cheeks, and her eyes were swollen and red. She pointed her gun at him.

"Amanda, stop! Don't do this. Just put the gun down."

"You made a mistake," she said, her voice cracking. Then she screamed it. "You made a mistake!"

"Amanda, easy. Please. Just put the gun down."

"He was innocent. You killed an innocent man, and now you're out here celebrating it. You're a murderer!"

"Amanda, wait. Listen to me. Please, put the gun down. If you want, we will go inside and I will listen to everything you have to say. Just put the gun down."

"You didn't find the locket. How can he be guilty if you didn't even find the locket?"

"Jacob," said Nick.

Jacob held up one hand to keep him back, but never took his eyes off Amanda.

"Amanda, that's good. That's something we can talk about. Put the gun down, okay, so we can talk about it. Just put it down."

"He was innocent," she said. "My Jerry was innocent." Then she put the muzzle to her chest.

Kelly screamed.

"No!" Jacob ran forward, but he was too late. Amanda fired and collapsed onto the ground.

Jacob put his hand over the wound and tried to staunch it, but there was too much blood, too much damage. She wasn't breathing, and when he put a bloody hand up to her neck he couldn't find a pulse.

"She's dead," he said, and rocked back on his heels.

Barry came over and checked again for a pulse. Then he forced Amanda's eyes open and examined the pupils.

"Ah, Christ," he said. "Jacob, she's turning already." He backed away from the corpse just as it started to twitch.

From somewhere in the crowd somebody groaned miserably. Then the thing that had been Amanda Grieder climbed to her feet and lurched toward Barry.

"Jacob . . ." he said. "A little help."

Jacob stepped up behind the zombie and put a bullet in her head. For the second time, Amanda Grieder dropped to the street, lifeless and still.

Jacob swallowed hard as he holstered his weapon. He stared down at the body and it was like looking at Jerry Grieder all over again. Blood dripped from his fingers, pattering against the pavement.

Jacob turned away from the body.

Down at the end of the street, the officers of the watch were running his way, their rifles clutched in their hands.

part two
OUTWARD BOUND

6

By the time Jacob turned onto the Banises' street, it was pouring. His umbrella did little good. No matter how he held it or what direction he turned, the wind somehow managed to curl under the rim, soaking his shirt and face. And what the wind didn't get on him, the puddles in the street did, leaving him cold and wet and utterly miserable.

He was getting a headache. A bad one. He walked around most of the time now with his head full of lists. Planning for the expedition had become pretty much a full-time job, and a seemingly endless exchange of what to leave in, what to leave out. Everybody had advice for him. Everything from the paperback Westerns David Sachs kept giving him, saying he should learn what to carry on the trail from those, to Jenny Oldham's quaint idea of having them bring along a covered wagon. ("It worked for the pioneers," she was fond of saying, "it'll work again here.") The latest idea came from Walter Mayfield. Walter ran the livery, and he was supplying the horses, and he sat on the town council, and his wife, Esther, was supplying the expedition with two hundred pounds of beef jerky, so he pretty much had to be listened to. His idea was to equip every member of the expedition with two horses, one for riding and the other as a pack animal. Jacob hadn't laughed in his face, partly out of respect for the man's position in the town and partly out of exhaustion, but the urge to do so had been there nonetheless. Instead, he'd mustered what little patience he still had and tried to explain that while every member of the expedition knew how to ride— you didn't grow up in Arbella without learning how to ride a horse—not all of them were competent enough to manage two horses over uneven terrain and still be able to deal with zombies, should they run into some. But Walter was unwilling to let the suggestion go, so Jacob promised he'd consider it and added it to an already huge list of headaches he would have to deal with eventually.

Though technically he wasn't off the clock, he was counting on tonight to recharge his batteries. Tonight's meeting was going to be fun, not work. Or at least it would be once he got out of the rain. So he hurried on his way, his head bent low as the rain sizzled and popped against the top of his umbrella. It was coming down so hard, and made so much noise, that he almost missed it when someone called his name.

He stopped, annoyed at being detained, and looked around.

Maggie Hester was trotting toward him, her arm over her head in a vain attempt to keep her hair dry.

Jacob held the umbrella out to cover her.

"Thank you," she said as she slid in beside him. She had something in her hands. "I wanted to ask a favor, Jacob."

"Yes, ma'am." He had to yell to be heard over the rain. "What can I do for you?"

She held out a plastic baggie, the kind with the locking seal at the top. Plastic baggies were a valuable commodity around Arbella, and this one had obviously been reused many times. The plastic had turned white and nearly opaque, but Jacob could see a slip of paper inside.

He took the baggie from her. "What's this?"

"Is it true you're going to Little Rock?"

"Yes, ma'am. That's the plan anyway. That'll be our southern terminus before we head back here."

Ms. Hester was in her seventies. She was a stocky woman with wide shoulders and the kind of bosom that made Jacob wonder why she didn't have back trouble. She was ordinarily an animated powerhouse, the kind of dowager who blows into a room like a summer dust devil. But that energy was gone from her now. Her expression was a pained one, and she looked small to him, standing there all soaking wet. He studied her face, her red, puffy eyes and runny nose, and he wasn't entirely certain the dampness on her cheeks was rainwater.

"That's the address for my old house back in North Little Rock," she said, nodding at the baggie.

"Yes, ma'am?"

"I was wondering, if you get a chance, would you go by there please? It may not even be there anymore, but if it is . . ." She trailed off. Her lips were trembling.

Jacob doubted they'd have much of an opportunity for side trips, and he was about to tell her as much when she started talking over him.

"We had to leave so fast. You don't remember those days, I know, but it was so crazy when . . . when . . . when we left. I didn't even get a picture of my daughter. At the time, it didn't seem important, you know, with everything coming down around us like it did. I thought I'd always have her with me. That she would outlive me. I was wondering, if you could make the time . . ."

Jacob had known Maggie Hester his entire life. She'd even taught his pickling and preserving class back in school. But he'd never heard anything about a daughter. She'd lived alone as long as she'd been here in Arbella. It wasn't hard to figure out her situation, though. A lot of people lost their families during the First Days. Jacob's own dad had died on the way to Arbella. He was only three at the time and had no real memories of the man, but his mom sure did.

Jacob slipped the baggie inside his jacket. "I'll make the time," he said.

She seemed to deflate right in front of him.

"Bless you," she said. "You have no idea how much this means to me, to all of us, that you're going on this expedition. We're so very proud of you."

Before he could respond, she turned and trundled back through the rain to her house.

Jacob watched her go.

When she was back inside, he turned, bent his head against the wind and rain, and pushed on.

But he only made it a few feet before he stopped and let out a gasp.

There, on the pavement, was the dark stain left behind from Amanda Grieder's suicide. The hard freezes of February had given way to a rainy March. It had rained a lot since that night. Nearly every day, in fact. He stared at the stain and wondered why the rain hadn't washed it away.

Nobody blamed him for Amanda's death. Quite the contrary, nearly everybody who was there, and nearly everybody who only heard about it later, said they thought he'd done everything he could to talk her down. And when she came back, he'd done the right and proper thing, putting her down with decision and dignity. A few had even said it was just another indication that Jacob Carlton was one of the best of his generation, the kind of man who exemplified the grit and get it done attitude that brought the First Generation safely to Arbella.

He alone blamed himself for Amanda's death, and there was no getting past that. Some wounds are slow to heal.

And some never heal at all.

7

Kelly greeted him at the door with a Mason jar full of her homemade gin in her hand. "Welcome, stranger," she said. "You thirsty?"

"God, yes."

"Barry," Kelly yelled into the house. Her home was lit by the warm buttery glow of dozens of candles and filled with the chatter and laughter of a small dinner party. "The boss wants a drink."

"On it!" Barry called from the kitchen.

"Here's a towel. You can put your umbrella over there, but leave your boots outside. I don't want you tracking mud in my house."

The other members of the expedition were already crammed in around the Banises' dining room table. There was a chair open at the head of the table, opposite Taylor's chair. Barry stuck a gin and tonic in his hand and pointed him toward the open chair.

"Welcome, boss."

"Thanks, Barry."

Jacob sat down at the head of the table. The others were

still talking amongst themselves. Only Taylor was watching him, another matchstick tucked securely in the corner of his mouth.

"You're late," Taylor said.

"I was figuring out the ammunition inventory with Steve. Looks like we're only gonna be able to bring about forty rounds each. The rest has to stay here to leave enough to defend the walls."

"Only forty rounds?" Barry said. "That's not enough, is it?"

Jacob shrugged. "It's what we've got to work with."

"Can't we gather some, you know, while we're outside the walls?" The question came from Bree Cheney, the gorgeous, bubbly blonde Nick Carroll had recommended for the post of medic. Her job at the Peach Orchard Farm was that of veterinarian, which meant she'd be able to help out with the horses, but she'd also been shadowing Dr. Gary Williams for a few years now, and by all accounts she was very good at what she did. Though clearly, from her question, salvage was not her bag.

Jacob glanced to Frank Hartwell, the engineer for the expedition and Jacob's old boss back when he was working with the salvage teams, figuring he'd want to answer that. Hartwell was a strong, bulky man of fifty. His hair was graying at the temples, but his full beard remained perfectly black. At first he'd refused coming on the expedition, saying that he was too old, but he was one of the most levelheaded men Jacob knew, and nobody in town could match his knowledge of the wasteland, and in the end, Jacob had insisted.

Hartwell nodded and churched his fingers together in front of his lips. "It's certainly possible that we could find some ammunition while we're out, but you can't hang much hope on that. The chance of finding the right caliber, for instance, is remote at best. It's possible we could stumble on a gun store or a sporting goods store that hasn't been looted down to the floor tiles, but not all that likely. And even if we did find a pile of the right caliber ammunition at one of those places, the stuff is going to be thirty years old. It's had plenty of time to rust and corrode. It might not even fire anymore. Or worse, it might blow up in our face."

"So what's the alternative?" Kelly said. "I mean, forty rounds apiece isn't much if we find ourselves in a bad mess, right?"

Several of the others started talking at once.

Taylor rapped his knuckles on the table and that quieted down the room. "Leave it all here." He nodded to Jacob. "Tomorrow, when you talk to Steve, tell him all the ammo stays here for civil defense."

Nobody spoke. There were nervous glances around the table.

"All of it?" Jacob said. "You're sure?"

"I am," Taylor said. "And don't worry, I got us covered. Shortly after you got the council's permission to organize this trip I went to Billy Evans over at the machine shop and asked him to gather up all the damaged shell casings he could find. He got a whole mess load of 'em from the school's shooting range and he's been retooling them ever since. I'm told he's reloaded enough to give us seven hundred rounds apiece."

"Seven *hundred*?" said Barry. "You're kidding. That's amazing."

"Well, most of us will have fourteen boxes of fifty rounds each." Taylor pointed at Eli Sherman and Max Donavan, two groomers from Walter Mayfield's livery. Neither man had turned twenty yet, but both were known to be equally good with horses, fists, and rifles. They were along for muscle, mainly, and to help Bree Cheney care for the horses. "You two," Taylor said. "I'm told both you men are crack shots. That true?"

The two men stiffened.

"Uh, yes, sir," they both stammered as one.

"Good. I set aside a thousand rounds each for the two of you."

Eli and Max looked at each other with equal parts delight and shock. The notion that the Great Sheriff Taylor had just publicly complimented them had left them both a little starstruck.

"I expect you'll make every round count."

"Yes, sir!" Eli said.

And from Max: "You can count on it, sir."

"Good." Taylor glanced across the table to Jacob. "And, what's more, Billy tells me he was able to make the rounds subsonic."

Jacob's eyebrows went up.

"What's that mean?" Bree asked.

"Slower than the speed of sound," Eli said, and slapped Max on the shoulder as the two shared a grin.

Bree gave him the finger. "I know what subsonic means, you little jerk. I mean why is it important that a bullet is subsonic?"

Jacob started to answer, but Frank Hartwell interrupted. His tone was quiet and patient, and to Jacob at least, who knew how gruff the man could be in the field, it was pretty obvious he had taken a shine to Bree.

"When you fire a gun," he said, "it sounds like it makes one loud bang, but it actually makes two. The first is the explosion that happens when the firing pin hits the detonator and the charge explodes. The second one, the loud crack that carries for miles, is the sonic boom that comes with the bullet breaking the sound barrier."

"So it'll be like having a silencer or something?" Bree asked.

"Not quite," Frank said. "But at least the sound won't carry for miles. It's definitely a good thing, even if it does decrease the range of our weapons a bit."

That brought appreciative smiles and nods from the others around the table. Jacob felt relieved as well, but he was troubled by the way Taylor had chosen to unveil his information. Jacob had shared everything with Taylor. He'd held nothing back, but clearly information wasn't flowing both ways. If they were supposed to be coleaders of this expedition, this wasn't the best kind of start Jacob could think of.

He felt like he had to retake control of the meeting.

"Is everybody ready to begin?" he asked the group.

Nods all the way around the table. The mood had turned light again.

Jacob surveyed the group. "So, this is what I want to do tonight. Most of you know each other quite well, or at least know of each other. That's good. But I want to lay out officially why you're all here and what you'll be doing. I thought we'd go around the table and introduce ourselves."

Jacob turned to Nick seated at his right.

"You want to start us off?"

"Uh, sure," Nick said. "So, yeah, I'm Nick Carroll. I draw pretty good, so they hired me on to make maps." He looked at Jacob with his patented wicked grin and shrugged. "I don't know. I guess that's about it."

Jacob shook his head. "Don't let him fool you, folks. Despite all the evidence to the contrary, Nick here actually has a brain. Most of you probably know already that he's pretty good at drawing, but he's also got a thing for maps, so I'm hiring him on as our cartographer. On top of that, he's got some expertise outside the wall. Sheriff Taylor and I have worked closely with him, and with Frank over there, to figure out our route, which we're gonna go over here in a sec."

He turned to Kelly. "You want to go next?"

Kelly smiled at the room. "I know most of you already. I'm Kelly." She gave a little wave. "This is my husband, Barry." Barry dutifully raised his hand in a drunken salute. "We supervise production and research over at Howth Farm, which I guess makes us as close to botanists as anybody you're gonna find here in this town. Obviously, we won't be able to carry all the food we need for the trip, so our job will be to tell you what stuff is safe to eat. Also, we're going to be doing frequent soil samples for CDHL levels." She gave Nick's shoulder a pat. "We'll be tabulating our data with Nick here, and hopefully, after we're done, we'll know the right direction for expansion."

"Excellent." Jacob pointed to Kelly's right and said, "Frank . . ."

"Yeah. Thanks, Jacob. Okay. My name is Frank Hartwell. I was Jacob's boss about ten years ago, before he went off and left me for the law. My specialty is salvage. I take what's gone bad and make it new again. At least in theory. I'll be working with Jacob and Sheriff Taylor to see if there's anything we encounter out in the wasteland that Arbella can use."

"Like what?" asked Max.

Frank shrugged. "Well, anything. Motors, gasoline, door knobs."

"Door knobs?" Max said.

"A joke, son. The point is we have no idea what might prove valuable. I've been collecting a list of requests, and we'll try to find that stuff, but salvage is all about thinking out of the box. There's no telling what can be repurposed into what. You just take it as it comes."

"Yeah, but it's a question of who takes it, if you know what I mean. I didn't sign on to carry a bunch of junk all over the wasteland."

Frank turned in his chair and looked like he was about to read the kid the riot act. Jacob stepped in before that had a chance to happen. "It doesn't work that way, Max," he said. "When you do salvage like this, if it's something there's no way you can carry, you just record the location of the find, hide it or disguise it if you can, and then report back to town for the proper resources to go back out and get it. We don't have a whole lot of gas, but we've got enough to power a truck to go out and bring something back, provided it's worth it."

Max mulled that over. "So, I'm not gonna be carrying a bunch of junk all over zombie country, right?"

"Right," Jacob said. "We're not bringing you along as a pack mule, don't worry."

"Oh. Well, okay then."

They worked their way through the rest of the introductions—Owen Webb, anthropologist; Andy Dawson, the town's main reporter—before Jacob ordered the table cleared so they could unveil a giant map of Missouri.

"Nick," Jacob said, "you want to start us off?"

Nick cleared his throat. "Yeah, you bet." He ran a finger down the right side of the map. "Obviously, this is the river, and this bend here, where it says New Madrid, that's us. The first leg of the journey is to take Highway 55 here up to where it meets Interstate 55. From there, we'll follow the interstate up to Sikeston. We're figuring that should take about a week."

"A week?" said Andy Dawson. "Why a week? That looks like a straight shot to me. What is it, about thirty miles?"

Andy was a talented carpenter. He'd actually rebuilt the front steps of Jacob's mother's house, which is why Jacob thought of him for this expedition—though not in his capacity as carpenter, but as a journalist. On the recommendation of David Sachs, Jacob had read the *Journals of Lewis and Clark* and had come away with an appreciation for the fact that they were going to need someone to chronicle the expedition. Jacob could barely force himself to write a full police report, much less something book length, so he'd turned to Andy Dawson, one of four part-time journalists for the Arbella *Weekly News*.

"It's closer to fifty miles," Jacob said. "But it's hard country. I remember there were places so overgrown that you couldn't even tell where the highway used to be. You'd see these big eighteen-wheelers standing in the middle of a sea of grass like shipwrecks and that was about the only clue there was ever a road there." Jacob glanced across the table at Frank Hartwell. "You've been out there recently. Is it still that bad?"

"It's gotten a lot worse, actually," said Frank. "Once nature starts taking over, the rate of encroachment speeds up exponentially every year. In some places the grass grows shoulder high. Fires happen every once in a while, usually near the end of summer, so there won't be that much scrub brush to contend with, but the grass and the sunflowers come back pretty fast, especially after a rainy spring like we've had. It may not look all that far, but we'll need that week."

"And remember," Jacob said. "This isn't a race. We're doing this to get a good look around. I want to take our time, give everybody a chance to get used to living on the trail."

"What about zombies?" Bree asked. She looked around the table nervously.

"There's always a chance," Frank said, his baritone softening just a little. He pointed to Sikeston on the map. "I was up in these parts about three years ago, and we ran into a herd of seven of them. And then there's the really big herd that Jacob fought back last month. So, yeah, they're out there. We'll have to be on our toes."

"What do we do if we see them?"

"Just fall back on the training you got in school," Frank said. "We avoid them as long as we can, and we only fight them if we absolutely have to."

"Silent running is the rule here," Jacob added. "I want you guys to take this first week to acclimatize yourself to life in the wasteland. Get comfortable on the trail. But keep in mind that comfortable is not the same thing as having a party out there. We'll exercise noise discipline the entire time we're outside the wall. Use the hand signals you were taught in school whenever possible. Talk only when necessary, or when it's obvious we're alone. But if you do talk, do so quietly. Remember: Anything can happen, and it often does."

Bree glanced down at the map, clearly nervous.

"Look," said Frank, softening his voice another notch, "we're not trying to scare anybody. I think you'll find, once you get out there, that the wasteland isn't all that bad. Parts of it are, yeah, but most of it is actually kind of beautiful. The fish have made a tremendous comeback, for example. There are streams so thick with trout you could almost walk on their backs to cross to the other side. Plus"—he drew an imaginary circle on the map with his index finger—"this part in through here is all a known element. We've been exploring it for years, so I'm not planning on any huge surprises."

"What about this area here?" asked Andy, his finger on the open country north of Sikeston.

Frank nodded thoughtfully, as though considering how to answer. He stroked his beard and heaved his broad shoulders. "Well, that's kind of the point of this whole expedition, isn't it? This is Highway 60," he said, and drew a line across the map. "Once we get out beyond that point, we're in undiscovered country. Nobody I know has been beyond there."

They all regarded the map with a newfound respect.

Jacob looked around the table and realized the full measure of what they were about to do was finally sinking in. "But we're ready for that," he said. "Everybody at this table has been trained to take care of themselves, and each other. That's our Code. *Everybody works, everybody watches the other guy's back.* Just remember that, and we're gonna make this expedition as big a success as Arbella herself."

Frank Hartwell nodded.

Max and Eli traded huge grins.

Even Bree seemed to relax a little.

"Well, I want another drink," said Barry. "Anybody else want some?"

A few held out their glasses, including Jacob. Barry rose to collect them, but before he could leave the table, Owen Webb spoke for the first time.

"I have a question," he said.

He seemed intensely serious, his frown in marked contrast to the rest of the room. Those few who were standing sat back down and listened. Owen was coming along as the expedition's anthropologist. He had been a brand new anthropology professor at the University of Arkansas at Little Rock when the First Days happened, but since coming to Arbella he'd settled into teaching reading and candle making to the children over at the school. Out of the entire group he was the only one Jacob had not personally recruited. In fact, he came to Jacob, and over the course of one long discussion while he helped Jacob mop the floors in the constabulary's jail cells he made a convincing case that he could offer a unique perspective on the world they were likely to find. Only two other members of the group, he reminded Jacob, were old enough to remember the world before the First Days. The younger members would undoubtedly have questions about the ruins they saw. Who better to answer those questions than a professor who taught about the way people used to live?

It was a convincing argument, and it had grabbed Jacob the same way Owen had grabbed the group at the table.

Once he had everyone's attention Owen said, "What about first contact?"

"What do you mean, first contact?" asked Max. He looked around the table. "What's that mean?"

"You know," Owen said, "with other people. We can't be the only Arbella out there. Surely others have survived, and thrived, just as we have. What happens when we make first contact with them?"

Jacob looked around the table. "That's a good question," he said. "Any thoughts?"

"Well," said Frank, "we've never run into anybody, and my crews and I have spent a lot of time out there."

"But it is possible," Owen said. "Even likely. It's like looking up at the stars and wondering if there's someone else out there. It's just not statistically possible that we are the only pocket of civilization to have survived. I think we need a plan for if, and when, we make that contact."

"I think we should probably try to avoid any settlements, don't you think?" Kelly said.

"Absolutely," Barry said.

"Yeah, me, too. I think that's a good policy in general," Nick said. "I'll, of course, record the location of any settlements we find. We could always arrange a future expedition to make the first contact."

"But it might be an opportunity to open trade," suggested Bree. "And if they've survived like we have, they're probably not the kind of people who would want to hurt us. I mean, right? They'd know that survival is a team effort, right? They'd welcome more team members."

Sheriff Taylor stood up.

All discussion stopped, and all eyes turned on him.

He leaned over the table and met the gaze of every person in the room. "Listen up," he said. "These are the ground rules. We make first contact only if we have to. We will record the locations of any settlements, as Nick suggested, but we will avoid first contact if at all possible."

Owen Webb started to object, but Taylor held up a hand to silence him.

"And I want to make sure that each of you understands this one thing. Under no circumstances are any of you to say a word about Arbella to anyone outside our circle. Not a single word. I will die before I give away the location of our home, and if you are going on this expedition, you better damn well do the same."

He scanned the room again, his gaze unflinching, the matchstick clenched tightly in his teeth.

"Is that absolutely clear?"

A few nodded right away, clearly cowed. Others, including Owen, Jacob, and Frank, slowly nodded a moment later.

8

They left Arbella on April 21st, and for that first week on the trail it seemed to Jacob more like a vacation than exploration. For one thing, his headaches were gone. There was no one else to make asinine suggestions that etiquette demanded he listen to. And all the public pressure of what to do and how to do it were finally a matter for the record. He'd taken action. He'd made the decisions. Now, finally, he was alone with the consequences of those choices. And he felt pretty damn good about it.

The last of the hard freezes were behind them, and spring had come upon them quietly as a cat. The mornings were cool and usually foggy, but the afternoons were mild. It got cold at night, but not even that had been much of an issue. Working closely with Nick and Frank, he'd charted out their course so that they always ended up close to some sort of structure by nightfall.

At night, they kept up a rotating guard, which had seemed a little silly that first night out, but proved useful during the second night.

Just before dawn, Owen Webb woke Jacob in a panic.

"Outside," he said. "Three of them coming up the road."

"Shhh," Jacob said, instantly awake.

He went to hand signals. *Just three. You're sure?*

Owen nodded.

They'd taken shelter inside an abandoned store that had once sold propane tanks. Frank Hartwell and his salvage teams had long since drained the tanks, but it was still one of the salvage teams' most popular stops on their treks outward from Arbella. It was set back from the highway by a good distance and offered some excellent places to hide the horses. It was also easily defended and afforded a fairly good view of anything coming up the highway in either direction.

Jacob went to the edge of the lot, keeping low between two large rusting tanks, and scanned the road where Owen pointed.

There were way more than three. Jacob picked shapes out of the darkness, eventually counting fourteen in all.

A fairly decent-sized herd.

There were only three before, Owen signed to him. *I promise*.

Something rustled in the grass behind them. It was Sheriff Taylor, coming up between the tanks, a black, mean-looking rifle in his hands. It looked sort of like an AR-15 with a collapsible stock, but it had a long, built-in suppressor on the muzzle and flip-up tactical sights. Jacob thought he'd seen every rifle in Arbella, but that one was a surprise

Jacob gestured at the rifle. *What's that?*

Taylor shook his head as if to tell him not now. The others were watching them from the storefront windows, crouched down out of sight. From somewhere behind the building, one of the horses caught the scent of the dead and snorted in fear.

Out on the road, several of the zombies turned toward the propane tanks and picked up their pace.

"Damn it," Taylor muttered. "Gonna have to go tactical."

"You can't shoot that many of them," Jacob said. "All the shots will attract every zombie in the area."

Taylor winked at him. "Just trust the old man, would you?"

Moving in a crouch Taylor stepped onto the road. A few zombies saw him and began to moan. But before they had a chance to start the feeding call that would attract even more of their numbers, Taylor began to fire.

There was no muzzle flash, no loud crack. The gun was nearly silent. It made a noise like somebody quietly snapping their fingers each time Taylor shot. And clearly, it was deadly accurate, for within seconds, motionless corpses surrounded Taylor, dark humps against the road.

Taylor scanned the countryside and, evidently satisfied, raised the rifle and calmly walked back to the storefront.

Jacob followed after him. "What the hell was that?"

Taylor smiled. "The old dog's still got a few tricks."

"No kidding. Where did you get that rifle?"

"A little something from before the First Days. Part of my private stash."

"I thought I'd seen every rifle in town, but I've never seen anything like that. What is it?"

"A Colt M4 carbine with a built-in suppressor. I railed it up a bit, but deep down it's just your standard M4."

"Those shots . . . it was so quiet."

"Special ammo. It's a 300 Blackout round, subsonic."

Jacob shook his head and laughed. The old man really did know how to make a splash. And then he saw the magazine sticking up from Taylor's belt. On the bottom of it was a white sticker with a happy face on it. Jacob pointed at it. "Never would have thought you'd have a sense of humor about bullets."

Taylor saw him pointing at the magazine and his expression turned serious. He stripped the magazine from the M4 and ejected the round from the chamber. Next he visibly and physically checked the weapon to make sure it was empty and then slid it back into his saddlebags.

He held out the two magazines, the one he'd just ejected from the weapon and the one with the smiley face, and said, "Look at those. Tell me what you see."

They appeared identical. That is, until Jacob turned the magazines upside down and examined the bullets loaded there. In the low light it was hard to tell what he was supposed to be looking for, but then he saw it. The bullets in the magazine with the happy face were a different caliber. They were bigger. Not by much, but definitely bigger.

Jacob looked at Taylor in surprise. Bigger bullets like these would seat into the chamber just like the properly sized bullets, but if it was fired, it would jam up in the barrel and probably blow up in the shooter's face. At the very least, it would ruin the gun.

"Why do you have these?" he asked Taylor.

"It's a nasty surprise if anybody ever gets the gun away from me and tries to use it on our people. When you get to be sheriff, this'll be your gun. Remember that."

Then he put both magazines in his bag, took a seat against the wall, and said, "Wake me up when the coffee's ready, okay?" And with that he lowered the brim of his hat down over his eyes and settled into sleep.

9

The encounter made them cautious, and it was slow going after that, just as Jacob had predicted. Morale remained high. But Bree Cheney, the pretty young blonde Frank Hartwell was so taken with, turned out to be the biggest surprise of all. Jacob had been a little worried about her before they started out, because she'd seemed so terribly nervous about what they might encounter, but she took to the trail right away.

At one point, just before sundown on the third day, she'd gone to the edge of the roadway—there was actual pavement still visible at that point—and faced the setting sun. A cool wind blew across the grassland, making it move like a sea of molten brass. Frank had brought his horse up next to Jacob's so they could study the map a bit, but the sight of Bree on horseback, her hair filled with burning orange light, had completely thrown him over.

She turned suddenly, her smile beaming. "Isn't it beautiful?" she said.

"Yes, it is," Frank had said. "Yes, indeed it is."

Jacob had chuckled at that, and then went back to his map.

The other big surprise was that the horses were managing the tall grasses without any real trouble, and everybody seemed to be doing okay with the long rides. He hadn't heard any complaints at all.

Except for Nick, of course. From Nick there were complaints aplenty. He was a decent rider, but made little secret of his low opinion of horses. His horse, a rugged little six-year-old piebald mare, seemed to share a similar lack of respect for him. The horse absolutely refused to cross the numerous streams left behind from the rainstorms that kept them stuck in Arbella for the whole of March and early April. Even small ones made the animal nervous. The horse would be doing fine, then suddenly rear back at the water's edge and fidget around like she was terrified of getting her hooves wet. The constant battles grated on Nick's nerves and more than once resulted in him threatening to punch the animal in the nose. Jacob suspected the mare was just trying to show him who was boss, and Max and Eli even told him as much, but rider and horse proved too hardheaded to give in to the other. They ended up falling into a rhythm where either Eli or Max would come up alongside the animal, grab the reins, and coax the mare through the stream. It irritated Nick to need the help, but it got them along.

And in the evenings, while they couldn't risk a campfire, they had Kelly's homemade gin to ease the bumps and bruises of the day. All in all, Jacob went into those first few days with the feeling that they had this thing in the bag.

But of course it didn't last.

They ran into trouble shortly after setting out on the fifth day. They'd had gloriously good weather for the first part of their trek, and it had spoiled them. Then it started to rain. It wasn't much, at first, but the clouds grew darker and darker, and the rain went from a mild shower to an apocalyptic event. The wind picked up. Rain lashed at their faces like shards of glass. Jacob pulled a tarp over his head and pinched it close beneath his chin. Turning to look down the line of riders, he saw the others doing the same.

The horses grew skittish. Nick's mare turned into a devil and got so uncontrollable that Max had to hand his pack animal off to Eli so that he could come up alongside to help control the horse.

Still, the animal bucked and snorted every time lightning fired in the distance.

After watching Nick get nearly thrown from his mount, Jacob made his way to the rear of the column and found Sheriff Taylor there, horse and rider with their heads down, trudging forward.

"I want to stop us up ahead," Jacob said. "There's an abandoned gas station there we can use to get out of the weather."

"Sounds good," said Taylor.

Jacob waited for more, but there was none. He regarded the man's quiet resilience and wondered if it was fortitude or merely bluster. Surely he had to be as miserable as the rest of them. Yet there was that iron look in his eye, and that flat, unflappable confidence in his voice, which always gave Jacob pause. You don't develop a reputation as the George Washington of your people without earning it, he thought, and maybe this was how you did it.

He turned his mare and headed back up the line.

"Listen up," he said. He had to yell to be heard over the wind. "There's an old gas station up ahead here. We're gonna stop there and wait out this weather. Is everybody doing okay?"

He heard grunts and grumblings from the others, which was good enough for him.

"All right," he said. "We're almost there."

10

They reached the gas station two hours later.

It was a rundown affair, barely more than a shell of the building it had once been. Grass crowded up against its walls, and trash lay thick on the floor. Shrubs were trying to grow through the broken windows and there was a faint, but noticeable, odor of rot and mildew. But they had just slogged through muddy rivers that had once been roads and had their faces lashed by rain, and they were glad for the shelter.

They tied up the horses under the awning that covered the gas pumps and most of the others went inside to push the trash out of the way so they had someplace to sleep. Jacob climbed on top of one of the gas pumps and scanned the distance. The rain made it impossible to see very far. The sky was so gray as to be almost black, and he could see flashes of lightning sparking on the horizon all around them.

"Looks like we're not going anywhere for a while," he said. Taylor was watching him from the doorway. "What do you think? Shall we just call this camp for the night?"

"Might as well," Taylor said. He gestured toward the garage bays. "We're blind to the west, though. Anything coming at us from that direction would be on us before we knew it. You'll need to post extra lookouts to cover that."

"Agreed," Jacob said.

"Also, I want you to have everyone turn out their gear and make sure nothing got wet that wasn't supposed to. That storm came up on us fast and I know some of these folks haven't been all that careful packing their kits."

"Okay. Sure."

Taylor nodded and went inside without saying another word.

Nick came up behind Jacob. "What's that all about?"

"What's what all about?"

Nick gestured toward the doorway Taylor had just slipped through. "You and him. Trouble?"

"Why would there be trouble?"

Nick shrugged. "I don't know."

"Of course you do. You said it. What did you mean? Why would there be trouble?"

"Well, we've got two leaders. Supposed to have two, anyway. But from where I'm standing it looks like he's treating you more like a first officer than a partner."

"That's not what's happening," Jacob said flatly.

Nick shrugged again.

"It's not," Jacob said.

"Okay. I'm just telling you what it looks like from over here."

"Yeah, well, it's not."

Nick looked out across the rain-swept parking lot and sighed. "I just think you need to be careful is all. The whole point of this was to help you transition into the sheriff's job. You can't do that if he's never gonna step down."

"The point of this is not to make me sheriff."

"You know what I mean. The point of having you guys share leadership of this expedition. That was a mistake, if you ask me."

"He either came along or we didn't go. Both he and the council made that plain."

"That's just the council doing what he tells them."

"Nick, where's this coming from? If you had all these doubts, why'd you come?"

"Look, I'm not trying to start anything. I'm just thinking out loud. But I will say that you need to start thinking about who's actually in charge around here. Because so far, it looks like Taylor's using your opportunity for transition as his last stab at glory."

"How can you say that? He's not a glory hound."

Nick laughed. "Jacob, if you believe that, you don't know much about leadership. You really think a hero like Taylor over there is gonna sit back, content in his dotage, while some young hotshot steps in and takes all the glory?"

Jacob had no words. He just shook his head in exasperation.

"Just think about it. That's all I'm saying. Pay attention to what's coming."

Nick walked inside and left Jacob feeling angry and defensive, mainly because now that the words had been said out loud he knew them to be true. He'd seen it back in Arbella, during their meetings, and he'd seen it in little exchanges like the one he'd just had, ever since they took to the trail. Nick was right about one thing: Something would have to be done about it.

He sighed and turned to watch the rain sweep in silvery sheets across the road.

Gradually, he became aware of Max and Eli lurking near the door.

"What's up?" he said over his shoulder.

"Hey, boss, is it true we're camping here tonight?" Max said.

"Yep."

"You mind if we get the horses cleaned up?"

"Yeah," Jacob said. "Here, I'll give you a hand."

11

After helping Max and Eli with the horses, Jacob went inside to make himself something to eat. Kelly and Barry were off in a corner, setting up their equipment. Andy Dawson had one of his journals open on his knees and was busy scribbling notes about the ride. And over by the entrance to the garage bays, Bree was giggling at something Frank Hartwell had just told her.

Jacob couldn't help smiling at that.

A month ago, hell even a few days ago, he would have told Frank he was just a big hairy dog barking up the wrong tree, but to Jacob's surprise, Bree seemed to enjoy the older man's attentions. They'd become quite comfortable together, in fact, usually riding side by side on the trail.

The way Jacob figured it he didn't have much reason to be surprised. Frank was twenty-three years older than Bree, true enough, but that wasn't that weird. The day-to-day reality of life in Arbella had led to stranger unions, to be sure. If old Frank got cozy with a hot young blonde, more power to him. Plus, it was fun to watch Nick grumble about being cock blocked.

After a meal of peppered beef jerky and dried apricots, he arranged the lookout schedule, found a spot in the corner, pulled his hat down low over his eyes, and drifted toward sleep thinking about what Nick had told him. Maybe it was true what he said about Taylor using this expedition for his own glory, and maybe it was just Nick lashing out in frustration because Frank was taking the woman Nick had wanted for himself. He'd just have to wait and see.

But there was no use trying to worry it all out now. He'd learned back in his days with the salvage teams to get sleep when he could, and so he settled into his corner spot and went to sleep with the music of the rain playing on the roof.

12

When he woke it was dark and the rain had stopped.

He pushed his hat back in place and listened, straining his senses against the night, unsure exactly what had brought him out of sleep. Outside, the horses were nervous. He could hear them bumping against each other and the gas pumps. A metal sign hanging from a chain by the doorway moved in the breeze and rattled against the wall. He felt an odd humming in his teeth, like a vibration. It was so subtle he thought maybe he was imagining it, or maybe he was getting sick, but then he noticed Andy Dawson's pen moving across the cover of his notebook. It was turning slightly with the vibration, which was getting stronger.

Not louder, because there was no sound, just stronger.

Soon the others stirred.

"What's going on?" Kelly asked.

"Shhh," Taylor said. He was standing near the door, rifle at the ready. He looked back at the others and held up his left fist, the sign to go to hand signals only.

Jacob was on his feet, rifle in hand, in the next instant.

The others followed his lead.

The vibration was growing stronger, and it was starting to hurt. The filling in Jacob's tooth felt like it was trying to rattle itself loose.

Andy let out a whimper.

The rear windows suddenly filled with four bright white lights. The lights drew up close to the building and stopped. Max took a few steps toward the window, his hands up in front of his face to shield his eyes.

"What in the hell . . . ?"

Jacob grabbed him by the arm and pulled him back. "Get down," he said. "All of you."

But before any of them could move, the lights slowly and silently rose into the air and disappeared, dropping them into near darkness again.

Only the vibration remained, and that continued to get stronger and more painful. Andy's pen was almost dancing on the floor. One window still held a shard of glass in its frame, and that suddenly popped and fell to the floor. The tin cup from somebody's mess kit rattled on a plywood shelf before it too fell to the floor. A worn metal sign secured to the door to the garage rattled hard against its bolts, then broke them, and flew to the ceiling. So did the tin cup, and forks and spoons and everything metal in the room.

There was a loud click, like heavy gears falling into place, and then a blinding flash of light hit the entire building. Nobody moved. Nobody spoke. Jacob was so scared he felt like his feet had grown roots, holding him firmly in place. He tried to look out the window, but it hurt too badly and he had to turn away.

Then there came another loud click and the flood of light changed to a softer, but just as brilliant pattern of colored lights that moved away to the south. All the metal that had rushed to the ceiling came crashing back down to the floor.

A moment later, Taylor and Jacob were rushing out the

door, pushing their way through the thoroughly terrified horses and out onto the road.

Gliding silently about a hundred feet off the ground was an immense airship. It seemed to take forever to pass overhead. More and more of it came into view. Every inch of it sparkled with colored lights. Jacob thought he saw something black and long and made of metal under the lights, like a long rectangular box, but it was impossible to tell for sure. And then a loud series of pops, like the wind catching a sail, filled the air. The colored lights suddenly went dark, and vast cloth sails, like wings, lowered into place.

Jacob watched it glide away, the only noise the wind popping in its sail-wings as it picked up speed.

Thirty seconds later, it was gone.

From behind him, someone spoke. "What in the hell was that?"

13

Nobody spoke. Not at first.

Jacob looked around the group, and saw his own shock and terror staring back at him. Even Taylor looked rattled. With the airship gone they seemed to have been consumed in an exhalation of darkness, though enough starlight filled the sky to cast a silvery light over their faces. A breeze gusted in off the grasslands, carrying the scent of rain. Above them, to the east, Orion the hunter was climbing the sky from the horizon, one foot in the vast reaches of space, the other digging for purchase on the edge of the world.

It was almost like nobody wanted to speak, or was afraid to.

And then one of the horses bumped into one of the other horses, and the sudden contact sent a wave of panic through their number. One horse reared and whinnied.

Eli rushed over to calm the animals, and eventually they fell silent again.

But the commotion had loosened everybody's tongue.

Owen Webb put a hand to his forehead and paced in a circle. "Seriously, what the hell was that?" He'd been sleeping on his windbreaker before the encounter and it had messed up his hair, half of it sticking out every which way and the other half mashed flat against the side of his head. Between his crazy hair and the pacing, he looked like a man about to unhinge.

"I think we all know what that was," Andy said.

"We do?" Owen snapped back, wheeling around to face him. "Please, enlighten me then, because I have no idea what the hell I just saw."

Andy said nothing. He looked around at the others for some sign that others were thinking the same thing he was.

"Motherfucking space aliens is what it was," said Eli.

Andy motioned at him with a *Thank-you!* gesture and turned back to Owen.

"That wasn't a spaceship," Owen said.

"It wasn't? You just said you had absolutely no idea what it was. So what was it?"

"I don't know!" Owen said. His voice had turned shrill and he was near to screaming.

"Quiet!" Jacob barked. He stepped between the two men. "Everybody keep your voices down. That thing made enough light to attract every zombie in the area. I think we need to move out."

"But . . . to where?" asked Bree. "I mean, shouldn't we, I don't know, go back?"

"Why would we do that?" Barry said.

"Well . . . I don't know, that thing. That was scary. Shouldn't we tell somebody?"

"Like who?" Barry said. "And what would we tell them? That we saw an alien spaceship?"

"I'm not at all convinced that's what we saw," Owen said.

"You have no idea what we just saw," Andy said.

"Neither do you. But I know it wasn't space aliens."

"You saw what it did. The lights. All the metal stuff rising to the ceiling. Those great big sails."

"What's a spaceship need cloth sails for?"

"I don't know," Andy said. "I didn't build the damn thing."

"Enough," Taylor said. He stepped into the middle of the group. The others fell silent, waiting for him to speak. "I don't know what that thing was," he said, and made a point of looking right at Andy and Owen. "None of us knows what that thing was. But I know this. It put out enough light to attract every zombie around here, just like Jacob said. We need to be ready for that. I want everybody to gear up. We're moving out in ten minutes. If we're gonna have a fight, I want to be ready for it."

"But where are we going?" Bree asked. She looked at Frank. "Shouldn't we go back to Arbella?"

"We're continuing with the mission," Taylor said.

"But we don't know what that thing was," Owen said. "What if it comes back?"

"That's exactly the point," Taylor said. "We don't know what it was. It could be a threat, or it could be something else. We just don't know. But if there's a threat to Arbella out there I damn sure want to know what it is. We'll head back when we have some answers, not before. Now everybody get ready to move out."

14

They traveled in silence the rest of the night and arrived on the southern outskirts of Sikeston shortly after first light.

Max was out front, riding point. All the other Arbella men had made an effort to shave in the evenings, when they made camp, but Max had not. He was sporting a splotchy mustache and beard that might grow into something big, but at the moment only made him look unkempt.

He stopped his horse, turned in his saddle, and motioned for the group to stop. Then he turned his horse and came back to where Jacob and Nick were waiting.

"Looks pretty quiet," he said. "What do we do?"

Jacob scanned the city. It was too big, too spread out, to see all of it at once, but what he could see looked quiet and deserted. Most of the buildings were low, rectangular concrete boxes with grass and spindly shrubs climbing up the sides. Few of the buildings were more than two stories high, though there were some larger ones here and there that Jacob guessed had been hotels back before the First Days.

Nick had his map open on the back of his mare's neck. "There's this road here," he said, and pointed to a thick yellow line that cut the town into two more or less even halves. "Malone Avenue. It looks like it runs all the way through town. I was thinking we could get on that and head west. That'll take us by the airport, here, where we can let Frank look around for whatever he can find."

Nick looked to Frank and the older man nodded.

"Okay. Then we head west again. That'll put us here, in the middle of town. I was looking at some old photographs and it looks like they had a tractor supply store, a farm and home store, and a couple of other places that might be good to check out. After that, I thought we'd head north up to here and check out their medical center."

Jacob glanced around the group and got nods all the way around.

"Okay," he said. "Let's move out."

Once they entered town, they formed a single column, Jacob and Max riding at the head of the line, while Eli and Sheriff Taylor brought up the rear. Most of the trail up from Arbella had been over grass-covered roadways, which masked the sound the horses' hooves made on the ground. And even in those places where the pavement remained uncovered, the whistling of the wind had been loud enough to conceal their movements. But that wasn't the case here in town. Weeds grew up from the cracks in the roads, but nature had yet to reclaim them. The sound of hooves on pavement echoed off the windowless buildings on either side of the road, making Jacob more and more nervous. Glancing back down the line, he could see his worry reflected back at him from the others, but there was little they could do about it except keep a weather eye open for trouble.

Their luck held out all the way to the airport. Sikeston seemed as quiet as the grave. The only things moving were the birds, and there were plenty of those. Ravens, mostly. They'd seen several sitting atop the sign welcoming them to the airport, but there were many more on top of the three main buildings that made up the airport's business center. They looked down on Jacob and the others with haunting, dead stares, completely unafraid of the intrusion into their home.

But looking past the birds there didn't seem to be much they could salvage. The buildings had long ago been hollowed out and stripped down to the lath, and the runway was wrinkled and cracked. Here and there they saw a few small planes, but they were little more than rusted heaps. One even had a mulberry bush growing out of the frame that had once held its windshield and a carpet of green clover growing on its wings.

"Any chance there's gas in the underground tanks?" Jacob asked Frank. If there was anything salvageable around here, it would be that.

"Maybe. Though it looks like this place has been cleaned out already."

"Where do you suppose those would be?"

Frank turned toward the hangars. "Over there'd be my—"

He cut himself off and pointed at the tree line beyond the hangars.

A dead woman had just stumbled out of the trees. She was badly decomposed, her clothes nothing but dirty rags embedded into her rotting flesh. The decomposition was so complete her legs could barely carry her, and every jerky step sent a shudder through her body that seemed like it might cause her to collapse. But she staggered on, one clumsy step after another.

Jacob scanned the tree line, looking for more. One thing they'd learned about the undead over the last thirty years was that they tended to group together. They sought each other out wherever they could, gathering into progressively bigger and bigger herds. Some of the First Generation told about seeing herds so large they shook the ground when they walked and made such a horrible moaning they could be heard for miles. Herds like that didn't exist anymore—at least Jacob hoped they didn't—but he had no doubt they once did.

Still, it only took one. A bite or a scratch from a zombie wasn't necessarily fatal, but the infection that usually resulted from a bite was. Back in grade school, one of his shooting instructors had described zombies as walking petri dishes full of just about every deadly bug known to man, making their bites almost as dangerous as that of a venomous snake.

But surprisingly, this zombie seemed to be by itself. It staggered slowly across the parking lot, making it almost halfway before tripping over a rusted pipe and falling face-first into the weeds.

It tried over and over again to get back on its feet, but couldn't manage it.

Jacob was about to go over to it and crush its head when the first ravens lit from the business center and began circling the still struggling zombie.

More followed.

Soon an enormous flock of them circled in the air over the dead woman.

"What are they doing?" Kelly asked.

"I don't know," Jacob answered. He looked to Frank. "You ever seen that before?"

"No."

Jacob turned to Sheriff Taylor, who answered with a single shake of his head.

The first few birds had already landed next to the dead woman by the time Jacob turned back. One of the birds darted forward and stabbed at the dead woman with its beak. The zombie raised one feeble arm, but it didn't come anywhere close to the bird.

More darted in, pecking at the zombie.

Jacob heard angry squawking and a furious rustling of

wings, and then the birds rushed in as one and started to tear the zombie apart, fighting over the leathery scraps they had ripped away in big strips. The zombie thrashed and writhed to the last, but it never had a chance against so many.

It took the birds less than two minutes to strip the carcass down to the bone.

When they were done, the birds went back to fighting amongst themselves.

It was a chaotic scene, and one that held them all with a shocked and rapt fascination.

"I've never seen anything like that," Frank said.

Beside him, Bree shuddered. "It was awful."

Frank turned to Sheriff Taylor. "Why do you suppose they attacked that zombie like that? Ravens are carrion birds. That thing was still moving."

"I've never seen anything like that," Taylor said.

"I guess they smelled the decomposition," Barry said.

Taylor shook his head. "That's possible, but birds cue off of movement more than smell, don't they?"

"Raptors do," Barry agreed.

Taylor surveyed the blackened skeleton that was all that remained of the zombie, and shook his head. "I don't think we should stick around here to discuss it," he said. "Where there's one of those things, there's probably a hundred. We should make ourselves scarce."

"Are we going to ride out of town?" Bree asked.

Jacob glanced at Taylor, who nodded.

"That'd be the smart thing to do," Jacob said.

"But . . . what about the medical center?" Bree asked. She looked from Jacob and Taylor back to Frank, like she hoped he'd back her up. "I wanted to see if there were any medical supplies there we could salvage. There are things we need back in Arbella. Syringes and IV bags. A defibrillator, if they've got one. That'd be the Holy Grail, actually."

"She's right," Taylor said. "We can't pass up a chance to

collect medical supplies. Nick, you said the medical center was north of town?"

"North of where we were. It should be due west of us now, across that field there."

"Okay," Taylor said. "We'll head there first. We make it quick though. We grab what we can and we get out."

"Thank you, sheriff," Bree said.

"Absolutely," he said. "Let's hope it's worth it."

15

Thirty minutes later they reined up in front of a wall of concrete barriers two stories high. The walls were pocked with bullet holes and brown, woody vines were growing up its moldy face, but they could still see the word *LIARS* written in spray paint all over the walls.

"What's that about?" Jacob said.

Nick came up alongside him. "No idea. Let's ask the anthropologist." He turned in his saddle and called out to Owen. "Hey, professor, what's this all about?"

Owen stared up at the walls, and then scanned their length in both directions. Evidently whoever built the wall hadn't had enough concrete sections to surround the hospital. There were gaps, and those gaps had been filled with buses and intermodal cargo boxes and anything else the builders had been able to put their hands on. But the word *LIARS* was painted over all of it.

Owen glanced at the ground where, even now, thirty years after the First Days, shell casings could still be seen rusting in the grass.

"Looks like they put up a pretty good fight. If they were

shooting toward the hospital I would imagine they must have rounded up most of their undead and kept them here in the hospital. These shell casings and bullet holes in the walls are probably from them trying to keep the zombies inside."

"Yeah, that's pretty much obvious," Nick said. He waved a hand toward the wall. "What's with the *LIARS* written all over the place?"

Owen's eyes narrowed.

Jacob had been watching the two men during their time on the trail. They'd taken a strong dislike to one another. On Nick's side, that dislike came out as name-calling and mockery. Owen just did a lot of squinting and muttering.

Yet another problem he had to add to his list.

Owen said, "I haven't seen any specific mention of liars, but I think I can infer what they meant here. During the First Days, there was a lot of talk of finding a cure. Everybody had lost somebody they loved. People were desperate for a way to bring them back."

"How do you cure a zombie?" Nick said. "They're dead. There's pretty much no cure for that."

Owen took a long moment to answer.

"Everybody wanted a cure," he finally said. "Yes, they were dead. Yes, there's no coming back from that. But people don't always think right when it comes to losing the people they love the most. And when you see them walking around, it's even harder to think of them as dead, even if you know it academically. Remember, knowing something and feeling something are very different. Every night on the news you'd see some segment on how close they were to a cure. I think we all knew it was a lost cause, but when your six-year-old daughter is wandering around the backyard with a piece of your ten-year-old son hanging from her lips, you find yourself willing to hang a hope on finding a cure."

Owen's face had turned red, and his breath whistled in his nose. Jacob watched the pain play out on the man's face, and he was reminded yet again of what it meant to live in a small town. You know everybody, and everybody knows you. But nobody knows the real you, the deep-down dark places that you go to when you're on fire with hurt and lost in the pain of memory. That belongs to you alone, even when you give it voice.

To his credit, Nick said nothing.

Owen looked up at the wall and studied the graffiti written there. "This," he said, his voice thick with emotion. "This is the work of an angry people. You can see their wrath all along this wall. They wanted to believe there was a cure, and what they got instead of the results they'd been promised, was more death. Is it any wonder they did this?"

Nick glanced at Jacob, clearly a little embarrassed. At least the man had some sense of shame.

Jacob nodded. "Thanks, Owen. That explains it just fine."

Owen didn't say a word. He just turned his horse around and went to the back of the line.

16

The south side of the hospital, the side that faced into town, had taken heavy damage. One of the concrete sections had fallen over, creating a big hole, but there were numerous other gaps as well. Jacob scanned the area for trouble. Everywhere he looked, he saw burned-out cars and trucks, and the ground was covered with thousands and thousands of rusted shell casings. There'd been some bad fighting here, back in the day.

"Bree, do you have a pretty good idea of what you need?"

Their medic rode up, Frank Hartwell by her side. "I have a wish list," she said. "If I'm able to find anything on it is anybody's guess."

"Okay," he said. "Well, it's getting to be about noon. I'll give you an hour. Sound like enough time to look around?"

"Should be, yeah."

"Frank, you're going with her, right?"

"Yep."

"Okay. Max, you, too."

"You got it, boss."

The three of them dismounted, climbed through the wall,

and crossed the overgrown field that had once been the front lawn of the hospital. The front doors had long ago been knocked down and they slipped inside without incident.

"You think this is worth the effort?" Kelly asked. "I mean, thirty-year-old medical supplies?"

Jacob shrugged. "It'll be worth it if she finds that defibrillator she was talking about. Even if it doesn't work, we could rebuild it. We could save lives with one of those."

He climbed down off his horse and the others did the same. They tied the animals off in a small field where they could forage for some grass. Then Jacob and the others took a seat in the middle of the road and shared a lunch of beef jerky and pickled vegetables.

Jacob was trying to get at the last piece of cauliflower in the jar when the ravens came back. They landed on the top of the wall and on the nearby roofs, hundreds of them. Several of the horses got spooked and started making noise.

Jacob stood up and turned in a circle, watching the birds land on every available roosting point.

Within seconds, the birds were all around them.

"I don't like this," said Nick.

"No, me either," Jacob said.

Taylor grabbed Eli by the shoulder. "Go into the hospital and find the others. Bring 'em out here as fast as you can."

Eli ran for the hospital.

Taylor pushed the brim of his hat up with his thumb as he looked around. "Damnedest thing I ever saw."

"Uh-oh," said Barry. "Hey, guys, we got trouble."

Barry pointed off to their left. A gray-haired man with dark stains all over his clothes was walking their way, his gait too slow to be normal, his arms and legs too stiff. Behind him, two more men staggered out of the shadows.

Suddenly, the birds began to squawk excitedly.

Several hundred of their number took to the air and circled overhead.

The three zombies stepped into the street. Jacob went for his rifle, but Kelly put her hand on his.

"Wait," she said. Kelly turned to Barry. "I think they're changing their predation ecology."

As they watched, the birds dipped toward the zombies, dive-bombing them, pecking at them a little at a time with each pass. Jacob had seen the same thing back in Arbella every time somebody's dog got too close to a blue jay's nest. The birds would dive-bomb the dog relentlessly, pecking at its back just where the tail starts. The dogs would go from angry and frustrated to hurt in just a few passes, and the next thing anybody knew the dog would run away, yelping the whole time.

But this looked somehow a little different, a little more like lions moving in to make a kill on some oversized prey.

The zombies grabbed at the birds, but caught only air. They were too slow, and the birds struck with the lethal precision of predators. Soon one of the zombies collapsed to its knees, only to be knocked facedown under a furious pounding of black wings. The birds started to devour it, even as it continued to struggle.

The other two zombies went down moments later.

Soon there were three knots of ravens, tearing and pulling the corpses apart.

"My God," Kelly said, stepping forward with a hand over her mouth. She turned back to the group. "Galapagos," she said.

"Yes!" Barry said, clearly impressed. "Darwin's finches reinvented for the apocalypse."

"What does that mean?" Jacob asked.

"They're evolving," Kelly said. She was so excited she was trying to talk with her hands. "They're showing adaptive behavior."

Jacob glanced at Nick, who only raised his eyebrows again. He was no help.

"I don't understand. What's Galapagos?"

"The island chain where Charles Darwin first worked out the theory of evolution. That's what's happening here. These birds are evolving. It's . . . it's like this. Ravens are opportunistic. They always have been. They have this huge range in their diet, everything from carrion to blueberries; they'll eat anything. They've coexisted with humans since before we started keeping track of things like that. But in all that time, we've known them as scavengers. They'll eat anything. They are the rats of the skies. But it's usually what we leave them. The corn growing in our fields or the trash in our alleys. But these birds, they've found their own way. They're living off the dead. Don't you see?"

No, he didn't see, but he was trying. Jacob shrugged and said, "That they're eating zombies . . . ?"

"Yes!" she said. "That's huge. They've gone from being our pests to being our predators."

"Not *our* predators," Jacob said. "They're eating zombies."

"Ravens are intelligent," she said. "But they don't know the difference between zombies and humans. That's what's so incredible about this. Consider it from a bird's point of view. The thing that has spent ten thousand years chasing them from the cornfields is now dinner. It walks around smelling dead, yet still it walks. Can't you see how huge that shift is? They've done more than change their diet. They've taken an environmental catastrophe and turned it into a niche to guarantee their own survival. They're evolving."

Jacob thought on the implications of that, but he quickly realized he was out of his depth. It had been that way between them back when they were seventeen, and things hadn't changed much twenty years later.

Except that maybe the gap between them had grown more pronounced.

She turned away from him and spoke in hurried, excited

whispers with Barry, the two of them like kids with a new toy.

"Oh, shit," Owen said. "You guys . . ."

The ravens had suddenly taken flight in a roar of beating wings and angry squawking. They filled the sky.

Jacob saw why they'd launched a moment later. The houses to the west had once been small, comfortable one-story homes of red brick and wide lawns. The bricks still stood, but the lawns had turned to riot. Grass and wild shrubs grew shoulder high, and they'd covered the movement of a small army of zombies.

As Jacob and the others watched, zombie after zombie stumbled from the overgrown lawns. They staggered out of the tall weeds, and then locked in on the hospital and moved that way. There had to be forty of them at least. And then Jacob saw why the zombies were passing them by and heading for the hospital, where Bree, Frank, and their escorts had just launched themselves from the building's darkness. They were running through the tall grass as fast as they could go, trying to make their way back to the group, and it was driving the zombies insane with bloodlust.

Some believed that zombies keyed on movement as much as they did on sound. Jacob had heard stories from some of the salvage team guys about going perfectly still and quiet while a zombie herd moved around them, a stone in the middle of a stream, but he'd always thought that the same kind of talk as someone who claimed they had to walk five miles to school, in the snow, and uphill both ways.

Evidently, though, it was true, for Bree and the others weren't going to make it. The zombie herd was already at the wall and closing in around them.

Bree and the others stopped.

Frank put himself in front of the group and swung his rifle down from his shoulder.

"Rifles," Jacob said.

"No," Taylor said. "Belay that order."

He walked to his horse and pulled the carbine from his saddlebags.

He slapped a magazine into the receiver and charged the bolt. Then he rushed into the herd, firing as he moved, every shot deliberate and controlled.

And so damn quiet.

His shots sounded like a muffled cough, barely audible. Taylor charged into the herd and it never occurred to Jacob that he was watching a man in his seventies doing the shooting. He moved like a trained solider. Rather than give in to the excitement and confusion, all his movements were made with deadly precision.

Three zombies noticed Taylor coming up behind them and turned on him.

He put them down with perfect head shots.

When they fell, the others turned on him. Half the herd, maybe twenty of them, were still headed toward Bree, Max, Frank, and Eli, but the others were coming for Taylor. He never slowed his pace. The herd swarmed around him, but he kept a straight line for the hospital's front door.

In school, Jacob's tactics teachers had emphasized the importance of creating distance. Never let a zombie get too close to you. Create distance, take aim, and make your shots count, they'd said. But Taylor was doing exactly the opposite. He moved in close and fired, then turned, and fired again. Several times Jacob lost sight of him as the zombies closed in around him, until he'd suddenly erupt from their massing, gun blazing. He didn't stop moving until he reached Bree and the others. Once there, he slapped in a new magazine, turned to face the approaching crowd of zombies, and systematically gunned them down.

When the shooting was done, the street and the field in front of the hospital were littered with bodies. Jacob quickly lost count of how many of them there were. Certainly more than the forty he'd seen at first. Most lay in heaps on the ground. Some were slumped over the barricades. Others were face up in the grass, their arms bent at wrong angles, their heads caved in and misshapen from the gunshots.

Taylor walked from body to body, sometimes pausing to push one over with the muzzle of his weapon. Then he motioned for Bree and the others to follow him back to the horses.

Jacob stared at the carnage. Nick came up beside him.

"What do you think?" Nick said.

"That was amazing."

"Damn straight it was. Sheriff Taylor with a gun is like Picasso with a paintbrush." He turned and gave Jacob a pat on the shoulder. "You sure you're ready to be sheriff?"

Jacob could only stare at what Taylor had done. Picasso with a paintbrush was just about the perfect description for what he'd just seen. He was still staring at the bodies in the grass when Sheriff Taylor stepped over the barricade, Bree, Max, Frank, and Eli coming up behind him. All four of them looked thoroughly rattled, though it looked like Bree had found her defibrillator.

"Time to move out," Taylor said. "Everybody saddle up."

He went to his horse and stuffed the carbine into his saddlebags.

In the distance, a police whistle sounded. Three short, sharp blasts. Everybody turned toward the sound.

"What the hell was that?" Nick said.

The three whistle blasts sounded again, and this time, they were followed by a huge collective moan, as though from hundreds of voices.

"Look at that," Barry said, and pointed toward town where a vast dust cloud was rising into the air. The moaning was getting louder with every passing moment.

"That's a big herd," Taylor said.

"What do we do?" Kelly said.

"We'll make too much noise trying to run from them," Jacob said. He looked over at Taylor and pointed down a side street. "I suggest we head down that way, hide between the houses. A herd that big'll probably keep moving down the main road."

"How do you know that?" Kelly asked.

"They're a herd. They'll follow along wherever the main body goes."

Before anybody could argue, the whistle blasts came again. And the sound of dogs barking.

"What is that?" Nick asked.

"We should be somewhere else," Taylor said. "Jacob's right. Let's head down that way."

Jacob dug his heels into his mare's flanks and she took off at a fast trot. The others followed along behind him. He took them halfway down the block, glanced back to make sure they had gone far enough, and then turned them into the alley between a pair of houses.

Jacob climbed down off his horse, pulled his rifle from his saddlebags, and walked back toward the front of the house.

"Where are you going?" Nick asked.

"Lookout," Jacob answered. "Just in case."

Taylor pulled out his own rifle and followed him.

The two men got down on their stomachs behind the bush and watched the intersection at the end of the street. But it wasn't zombies they saw first. A lone rider appeared, working his horse back and forth across the intersection, blowing the whistle as he moved.

"What in the hell is he doing?" Jacob asked.

Taylor shook his head, clearly as confused as Jacob.

But then the rider reined in his horse. He was staring at something over by the barricades. He turned his horse off the road and into the field in front of the hospital. He stopped again, and then dismounted.

"What's he doing?"

"He sees the bodies."

Sure enough, the rider knelt next to one of the corpses Taylor had put down, grabbed the thing by the chin, and turned its face first one way and then the other.

He stood up and looked around.

But there wasn't time for him to investigate. The first zombies stumbled into the intersection a moment later, and he was forced to mount up again. He blew the whistle again, two short blasts, a pause, and then two more blasts, and rode north at a slow trot, a gigantic herd of the undead at his heels.

"He changed the pattern that time," Jacob said. "Did you hear that?"

"Yeah."

"Why'd he do that?"

Taylor shook his head. "Don't know. Signaling somebody maybe. No way one man could work a herd that big. He's probably got some wingmen."

"Great."

The zombies coursed through the intersection like a black river. Their collective moaning sent up a wall of noise that sent a chill over Jacob's skin. He'd heard stories from the First Days about people locked up in their attics while the dead filled the streets below, how the noise was so loud they were sometimes forced to go days at a time without sleeping, how it could drive a man so far over the edge he'd put his gun in his mouth. He looked back at the others in their group and saw several with their hands clapped over their ears. Jacob couldn't blame them. He'd only been in the presence of that horrible moaning for a few minutes and already he felt jittery and sick with adrenaline and fear.

Then some of the undead tried to wander away from the main road. He stiffened. For a second Jacob thought he might have guessed wrong about them sticking with the main herd, but then a dog came sprinting into view. It stopped in front of the small pack of wanderers and barked furiously. It moved closer to the main herd and barked again.

The wanderers dutifully turned around and gave chase.

"I can't believe that," Jacob said. "Why in the world would they be herding them?"

"Maybe to keep 'em away from wherever that rider's from. He's like a diversion, you know?"

"Yeah, maybe."

Taylor turned back to the herd, his mouth working slowly, like he was trying to keep count. It took nearly an hour and a half for the main group to pass, and even after that stragglers came along in progressively smaller packs.

They watched another few minutes, but when no more came into view, they went back to the others.

"Well?" Kelly asked. "What'd you see?"

"The biggest herd I've seen," Jacob said.

"How many?"

Jacob looked at Taylor and shrugged. "I don't know."

"Half a million," Taylor said. "Maybe more."

"That's impossible," Kelly said. "How could there be that many?"

"I remember working crowd control at the Razorback games. We'd load sixty thousand people into that stadium in less than thirty minutes. I know what a crowd that size looks like. The herd I just saw was easily twenty times that number."

"That's not all, though," Jacob said. He told her about the rider with the whistle and the dogs. "It looked like he was guiding them north, out of town."

"That's the direction we were supposed to go."

"Yeah," Jacob said.

He glanced at Taylor. The sheriff reached into his shirt pocket and took out a matchstick. He jammed it into the corner of his mouth and chewed on it while he thought.

"So what do we do?" Nick asked. "We can't very well head north again. Not with all those zombies going that way."

"I think we should go home," said Bree. She looked guiltily around the group, and then lowered her head. She seemed near tears. Frank guided his horse next to hers and held out a hand for her.

"Jacob," Nick said. "What do we do?"

Jacob climbed up on his horse, but didn't answer right away. If he was honest with himself he had absolutely no idea what to do. Nick was right. They couldn't very well head north, not now, not with that herd moving that way. And they couldn't head home, as Bree suggested. So far they'd seen strange ships in the sky and zombie-eating birds and cowboys wrangling more zombies than they thought were left in the world, but they couldn't explain any of it. They had questions, lots of questions, and so far absolutely no answers.

"I say we find a place to hold up for a while," Taylor said. "One of these houses maybe. Or one of the buildings back in town. We can spend a day or two here. That'll put some distance between us and that herd and give us a chance to rest the horses."

Jacob looked around the group and saw nearly everybody nodding in agreement.

"All right then," he said. "Nick, you got any ideas?"

Nick took the map from his pack and studied it for a long moment. Finally, he pointed west. "If we follow this street that way it meets up with Kings Highway. We can take that south to Malone and head west from there. We should be able to find something there."

"Like what?"

"I don't know," Nick said. "A hotel, maybe. Maybe a business with a closed in lot where we can graze the horses."

"Okay." Jacob looked around, and as nobody else had anything to say, he made his decision. "Okay, we'll do that."

"Let's move out single file, and keep it quiet. Hand signals only until we get somewhere safer than here. Max, you want to take point?"

"Yes, sir, boss."

"Eli, bring up the rear."

The younger man still looked rattled from nearly getting killed back at the hospital, but he rallied and nodded.

They took the horses out at a walking pace, careful to stay close to the houses where they had trees to cover them. Kings Hwy had figured large on the map, but it was little more than a two-lane suburban street, littered with debris and choked with tall grass, as was most of Sikeston. The tree cover had been dense on the other street, but it thinned out dramatically here, affording very little cover. Jacob, feeling dangerously exposed, ordered the group to split in two and move as close as possible to the rotting houses on either side of the street. He let Max take one column, while he took point on the other, Taylor, Kelly, Barry, and their journalist, Andy Dawson, coming up behind him.

The afternoon had grown hot, and pollen and dirt stuck to his sweaty skin and clumped in his eyes and in his nostrils. The street was quiet, no wind to whistle through the empty buildings, but the silence didn't hold. Two brown dogs trotted into the street about fifty yards ahead of them, their heads bent down, eyes narrowed on the Arbella riders. The dogs uttered a series of stuttering growls that quickly turned into furious barking.

"Shit," Taylor muttered.

He raised his rifle and Jacob nodded. It would have to be done. They couldn't let the dogs go on making that noise.

But then something whizzed by Jacob's ear, struck the corner of the house next to him with a wet thud, and blasted off a big piece into the grass beyond. Three more shots popped next to him, like somebody breaking sticks, and only then did Jacob realize they were being fired on.

But the shots weren't accurate. He couldn't even tell where they were coming from.

Jacob had been in plenty of scrapes. He'd even had some combat training after graduating school, back when he thought salvage was going to be his life's work, but he'd never actually taken live fire before. Now he was in the middle of it, and the only thing he could think was: Huh, so this is how it feels.

Then another round struck the house next to him, punching a huge hole in the wall, and Barry let out a groan loud enough to be heard across the street. Jacob turned around angrily, ready to berate the man, but stopped short when he saw the piece of wood sticking out of Barry's cheek. Seeing all that blood cleared his head in a hurry. Jacob remembered his training and knew a man on horseback made a huge target. They needed to find cover, and fast.

Meanwhile, Barry was turning pale. He had slumped over in his saddle and looked close to falling to the ground. Jacob turned his horse and came up alongside Barry. He grabbed the injured man's reins. Kelly was beside him, trying to help him, but she had no idea what her husband needed. She only saw his distress.

"I've got him," Jacob said. "We have to get off this street."

"Where?" She turned toward the whooping and the screaming. "Jacob, what are they doing?"

"Over here," Taylor said. He was about ten yards away, near the gap between two houses, his rifle leveled at the chaos in the street. "Come on, move!"

Taylor was about to turn the corner when they heard more screaming from across the street.

Gunshots, pistol fire from the sound of it, came seconds later.

Three riders, men dressed in jeans and long-sleeve denim shirts and floppy cowboy hats, came tearing out of a gap in the houses. They drove their horses right through the other

Arbella column, sending Max and Nick and the others scattering in half a dozen directions at once.

Complete chaos followed. The riders fired as they charged, but they weren't trying to hit anybody. They were shooting into the air, and to Jacob they looked more like a bunch of drunken ranch hands out for a joyride than an organized cavalry. But they were brutally efficient at what they were doing, and soon, Nick and the others broke in panic.

More riders, a dozen at least, came up from behind, yelling and shooting like the first three. A man in a red T-shirt and black baseball cap seemed to be the leader. He motioned for the riders to fan out, which they did, yelling and firing their guns like madmen.

Jacob wrestled with Barry's horse, but the shooting and the yelling had spooked it badly and it fought against the reins. Then the horse turned on him suddenly, pushing his own horse sideways so that he was facing the middle of the street. Owen, the anthropologist, had tried to make a break for it. He spurred his horse and the animal took off at a full gallop down the street. But Owen was not a great rider, and his pursuers looked like they'd been born on horseback. They caught him easily, circled him, and yelled for him to dismount.

Owen was clearly terrified. Jacob could see that. His face was a twisted grimace of fear and confusion. He spun his horse around in mad circles, but he was blocked at every turn.

"Get off your horse," the man in the red shirt demanded.

One of the other riders, a kid of about eighteen, darted forward and grabbed Owen by his coat.

"He said, 'Get off!' "

The next instant Owen tumbled from his horse, landing painfully on his back.

The younger rider slid down from his horse with a rope in his hands.

Owen didn't give him a chance to use it though. He jumped to his feet and ran screaming down the street.

"You better get back here!" the guy in the red shirt said.

The young man with the rope started to chase after Owen, but the other one told him to stop. "Just shoot him," he said. "That one's too old anyway."

Another man raised a rifle, leveled at Owen's back, and dropped him with a single well-aimed shot.

"No!" Jacob yelled.

A few of the riders turned his way. The man in the red shirt pushed the brim of his ball cap up with his thumb. He was a stern, leathery-faced man in his early thirties, big and tough looking. He motioned for two of his henchmen to move on Jacob and the men peeled off to try and flank them.

"Jacob, this way!" Taylor yelled. "Bring him. Hurry!"

Jacob grabbed Barry's reins and this time was able to bring the horse under control. He motioned for Kelly and Andy to go ahead and he followed after them.

Meanwhile, Taylor provided cover for them. He fired his suppressed rifle and one of the men trying to flank them went down to his knees and folded over into the long grass. Taylor fired again, hitting the younger man who'd shot Owen. The kid went down screaming.

Jacob and the others got around the side of the house as fast as they could, but it was slow moving with Barry. He rocked like a drunk in the saddle, his groans of pain audible even over all the shooting and yelling back in the street.

"Hurry!" Taylor yelled back at them.

"What about the—"

But Jacob cut himself short. Taylor's head had snapped back. The rifle slid from his hands and he sagged forward.

"No!" Jacob said.

He handed Barry off to Kelly and Andy and rushed to Taylor's side. He grabbed the sheriff's arm and held him up, but Taylor's neck had gone slack and his head lolled on his shoulders. He'd been shot in the mouth. The bullet had ripped part of the man's cheek and exploded his teeth like dice tossed down his throat. He tried to speak, but only managed a gargling sound that soon turned into coughs.

"Sheriff Taylor," Jacob said. "Stay with me, sir. Stay with me. Can you hear me, sir?"

But he couldn't. Not anymore. Even as Jacob talked to him, pleaded with him to fight, the light faded out of the man's eyes and he went blank.

"No!" Jacob said. "Sheriff Taylor, no!"

A man crashed his horse into Jacob, grabbing him hard by the shirt collar.

"Get off that horse," he said, and tried to pull Jacob out of the saddle.

Jacob grabbed the man's arm and shoved him hard. But the man wouldn't let go. He reached over with his other hand and pulled Jacob down even as the man's horse backed up. Jacob was yanked right out of the saddle and thrown to the ground.

He quickly rolled to one side to avoid getting trampled by the horses, but when he tried to run around the man to get back on his own horse, he got the heel of the rider's boot in his face.

His vision turned purple and he couldn't stand up.

He'd never been hit so hard in his life.

From the ground he saw the rider charge Kelly and the others. He knocked Barry from his horse with ease, and then wheeled on Kelly. She slapped at him when he tried to put his hands on her, but he dismounted her in seconds.

When he turned on Andy he flinched. The journalist had a pistol in his hand. He was trying to aim it at his attacker, but his hand was shaking uncontrollably. The fear on his face was horrible to behold. The other man yelled, "Fuck!" and pulled a pistol of his own from inside his shirt. The two men fired as one and both went down.

Jacob saw his chance and took it. He climbed to his feet, grabbed Barry, and told Kelly they had to move.

"Where?" she asked.

"That way," he said, and gestured toward an overgrown lot that contained row upon row of concrete walls. He ducked a shoulder under Barry and took his weight. To Kelly he said, "Go that way. We'll try to hide."

They ran as fast as they could while carrying Barry, but long before they made cover Jacob heard one of the riders yell: "Go on, get him!"

The growling of a pack of dogs followed close behind.

Jacob looked back to see several dogs running in his direction. They overtook him a moment later and tore into him. He fell to the ground and covered his face with his arms, twisting one way and then the other as the pack tore at his clothes and his skin, ripping him to pieces.

"You, dogs, back!" someone said. "Go on, back!"

The dogs stopped biting him, and they backed up, but they didn't stop growling.

Jacob rolled over and slowly pushed himself up to his knees. His clothes, and his arms beneath, were a shredded mess of blood and torn cloth. He looked over at Kelly, who was holding her husband in her arms. She too was covered in blood and fresh wounds.

Jacob looked around.

The dogs had him surrounded, all of them growling, teeth bared.

Then the man in the baseball cap rode up. The others parted way for him. He told the dogs to shut up and they all went silent, though not a one of them looked like it had lost the desire to tear into Jacob once again.

Jacob stared up at the man through a veil of his own blood.

The rider had a hardened look about him, like a man well

used to fighting his own fights, though he also wore the practiced air of one comfortable with giving commands.

"We'll keep those three," the man said. "Search them, and make sure their belongings are secure."

One of the other riders came up alongside him, holding Taylor's 300 Blackout. He held it out to the leader, the man in the black ball cap. "Casey, one of 'em had this."

Jacob caught the name.

Casey took the rifle and looked it over, clearly impressed. "Which one of 'em had this?"

"Old guy back there. He's dead."

Casey grunted and nodded. "Nice gun. Built-in suppressor, military stock." He ejected the magazine and checked the rounds. "Reloaded ammo. Good job of it, too." He turned his horse to face Jacob and the others. "Who reloaded this ammo?"

Nobody said anything.

"You," Casey said, nodding at Jacob. "Where you from?"

Jacob just stared at the man.

"I asked you a question."

"No hablo Inglés."

Casey laughed, and the others did, too. "Wow, we got us a comedian." Casey handed the magazine to one of the other riders, and then turned back to Jacob. "You and I are gonna have a good time getting to know each other."

Then he flipped Taylor's carbine around and smashed the stock down on the bridge of Jacob's nose.

For Jacob, everything went black.

part three
TRACTS AND BRIDEMEAT

17

Jacob, Kelly, and Barry were led back to the street. Nick, Bree, Eli, and Max were already there, surrounded by riders who had them at gunpoint. Now that the fighting was over, most of the riders looked tired and bored. Kelly had to support Barry. The wound in his cheek was bad. They hadn't been able to remove the piece of wood impaled there, and his face had swollen up around it and turned an angry shade of red. Jacob limped along as best he could, but there was blood in his eyes and his mouth and his vision was fading in and out. Everything seemed to swirl around him. His arms hurt the most though. The dogs had really torn him up.

When they got to the others, Bree rushed forward to examine Barry and Jacob. "Jesus," she said. "What did you bastards do to them?"

"Just a little getting to know each other party," Casey said. "Now get back over there."

"Both of these men need medical help."

He adjusted his ball cap as he leaned back in his saddle. "Well, I don't see no doctors around here. My guess is they're just fucked."

"I'm a physician's assistant. Let me help them."

Casey laughed at that. "You hear that, boys? Missy here is a doctor." He looked around and the others laughed with him. Then he turned back to Bree and chewed on his bottom lip, regarding her all over again. "You're a pretty little thing, ain't you?"

Bree didn't respond.

"Well," Casey said, "if you're gonna help him, go on and do it."

"I need my pack. And I need clean water to rinse out these wounds."

"That ain't gonna happen, princess. We gotta move out directly. You do what you're gonna do right here, right now, with what you got. And then we're outta here."

"Can I at least have some water from your canteen?" she asked.

"No, you may not," he said. "You may be a hot little number, but you need to mind your place. You don't ask a free man for nothing, you hear?"

"We're all free men," she said.

"Sweetheart, you definitely ain't no man. And as of right now, ain't none of you free. Now get busy with whatever you're gonna do."

Jacob's head was a soupy mess, but at Bree's mention of her pack he rallied a little. He looked around, and for the first time realized that he and the others had been roughly searched and their belongings seized. He hadn't even been aware that they'd searched him. Everybody's clothes were in disarray. Nobody had their backpacks anymore. Through the blood and dirt he saw the riders holding the Arbella party's horses by the reins, their belongings hanging off the saddle horns. He saw Bree's defibrillator near the front door of a house on the far side of the street, smashed to bits.

He groaned.

"Are your ears ringing?" Bree asked him.

"Yeah, a little."

"Does everything feel kind of slowed down, like you're moving in slow motion?"

He nodded.

"I think you have a concussion. I want you to stay awake, okay? I'll help you as soon as I can. Just stay awake."

"They killed Sheriff Taylor," he said.

"I know," Bree said, her voice was thick with emotion, but she was fighting hard to keep it together. "They shot Frank, too. He was trying to hide me under a house when they . . . they pulled him into the grass and just shot him."

Jacob struggled with what to say. The words felt unreachable, lost in a fog in the back of his mind.

"Jacob," Bree said. She gently patted his cheeks. "Hey, stay with me, okay? Stay awake."

"We're moving out now," Casey said. He turned to one of the younger riders and said, "Get 'em tied up and ready to move out."

"Where are you taking us?" Bree demanded.

"You're coming with us, little lady."

"You have no right to force us to go anywhere. We never did anything to you. You attacked us for no reason. You had no right."

He turned to the rider beside him. "You hear that, we got no right?"

"We're bad people, I guess," the rider answered.

"Why are you doing this to us?" Bree said. "What's wrong with you people?"

"We're surviving. Doin' the best we know how."

"You had no right to attack us. We weren't doing anything to you. We're not out here to hurt people."

Casey had been smiling, but he seemed to have lost interest in the conversation. His expression turned mean. "Right ain't got nothing to do with nothing," he said. "And if you're not looking to do what's necessary to stay alive, then that's your own damn fault. We're moving out."

"But these men aren't well enough to travel."

"They'll travel," Casey said. "They'll keep up or they'll get shot." He turned his horse and trotted off.

"Bree," Jacob said, his voice sounding slow and thick. "Don't."

"Jacob, they killed Frank. They killed Sheriff Taylor. They had no right."

"We live to fight another day," he said.

A few moments later somebody grabbed Jacob's wrists and lashed them together with a yellow nylon rope. It cut into his skin, but he was too out of it to feel pain. Somebody pushed him along, and before he knew it, he and the other Arbella survivors were being led single file down the road, flanked by riders.

18

They saw the birds first, the ravens, circling low over a dark line of vehicles at the edge of town.

It was getting near dark, but it was still hot. Dust rose up from the road in sheets and matted to his bloody face. It got in his eyes and his nose and his mouth, making him miserable. His head was pounding, yet even with the pain he could barely keep his eyes open. Without the occasional jerk on the ropes that bound his hands together he might have fallen over and passed out right there. As it was, he hobbled along in a daze, his one clear thought one of surprise that a blow to the head from a rifle butt could cause such intense and persistent pain.

Eventually, the caravan of vehicles came into view. They were a mismatch of wagons and RVs cobbled together from a bizarre collection of flatbed trailers and pickup truck beds and motorcycle tires, perhaps three hundred vehicles in all. And in between and all around the vehicles were packs of dogs and dirty children and men and women in filthy clothes. But Jacob could smell meat cooking over a fire pit, and the fragrance was enough to bring him part of the way back from the haze into which his mind had slipped.

Seated in a lawn chair out in front of the vehicles was a fat woman of about sixty. She wore a peach-colored dress and brown cowboy boots. Her hair had mostly gone to gray and she'd cut it short and parted it to one side, like a man's. She was sunburnt and irritable looking, the way some heavy people can be in the hot sun, but she watched the approaching group with interest.

Casey, the leader, got down from his horse and gave the woman a kiss on her cheek.

Glancing back toward the line of vehicles Jacob saw one of the bigger RVs had "Mother Jane" written across the side. Wasn't hard to figure out who this was.

She studied the Arbella survivors and didn't look pleased. "Our scouts said there were eleven of them."

"There were. They put up a fight." He held up Sheriff Taylor's rifle. "Found this on one of them."

"Which one."

"He ain't one of these. Wesley had to shoot him."

Mother Jane grunted. "Well, them two young ones'll make good tracts." She pointed at Barry. "That one with the messed up face, though, you might as well shoot him now."

"No!" Bree said.

"Just putting him out of his misery, sweetie."

"But I told you, I can help him. I just need my kit."

For the first time, Mother Jane seemed interested. "What kind of kit?" She turned to Casey. "What's she talking about? What kind of kit?"

Casey was about to answer when Bree spoke up. "My medic bag. Your dragoons took it from me. They won't give it back."

" 'Dragoons'?" Mother Jane said. "Seriously? You ain't from around here, are you, sweetie?"

Bree held her tongue.

"You some kind of doctor?" Mother Jane asked.

"She said she was a 'physician's assistant,' " Casey said.

"What's that mean?" Mother Jane asked.

"It means I can help him."

"No, no. What's that mean, *physician's assistant*? I remember those back before everything went to shit." She gave Casey a gentle slap on the hip with the back of her hand. "You remember that Indian doctor I used to take you to? What was his name, Vanketswar or some such crap a soul couldn't never wrap a tongue around. I kept wanting to call him doctor, and every time he'd correct me and say he was a physician's assistant. Said he'd gone through med school, but hadn't done a residency. That sound about like you, sweetie?"

"Something like that," Bree said.

"You mind telling me how that is? I've taken this caravan all over this country, and I ain't seen a med school nowhere. Unless you're one of them airship people, and you don't look like them."

Bree said nothing, but she did glance back at Jacob.

Mother Jane caught the glance, and stood up. The ravens that had clustered around her took to the air with a furious beating of wings. She moved with a ponderous waddle as she approached Jacob. She looked him over, checking out the jeans without holes or frays at the pant legs, his sturdy boots, even lifting one of his hands to examine his fingernails.

"Where you people from?"

No one answered.

"You ain't road people. Where you from?"

Jacob didn't answer.

"You folks ain't eating until I get an answer. Where you from?"

"Arbella," Jacob said.

"Where's that at? I ain't never heard of no Arbella."

"South of here," Jacob said. He could feel others staring daggers at him, and he only hoped they'd follow along with the lie he was about to tell. "It's south of Little Rock, down near Texas."

"Arkansas?" She scoffed at that. "What are you doin' way up here?"

"We're explorers," he said. "We're looking around to see what's out here."

At that she laughed. Everybody did. Even the ravens seemed to shiver with excitement.

"Oh, that's good," she said. She patted his cheek, hard, sending a wave of pain through him. "Don't you worry, young man. I trek this caravan all over this land of ours. We cross her diamond deserts and her wheat fields rolling sometimes three times a year. You want to know what's out here, you're gonna find out."

She returned to her lawn chair and dropped into it with effort.

One of the ravens squawked next to her and she reached over to stroke it.

"Go on," she said, motioning to Casey. "Get them out of my sight. Oh, and you," she said, gesturing toward Bree, and then to Barry. "You fix him, I may have a job for you. Physician's assistant. Shit."

19

They were taken to the front of the caravan and told to sit. About forty other men, women, and children were already there, all of them with the quiet, fearful look of slaves. A few armed men on horseback rode around the periphery of the gathering, but they didn't seem especially watchful and, curiously, none of the slaves seemed all that eager to run.

They sat in the grass and one of the riders brought Bree her medical kit. She started working on Barry as Kelly looked on.

Poor thing, Jacob thought, watching her. Whatever there had once been between them was truly ancient history now. He saw the worry, the pain, the frustration, the love in Kelly's eyes when she looked on her injured husband, and Jacob knew where her heart was. No question about it. He'd been foolish to think otherwise.

Bree turned Barry's face to one side, exposing the piece of wood that had lanced through his cheek. The whole side of his face was red, and he was sweating badly. His pupils looked dilated and he was drooling blood. Some of it had already caked dry on his throat.

"He's in shock," Bree said. "We're gonna have to get that wood out of there. It looks like the bleeding has pretty much stopped, but I don't like the way it's swollen up like that."

"Do you think it's infected?" Kelly asked.

"I don't know. Maybe. That redness is a bad sign. I need water to clean this wound. It needs to be as sterile as possible, too, otherwise we're just making the risk of an infection even worse."

Jacob looked around. A young girl of about seventeen, dirty and malnourished, was huddled in a fetal ball a few yards away, a hacking cough shaking her whole body. Beyond her was a man in his early twenties, just as dirty as she was but clearly not as starving. He watched the young girl with something close to contempt on his face.

"Hey," Jacob called to him. "Where can we get some water around here?"

The man glanced at him, but said nothing.

"Hey, come on. A little help here. This guy's in shock."

"Everybody needs something, pal," the man finally said. "And if I had water, you really think I'd give it to you?"

"What the hell?" Eli said, and started to stand.

Jacob put a hand on his arm. "Easy," he said. "Let it go."

Eli sat and cussed under his breath. Then he turned on Jacob and said in a forced whisper: "I don't get it. Look at the guards they got around here. How hard would it be to slip away? We could do it right now if we wanted to."

"We wouldn't get far. They've got horses, we don't."

"Me and Max could steal some. We could meet the rest of you someplace, and then we make a run for it."

The pain flared up again, and for a moment, Jacob was nearly blind with it. Everything went white. Even the dog bites on his arms, which had gone practically numb compared to his headache, were starting to ache anew. He'd lost a lot of blood, he knew that, and his wounds would almost certainly need stitches.

"Hey, boss, you okay?" Eli asked.

Jacob had to work to catch his breath. The pain gradually faded, and at last he was able to nod. "I'm all right," he said. "It hurts. I gotta tell you, I'm in no condition to travel. And I know Barry isn't. We need to get him better before we do anything."

"Okay then, we wait until Bree fixes him up. Then we get the fuck out of here."

"Agreed. I don't want to be around these people any longer than I have to. In the meantime, we need to keep our eyes open. I want to figure out how these people work, what their deal is."

Kelly turned from Barry and wiped her eyes. They were red and puffy, and she seemed to be holding on to her composure with both hands. "You shouldn't have told them about Arbella," she said. "Sheriff Taylor said nobody finds out about our home."

"What was I gonna do, Kelly? Did you think she was just gonna stop asking?"

"But now they know the name of our home."

"Which doesn't appear on any map."

Nick groaned. "Except the ones in my pack. I'm sure they're probably searching our stuff right now."

Jacob put his face in his hands. "Crap," he said.

"It's not your fault, Jacob," Nick said. "Even if we'd lied about the name of our town, they'd have found out the truth from my maps."

"Well, what happens if they try to attack Arbella?"

Jacob looked around the group. The horror of what might happen should these people attack Arbella was on all their faces. It was true they had probably only two hundred riders, but that didn't mean they couldn't do some serious damage. Arbella's defenses were set up to guard against zombies, not human strategy. There were no hidden shooting positions, no turrets or battlements. Shooters on Arbella's walls stood in the open, to allow for ease of aiming against targets too stupid to use stealth. Even if Mother Jane's boys attacked in a straight-up fight against Arbella's walls, losses on both sides would be huge. And if they decided to sneak in through some of the more sparsely covered sections of the wall, it would be a bloodbath.

"If we see them going towards Arbella, we'll have to escape and get back home to warn them. We could do as Eli suggested, send him and Max out ahead. Even if Barry and I aren't ready to travel, the rest of you should go. Maybe you could just do a dead sprint back to Arbella."

Before anyone could respond, Mother Jane's ravens descended on the slave area. The giant black birds lit on every available perch.

"What's this?" Nick asked.

"Do you think there are zombies nearby?" Kelly asked.

Jacob doubted that, but he didn't say as much. He'd risen to his feet and was looking around the darkened clearing in which they'd been put. Slaves were coming out of the woodwork, many more than there'd been when they first arrived here. There were perhaps two hundred in all, which he didn't like because that meant he'd probably underestimated the number of riders as well. And there were dogs, too. He could see them watching from the edges of the circle, waiting for something.

Soon about twenty guards descended on the slave quarters. Two of them carried a battered orange canoe full of root vegetables and some half-eaten joints of roasted meat out to the middle of the slave area and dropped it on the ground.

"Is that supposed to be our dinner?" Kelly asked.

"God, I'm hungry," Nick said. "I wonder where we line up."

Slaves moved in on the guards carrying the canoe. One of the men dropped his end of the canoe and pulled a black nightstick from his belt. He used it to beat the slaves that got too close.

The other man dropped his half of the canoe and then the

two men retreated, leaving the slaves to descend on the meal en masse.

Many fights broke out.

Jacob saw a woman pull a piece of meat from the boat and then get beaten by two other women intent on stealing it.

A boy of about eight was knocked to the ground and kicked repeatedly in his back and ribs as he desperately tried to hold on to something that looked like the blackened remains of a potato.

"Oh, God," Kelly said.

But that wasn't the worst part, not to Jacob's mind anyway. The worst part was the laughing and cheering that went up from the riders and their women, who had gathered around the edges of the clearing and were obviously having a grand old time watching the slaves beat the daylights out of each other.

"These people are animals," Kelly said. "Is this what happens to us after just thirty years?"

They were all on their feet now, all but Barry, watching the melee, the disgust plain on their faces. None of them noticed the young riders coming up behind them until they were standing next to Kelly and Bree. "Come on," one of the riders said to Bree.

"Let go of me," she said, and yanked her arm away.

"Hey!" Jacob said. He moved on the men, but several of them pulled pistols and leveled them at Jacob and the other men.

"You ought to give it a try," one of the men said. "See how it works out."

"Let go of me," Bree said.

"Not likely. I'm gonna give you a roll around the mattress. Try me on some bridemeat."

"The hell you are!" Bree said. She struggled and kicked with everything she had, but there were three big men holding her.

Jacob saw Casey watching the exchange. He looked powerfully drunk and regarded the events unfolding in front of
him with a genuine lack of interest.

"Hey, your name is Casey," Jacob said.

Casey wasn't wearing his ball cap, but his hair still had a
sweaty curl in it where the edges of the hat had been. He
looked back at Jacob with plain contempt on his face, but he
said nothing.

"Please," Jacob said, dropping the tone of his voice, trying to sound respectful of Casey's authority over this place.
"Make them stop. They can't do this. It's not right."

Casey regarded him for a long moment.

"I keep hearing that from you Arbella people, that it ain't
right. I don't know what kind of lives you folks lead down
there in Arkansas, but up here, you don't go around telling a
free man what's right and what's not. 'Round here, a man
makes his own right."

Behind him, more riders gathered. Many of them were as
drunk or drunker than he was.

All of them were armed.

"Please don't let them do this," Jacob said.

"You're done talking. You fellas just mind your place
there. My boys are gonna have a little fun time with the
bridemeat there."

"The hell you will," Jacob said.

Casey pulled Sheriff Taylor's rifle from his shoulder and
leveled it at Jacob. "I told you you're done talking. Now if
you don't want to start dying, I suggest the lot of you take a
few steps back."

Before any of them could move, Barry climbed to his feet
and charged one of the men holding Kelly's arms behind her
back. "Get your hands off my wife!" he screamed, and his attack was so sudden the rider couldn't react. Barry knocked the
man to the ground and then started swinging wild punches at
the other men.

In a flash, Max joined in, too.

But they didn't last long. As calmly as a man would watch a sunset, Casey turned the stolen rifle and shot both men in the chest, three times for Max and six for Barry, the gun quiet as a snake in the grass. Barry, delirious as he was with the pain and the spreading infection and his love for his wife, fought even as he fell to his knees.

"No!" Kelly screamed, and broke free from the men holding her and went to her knees beside her dead husband. She put his head in her lap and rocked him back and forth, wailing so loudly the rest of the slaves stopped fighting, and even eating, to turn and watch.

Casey shouldered the weapon. To the men holding Bree he said, "You boys go and have your fun. Make sure and hold her down, though. The way she's kicking, she's liable to break something."

He motioned to one of the men who had been holding Kelly.

"Go and get two ropes. Hurry now."

The man ran off in a hurry.

Bree fought all the way to the RV, and the men had a tough time getting her through the door. She grabbed hold of the doorframe and wouldn't let go. They had to pry her fingers loose one at a time to finally get her inside.

A moment later, the young rider returned with the rope.

"Go and fetch some of them slaves over here."

"What are you doing?" Jacob asked.

Casey ignored him. When the slaves ran up, he motioned for the young rider to hand them the ropes. "Take these two bodies over to the clothesline and tie them up on the posts scarecrow fashion. Best hurry. They're liable to make the change here pretty soon."

The slaves dragged the bodies away, even as Kelly tried to hold on to Barry.

"Make her shut up," Casey said to one of the riders.

The man took out his nightstick and advanced on Kelly, but Jacob got there first. He picked Kelly up and held her in his arms, her face pressed into his chest. She was sobbing and shaking uncontrollably.

"I got her," Jacob said.

Casey huffed, then turned and walked away.

Jacob called out to him, "How can you do this?"

"String 'em up?" Casey asked.

"What's wrong with you?" Jacob said.

Casey shrugged. "Mother Jane's birds gotta eat, too." He walked away, leaving them standing there in shock.

And then, from the RV, Bree started to scream.

20

It took a long time for the birds to eat enough of Barry and Max for them to stop struggling against the ropes that bound them. They had stripped the zombie carcasses to the bone in less than two minutes back in the town, but now, the ravens seemed to be enjoying the meal, taking their time about it. Jacob and the others couldn't watch, but they couldn't escape the sound of it either. Max went on groaning, even after they'd stripped most of his flesh away.

Kelly was inconsolable.

Bree had come back to them with a black eye and a fat lip. Her shins and wrists were bruised, and there was blood dripping from one ear. She wouldn't speak, wouldn't let anybody touch her or even get near her. She crawled inside her shell and stayed there.

Jacob blamed himself. From Sheriff Taylor to Barry to Bree over there, it was all his fault. There was the Code, a promise to always have the other fella's back, and he had failed to live up to that code. Taylor and Barry and the others were dead because he had failed, and Bree was broken for the same reason. And now, Arbella's very existence was threatened, all because he had failed to live by the Code he'd been raised with.

He glanced at Bree and just as quickly looked away. She hadn't cried since they brought her back. She had taken a seat against a fifty-five-gallon drum and hugged her knees and stared off at a spot only she could see. In the starlight, Jacob had caught the emptiness of her stare and withered before it. He knew somebody needed to try and reach her, but the thought of speaking to her terrified him. He just knew he would say the wrong thing, and that he would probably only make it worse for her, and that crippled him.

The same was true with Kelly. She'd been open, letting him hold her, but she hadn't said a word either. She spent most of her time sobbing, either to herself or into his shoulder, but then she would suddenly lash out and bang her fists against her thighs while her face twisted in rage. All of it left him feeling helpless.

Eli had asked him what they were going to do now, and he'd been unable to answer. He'd tried to mask his indecision with anger, but he was sure he hadn't fooled anybody. He'd failed them, and they all knew it.

"We need to get out of here tonight," Eli said. "If we don't get out of here, we're gonna die here."

"I . . . I don't know," Jacob said. "We could all get killed before we make it ten feet from here."

"Are you kidding? We can easily make this. Look at there, they don't even have guards posted. They're all down there getting wasted. You guys could slip off that way. I'll steal some horses and meet up with you. We'll be on the way back home before they even know we're gone."

"But they'll follow us. They have Nick's maps. They'll know where we're going."

"Then we'll go somewhere else. Or we'll ride like mad and keep a pace they can't match. But, Jacob, come on, we have to get out of here."

"They have dogs, too."

"Yeah, and we can find sticks or something to take care of those."

"I guess . . . I don't know." Jacob put his face in his hands. This was so hard. He felt miserable. "I'm so sorry, you guys. I'm so sorry."

Eli threw up his hands in a *What the hell?* gesture.

"What are you sorry for?" Nick said. He'd been sitting on a plastic egg crate, watching the young girl with the hacking cough. She was still curled up in a fetal ball, and even though the temperature had dropped dramatically with nightfall, she was sweating badly.

"I'm sorry. This whole thing . . . it was a bad mistake. I'm sorry. We should never have come."

"Jacob, come on," Nick said. "What would Taylor have done? That's what we need to ask ourselves. What would the old man tell us if he were here right now?"

"I don't know."

"Well, I'll tell you what he'd say," Eli said. "He'd tell us to do everything we could to protect Arbella. He'd tell us we should die trying, if we had to. We need to get out of here, and we need to warn the folks back home. And we need to do it tonight."

Jacob didn't respond. He felt like he couldn't. Nothing he could say would come out right.

"What the hell?" Kelly said. "Jacob, what the hell is wrong with you?"

She sounded shrill, but he didn't dare tell her to keep her voice down. He could barely hold her gaze.

"Seriously, what the hell is wrong with you? Where's all this it's all my fault crap coming from? Since when do you get to play martyr?"

"I'm not playing—"

"Like hell you are. You're sitting there acting like all this is your fault. Well, I say bullshit to that. Every single one of us volunteered to come on this expedition. I've been begging for this since I was seventeen. We all agreed to the route, to all of it. Stop moping, Jacob, and fucking grow a pair." She glanced over at Bree, and then at the clothesline, where a few bits of flesh still clung to her husband's skeleton. "Some of us have lost a lot more than our pride. We need to make a decision."

Nick leaned forward. "Jacob, come on, buddy. Eli's right. This is what Taylor would do."

Jacob felt like he was on autopilot. He nodded without even realizing he was doing it. "So we're ready to go? No supplies, no weapons. Just like this?"

Off in the corner, Bree stood up.

The others looked surprised, but stood up as well. Only Jacob remained seated.

Finally, he stood up, too. He looked around the group, and though they looked ragged and beaten and tired beyond measure, they were nonetheless determined. He felt a rush of pride in them, even as he continued to hate himself for the weaknesses he'd shown.

"Eli," he said, "go and get us some horses." It was spring, so he looked toward the southern horizon to find the constellation of Virgo. Out in the grasslands, with no electric lights to pollute the sky, the stars were bright and the night sky a blaze of blues and gray and molten reds. The Milky Way was like a paint stripe across the sky. He pointed to the star that marked the reclining virgin's left breast. "There. We'll follow Spica, in Virgo. We'll keep that line until you come up on us."

Eli glanced toward the horizon until he found Spica, and nodded. "Okay, got it."

Jacob and the others ducked down into a crouch and moved as quietly as they could toward the edge of the clearing.

No one stirred. No one raised a hue and cry.

They reached the high grass of the prairie and tried their best to melt into it.

Only then did they get the first indication that something was wrong. They heard a man's voice yelling, "Runner! Runner!" and then the sound of a struggle.

Jacob looked back to see that one of the slaves had tackled Eli. The two men were rolling around in the grass, not so much fighting as wrestling.

The slave managed to pin Eli to the ground and began yelling to beat the devil. "Help! Help!"

"What the hell?" Jacob said. "No. No."

It took a long moment, but eventually several drunken riders descended on the scene. They were feeling rowdy, but they seemed to know better than to get into the middle of a slave brawl.

Casey showed up a moment later.

The slave on top of Eli had held his tongue until Casey appeared, but he spoke up as soon as he saw the leader of Mother Jane's Boys.

"He was gonna steal some horses," the slave said. "I heard him. Him and the others, they were gonna steal some horses and head south to Spica."

"What's Spica?" Casey said.

The slave took a moment to answer. "I don't know. They said they'd meet him there. They went off that way."

Casey followed the direction of the man's gaze. "That true?" he yelled, head thrown back. "You out there, Jacob? If you are, you best show yourself. I won't kill ya if you show yourself." He turned to the rider behind him with a drunken grin. "Gonna fuck him up, but I ain't gonna kill him."

Down in the grass, Jacob could only pound his fists on the ground in bootless rage. What was he supposed to do? They were helpless here, pretty much no options at all.

"We cut our losses," he said. "We surrender."

"No!" Kelly said. "They'll kill us."

"They know we're here," he said. "We don't have any-where to run."

"But we can't give up."

"We're not giving up," Jacob said. "We're living to fight another day."

He stood up, his white shirt turned silver by the starlight. He glanced over his shoulder and saw the others doing the same.

"Come on back," Casey said. "Come on, this way."

They trudged back up to camp. They'd made it perhaps fifty yards, and Jacob fumed at the coincidence. They'd made it maybe fifty miles under Taylor. Under his leader-ship—because it was bullshit to pretend at this point that they'd been co-authors of this plan—the survivors had made it roughly two percent of the distance they'd made under Taylor. Because it had been Taylor who led them, he realized that now. He'd only been a puppet, if that. In truth, he was probably less than that.

He certainly felt less than that right now.

One of the younger riders, one who was tremendously drunk, climbed down from his horse and pulled the slave off of Eli.

When Eli tried to charge him, the rider produced a pistol and pointed it at his chest.

"Yes?" the rider said. "You had something you wanted to say?"

Eli said nothing. He raised his hands in the sign for sur-render.

Casey rode forward then and scanned the Arbella survivors. "I give you guys a week," he said. "We probably shouldn't even bother to feed ya."

He nodded toward the slave who had alerted them to the escapees.

"What's your name?"

"Walker," the slave said.

"I didn't ask you what you do for us, I asked you your name, son."

Laughs from the assembled riders. And more were coming down from the back of the caravan, men and women, all of them laughing like they'd been lit on fire with booze.

"My name's Walker, sir. Chris Walker."

Casey leaned back in his saddle and sighed. He almost seemed magnanimous when he spoke. "Well, Chris Walker, you think you might want to be one of Mother Jane's Boys?"

"Yes, sir!" Walker said. "You know it."

"You think you could kill a man who's broke the peace of our camp?"

"Yes, sir. In a heartbeat."

"A heartbeat? Well. All right then." Casey leaned back on his saddle and pulled a pistol from his waistband. He twirled it on his finger, catching it so that it ended up with the butt of the gun pointed at the slave. "Here you go. Take this."

Walker, the slave, didn't seem to know what to do. He took a few steps toward Casey, but didn't reach out for the weapon.

"Go on, take it."

The slave reached out for the weapon and took it in his hands.

He held it like it might break, clutched to his chest, uncertain about what he was supposed to do.

"Go on," Casey said, motioning toward Eli. "He was gonna steal our horses, right?"

"He was."

"And the horse is what?"

"The horse belongs to the rider," Walker said, like it was something he'd learned at his catechism.

"Can you do what's got to be done, Walker?"

Walker looked stunned, like somebody had just thrust a major award into his hands. "Yes," he said. "Yes, I can."

"All right then. Put a bullet in that little shit's head. Let's be done with it."

Walker stepped up next to Eli, leveled his weapon, and without the slightest preamble or hesitation, fired a single shot into Eli's face.

Jacob lunged forward, but Nick held him back.

"Don't," Nick warned.

Casey glanced at Jacob and smiled. "You folks should get some sleep. Probably gonna have some tract work for you come the morning." He gestured at Walker. "Put that one on a horse. He's one of us now."

And with that he turned and rode away.

21

The next morning, at first light, one of the free women came into the slave corral and hollered for them to wake.

Jacob climbed to his feet. He'd slept little, and he was exhausted. He was thirsty, and so hungry he had the jitters. The ringing was gone from his ears, but his head still ached. They'd used some of the bandages and disinfectant in Bree's med kit to wrap up his arms where the dogs had bit him, and now they were soaked through with blood. It hurt so badly pulling them off, his hands started to shake.

The wounds were bad, and deep, too. He should have had stitches, but Bree was obviously in no condition to do it, and Kelly was a mess, too. Nick had tried, but he had the grace of a bull and all he'd managed to do was make a few of the wounds messier than they already were. In the end, Jacob had given up and just wrapped himself in bandages. He would have to do that again pretty soon and just hope for the best.

From behind him, Kelly groaned.

She was staring at the clothesline where Barry and Max's skeletons were still lashed to the end posts. They'd been picked nearly clean, but they were still black with blood and little bits of cartilage still clung to the bone.

"Oh, man," Jacob said. He turned to Nick and motioned toward the bodies. "You think we can find some shovels around here somewhere?"

"Yeah, maybe," Nick said.

Four of Mother Jane's Boys were coming up behind them. One of the older men, a big-bellied man with sunburnt arms and a huge gray beard, said, "Ain't no slave getting buried around here. Just take the carcass out in the tall grass and leave it there. Something'll come along and eat it."

"And you ain't gettin' no shovels, neither," said one of the others. He was half the age of the fat man with the beard, but otherwise looked just like him. Father and son, probably, Jacob thought.

"It's scrapers for you this morning," the older man said. "Now go on out in the grass there and do your business. Be quick about it."

"My business?" Jacob said.

"You gotta piss or take a shit, now's the time to get it done."

"What about food?" Nick asked. "What about water?"

"You get water once you start working. As to food, slaves eat at night."

A few minutes later, Jacob and the others were given thin plates of hard plastic and told to scrape the sides of the caravan's many vehicles. The ravens had perched all along the caravan during the night, and just about every vehicle had thick runners of bird shit dripping down the sides.

For Nick, it was too much. "That's stupid," he said. He threw down his scraper. "I'm not doing that. I won't."

"Nick . . ." Kelly said. "Careful."

The woman who had given them the scrapers didn't reply. She just took a step back and called to a man standing nearby.

"Bobby, a little help."

Bobby came over. In his ratty jeans and the filthy T-shirt and the baseball cap with a tractor on it he was wearing what seemed to be the uniform for Mother Jane's Boys. And like most of the others, he was a powerfully built man with a big gut and arms like slabs of meat.

"That one," the woman said, and pointed at Nick.

"Go on and shoot me, if that's what you gotta do. But I'm not your slave. I won't do shit for you people."

The man advanced on Nick, who raised his fists.

Nick was fast with his fists, Jacob remembered that well enough, but Bobby was faster. He moved quickly for such a big man, and when Nick took a swing at him, he dodged it with surprising ease.

Then he moved in close with a flurry of uppercuts to Nick's ribs. He stayed away from the face, focusing on the body. Jacob watched the beating with sickness in his heart. He couldn't even jump in to help. Other riders had come up to watch the show, and all of them had their hands resting on the butts of their pistols.

Nick was coughing up blood by the time the man stopped hitting him. When it was done, Bobby picked Nick up by the back of his shirt and pressed his face into one of the runners of bird shit dripping down the side of one of the wagons. He grabbed Nick by the hair and moved his head up and down the side of the wagon. Then he tossed Nick to the ground and said, "Congratulations on your first cleaning."

Nick rolled over onto his back, holding his ribs and moaning in pain.

"None of them eat or drink until that one works," Bobby said.

By mid-morning, Nick had recovered enough to get back on his feet. He couldn't lift his arms over his shoulders, but he did manage to work his scraper a little. Enough that water was finally brought to them.

Jacob felt broken to his core. He was utterly demoralized. He couldn't even look at the others. Every time he tried, he felt so sick he wanted crawl inside a hole and hide. The dog bites on his arms bled through the bandages, but he didn't do anything about it. He wanted the pain. And he suspected the others wanted him to hurt, too. Despite what Kelly had said the night before, he knew they blamed him for this. How could they not?

The thought of it overwhelmed him like a fever, and he thought for the first time that he understood why Lady Macbeth had scoured her hands to the bone and never gotten that damned spot out. Like her, the blood on his hands was not ever going to go away.

Somehow, whether accidentally or through some subconscious desire to be away from them, he'd lost the others. He looked around and realized he'd moved down the row of wagons, scraping and scraping, without paying attention to the world around him. Now he looked around. Off to the west the sky was darkening, as though rain was headed their way, and gray tattered clouds moved across the horizon like columns of smoke. The town of Sikeston, birthplace of all his troubles, slumbered quietly in its desolation in the near distance, and it occurred to him, as his gaze wandered over the empty buildings and overgrown streets, that desolation could be part of one's internal landscape as well. He'd never realized that desolation could be contagious, or that it was possible to hurt so badly.

He heard men laughing and ducked behind one of the wagons. There were voices coming from the other side of the RV next to him, and among them was that of Casey and Mother Jane. He got down on his stomach and crawled under the RV. There were crates on the ground on the other side. He could see people sitting on them, or their legs at least. And beyond them, seated in her lawn chair under a fold-out awning, one of her ravens perched on the back of the chair, was Mother Jane.

"This town was a bust," Casey said. The man was pacing back and forth in front of Mother Jane's chair. He would come in and out of Jacob's view every few seconds. He looked worried and upset. "We lost five good men, and we didn't find those parts we was looking for. Without that pump in working order, we're gonna have to find some other way to get clean water."

"We'll find another pump, Casey. If not here, then in Dexter, or the next place. It'll be all right."

"So then, you've decided? We're heading west again?"

"No, I ain't decided. That's what we're here to talk about."

"Linda's gonna have her baby any day now," Casey said. "We need to be somewhere safe for that to happen."

"Stop worrying so damn much, Casey. Jesus a' mighty, you make a woman's head spin the way you pace like that. Women have been having babies for thousands of years. Linda's gonna do just fine. Hell, I had you on the living room couch, nobody but the ambulance driver there to deliver. Linda's got all the comforts in the world here. Plus, she's got that physician's assistant we picked up in Sikeston."

Mother Jane reached up and stroked the raven at her shoulder. Then she watched Casey pace.

"By the way," Mother Jane went on, "I heard some of your riders used her as bridemeat last night."

"Yeah, that's true."

"And you let it happen?"

"She's a slave. Don't make no difference how she feels about it."

"Casey, you ain't a dumbass, so stop acting like one. She's a cute little thing all right, but if she's got any medical learning at all, it'd be good to have her around if Linda has trouble. I'm not saying she's gonna, just a precaution. Some times babies don't come along all that easy. You tell your rid ers they can have their fun somewhere else. But they leave her be."

"That's gonna be hard to do. I heard a lot of the boys al ready calling dibs on her for tonight."

"You see that they stay away," Mother Jane said. "If you give a Goddamn about that baby of yours, you see to it. It's hard for a girl to do any doctoring when she's too busy wor rying about being raped by a bunch of drunken rednecks."

"All right," he said. "But I still say we need to find some place safe to hole up. I don't want to be on the road and come across another caravan. A fight right now would be bad."

"We'd do just fine," said one of the men along the far wall.

"You think so, Hank? Do you now?"

"I know ain't nobody gonna fight us and win."

"Yeah? Maybe not, but you really think we'd come out ahead after a standup fight, even one we win?"

"Why wouldn't we?"

"Because we're low on everything, ammunition to med ical supplies to food. Most of our vehicles are held together with rust and a prayer. We got more dogs and slaves than we've got food to feed 'em with. We'd win any fight we pick, that's true, but we'd be left with wounded, and right now, with no medical supplies and no fresh water, we'd find our selves up the creek. You know what I mean?"

"So where do you want to go?" Mother Jane asked.

Casey stopped moving. "I say we go north, up to Scott City. It's on the river. It's close. We'll have access to fish, and deer. Fresh water, too."

"Why not head to that Arbella place those slaves was talking about?" Hank asked.

Mother Jane raised an eyebrow. "Why not?"

"I just told you," Casey said. "We can't afford a fight right now."

"Who said anything about fighting 'em?" Hank asked. "They're explorers. That's what that one guy said. That means they don't know what's out here. That means they're sheltered. And if they've been sheltered all this time, that must mean they've got a pretty good thing going back home."

"Not necessarily," Mother Jane said. "He was lying about them coming from Arkansas. I saw the maps in their backpacks. They come up from New Madrid. Ain't but fifty miles south of here."

"So it's close, right?" Hank said. "At least as close as Scott City. And it's on the river, just like Scott City. Sounds like some low-hanging fruit, if you ask me."

Mother Jane looked at Casey. "Ever since you was boys you couldn't agree on nothing. Fight just to fight."

There was a sudden commotion from somewhere behind Mother Jane, and everybody in her court moved to see what it was.

"Michael's back," someone said. "Been riding hard, too, looks like it."

A few seconds later, a young blond kid of about sixteen came into the circle standing around Mother Jane. He was winded, and covered head to toe in sweat and grime. His hair had the molded shape of one accustomed to wearing a hat, but there was no hat.

"What's got you all in a bother?" Mother Jane asked.

"Herd's coming," he said. "They're close, too."

"What?" she said. She looked at another man standing against the wall. "Thomas, you were supposed to lead them away from here."

"I did, Momma. I led 'em a good ten miles north of here before I let 'em go on their way."

"Well, they're coming back," Michael said.

"That's impossible."

"Go see for yourself if you don't believe me. Got a dust cloud big as can be rising up over the hills due north of here."

"How far away?" Casey asked.

"I put about three miles on 'em to get here," Michael answered.

Mother Jane stood up. Her ravens took to the sky. "Pack up the wagons," she said. "We're headed due west, to Dexter."

22

The caravan turned into a frantic hive of activity. Jacob was able to slip back to the slave area unnoticed, where he found the others waiting, confused, trying to figure out what they were supposed to do. The other slaves were packing up the few belongings they'd managed to squirrel away—a blanket here, an extra coat or hat there—but the Arbella survivors had nothing like that.

Kelly was the first to see Jacob. "Oh, my God, Jacob, what's going on? Where have you been?"

"We have to get ready. They're moving us out right now. The herd's coming back."

"What?" Nick asked. "But how? Didn't they lead it out of town?"

"I don't know," Jacob answered. "One of their riders came back saying they were only three miles away."

"Where did you hear that?" Kelly asked.

Jacob took a breath and told them about the conference he'd overheard. "They said we're going someplace called Dexter."

"Yeah, it's due west of here," Nick said. "I don't know

why though. There's nothing there. Not according to the maps, anyway."

"They must know something we don't," Kelly suggested. "They've seen more of this land than we have."

"Maybe," Nick said. He didn't look convinced though.

"They're looking for some kind of pump," Jacob said. "I heard Casey say that the one they've got is busted. Apparently, they need a new one or they're not gonna have any drinkable water. And his wife is about to give birth. He was looking for some safe place to halt the caravan while that happens. There are other caravans out here, too. Apparently they fight each other whenever they meet."

"Not good," Nick said.

"So what do we do?" Kelly asked. "Do you think we can use the herd as cover to escape?"

She looked at Jacob and he felt himself lock up inside. Make the decision, he told himself. He knew exactly what he was supposed to do, but he couldn't make himself speak the words aloud.

He didn't get the chance anyway, for just then some of the riders came around with tangles of leather straps in their hands. They grabbed Jacob and Nick and pulled them to the middle of the slave clearing, where the bodies of Max and Barry still stood.

"Put these on," one of the men said.

"What? What is this?" Jacob asked, holding the knot of leather straps up in confusion.

"Put it on," the man repeated. "You're on tract duty."

When he still didn't understand, the man grew angry and turned him around. Then he tossed the straps over Jacob's shoulder and cinched the buckles tight at his back. Only then did Jacob realize he was wearing a crudely modified draft horse harness.

"What the hell is this?"

"Stand still," the man said, and then clipped a series of

leather reins to him. Other slaves fell in line, all of them wearing similar harnesses, and before Jacob knew it, he and Nick were tied in as draft animals, and told to start pulling.

"You tracts better get to moving," one of the free men said. He marched up and down the line of slaves, yelling at them like a drill sergeant. "If those zombies catch up with us, we're all running and leaving your dumb asses here to slow 'em down. Now move!"

Jacob glanced behind him, trying to spot the advancing zombies. He could see the dust cloud rising high above the line of vehicles, and he could hear the distant moan of the herd, but they had hooked him to a flatbed trailer topped with a huge orange tent, and it dominated his view.

Beside him, Nick had stopped pulling.

"What are you doing?" Jacob said.

"Look at her," he said, and pointed at the young girl they'd seen that first night. She was still coughing her lungs out and curled up in a ball like a wounded animal. "Hey, what about her?" Nick said to one of the free men.

The man didn't even look at her. "She either walks or gets eaten."

"You can't do that," he said. "There's room on the trailer. Throw her on there. Come on, man, show some decency."

"Why don't you show a little enthusiasm for pulling? You ain't got much time before that herd is all over this place."

"Let me carry her," Nick said.

"What?" the man said.

"Nick, what are you doing?" Jacob said.

Nick ignored him. "Let me carry her. If you won't let her ride, let me carry her. It won't put you out any."

The man looked like he was actually giving it a lot of thought. Finally, he shrugged and said, "Yeah, sure. Go ahead. But if you don't keep up, we'll cut you loose and let you both die."

"Fine," Nick said.

He tried to veer off toward the girl, but the other slaves wouldn't budge from the line they'd set.

Nick turned to the man behind him and said, "Hey, come on, give me slack."

The man just shook his head and bent into his work.

Nick fought against the reins, but they held him firm.

"Hey," he yelled to the girl. "Come on. Come to me. I can't reach you. You have to come to me."

At first, Jacob thought the girl was just going to lie there and watch them, but then she slowly lumbered to her feet and stumbled into Nick's arms. "That's it," he said. "Got you." And he put her over his shoulder.

He glanced at Jacob and winked. "It's the Code, right? Everybody watches the other guy's back."

Before Jacob could respond, a huge swell of voices rose from the caravan behind them. At first he thought the herd had caught up with them, and the people back there were being slaughtered, but then he saw slaves and free men alike with their faces turned to the sky. Some of them were pointing.

Turning as much as the harness allowed, he saw the airship—or one just like it, he thought—gliding soundlessly toward them from the east. It was immense, like one of those aircraft carriers he'd read about back in school, and the span of its cloth wings was many times its length. Even at this distance, he could hear the faint popping noises the wings made in the wind.

The huge airship moved with the silence and grace of a bird riding the thermals. When they'd seen it the other night, it had been brightly aglow with neon lights of every hue. It had sparkled like a diamond in the sky. But now, it seemed far more a machine of unimaginable power than some glittery jewel. The top of its hull was made of curving black sheets of metal that dappled in the sun. A row of tall turrets and towers and sensors ran down the spine of the ship, end-ing in a giant rectangular tower that might have been a caudal fin, or just as easily might be something else.

The underside of the ship was in stark contrast to the top. Whereas the towers and turrets on the top of the ship were restricted to a narrow line running down front to back along the spine, the underside had an almost skeletal appearance. There were lights all along the length of it and blinking out from every nook and cranny. They just weren't as bright as they had been during the night. Jacob couldn't see weapons anywhere down its dull black metallic hull, but he had little doubt they were there.

And then, without making a sound, the airship changed course and veered toward the approaching herd.

For the first time, the airship made a sound, a long, low bass note that Jacob felt in his bones more than in his ears. He, and all the other slaves yoked in with him, took a few steps that way.

They caught themselves at the same time. Jacob shook his head. He'd felt like something had grabbed his guts and pulled him.

From behind him, Kelly said, "Jacob, did you feel that? Did you? It was like it was pulling me. I can still feel it."

She closed her eyes, spread her arms, and let out a long, slow breath.

And fell forward two steps before catching herself.

She opened her eyes. "If you stop thinking about it, it pulls you."

Kelly ran up to him, excited, despite all that had happened. "And did you see those sails, the way they reflected the sunlight. I think those are solar sails. They generate electricity from the sun. Back home, we've been working . . ."

But she stopped there.

Jacob read the pain in her face and knew her memories were flooding back again, grief hitting her with all its suddenness and cruelty.

He looked away, embarrassed.

On the opposite side of the caravan, slaves and free men alike had walked away from the vehicles, pointing and cheering. The herd, in all its enormity, had turned like a school of fish to follow the great metal beast as it tracked its way across the sky.

The diversion, they all realized as one, had bought them some time.

In the excitement of the moment, nobody but Jacob noticed Bree walking along the backside of the vehicles. She had no interest in the airship. Her gaze was fixated on something Jacob couldn't see inside the open door of one of the wagons.

"Kelly," he said, and nodded toward Bree.

"Oh, no," Kelly said. "No. No, baby, no."

But it was too late. Bree had reached the door, leaned inside, and came out holding a black revolver that looked as big as her forearm. Holding the gun in both hands she walked like a woman in shock through a gap in the caravan to the other side, where Jacob saw two of the men that had forced themselves on her the night before.

What followed seemed to him to play out in slow motion. Bree called out to the two men. They turned at the same time, the joy of watching the airship route the zombies away from them still shining on their faces, only to have that shine change to terror at the sight of the pretty little blonde with the dead stare and the enormous gun.

She leveled the weapon at the nearer man's balls and said, "I've got something for you," and fired.

His legs flew out from under him and he landed face-first in the grass.

Then she turned on the other man. She was probably aiming for his balls as well, but she only managed a gut shot. Still, the man folded into a ball, a hollow scream dying on his lips. She fired twice more, silencing that scream forever-more.

By then other free men had got their wits about them and pulled their weapons. From somewhere near the head of the column Jacob was pretty sure he could hear Casey screaming for them to stop, but it didn't happen. A dozen gunmen at least opened fire on her, causing her body to jitter and dance with the music of bullets.

She finally went down under the spray of lead, the huge pistol falling useless in the grass. Her face was a pale and twisted mask of pain and, strangely, the glory of release.

Jacob turned away. Failure and self-loathing and contempt for his own inadequacies overwhelmed him, and it was all he could do to keep from screaming.

"What the fuck is this?" cried Mother Jane.

Jacob opened his eyes.

The matriarch was storming down the line of wagons, swollen and pained ankles be damned.

"Who shot her?" she demanded. A pause. "Well? Who the hell shot her?"

She stared around the group of free men, all of them with their rifles still smoking.

No one spoke. No one dared to.

"Goddamn it," she said. She turned on Casey, who was right by her side. "You see this? Do you see this? You remember this when that baby comes. You remember this right here."

She looked around at her boys, the disgust plain on her face.

"Damn wasted opportunity is what that is. Damn shame."

And then she stormed off to her wagon.

23

They pulled the wagons for hours at a time, resting only long enough for a taste of tepid water. There were eight slaves in Jacob's team, tracts, as the pullers were called. At times he was able to see portions of the caravan ahead and behind him, and he saw that horses pulled the heavier vehicles, the RVs and bigger trailers. The smaller trailers, like the one they had him yoked to, had human tracts.

It was exhausting, mind-numbing work, and when they at last pulled up to the outskirts of Dexter, just before sunset, Jacob felt like his legs had turned to water. Every inch of him was wet with sweat and grimed over with road dust. His clothes were already showing signs of wear, and it was little wonder the other slaves looked as tattered as they did. If only one day of tract work had done this to him, it was a wonder the others still had what little rags they had left. It was a wonder they were alive at all.

But Jacob said nothing by way of complaint. All the work he had done Nick had done, too, and he had done it while carrying the sick girl. Jacob had heard him talking to her, reassuring her, but she'd said little beyond a few pained grunts and moans.

After they made camp, all he wanted to do was fall over and go to sleep, but he knew he couldn't afford to do that. If he was to survive here, with these people, he'd have to learn their ways. And so he stayed awake, and alert, watching and listening for anything he could use to stay alive.

Throughout the day he'd seen riders ranging across the prairie, and occasionally he'd heard the clap of a distant rifle shot. Evidently they'd been hunting, for there were campfires burning throughout the caravan, and he could smell the succulent aroma of roasting meat. Water seemed to be in short supply, though. Clean water at any rate. The water they'd been given was cloudy and warm. And probably loaded with bacteria, he thought. Kelly had warned him about using it to clean out the dog bite wounds on his arms, but there was little else he could do. Already the wounds were turning fiery red and raw looking, and in places he saw boils forming. Without clean water, the infection was likely to spread and swamp him over.

A lot like it had done with the sick girl Nick had carried all day.

Which was another thing.

Nick seemed to have made it his mission to care for the girl. He'd set her up on a flat section of grass and put a coat under her head for a pillow. He'd fought another slave for a pitcher of water, and now he was giving it to her a few small sips at a time while mopping the sweat away from her forehead.

"She's burning up," he said to Jacob.

Kelly grumbled beside him. "Nick, what are you doing?" she asked, gesturing at the girl.

"She's sick," he said, like that explained it all.

"We'll all be sick soon, I think."

"Yeah, but she's sick now, and none of these people will help her. It's inhuman the way they treat each other."

There was no arguing with that. Jacob hadn't stopped wondering the same point since the moment they met their first rider. How could people live this way? Why would they want to live this way?

Growing up in Arbella, he'd been taught that survival was a group effort. Everybody pulled his or her weight, everybody looked out for the other guy. There was no room for those who wouldn't work, and there was no room for those who betrayed the trust of their fellow man. To live like these people did was to invite misery and death.

And for those it didn't kill, life wasn't worth living.

But for now, he thought, it was his life, too. Until he and the others could figure out a way out of their situation, they all had to live here.

"What's her name?" Kelly asked.

"She said it was Chelsea."

"She's just a girl," Kelly said. "She can't be more than seventeen."

"About that, yeah."

"She won't be well enough to come with us when we bust out of here." Her voice had dropped to a whisper as she said it. "I'm thinking we go tonight."

She glanced at Jacob, and then at Nick.

Both men nodded.

"You shouldn't," Chelsea said.

She rolled over to face them and tried to sit up. Her dark brown hair was long and stringy and dirty. She looked weak from hunger and bleary eyed with fever, and when she spoke, her voice had a tremor to it.

"They'll be watching you tonight."

"They haven't posted guards," Kelly said.

"They don't have to. The slaves will be watching you.

They want you to try to escape. All of them will be wanting to do what Chris did."

"Who's Chris?" Jacob said.

"My older brother," she said. "The one who shot your friend yesterday and was made a rider for it. The others will be waiting for a chance to do the same."

Jacob and Kelly traded a worried look. A quick glance around the slave area was enough to back up what she said. The others were watching them. Not overtly, not making a scene of it, but they were watching.

"I don't understand," Nick said. "He's your brother? Why didn't he take you with him when they made him part of their gang?"

"It doesn't work that way," she said, and hugged her belly and groaned. She coughed hard, and when she could finally open her eyes again, they were red and teary from the pain. "You have to be invited into their family. They wouldn't want me."

"But he's your brother."

"Not anymore. Not for a long time. This life changed him."

"Yeah, I bet," said Nick. Something caught his eye. "Hey, check that out. Looks like dinnertime."

The nightly ritual began again. The ravens descended on the slave area. Dogs and more slaves began to appear at the edges of the encampment. The canoe was brought in, and this time it looked mounded with meat. The foraging parties had done well, apparently. Free men and women, fewer this time around, but still plenty, gathered to watch the show.

"God, I'm hungry," Nick said.

"We all need to eat something tonight," Jacob agreed. "We're gonna have to go in there and fight it out."

"Oh, God," Kelly said. She looked positively ill with dread.

"You stay here with her," Jacob told her. "Nick, you think you're well enough to help me out?"

"Hell, yeah," Nick said. "Let's go get dinner."

24

In the morning the scraping drill started over.

Jacob and the others went about their work like it was the only thing on their mind, but they were actually trying to repeat the bit of intelligence gathering that Jacob had lucked into the day before.

Right away they got lucky.

As they were scraping down the sides of one of the RVs, a rusty metal Airstream, two free women emerged.

"It'll be any day now," said the first woman. She was heavyset, with a red face and flabby arms and gray, wiry hair that stuck out in all directions. "I'm worried that the baby hasn't dropped down more than it has."

"Maybe it's just a big baby," the other woman said. "Happens with the diabetes."

"Yep," agreed the first woman. "Let's just hope we can stay here for a while. A week at least. Give Linda a chance to recover after that baby finally comes."

Whatever the other woman's response might have been they didn't hear. The two women went around a corner and were out of earshot.

"I bet that's Casey's wife they're talking about," Jacob said.

"Yeah," agreed Kelly. "Sounds like we're going to be here for a while. Might give us a chance to figure out how to slip away."

"And go where?" he said.

"Away from here," she said. "God, anywhere but here."

"Yeah, but where? Seriously, we can't just go off half-cocked like we did before. If we make a blind run for it, they'll catch us in no time. We might as well shoot ourselves and save them the trouble."

"What are you saying, that you don't want to escape?"

"No, of course I want out of here. I'm just saying we have to be smart about it. Even if we steal some horses, there's nothing around here but grassland. Once we get out in the open, we'd be visible to God, man, and everybody. Even these assholes."

"So what do we do?"

"I don't know," he said. He glanced toward the town of Dexter. What little of it he could see was in the process of being consumed by ash and dogwood trees. Here and there he could make out a few one-story buildings, some shops, in the distance a water tower, but little else. "Over there, maybe," he said. "That'd be our best bet. Find some attic or cellar somewhere in there and hide until they decide to move on. They're caravan people, prairie Bedouins, so they won't spend forever around here looking for us. We wait them out, and then we go back home."

"Is that really as good as we can do?" Kelly asked.

"If there's something better, I don't know it."

After a long hesitation, she nodded in agreement.

They scraped around to the other side of the trailer, and there they stopped again. There was a large pit fire burning about twenty yards away. A large section of chain-link fencing had been stretched over the fire, and a handful of slaves were sitting sullenly, watching for pots of all different shapes and sizes to come to a boil.

"Good Lord," Kelly said. "Is that how they clean their water?"

"I guess so."

"What are you two doing here?" came a voice from behind them.

It was Casey, and next to him was Mother Jane.

Jacob was about to make some lame excuse about working, but Kelly didn't give him a chance.

"Is that how you clean your water? In pots and pans?"

"Gotta boil the water if you want to get all the bugs and shit out of it," Casey said.

"Well, yeah, but . . . it's not very efficient."

"What do you mean?" Casey asked.

"Well, like look at that. You've got what, about twenty gallons there? The average person needs a gallon of water a day. More if they're active. Horses need even more. And you've got plenty of both around here."

"What's your point?" Casey looked close to losing his patience.

"Only that . . . why don't you have a still?"

"You mean like for making whisky?"

Kelly nodded. "Well, yes, you can use a still for making alcohol. But you can also use it to clean huge amounts of water in a single batch." She pointed at the fire pit. "Doing it that way would take you all day to make enough water for this camp. But if you had a large capacity still, maybe one you mounted on a trailer, you could clean a week's worth of water in a few hours."

"Yeah, that'd be nice," Casey said. "But this isn't Kentucky. We can't go out and find a still someplace."

"You don't need to," she said. "You just make one. It's easy."

"Out of what?"

"Sheets of copper are the easiest thing to use."

He laughed. "You see any of that around here?"

She looked at Jacob and shrugged. "I don't know. Any ideas?"

"You got a ton of fifty-five gallon drums around here. You could use those. You could make a really big one if you had an empty propane tank and the exhaust pipe off a pickup truck or a tractor. It'd take some serious cleaning, but that would make a giant one."

Casey frowned. "I saw a place in town that sold propane. They had a bunch of big tanks outside. How long would it take you to build something like that?"

"As long as everything was cleaned first," Jacob said, "I don't know, a few hours. I'd need some kind of welding torch, but it wouldn't take long."

Mother Jane had been listening to all of this with growing interest, but now she just shook her head in disgust and said, "Wasted opportunity. I done tole you, Casey, wasted opportunity."

25

Later that afternoon they brought Jacob everything he'd said he'd need to make the still, and true to his word, by nightfall, he had it done. It was a simple column still, made of a fifty-five gallon drum and the exhaust pipe from a pickup and a length of garden hose. It was a big version of the kind he'd seen Kelly use for the last ten years whenever she made up a batch of the gin she did so well.

It took Kelly the better part of an hour to show them how to use it, and that was pretty much all it took. They had it up and running and the first batch of clean water ready by the time she was done with teaching them how it worked.

Casey came over, gave the still a dubious look, tasted some of the water, and finally nodded. "That's not bad," he said. He looked around at his fellow riders, the inner circle, from what Jacob had been able to discern and nodded. "A little smoky, but not bad."

The others laughed and gathered round to fill their cups and canteens.

Casey stepped away from the still, drinking more water

from a metal cup, and raised it to Jacob and Kelly in a toast. "This is good shit. You two done well."

Kelly could only frown, but Jacob saw an opportunity.

"Where we're from we have a law we live by called the Code. It says that everybody works, everybody does their fair share, everybody watches out for the other guy, and nobody steals from anybody else."

"Sounds like a regular fucking love-in," said Casey.

"It works for us," Jacob said.

"Yeah? How's it working out for you now? 'Cause from where I'm looking, you guys are pretty fucked."

"I'm hoping that's not the case," Jacob said. Casey had given him exactly the opening he was looking for. "I was hoping, if we did this for you, you'd do something for us."

Casey's eyes narrowed suspiciously. "Like what?"

Jacob showed him the bloody bandages that made his arms look like a mummy's. "I need fresh water for what your dogs did to me. I need to rinse these wounds out on a regular basis."

"And we've got others with us who need fresh water, too," Kelly said, picking up on Jacob's thread. "Clean water could make all the difference in the world to us, and now you can make enough to float this caravan across the prairie." She even borrowed a line she'd heard Nick use on one of the riders. "It wouldn't put you out any."

He looked them over, but his expression showed little beyond disgust. "I'll consider it," he finally said.

"But we need it tonight," Kelly said.

"And I said I'd consider it. Now get the hell out of my face before I shoot your boyfriend here and turn you over to the boys as the evening entertainment."

Jacob put a hand on Kelly's wrist. "Come on," he said.

She gave him a nasty scowl, then reluctantly turned and walked with Jacob toward the edge riders' campsite.

"Wait a minute," Casey said.

Jacob and Kelly stopped and turned.

"Your name's Jacob, right?"

"Yes."

"This Code you talk about, it sounds like you people have got it all figured out."

"No," Jacob said. "We've found something that works for us." He gestured toward the still. "And now, it works for you."

Casey smiled. It was a nasty, slippery smile, like that of a man always on the lookout for a weak spot, a way to overcome his opponent, and he just found that spot.

"But it doesn't work," he said. "Does it?" He paused a moment, looking at them both, still wearing that greasy smile. "It ain't done jack shit for you people, has it? You know why?"

"Why?" Jacob asked.

"Because out here, there's a different Code. Out here, a man makes his own way. He doesn't get to rely on the welfare of a bunch of do-gooders. A man pulls himself up by his bootstraps, or he dies a slave. How's that for a Code?"

"It sounds barbaric," Kelly said.

"And yet you come asking me for water." Casey looked down his nose at both of them. "You two go on back where you belong."

"What about the water?" Jacob asked.

"I told you. I'd consider it. Now get your ass back with the slaves before I put a bullet in your gut. Go on, get!"

Casey met Jacob's stare, daring him to react. But Jacob didn't rise to the bait. He simply turned around and started back to the slave encampment. But they'd only gone a few yards when the fat woman with the gray, wiry hair they'd seen earlier that day came trotting around the corner. She saw Casey standing in the middle of the group and ran straight for him.

"Casey, it's time."

So that was it, Jacob thought. He's anxious, not insane.

"What . . . what do I . . ?" Casey said, stammering.

"She's asking for you. Come on."

Casey let the old woman lead him away, never even glancing at Jacob and Kelly. When they were gone, one of the free women came up to them and said, "That still's gonna really help us out. Thank you."

"Yeah, sure," Jacob said.

The woman lowered her voice to a whisper. "If you go around the side there and wait I'll bring you some fresh water and some deer meat you can take back with you. It's past dark so I think you already missed feeding time."

"That'd be nice, thank you," Kelly said.

When they returned, they found Nick with a fresh black eye. He was holding his ribs.

"What happened to you?" Jacob asked.

"It's easier to get a meal when there's two of us," he said. "Where'd you get all that?"

"One of the Family gave it to us."

Jacob glanced over at Chelsea, who was sitting up, hugging her knees, watching them. Her fever had broken, thanks to some of the meds in Bree's kit, and she looked to be feeling better. Still pale, still sore, but much better.

"We got enough for you, too, Chelsea." He held out one of the jugs of water. "Come on over here and join us."

She looked distrustfully at the water, then at Nick.

"It's all right," he said. "Come on."

She sat down next to Nick. "You people are nice. Thank you."

"You're welcome," Kelly said.

Chelsea took one of the pieces of deer meat and tore into it eagerly. She hadn't eaten in days, Jacob guessed, and it showed. Clearly, she was starving. He almost joked with her to slow down, enjoy it, but that would have been cruel. Instead, he just traded a smile with Nick and offered her the water jug, which she drank with equal gusto.

After she put the water jug down, she said, "Nobody shares anything around here."

"It's our way," Jacob said. "Everybody works, everybody does their share, everybody watches the other guy's back."

She nodded as she took another bite of the venison. "Nick told me about that," she said. "Your home sounds such a lovely place."

"Where is your home, Chelsea?" Kelly asked. "Were you born here, in this caravan?"

"Oh, no. I belonged to another caravan before this one. This Farris Clan sold my brother and me to Mother Jane about four years ago."

"The caravans trade back and forth?" Jacob asked. "When I overheard them talking yesterday, they made it sound like they're at war with the other caravans."

"Most of the time it is war," she said. "But sometimes they trade, if they know each other."

"How many caravans are there?"

Chelsea shrugged and took another bite. "Nobody knows."

"Well how often do you see other caravans?"

"Not very often. In the time I've been here we've seen four others."

"And do they all use slaves?" asked Kelly.

Chelsea nodded. She was almost done with her venison and eyeing the rack of short ribs next to Jacob.

He slid them over to her.

"Really?" she said, her eyes wide.

"Yeah," he said with a chuckle. "Eat. Enjoy."

"I can't believe that about the slaves," Kelly said to Jacob. She pursed her lips in disgust. "Barbarians." She caught herself then and turned to Chelsea. "I'm sorry. I didn't mean to insult you. It's just that I find this kind of existence, and the keeping of slaves, to be brutal and degrading."

"Oh, you're not offending me," Chelsea said. "Slavery is anathema to the human condition."

Jacob glanced at Kelly, who raised her eyebrows in surprise.

"Anathema?" Jacob said.

"Yes," Chelsea said. "It means something held in contempt or abhorrence."

Nick laughed.

"I, uh, yes, I know what it means," Jacob said, catching himself. "It's just that I didn't expect to hear it . . . out here."

"Why not?" Chelsea asked, oblivious to his attempt to dance around insulting her. "Injustice anywhere is a threat to justice everywhere."

"Well," Jacob said, "yes, I believe that."

"No," Kelly said. She gave Jacob a frustrated look. "Good for you you're good at being a cop. Book learning never was your thing. That's the keynote line from Martin Luther King, Jr.'s 'Letter from a Birmingham Jail.' " To Chelsea, she said: " 'We are caught in an inescapable network of mutuality, tied in a single garment of destiny.' "

"Oh, yes," Chelsea said, brightening. "You've read it."

She tore one of the ribs from the rack and her eyes rolled up into her head as she ate.

"That's so good," she said.

"Yes, Chelsea," Kelly said. "I've read it. I read it back in school. It meant a lot to me then, and it's been close to my heart ever since. But please forgive me for sounding condescending or rude, but I'm surprised that you've read it. I'll be absolutely honest and say that I'm surprised you know how to read."

Chelsea was about to eat another rib, but that last part struck a nerve. She frowned and said, "Of course, I know how to read. I speak three languages."

"I, uh . . . what?" Kelly asked.

"English, Spanish, and Mandarin. I'm fluent in all three. I can read and write in all three."

Nick had leaned back on his elbows and was watching the exchange with a bemused grin on his face, but upon that he sat up. "Where did you learn three languages, Chelsea?"

"Back in school."

"Oh," Kelly said. "Did the Farris Clan caravan have a school?"

"No way," Chelsea said. "They were religious nut jobs. The only lessons they ever taught were out of a paraphrased version of the Christian Bible."

"Chelsea, wait," said Nick. "I'm confused. Clearly you're a bright girl. Where did you go to school?"

Chelsea didn't answer. She lowered her head and put the ribs back on the plate next to Jacob.

"Chelsea?" repeated Nick.

"I'm not allowed to talk about it."

"Why not?" Nick said.

"It's the law of my people."

Nick started to speak, but Jacob put a hand on his shoe to quiet him.

"Chelsea," he said. "In Arbella, we have a similar rule. Nobody says anything about Arbella to anyone not part of our group. When we first sat down, and I heard from you that Nick had told you about our home, I was upset. But I'm not upset now because after hearing you speak, I realize that there are people out here in the wasteland worth getting to know. Maybe we can help each other. I'm willing to try. Are you?"

She shook her head. "I'm not supposed to."

"It's okay," Jacob said. "We won't force you to say any-thing."

She looked up, surprised. "You won't?"

"No. You should know that about us by now. That's not the kind of people we are."

She looked from Jacob to Kelly and finally back to Nick. He nodded. "It's true," he said.

She looked uncertain still, but at last she said, "I was on-board an aerofluyt that crashed. The *Darwin*. Chris and I were just a few of the survivors. Our parents and a bunch of others died. Chris and I hung around the wreckage for a few days, hoping for a rescue team, but they didn't come in time. The Farris Clan came upon us while we were trying to pick soybeans from a pasture, and before I knew it, seven years had gone by and now I'm here."

She stood up to go. Her voice had grown unsteady and charged with emotion, and Jacob got the feeling there was a hoard of hurt and pain buried deep in that girl just waiting to bust out.

"Wait," Kelly said. "What's an 'aerofluyt'?"

Chelsea stopped and made a half turn toward Kelly. "You know the big airship you saw the other day?" she said. "That's an aerofluyt."

26

"Hey, wake up."

Rough hands were shaking him. Jacob jumped to his feet, still half asleep but ready to fight. There was a time, not too long ago, when he would have grunted and rolled over in his bed, telling whoever it was to go away and let him sleep. But not now. Two weeks in the wasteland didn't seem like much, but it had changed him.

"Easy," said the man who'd woken him. It was one of the riders. In the dark it took Jacob a moment to recognize Casey.

Jacob sat up uneasily, waiting for a hammer to hit from somewhere out of sight.

"What do you want?" Jacob said, lowering his fists. Aggression toward a member of the Family was an easy way to get killed.

On the ground beneath him, Kelly, Nick, and Chelsea stirred.

"We need a doctor," Casey said.

"None of us are doctors," Jacob answered back.

"It's for Linda, my wife. The birthing is going hard for her. Momma says if any of you knows anything about doctoring, you're needed real bad."

"We're not doctors," Jacob repeated.

"Look," Casey said. "I know you been treated hard. That's our way. I can't help that. But Linda, she's got the diabetes, and it makes the baby real hard to get out. Our midwives don't know what else to do. Momma thinks they're both gonna die if she don't get some real help."

"The woman you raped and murdered could have helped you," Kelly said, rising to her feet. "But I guess it's too late for that now, isn't it?"

To his credit, Casey didn't become enraged.

He hung his head low and looked every bit like a man with his hat in his hand.

"The woman and baby that's dying back there, they didn't do nothing to you people. They didn't hurt you. They didn't do nothing. Please, if you know how to help, we could really use your help."

Jacob didn't hesitate. And he didn't bother looking to the others for confirmation.

"We can't help you," he said. "You murdered the only doctor we had."

"What about that Code you told me about? Everybody watches each other's back. Isn't that what you said?"

"Yep, that's what we said."

"She's dying," Casey said. In the dark it was hard to tell if there were tears on his face, but his cheeks did seem to shine in the starlight. "She needs help."

"That might have been possible before you raped and killed our medic. But now, you got nothing but us, and there ain't a one of us that knows the first thing about birthing a baby. What was it your mother said? This is a missed opportunity?"

Jacob waited for the man to lash out at him, to beat him senseless.

But that didn't happen.

Instead, Casey simply rose to his feet and turned back toward the darkness. "I'll remember this," he said over his shoulder. "I promise you that. I'll remember this."

27

Jacob had already caught on to the routine.

At sunup a free woman would come to the slaves—it still rankled him that he could saddle himself with that word—with a large box full of scrapers. She would select a handful of slaves, generally the new ones, like Jacob and the others, and those she didn't like or thought lazy, like Chelsea, give them the scrapers, and send them off to clean. Other slaves were sent off to do other tasks.

When they were done scraping, they would return the scrapers and then get used for other mundane jobs around the encampment, everything from wood gathering to cleaning out the toilets to hauling around supplies or fixing broken things.

It was hard work and it was demeaning in the worst way. To get past it, you could turn off your mind and give in to the soul-sucking boredom of it all, or you could hold the indignation and rage inside you like a flame, letting it burn you.

Jacob wanted to believe he'd always have that flame inside him, but as he watched the other slaves waking up and waiting for the day to start, he wondered how long he could keep it burning.

What would ten months of a life like this do to a man?

What about ten years?

It scared him, the things that might happen, the life he might learn to accept.

But the free woman with the box of scrapers didn't come when she normally did. Instead, Chris Walker, the former slave who'd stopped their escape two nights earlier, rode up on his new horse. He'd taken a bath and changed his slave rags for some real clothes, and with it put on an air of arrogance that was almost palpable.

He rode right through the middle of the slave encampment, his horse's hooves stabbing at the grass as he told them all that there were to be no fires after noon. If they had any reason for a fire, they needed to get it done before then.

His message delivered, he turned his horse to get out of there as fast as he could, but was forced to stop when he came face to face with his little sister. Chelsea was standing next to Nick, staring up at her older brother.

A long, cold moment of silence passed between them.

"You look like you're feeling better," he said.

"A little, yes."

He nodded. Perhaps he wanted to say that he was glad, but something held him back. He lifted his chin and said, "Good. At least we can finally get a little work out of you. Now stand aside."

"Wait," Nick asked. "Why can't we have any fires after noon. What's going on?"

Walker looked down his nose at Nick, and seemed to debate with himself for a moment whether it was beneath him to answer a slave's question or not.

His horse pawed at the ground impatiently.

Finally, he said, "The herd is coming back. Our scouts

think they could be here as early as this evening, but probably sometime in the morning."

"The herd?" Nick said. He looked over at Jacob and Kelly, the alarm plain on his face. "Why aren't we moving then? We should be getting out of here."

Again, Walker seemed to debate with himself about how to handle this slave and his questions. His new mantle of authority wasn't fitting well.

"That ain't for you to decide," he finally said.

Studying him more closely now, Jacob noticed the discomfort in the man's voice as he forced himself to say *ain't* instead of *is not*, like he was wearing shoes that were too small. It was a reminder to Jacob that Walker had received the same education Chelsea had. There was a civilized man on top of that horse, and he was teaching himself to be a barbarian, to survive even if it meant letting his own family be damned.

To Jacob, it was disgusting.

"Stand aside," he ordered Chelsea and Nick. "There's a free man coming through."

Jacob watched him ride back to the far side of the encampment, and it amazed him that Walker and Chelsea could be so different.

It had taken Chelsea much coaxing and their repeated assurance that her secrets were safe with them for her to finally open up about the home she'd known before becoming a slave.

She told them her home was on Galveston Island, though her people called it Temple, and not Galveston. That made sense to him, coming from Arbella. You can't build a new world without new names, because naming is building the world anew. Even the Bible taught that. Hadn't Adam been called upon to name all the things in his world?

But there was more than new names for old places. What

Jacob's people commonly referred to as the First Days, Chelsea's people simply called the War. Jacob and the others, especially Kelly, peppered her with questions about where her people came from and how they'd managed to become so advanced as to create airships like the ones they'd seen, but her answers were frustrating. For as clearly amazing as her education had been, she was only eleven when the aerofluyt she'd sailed on crashed, and her memories were that of a seventeen-year-old girl looking back on a world she knew only as a child.

To Kelly's questions of "But how do they work? What powers them?" and "How come they don't make any noise?" Chelsea could only shrug.

"I don't know," she said. "Chris took some engineering courses. I remember him saying how much he hated those. He could probably tell you more. But the aerofluyts aren't the thing I miss the most. I remember we also had these really pretty clipper ships that would sail around the Gulf. My parents were both scientists—well, everyone that lives in Temple is some kind of scientist—and I remember my dad telling me that those clipper ships sailed all over the world. I thought they were so beautiful. Sometimes, when my classes let out for our morning break, I would see them out on the water, unfurling their sails. It was gorgeous."

Everything she said generated more questions, but it was Kelly who was the first to ask them.

"How did they lead the zombies away from us?" Kelly asked. "The, what did you call it, the aerofluyt? How did it lead the herd away from us? That was amazing."

"Oh," Chelsea said, "I know that one. Basic morphic field theory is one of the first things they taught us about zombies."

"Morphic field theory?" Kelly said.

She'd made it into a question, but Jacob had known Kelly

a long time. He recognized when the snarkiness in her was about to surface.

Chelsea nodded eagerly. "Mm-hmm. The idea that a neuro-electric field in the reptilian core of the brain links all sentient organisms is the basis of all zombie research. Once the higher brain functions are destroyed, all that's left is that reptilian brain core. The zombie becomes little more than a pawn, open and receptive and completely dependent upon the morphic field that connects it with every other zombie out there. Control that morphic field and you control the zombie."

"I . . ." Kelly trailed off.

She was chewing on her lip and bouncing like a kid who has to go to the bathroom.

Jacob couldn't help but smile. Knowing her as well as he did, he saw that she was log jammed. There was so much in her that she wanted to spill out it was getting caught up in her throat.

He decided to play her straight man.

"I was under the impression that morphic field theory was junk science," he said. "Like astral projection and astrology."

Kelly, still trying desperately to bring herself under control, managed to nod.

"I don't know what astral projection is," Chelsea said, "but morphic field theory isn't junk science. It's a proven fact, same as geologic stratigraphy and geometry and evolution. Calling it a theory simply means we're continuing to define our understanding of how it works, not that its truth is in doubt."

"Yes, but what facts are there to support morphic field theory?" Kelly said. "That idea's come up before and there's nothing to support it."

"Of course, there is," Chelsea said. "You've seen the

zombies form into herds. That's why. It's also the reason why head shots kill them. Knock out the reptilian core and you knock out the source of the morphic field that connects an individual zombie with all the rest."

"But there's lots of reasons why—"

"And you've felt it yourself," Chelsea said. "Remember when the aerofluyt went over us? You heard that deep humming sound it made. You felt the way it pulled you? That's morphic field theory at work."

Once she got talking, she couldn't stop. She looked around the circle of new friends and beamed a radiant smile at them.

"All of those aerofluyts are equipped with morphic field generators," she went on. "That's how they manage to control the great herds. I remember my mom telling me that they steered herds away from human settlements whenever they could. I always liked that. It's a lot like what you said, about how you always watch the other guy's back."

Jacob had nodded to that, even as Kelly dug in with more questions.

Remembering what she said made him think of Chris Walker's warning that the herd was coming back. It was possibly an opportunity to escape, and he said as much to the others.

"How?" Kelly asked. "Won't they just send out a rider to shepherd the herd around us, like they did in Sikeston?"

"Probably," he said. "We'll just have to find a way to bring them to us."

"You're saying bring the herd down on this caravan?"

He nodded.

"That'd be suicide," Nick said.

"Or a way out," Jacob countered.

"But how?" Kelly asked. "Make a loudspeaker or something? I wouldn't know how to do that. And even if we did, the Family would shut us down before we could do any damage."

"I was thinking a smoke grenade."

"A what?" Kelly said.

"Remember when I used to cheat off your tests in chemistry," he said. "You're the smart one. Figure it out. What do you get when you mix potassium nitrate and sugar together?"

She thought for a second. "I don't know, low-grade gunpowder?"

"Which sends up a lot of smoke, right?"

She nodded. "Yeah, I guess so. But where would we get potassium nitrate?"

He pointed at the bird shit. "Mother Jane's flock makes plenty of it right here."

"Yeah," she said, suddenly excited, "that's right! It would make really weak gunpowder, but that's exactly what we'd need. It would make lots of smoke, but no bang." He could see the wheels turning in her head. She was already running through the procedure. "The only thing is the sugar. Where are we going to get that?"

"I don't know."

Jacob turned to Chelsea.

"Any idea where we can get some sugar around here?"

"Maybe. How much do you need?"

Jacob considered that for a moment. "Possibly, what, five pounds?"

"Not even that," Kelly said. "You don't want too much sugar, or the mixture won't set. I'd say less than a pound."

"Oh, well, that's easy then. I thought you'd want like fifty pounds."

"They have that much around here?" Kelly asked.

"Sure. The slaves aren't allowed to have any, but they've got a whole trailer devoted to stuff like that. They've got sugar, baking soda, cornstarch, flour, whatever they need to cook with."

"Any chance they have a cast-iron skillet?"

"I don't know, but I can check."

"You can get in?"

"Sure. They're supposed to keep it locked, I guess, because there's a padlock on the door most of the time, but nobody ever fastens the lock. I guess they're in and out too much to worry about it."

Kelly glanced at Jacob, a huge smile on her face. "We just might be able to make this work," she said.

Before Jacob could answer, they heard a man's screams of rage coming from the far side of the caravan. Then the screams gave way to fists beating on the sides of an RV.

Jacob and the others started to head that way, their curiosity baiting them.

Though the dividing line between slave and free man was sharply drawn, it was a small community, and gossip spread quickly across social lines. They'd made it maybe halfway to the far side of the caravan, where Mother Jane and her Boys had their quarters, before they started to hear whispers that neither Casey's wife nor their unborn son made it through childbirth. Mother Jane's eldest son had just lost everything, and he was in a rage to beat the devil.

"I don't think we should get much closer," Kelly said.

"Agreed," Jacob said. "And I think now's a pretty good time to leave this place."

28

They worked throughout the morning, gathering bird shit and bringing it back to their part of the encampment in the pockets of their clothes.

Within a few tries, Kelly got good at eyeballing the right amounts.

Two handfuls of bird shit mixed with a scant handful of sugar, cooked over coals in a cast-iron skillet, yielded a gray pancake-looking disc that needed to be dried under the sun, but otherwise looked to be exactly what they needed.

All they lacked was the right opportunity to deploy them.

It would have to be timed just right. Too soon, and they risked the chance that the herd could still be shepherded around the caravan's hiding spot. Too late, and the zombies might not see them.

There was also the chance that the herd would pass them by in the middle of the night. That was what the Family wanted, Jacob was sure of that. The caravan would be dark, and quiet, and the herd would have nothing to draw them in. Morning would come with news from the riders that the herd had safely passed them by in the wee hours of the morning, with none of them the wiser.

It was a very real possibility, and one that would certainly write their death sentence if it happened; for Jacob knew, and had indeed heard rumblings from others, that Casey blamed him for the death of his wife and son. He had come begging for help, and while Jacob spoke truly that none of them had the medical knowledge needed to see his wife through the delivery, he was certain that Casey didn't believe a word of it.

All he would need was the thinnest of excuses to kill Jacob and the others, if not for justice, but for some misplaced need for revenge. The short answer was that they needed the herd to come through the area at morning's light.

Everything rested on that hope.

29

A curious quiet had descended on the camp.

Their evenings were usually filled with the yelling and laughing of the free men from the far side of the caravan. The Family liked to drink, and they got rowdy once the sun went down. But that evening was the first quiet one Jacob had heard. There was no singing, no fighting, no drunken fornicating. None of the normal noises. A sort of cowed quiet pervaded the community, as though everyone was stunned by the death of a mother and child and laid low by the surprise of it.

To Jacob, that seemed ironic.

He wondered how a people so eager to cause the deaths of others could be stunned by the death of one of their own.

It seemed like an exercise in hubris to him. But then, that didn't shock him. Mother Jane and her Boys were barbarians. Surely they had no trouble believing the world revolved around them.

Yet, hadn't he bccn the same, just a few days ago?

That thought caused him some disquiet. As a lifelong citizen of Arbella, he'd known a life of comfort and confidence that all around him shared the Code. And he'd gone forth into the wilderness believing that the Code would carry him through any situation, that it would be his spiritual guide. Yet, in the span of a few days, he'd stood by while a woman was raped and while another died in pregnancy. Did it matter that he was at gunpoint during the former, or technically unable to do much for the latter? He wanted to believe that it made a difference, but a part of him had doubts, especially about Bree's death. Justly or unjustly, he couldn't quite shake the idea that he was no better than these savages.

Wasn't he just a brute of a different stripe?

Those were the thoughts that haunted him as he stood the first watch, straining his senses against the night, listening for some sign of the coming herd.

No sign came, and at the end of his three hours, he glanced from Kelly to Nick.

Nick was sleeping with an arm around Chelsea, and that made him frown. Since their early twenties, Jacob had more or less realized that Nick had a thing for the younger girls. Not the really young, not the little girls, because that would be sick and wrong, but for the girls on the edge of womanhood, around sixteen and seventeen.

Kelly had even noticed it. She'd seen the attention Nick lavished on Chelsea, and to her it was troubling.

"He likes 'em young," Jacob said.

He'd meant simply to agree with her, but she'd gone on the offensive. "It's not cool," she said. "She's a child. He has no business getting intimate with her. It's . . . it just seems, I don't know . . . ewww."

His first instinct had been to defend his friend, but something made him stop short. It was a trend he'd first noticed right after they left school. At eighteen, they'd been farmed out as shadows to the various trades Arbella had to offer. Jacob had gone into salvage. Nick, because of his drawing ability and fantastic memory, had been pulled into the cartography school. Their evenings had been spent drinking and carousing with a bunch of girls just starting out in their new jobs. Jacob and Kelly had fallen together that first year out of school, and it had been fantastic. But Nick, Nick had remained fascinated with the younger girls still in school. At first, it was just the novelty of hanging out with the post-graduation kids that got him the girls, but as he got older, he got smoother, and soon at every party, every gathering, he had the latest cute girl from school on his arm.

That had gone on throughout their twenties without Jacob saying anything. After all, Arbella was a small community, and there simply weren't that many available people with whom to have a sexual relationship. But by the time they'd entered their thirties, even Jacob had stopped thinking it cool that Nick always found some cute seventeen-year-old girlfriend to bring to the parties.

He'd never said anything, nor had anyone else, to Jacob's knowledge, but Nick eventually stopped bringing the young ones around.

At the time, Jacob simply assumed Nick had finally grown up, and was going after girls his own age. But now, watching his friend with his arm over the girl's shoulder and his body spooned up close to hers, he wondered.

He knelt down next to Nick and said, "Hey, buddy, time to wake up."

Nick started and twisted around in his sleep. He blinked and then stared wide-eyed in alarm.

Beside him, Chelsea stirred.

"What's up?" Nick said, through a cloud of sleep.

"Wake up, man," said Jacob. "It's your turn."

"Huh?"

"For watch. It's your turn."

"Oh. Okay. Yeah, I got it."

"You got it? You sure?"

"Yeah," Nick said, sitting up. He ran his fingers through

his black hair. "Yeah, sure, I got it. Go to sleep, man. I'll wake you if I hear anything."

"You sure?"

"Of course, I'm sure," he said. He yawned and stretched. "Go to sleep, man. I'll wake Kelly next."

And with that assurance, Jacob let himself drift off to sleep.

30

Jacob woke to sunlight on his face. It took him a moment to mentally drop into gear, but when he did, he sat up in a panic. Nick was asleep again, still pressed up against Chelsea's backside. Kelly had curled up in a ball and pulled a frayed and muddy blue tarp over herself as a blanket.

He shook Kelly first, then Nick.

"Nick, what happened? Did you fall asleep?"

"Huh? What? Oh, crap. Oh, man, I'm sorry."

"You're . . . Crap!"

Jacob ran to the edge of the slave encampment and stared down the length of the caravan. Up near the road they'd used to come here from Sikeston he saw members of the Family walking in quiet groups, a horse-drawn trailer with a pair of bare pine wood coffins on it coming along behind the procession.

"Crap," he muttered.

He ran back to the others. "The Family is going out to bury Casey's wife."

"Oh, no," Kelly said. "That was our window."

"I know."

"So what do we do?"

Jacob listened, hoping beyond hope to hear at least the distant tramp and moan of the promised herd, but there was nothing. Only the sound of the wind whistling through the trees.

"Do you hear that?" he asked.

"I don't hear anything." Kelly said.

"No dogs barking." There were at least sixty that Jacob had seen around the caravan, and you could rely on there always being one or two barking at something, be it one of Mother Jane's ravens or chasing after some kids or just out of boredom. He went to the other side of the caravan and looked toward the corral. There were horses there, but at least half were missing. "They must have sent riders out to shepherd the herd, and taken the dogs with them."

"Nick, they said the herd was expected to pass east of town. What's out that way?"

"According to the map, just open country."

"And the town, how big is it? How far across?"

"Well, we're to the northwest. Straight shot across Highway 60, it'd be about a mile and a half to the other side of town."

"Okay, so not that far. If the herd was over there, and if they saw the smoke, we could see the first ones within, what, about thirty minutes?"

"Jacob," Kelly said. The way she drew out his name, he could tell she thought he was grasping at straws.

"Do we have any other options?"

"I don't know. That just seems like a mighty thin hook to hang our chances on."

"When are we going to have a better chance, Kelly? Most of the Family is at least ten minutes away. They'll be on foot. And most of the men who aren't at the funeral are off guiding the herd. This is our best chance. We light the smoke, get some horses, and make a break for it. With any luck at all, we'll be well south of here while the Family is trying to save themselves from the herd."

Kelly had seemed excited about the plan the night before, but now that it came time to put it in motion, she looked absolutely ill.

Nick looked doubtful, too.

Only Chelsea seemed unperturbed. But then, he figured that made sense. Neither Nick nor Kelly had gotten used to life as a slave yet. Chelsea had. She had seen how brutal and nasty and short life as a slave could be. But for Nick and Kelly, and for Jacob, too, this all still felt like a horrible nightmare from which they still had a chance of waking.

"We have to do this, you guys," Jacob said. "This is our last, best hope."

He looked at his old friends, and gradually saw their resolve taking shape.

He stuck out his hand between them, the way they'd done back in school, and Nick smiled. He put his hand on top of Jacob's, and Kelly followed a second later.

Nick gestured at Chelsea, and she did the same.

"All right," Jacob said. "Let's do this."

31

Jacob, Nick, and Chelsea went around the caravan as discreetly as possible, planting the gray pancakelike smoke grenades in places where they wouldn't be easily found.

Kelly was the best rider of the bunch, so she went to collect horses for them.

Jacob couldn't believe how careless the Family was. Perhaps it was because they were so preoccupied with the funeral and the passing herd, but it shocked him that they had left the camp virtually deserted. And as he planted the last of his smoke grenades, he thought how very sad it was that none of the other slaves had thought to use the opportunity to escape. Maybe it was true that some people learn to love their chains.

He stood and walked to the edge of the caravan, trying to look like he was busy fixing something whenever a free man or woman would pass. Fifty feet to his left, Chelsea did the same. Up near the head of the caravan, Nick, too, was finished and waiting for the signal.

And then he saw Kelly step into view.

She gave him a nod, and he nodded back.

They'd each taken a box of matches from the pantry trailer Chelsea had shown them, and as Jacob drew a match and knelt down to light the first grenade, he couldn't help but think of Sheriff Taylor. A flood of emotion came over him. Here, reduced to a simple stick of wood, was his George Washington, his Sam Houston. Everything he knew and valued and thought worthy of praise, could be summed up in this simple matchstick. Somehow it seemed overly simple and obscene to reduce such a great man to something so banal, and yet at the same time it seemed elegantly appropriate. Sheriff Taylor had literally meant the world to him, and now he was fit for burning.

For the first time since watching Sheriff Taylor die, Jacob felt like he was doing exactly what the grand old man would have done. There was a sharp scratch, and the blue spurt of the match catching, and he touched the flame to the grenade.

It began to hiss right away, and the flame caught a moment later.

Within seconds, a thick, gray, sulfurous-smelling smoke rose from the grenade, and as the flame spread, so did the smoke. Jacob ran to ignite the others, and within minutes, they had a full cloud of smoke rising from under the line of vehicles.

The quiet caravan turned into chaos. Slaves ran in every direction, most of them screaming, "Fire, fire, fire!" The few free men and women left in the encampment were no less frantic. They clearly had no plan for dealing with a fire, and after a confused few seconds falling all over each other, most ran to the open fields outside the caravan and turned to watch the thing burn.

Meanwhile Kelly came up with the horses. She stopped in front of them and handed off the reins.

"I found two rifles," she said.

"Outstanding," Jacob said, as he and Nick climbed onto their horses.

Only Chelsea was still on the ground.

"What's wrong?" Nick asked.

She looked uncertainly at the huge animal standing by her side. It was already jittery from the foul-smelling smoke drifting across the field, and it was picking up Chelsea's obvious fear. It beat at the ground with its front hooves and Chelsea let go of the reins and backed hurriedly away.

Kelly rode up beside the animal, grabbed the reins, and calmed it.

"Come on," she said. "You have to get up."

Nick jumped down from his horse and helped her up. "Just hang on," he said. "Keep your knees tight against his sides. We'll help you."

As he was about to get back on his own horse, one of the slaves ran out from between two vehicles and tackled him. The man immediately started yelling for help, just as Chris Walker had done when he tackled Eli.

"Get off me!" Nick said.

"Fuck no!" the slave yelled. "Help! Help! They're trying to escape!"

Nick twisted away from the man and jumped to his feet, but the slave wouldn't give up. He charged Nick with his arms spread wide for another tackle. Nick stepped into the man's charge and slammed his elbow down on the man's face, shattering his nose.

The slave gave out and sank to the ground. But even with his face a bloody mess he refused to let go. He threw his arms around Nick's knees and squeezed. Nick punched at the man. He drove his knees into the man's face, but still the slave held on, like a drowning man clinging to a pier. Finally, Jacob dropped from his horse, slid one of the rifles Kelly had been able to steal from the saddlebags, and brought it down on the back of the slave's head with a sharp crack.

The man collapsed, groaning, but still wouldn't stop. He rose drunkenly to his feet and lunged for Nick, but Nick sidestepped the charge and the man tumbled into the front legs of Chelsea's horse. The animal was still skittish from the smoke and immediately began stamping and punching at the man with his front hooves, catching the slave in the jaw with one of the strikes and snapping his neck like a twig. The man went down hard, arms and legs bent every which way and his head wedged over against the top of his shoulder. Blood ran from his mouth and nose, pooling in the grass beneath him.

Jacob and Nick both jumped onto their horses.

"You should have just shot the son of a bitch," Nick said.

Before Jacob could respond, they saw more slaves gathering around them. "Oh, crap," he said. Jacob turned his horse toward the head of the caravan and through gaps in the smoke saw free men with rifles running toward them, ducking behind cover every few yards as they came on. "They're behind us, too."

"Jacob, got a plan?" Nick asked.

"Not really."

Smoke drifted into Jacob's eyes and he turned his face away, squeezing his eyes shut. When he opened them, the slave with the broken neck was climbing to his feet, his head still tilted over at a painful looking angle.

"Oh, crap, we got problems," Jacob said.

Nick looked back at Kelly. "You got her?"

Kelly had Chelsea's horse by the reins. "I got her. You guys just find us a way out of here."

"Let's go this way," Jacob said, directing them back through the maze of vehicles.

The smoke was thick. They kept bumping into things, and the horses were difficult to control. Waiting for them on the other side were two male slaves, both of them with big sections of metal pipe in their hands.

Jacob leveled his rifle, aiming for the head, and instead shot the first man in the neck, the other in the chest.

"Are we shooting now?" Nick asked.

"Might as well," Jacob answered. "Not like we're gonna give away our position."

But then a gust of wind cleared away the smoke for an instant, and they saw the Family running toward the caravan from the road.

And Casey was leading the charge.

Jacob heard several shots and turned toward the head of the caravan. Free men with pistols and rifles were trying to get a bead on them through the smoke. On horseback, they made a target big enough for even an untrained shooter to hit.

"Come on, this way," Jacob said, and turned them back toward the slave encampment.

Jacob took the lead. They charged into the slave encampment, blind in the clouds of smoke, only to find themselves crushing headlong into a mass of slaves. Snarling faces, twisted with rage and desperation, swarmed all around him. Hands clutched at him, pulling at his clothes. Jacob twisted and kicked and punched with the rifle, but there were too many of them. They finally managed to pull him from the horse and he fell into a wail of kicks and punches.

As he went down, he saw Nick and Chelsea pulled down as well, but once he hit the ground he threw his arms over his head and pulled his knees in tight to protect himself from the kicking.

And then the kicking stopped and Nick was pulling him to his feet.

"Come on, we gotta go."

Bleeding and bruised all over, Jacob tried to make sense of what Nick was saying. His vision was a blur, but he saw Nick pointing to the west. Through a hazy screen of dissipating smoke Jacob had a view of a large group of zombies advancing through the tall grass, their feeding moans so loud they could be heard even over the gunfire the free men were directing toward them.

Jacob looked around for Kelly, but couldn't see her. All he could see were zombies closing in, pulling slave and free man alike to the ground wherever they found them.

Through the drifting screens of smoke Jacob saw Casey climb to the top of an RV and pull Mother Jane up behind him.

"Nick!" he yelled. "We need to go up!"

There was another RV nearby and Jacob covered them with the rifle as Nick pushed Chelsea up to the roof. A zombie staggered toward him, smoke curling off its back. Behind it were three more, coming up fast.

"Nick, hurry!"

"I'm going, I'm going."

Jacob raised his rifle and fired into the advancing zombies. He dropped two, but only winged a third. It spun halfway around and stopped walking, but then turned his direction, straightened, and stumbled forward again, its left arm hanging limp as a flag from a nasty shoulder wound.

"Jacob, get up here!"

He glanced to the roof of the RV and saw Nick with his hand stretched down to him. Jacob slung the rifle over his shoulder and caught Nick's hand.

Nick pulled him up to the roof just as a crowd of the undead clutched at his feet. Jacob kicked their hands away, gave it one last push, and landed hard on the RV's metal roof.

He rolled over onto his back and caught his breath. "Damn, that was close," he said.

Nick laughed. "You ain't kidding, brother."

Jacob got to his feet. The smoke grenades were starting to burn out, and big gaps in the smoke clouds started to appear. The crowd of zombies surrounding their RV was large, but there were many gaps in their number. They seemed to have gathered around a number of trailers and RVs, wherever the living had taken to the roof for shelter. Looking across the line of vehicles, he caught another glimpse of Casey and Mother Jane. They were both busy pulling members of the Family onto the roof of their RV, which was filling with people. Looking off to his left, toward town, he saw the main body of the herd coming down the highway. It was a black river of bodies that spread out to the horizon.

Moving through the zombies crowded around their RV Jacob saw several members of the Family. They were trying to find a way up, and a few were trying to get up on their RV, including Hank and a few free women he was trying to rescue.

"Help me!" Hank said, extending a hand up to Jacob. He was holding on to the sides of the trailer, already halfway up.

Jacob glanced at Nick, and an understanding passed between them.

He leaned over the side and met Hank's desperate gaze.

"Help me!"

Jacob kicked his hand, causing him to slide back to the ground with a scream of pain.

Zombies closed in on the noise, narrowing their circle around him.

"What are you doing?" Mother Jane screamed at them. "Help that man!"

Jacob made a point to meet her gaze, and then he kicked Hank in the face, knocking him flat on his back.

These zombies, the first of the herd to descend on their encampment, were the freshest and fastest of the bunch. When they attacked, they were vicious predators, snarling and tearing like dogs in a fight. They ripped into Hank with their teeth and fingernails, pulling him apart in seconds, his screams echoing over the roaring moans of the herd.

Other free men and women were trying to climb up as well. Nick and Jacob went around the edge of the RV, smashing with their rifles any free man or woman trying to gain the roof.

And then a smoke cloud dissipated and Kelly was there with the horses. She motioned for them to hurry.

There was still a gap in the herd, Jacob saw. They could make it.

"We have to go now," he said to Nick.

"How?" Nick said. "There's too many of them."

"It's now or never. Do it!"

Nick nodded. He waited for the zombies to fall on yet another member of the Family, and then slid down the side of the RV. He turned and motioned for Chelsea with an *I'll catch you* gesture.

When Chelsea was down in his arms, Jacob turned to see what was happening with Mother Jane and Casey. The two of them were staring daggers at him.

He gave them both a *Go fuck yourself* sign with his fingers and slid down the side of the RV. A zombie lashed out at him, but he managed to grab its arm, catch the back of the zombie's right foot with a sharp kick of his left leg, and sweep the dead man's feet out from under him.

The zombie landed flat on his back, but Jacob didn't stick around to continue the fight. He jumped to his feet and ran for the horses Kelly had managed to hold on to.

Once he was mounted, the group turned to the south and took off.

part four
THE WRECK

32

They rode hard for as long as Chelsea could handle it, which wasn't very far. Even with Kelly to help her, the poor girl could barely stay in the saddle. She was getting thrown all over the place and tiring fast, and to Jacob it looked like they were about to lose her. He came up alongside Kelly and gave her the sign to bring it to a stop. Kelly nodded, and as they slowed to a trot Chelsea slumped forward, her shoulders sagging. She looked beat to a pulp.

"We're out of sight now," Jacob said. "Let's stop here a second and figure out what we're doing."

Nick came up alongside Chelsea. "Hey, you okay?"

Chelsea tried to smile at him, but didn't quite manage it. She was out of breath and limp as a ragdoll.

"You did good," he said. "For someone who's never been on a horse before, you held on real good."

"You've never been on a horse before?" Kelly asked.

Chelsea shook her head.

Kelly traded a worried look at Jacob, and he knew exactly the thoughts playing out in her mind. Were they really about to take a hell-bent for leather ride through the wasteland with a little girl who had never even sat on a horse before? You've got to be kidding me.

He shared her concerns, but didn't let it show.

The horses had found a muddy rainwater stream running across what was left of the road and dipped their heads to drink, their sides still heaving from the hard run.

Nick said, "She'll do fine."

He pulled a canteen from the saddle, shook it, and heard liquid sloshing inside. He handed her the canteen and said, "Here, have a little water."

Chelsea took it, unscrewed the cap, and drank.

And promptly spit out. She coughed and spluttered and jutted the canteen back in his direction with a horrified and disgusted look on her face.

"What is it?" he said, taking the canteen.

"Ugh. That's whisky."

Nick frowned at the canteen. He took it, smelled it, and flinched away from it. "Whew!" he said. "That's some good lighter fluid."

He took a sip and shook his head. "Yep," he said, wincing, his voice suddenly strained. "The good stuff."

"Give me that," Kelly said. She took the canteen, sniffed at it, and drank anyway. Coughing, she replaced the cap and gave it back to Nick.

"That good, huh?"

Still coughing, she started to laugh. "That's absolutely awful. That's not bathtub whisky. Somebody made that in a toilet."

With a chuckle, Nick poured it out and looked down at the stream from which the horses were drinking. "What do you think?" he asked, rattling the canteen.

Kelly looked at the muddy water and shook her head.

"Yeah, I didn't think so either."

Chelsea's horse had drifted away from the stream and caught a whiff of the swill Nick had just poured out. The

mare shook her head and whinnied. Unable to control the
animal, Chelsea got scared again.

Kelly came up next to her, grabbed the reins, and settled
the horse.

"It's okay," she said to the young girl. "Here, lead him
like this. No, no, use your legs. Squeeze, like this."

With help, Chelsea got her horse turned around and they
headed back to the stream.

"That's good," Kelly said. "Yeah, like that. You got it."

Chelsea's horse calmed and fell in line with the others.

Kelly released the reins so Chelsea could take them up.
"How is it possible that you never learned to ride a horse?
Back where we're from, kids are taught to ride as early as
five. And it's part of school from day one. You got this fantastic education, but no horseback riding lessons?"

"It never came up," Chelsea said. "I mean, we've got
horses in Temple. I remember watching them run along the
beach. But I never had any real need to learn. Temple isn't
that big. You can either walk or ride a bike wherever you go."

"What about when you need to carry things?" Kelly
asked. "You know, like a bunch of stuff. What do you do
then?"

"Well, we have electric cars, so . . . you know." Chelsea
shrugged.

"Electric . . ." Kelly's mouth fell open in shock.

She seemed to have no idea what to say, which, in Jacob's
experience was definitely a first. He chuckled quietly. Kelly
glared at him, and rather than try to respond and make a fool
of herself, she turned her horse to the north and studied the
horizon for signs of pursuit.

"Can we stop here?" Chelsea said. "Just for a little while.
We must have ridden like ten miles."

"Not half that far," Nick said. "I'd like to put about twenty-
five miles between us and that herd before I'd feel good about
stopping. What do you think, Jacob?"

The countryside around them was flat and green, broken frequently by stands of trees and ponds and little rainy weather creeks like the one they were currently using to water the horses. There had been a state highway here at one point, but the years and the vegetation had long since reclaimed it. Now, only rusting and leaning metal mile marker poles remained to show where the road had once been.

Jacob panned slowly around, taking it all in. In their short but hard ride they'd seen more deer and birds and wild hogs than he'd seen during his entire time in the wasteland. And far off to the east, lost in the shadows of the trees, he saw a line of large, bulky animals that he couldn't make out because they were too far away. He thought of the elephants they'd seen on their trek up Highway 55, and what Owen Webb had said about all the zookeepers during the First Days who had released the animals under their care to roam the countryside, and he could only stare in amazement. It was such a strange world they'd stepped into, beautiful and terrifying all at once.

"We can't stop," he said. "Not yet."

"But I'm exhausted," Chelsea said.

"I know," Jacob said. "But it's not safe." He turned to Nick. "All the animals we've seen, they've all been going south."

"To keep ahead of the herd, is my guess," said Kelly.

"Mine, too. Nick, what are we gonna find if we keep heading south?"

Nick thought for a second, recreating his maps from memory. "Well, let's see, assuming we've gone about five miles, we probably have another five to go before we reach Bernie. About fifteen miles after that, if we keep going south, we'll come up on Malden. Malden might be a good place to head, actually. Highway 62 runs through there, and that would give us more or less a straight shot back to Arbella."

"How far?"

"Three days maybe, if we push it."

Jacob looked back to the north. The smoke was gone from the sky, but he knew they weren't very far from the herd. Their only hope was to put as much distance on the herd this first day as they could. Jacob and the others were limited on how far they could travel by horseback. Kelly had picked some strong animals, but even the hardiest of horses had limits. Twenty-five or thirty miles a day, especially over the rough and overgrown country they were traveling, was about the extent of what they could reasonably expect. But the zombies, moving on foot, would travel much slower. The fastest of them could do maybe three miles in an hour, and probably closer to two, but they never stopped walking. They never tired, never slept, never stopped, just kept on walking one step in front of the other, slowly, but inexorably making their way to their next meal. Any distance they put on the herd would be swallowed up during the night, while Jacob and the others were forced to rest. It was going to be close.

"Chelsea," Jacob said, "I'm sorry, but we don't have a whole lot of options. Stopping here, now, will get us killed."

She nodded.

Jacob nodded to Kelly. "What do you think, can we make Malden by nightfall?"

"You said it was, what, about twenty miles?" she asked Nick.

"About that."

"I think we can make that," she said. "The land is pretty flat, and I bet at least some of the road will still be usable."

"Okay then," Jacob said. "Let's head home."

33

Kelly was right about the road.

Another mile went by and they began to see bare spots in the high grass, and soon the grass gave way almost entirely, leaving only sand and patchy clumps of weeds here and there. In some places, they could even see asphalt.

They made Malden two hours before sunset. They were so far ahead of schedule that they even debated using the extra time to push east along Highway 62. But Kelly said the horses needed resting. They'd worked them hard, and they were going to work them hard again in the morning. Best to let them rest.

And so they rode out on Highway 62 just east of town, and stopped at a deserted farmhouse. During his salvage team days, Jacob had learned that commercial buildings, like gas stations and truck stops, tended to make the best choices for temporary shelter. Because of their industrial construction, they tended to hold up better to the ravages of time and weather than residential homes, which were more often than not made with wood frames and therefore subject to termite infestations and wholesale rot. And, because the architecture of commercial buildings was defined by their customer access function, they tended to have points of entry on only one side of the building, making them easier to defend against an undead attack, should that ever become an issue. But the farmhouse they found just outside of Malden was remarkably well preserved. It stood atop a slight rise, commanding quite a good view of the surrounding country-side, and its animal enclosures were hidden from the main road and still in pretty good shape.

And, best of all, there was a huge flock of feral chickens foraging in the yard. Seventy or eighty birds at least.

"Oh, God," Nick said. "I am so hungry."

"Me, too," Jacob said, watching the flock peck at bugs around the yard. He remembered nights of chickens and quail roasting in bacon fat on a cast-iron skillet and his mouth instantly started to water.

Kelly laughed. "You're going to try and catch a bunch of wild chickens? This I got to see."

"It's no problem," Jacob said.

"Oh, I'm sure it isn't. Not for a couple of tough guys like you. What's a couple of chickens up against you two?"

"Is that sarcasm?"

"Oh, never," Kelly said. She cast a mischievous smile his way. For a moment, in the low light of dusk, it made her look seventeen again. "I'd never dream of doubting you, Jacob."

Jacob rolled his eyes at her, and then he and Nick went after the chickens. They charged into the yard, thinking the feral variety couldn't be that much different from the domes-ticated birds they'd learn to catch, pluck, and field dress in their animal husbandry class back at school. But after the dominate cock spurred Nick, putting a nasty gash in his right arm and almost lopping off his left ear, and Jacob lost the hens when they took to the top branches of an ash tree, they realized they needed a better plan.

"We ought to just shoot them," Kelly said. She looked up

at the tree where about fifty of the birds had taken shelter. "That's only about twenty-five or thirty feet."

"It's an easy shot," Jacob agreed. "It's the noise that worries me."

"We haven't seen any signs of zombie activity all day. And the noise wouldn't carry that far, would it?"

"A few miles," Jacob said.

"At least that," said Nick.

"Well, do either of you have a better idea? We're all really hungry."

That much Jacob couldn't argue with. He stepped back from the tree, raised his rifle, and fired six times before the birds took to the air and flew to a nearby tree. They didn't stay there, though. They took to the wing almost immediately, and when they reached the next tree, repeated the process. In a matter of minutes, they were out of sight.

"I had no idea chickens could fly like that," Nick said.

"Me either," Jacob said. He motioned toward the fallen birds. "Come on, help me with this. I'm hungry, too."

Kelly found a package of sea salt in the kitchen and brought it out. "I didn't trust any of the other spices," she said. "But salt is a rock, so . . ."

"Sounds good to me," Jacob said.

They made a small fire and salted up the five birds Jacob had managed to hit and cooked them on a spit roast.

Jacob knew they were taking a chance with the smoke, but there was no arguing with their hunger, and the smell of the roasting meat was enough to forgive the bad tactics.

Forgive, but not ignore.

As soon as the birds were ready, Jacob got a bucket from the barn and filled it with water and threw it on the pit. Once the fire was out and the coals soaked to stop them from smoking, they went inside and tore into the birds, the four of them eating from plates Kelly found in the kitchen.

For Jacob, it was one of the best meals he'd ever had. He

sat back in his chair, and a plate full of bones stripped bare, and stifled a burp. "Oh, man, that was good."

Kelly laughed. She was seated on Jacob's left, Chelsea right across the table from her. Jacob, who knew Kelly pretty well, and who could tell Chelsea's comment about the electric cars had been bothering her all day, couldn't help but laugh when she finally brought it up.

"How is that even possible? In Arbella we had, what, like three gas-powered trucks that we could use for big projects, but usually only one was working at a time, and that because we had to cannibalize parts from the other two. I mean, the scale of production alone is just astronomical. Galveston Island isn't that big, at least from what I remember on the maps. There are a limited number of people who could live there, right? Just like in Arbella. How could your people create the industry necessary to build electric cars? And the aerofluyts we saw? And the clipper ships you described? How is that possible?"

"I don't know," Chelsea said. "I was ten when we left. But I know that my parents had one, and most of the families I knew growing up had one."

"Incredible," Kelly said. "It's just so hard to imagine."

Jacob couldn't help but smile. Poor Kelly, she was beside herself with a mix of wonder and jealousy.

"It's no more difficult to imagine than those huge airships we saw," Nick said.

"Aerofluyts," Chelsea corrected him.

"Aerofluyts," Nick said. "Sorry."

"You said your people renamed Galveston Island The Temple," Kelly said. "Is that like a religious thing? Are you Mormons, or Jewish, or something?"

Chelsea shook her head. "There's no religion in Temple. And it's just Temple, not *The* Temple. The founder of our community was a man named Dr. David Knopf." She looked at the others for some sign of recognition, but when it didn't come she said: "After the Provisional Government fell and it looked like the War was a total loss, Dr. Knopf led the surviving research teams and their families from Ohio to Galveston. Really, he was our town founder. There's a statue of him in front of our public administration office."

"Why Galveston?" Nick asked.

"Because it's an island," Kelly said. "They thought it'd be the safest spot to build a new community."

"Makes sense."

"And the Texas A&M maritime research campus was there," Chelsea said. "When Dr. Knopf and his teams moved in to the campus they started calling it Temple. I don't really remember why, but that's what they called it, and eventually the name just stuck for the whole island."

"What about the aerofluyts?" Kelly asked. "Why are they so big?"

"Well, they need to be to run the morphic field generator. That thing is huge. And plus there's a whole community living inside. All the scientists and their families. That's where I went to school, where we grew our food, where we went to the movies. You know. Lived life."

Jacob and the others traded a glance.

"What?" Chelsea said. "Did I say something wrong?"

"No," said Nick. "All of us have heard our parents talk about the movies, but none of us have ever seen one. Not one that we can remember anyway."

"Oh," Chelsea said. "Sorry."

Kelly, not wanting to lose the momentum of Chelsea's account, plowed on. "Tell us more about the aerofluyts," she asked. "Those huge wings are solar sails, aren't they?"

"Oh, yes," Chelsea said. "They provide nearly all the power the ship uses."

"Amazing," Kelly said. She looked pleasantly lost, like one caught up in a daydream.

Jacob said, "What do their engines run on? Are they powered by the solar sails, too?"

"I don't know," Chelsea said. "Partly, I think. Chris would know more than I do. But I do know they can stay in the air for months at a time, and they travel all over the Americas, monitoring the great herds, testing the land and the zombies they capture for signs that CDHL levels are going down."

"You know about CDHLs?" Kelly asked.

"Of course," Chelsea said. "They taught us about them in school. Plus, my dad was supposed to be a big deal in researching them. I remember him and my mom talking about them all the time, so I got it twice as much as the other kids."

But it wasn't CDHLs that had Jacob fascinated. It was something else she'd said.

"Chelsea, you mentioned the great herds. What can you tell us about them?"

"Not much, really," she said. "We didn't get a whole lot of that in school. But I do know from listening to my parents that there's the Plains Herd, which is the herd we just got away from, and the smaller herds up along the East Coast. Those are smaller because of all the barriers put up during the War. They've got all sorts of names, but I've forgotten most of those. And, let's see, there's the Desert Herd on the other side of the Rocky Mountains, and a few more in Mexico and Central America. But the really big one is the Great Texas Herd."

Jacob was almost afraid to ask, but his curiosity wouldn't let him avoid it. "How big is really big?"

Chelsea shrugged. "Nobody knows exactly. The numbers change pretty much all the time. Some zombies rot away. Others get lost and drift off. And all the while new zombies are made from the recently dead and find their way into the herd. Their numbers probably vary by several hundred or maybe even thousands from day to day. I do remember my dad saying once that he thought the Great Texas Herd might be fifty million, maybe more."

The full magnitude of her answer didn't seem to scare her at all, but it sent a chill down Jacob's spine.

"Your home sounds like such a wonderful place, Chelsea," Kelly said. "I'm still trying to wrap my head around it. An entire community built around scientific research."

Chelsea licked the last little bit of chicken grease from her fingers and nodded.

"Incredible," Kelly said, shaking her head.

To Jacob, it looked like someone had just sold her on a picture of paradise.

With the meal finished, they wandered off to find places to sleep. Jacob took the first watch. The house had several rooms, and he spent an hour walking the place, getting a feel for the layout. Kelly had found a spot in a small side bedroom and had managed to clear most of the dust and accumulated trash from one corner of the room. Nick had talked Chelsea into sleeping in his room. Several times Jacob passed the closed door to their room and heard the girl giggling, but when he heard the giggles change to moans of pleasure he couldn't take it anymore and went outside.

Three hours passed by as silently as the stars that wheeled overhead, and when his time was up he went back inside and woke Kelly.

"Your turn," he said.

She sat up without seeming groggy at all, like she hadn't even slept. "Are they finally done in there?" she asked, and nodded toward the bedroom Nick and Chelsea shared.

"I didn't hear anything when I came in," Jacob said.

Kelly frowned at the closed door. "That's not right," she said. "She's just a little girl."

"She's seventeen," Jacob said. "Girls younger than her get married in Arbella two or three times a year."

"She's not getting married," she said. "She's getting used

by a horny thirty-five-year-old man. It's not right. It's disgusting."

Jacob thought on that, and deep down he suspected that she was right. It felt like she was right. Still, that was Nick in there, his best friend, the man he trusted. "What do you want to do?" he finally asked her. It seemed like the easy way out, put it back on her, but he couldn't think of anything else to do.

"I don't know if there is anything we can do," she said after a long and thoughtful pause. "You can't tell a seventeen-year-old girl to stay away from a guy." Suddenly she was looking at him with a mix of anger and something akin to regret. It caught him by surprise. "I know that as well as any woman. Tell a girl that age that a guy is no good for her and she'll run to his side faster than a rumor in the night."

Jacob sat there in the dark, stunned and hurt. Was she talking about Nick and Chelsea, or about them? There had been a time, so many years ago now, but not so long ago that he couldn't remember every day of it, that they'd been Arbella's hottest couple. All the mysteries you could open up for the first time at seventeen, they'd opened up together. It had been a wonderful, magical, and ultimately heartbreaking summer.

Or so it was in his memory.

He'd always assumed it had been the same for her. But memory was a form of relativity, wasn't it? It depended upon one's point of view, both in time and space. The past, the present . . . hunger, desire, regret . . . they all played a part in building different vistas on the same battlefield that is teenage love. And what had seemed real, and powerful, and touched by an irresistible gravity to him—and, as he'd always envisioned it, for her as well—could be something else entirely from another's point of view.

The epiphany hit him like an earthquake.

It hurt.

It hurt badly enough for him to turn a shield toward her.

"Has he violated Arbella's Code?" he asked her.

Even in the weak silver starlight that leaked in through the open windows, he could see that the sudden hardness in his tone caught her off guard. She started to speak, but managed little more than a stammering and inarticulate mutter.

"Has he?" Jacob demanded, growing colder and sterner by the syllable. "Has he done anything against our laws?"

Kelly swallowed nervously. "No," she said at last.

"Then drop it," he said. "We're done talking, and it's your watch."

With that, he rose, turned, and left her.

He went off to his own little corner of the ruined farmhouse for a few hours of dream-haunted sleep.

34

"Jacob, wake up!"

Rough hands shook him from his sleep.

"Jacob, come on, buddy. We got problems."

Jacob scrambled to his feet. He'd been in deep sleep, but he was wide-awake in an instant. Nick had his rifle in his hand, clutching it by the breach. He had Jacob's in the other hand, waiting for him to take it.

"What's going on?"

"Zombies," he said. "I counted eight."

"The herd?" Jacob said. He couldn't believe they'd caught up with them already.

"I don't think so," Nick answered. "They were coming at us from due west, probably from the town. The ones I saw were looking pretty bad, like they were older."

Jacob nodded and took his rifle. He tried to move quietly, but the house was old and the floorboards creaked beneath his feet, even when he tried to put his feet down slowly and deliberately.

Where the hall connected to the living room he hesitated. It was still dark, an hour at least till sunup, and the house was steeped in darkness. But from somewhere ahead of him he could hear feet sliding on the wooden floor, and wood groaning beneath an unfamiliar weight.

Jacob craned his head around the corner. Halfway across the living room was a dead man, badly decomposed, his clothes rotted into his skin and his face little more than strips of dark flesh hanging from dull yellow bone. He was stumbling toward the hallway. Behind him, another dark form was climbing through the empty window.

Jacob turned to Nick and signed what he'd just seen. Then he swung his rifle around so that he could use it as a club, took a breath, and charged around the corner.

The first dead man was faster than he should have been. Decomposition as bad as his should have slowed the muscles considerably. No sooner had Jacob rounded the corner but the man was on him, hands up and clutching for him. Jacob reacted quickly though. He brought his rifle down on the man's face with enough force to snap the man's back, breaking the neck. The zombie stopped, head staring at the ceiling, but didn't fall. He just swayed there on his feet, unable to move.

Jacob swept the zombie's legs with a single kick, and when the thing lowered its arms, he drove the rifle down again three more times, crushing its skull. The second zombie had fallen heavily to the floor after coming through the window, and Jacob was able to smash his head to a pulp before he could regain his feet.

Looking through the window, Jacob could see three, no, four others coming up the slope of the lawn.

At the same time, hands slapped against the front door.

From somewhere in the back of the house, they heard a scream.

Both men went running. Chelsea was standing in the hall in bare feet, a blanket pulled over her shoulders.

Nick took hold of her as Jacob kicked in the door to

Kelly's room. Kelly was on her back on the far side of the room, using an upturned wooden chair to hold a zombie at bay. Three more were pushing their way inside the window directly opposite Jacob.

"Help me!" Kelly yelled.

There was no time for clubbing the zombies. Jacob saw that in an instant. He flipped the rifle around and leveled it at the head of the zombie trying to get at Kelly. He fired once, sending the thing sprawling into the corner. Then he turned his weapon on the zombies coming through the window and fired until each went down. He rushed forward, grabbed one of the moldering zombies by the remnants of the coat left on its back, and pulled it through the window to the floor. He leaned out the window and saw more zombies coming up from the road.

Kelly was still on her back. Jacob went to her. "Are you okay? They get you anywhere?"

"No, I'm okay."

He helped her to her feet, and then turned on Nick. "I thought you said there were eight of them out there."

"I saw eight."

"Yeah, well, there's a shitload of them out there now. We got to get to the horses and get out of here."

He went to the bedroom door, pushing his way past Nick and Chelsea. But no sooner had he entered the hall than the front door gave way with a crash.

Jacob stopped short.

"Okay," he said. "Not that way. Everybody out the windows. We'll head around back."

They scrambled through the windows and ran around the side of the house. Three zombies had gotten into the corral and were trying to force their way into the stables. Jacob ran ahead, jumped the fence into the corral, and swung his rifle at the first zombie to turn his way. The zombie fell back against the doors to the stable but didn't go down.

Jacob grabbed the rifle with both hands and smashed it down again on the zombie's face.

That did the trick and the zombie collapsed.

But not before the other two put their hands on him. Jacob teetered over backwards and went down hard. The zombies fell on top of him and the stench of their rotten bodies made him gag.

Nick was there the next instant, pulling one of the zombies off him.

Jacob had his rifle up in a port arms position, jammed up under the second zombie's chin to keep his rotted mouth away. With the other zombie off him, Jacob was able to push with his left hand and pull with his right, while at the same time twisting to his right. The zombie rolled off of him and landed on its back in the dirt. Jacob put his knees on the thing's chest and smashed the rifle down on its nose three times before it stopped moving. He stood up then, chest heaving, to see Nick rising from a kill of his own.

"Get the horses ready to ride," he said to Kelly and Nick. "I'll hold these off."

They nodded at him and ran for the stable doors.

"Wait," Jacob said, grabbing Nick by the arm. "Give me your rifle. I'm empty."

Nick handed it to him without hesitation and Jacob ran for the center of the corral. From where he stood he could see the yard filling with zombies. They came around both sides of the house like a river flowing around a rock. More were coming out the house's windows.

Jacob ejected the magazine from Nick's rifle and checked it. Eight rounds in the magazine, one in the chamber.

"You guys need to hurry in there!" he said.

He looked across the yard at the zombies closing in around him. The yard between the corral and the house was flat, but overgrown, coming up to the hips of the approaching zombies. Beyond the house he could see the skeletal remnants of a barn, starlight shining through its Swiss cheese roof. In between the buildings were large clusters of elms and ash trees that broke up his view of the field.

He'd have to make do.

Off to his left a zombie was climbing over the top rail of the wooden fence that enclosed the corral. The top rail gave way under the zombie's weight and the thing collapsed onto the next rail, bent over at the waist. The breaking wood made Jacob jump, and he fired off a bad shot that hit the zombie in its lower back. The thing fell face-first into the corral, rolled over, and stood up, completely unperturbed by the shot.

"Steady," Jacob told himself. "Easy."

He took a deep breath, steadied his front sights on the zombie's nose, and squeezed the trigger.

The thing's head snapped back and it fell to the ground.

He turned around, keeping his head on a swivel to cover every angle, and saw two dead women climbing the fence. A third zombie was a few feet to the left of them, but it was too badly decomposed for Jacob to tell what gender it was. It took two shots to put the first of the two women down, but he found his mark cleanly on the other one and dropped her with a single shot. The third zombie was having trouble climbing the fence, so Jacob turned his back on that one and focused on the others already on their way over.

"How's it coming in there?" Jacob yelled.

"Two more to go," Kelly answered.

"It's getting deep out here. Make it fast!"

Jacob fired two more shots, both direct hits. Had he fired six or seven shots? He wasn't sure; he'd lost count. Either way, he was running out of options. Four more zombies were climbing the fence, and dozens more were behind them.

"Come on, guys, hurry it up!"

"Almost there."

"Crap."

Jacob put down two of the zombies, but wasted his last

two rounds on reckless, over-the-shoulder running shots. He missed both completely and was forced to turn the rifle around and use it like a club.

He swung at one of the zombies and succeeded in knocking it down, but failed to crush its skull. It got up, half its head caved in, just as more dropped into the corral. He was surrounded now and they were closing in on him. One of them groped at his face with fingers that were nearly fleshless. Jacob grabbed the dead man's arm and felt it break in several places as he wrestled the zombie around in a circle. The thing was frail, but wouldn't go down, no matter how he tried to throw it off balance.

Realizing he couldn't make it fall, he twisted the thing's arm until he was behind it. He moved the zombie around the corral, using it as a shield as he ran it into other zombies, knocking them down or at least out of the way.

He was about to holler out again when the doors suddenly burst open and Kelly and the others came charging out. Nick was in front, a white metal bar in his hand. Behind him, Kelly held the reins to three horses, hers and Chelsea's in one hand and Jacob's horse in the other. Jacob ran for the empty horse while Nick swung his metal bar like a battle-axe, cutting his way through the crowd.

He reached the gate to the corral and kicked it open.

"Come on," he yelled.

Kelly and Nick spurred their horses as they crashed through the zombies, bounding for the gate. Zombies grabbed at their legs and hips, but they were already moving fast, and the dead fingers did little more than clutch at empty air.

Seconds later, they were through the crowd and galloping hard toward the road. The sun was coming up, and to the east the blacktop remnants of the highway were brushed with molten copper. Arbella was that way, Jacob thought, and for a moment, let himself dream.

Just fifty miles. So close.

But it might as well have been halfway round the planet. For coming up the road, and spreading out to form a line in the fields on either side of the road, were riders.

Riders they knew.

And Mother Jane and Casey were right out front.

35

They caught sight of each other at almost exactly the same instant, and for a moment, neither man moved. Jacob stared at Casey and Casey back at him, over a distance of perhaps a hundred yards.

And then Casey let out an earsplitting rebel yell and charged.

"Ah, Jacob," Nick said.

"Ride!" Jacob said, and they wheeled their horses as one and charged toward the dead town of Malden.

In the early morning light, shadows still pooled between the trees and the low one-story buildings. Jacob could see forms moving toward the road, but they were too far away for him to tell whether they were zombies or animals or more of the Family closing the net around them.

He chanced a look behind him and saw Casey closing fast. They were out of options. In another minute he'd be on them, and he'd be the only one with a loaded weapon.

"That way!" Jacob said, motioning to Kelly toward a low line of houses off to the right.

"Where?" she asked.

"Find us a hole," he said. "Anywhere."

With Chelsea's horse by the reins, she turned sharply to the right and went between the ruined shells of two homes. The vegetation was thick and it sliced into them as they charged into it. Jacob felt it pulling at his clothes, at his arms, at his face, but he urged them forward. It was their only chance to evade the riders on their tails.

"Hold on," Kelly said.

Jacob glanced forward just as Kelly and Chelsea jumped a leaning metal fence. Chelsea screamed and nearly flew out of her saddle, but Kelly was there to catch her. It was a bad landing, but Kelly got them under control and pointed the horses to the left, through a gap in the underbrush.

Jacob and Nick followed close on their heels.

They emerged onto the next street and found it just as overgrown as the last. Behind them they could hear Casey yelling for the other riders to close in, but they were having a hard time of it because of the underbrush. Kelly had done well threading a course through it. Now she was pointing down the lane, which was little more than a shallow area between two walls of encroaching trees, and motioning for Jacob to look. Six zombies, so badly decomposed they could barely walk, were staggering out of a house halfway down the block.

Can't go that way, she signed to him.

No, wait, he signed back. He motioned toward a gap in the vegetation that led over to the next street.

She rode up close to him, still holding Chelsea's mare by the reins. The young girl looked scared, but alert, and Jacob saw she was squeezing her knees to the horse's sides. She was learning.

"What is it?" Kelly whispered.

"Through there," he said.

She shook her head. "Too obvious."

"I know. That's what I'm counting on." He glanced over

his shoulder. Casey and the other riders had split up into small groups, perhaps realizing that their prey had used up all their ammunition, and were closing in on their position. "We need a distraction. Let's go."

She frowned, but he knew she trusted him enough not to ask questions.

She turned her horse and Chelsea's toward the gap and Jacob and Nick followed. When they emerged on the other side, Jacob asked Nick for the metal pipe he carried in his saddlebags.

"For what?" Nick said. "You already took my gun. What am I supposed to use?"

"Really? Come on, give me the pipe." He gestured toward a thick growth of trees to the west. "You guys go over there. Wait for me. Stay out of sight."

Reluctantly, Nick handed over the last weapon he had. He, Kelly, and Chelsea rode over to the place Jacob had pointed out and were instantly lost in shadow.

Good, Jacob thought. *At least they'll be out of sight.*

He guided his horse into a well in the vegetation and waited. Casey was a hard driver. There was no other way he and the other survivors from the Family could have gotten away from the herd and still managed to drive this far south unless they rode long and hard. And he clearly had some strategic sense, or at least some intuition, for he'd read Jacob and the others right in their intent to use Malden as their turning east point. But despite all that, he was brash. He believed absolutely in his own superiority, and he certainly thought he had Jacob on the run, unarmed and easy pickings. It was why he'd allowed his riders to split up into one- and two-man groups.

He dismounted from his horse and lashed the reins around a stout, low-hanging branch.

The saddlebags he'd inherited along with the horse had a set of wire cutters and some duct tape in them. He slid those into his back pocket, shifted the metal pipe to his right hand, and crept into position right at the opening to the gap. He heard twigs snapping in the underbrush and he clutched the pipe tighter, praying that he'd read Casey and the other riders correctly.

Thomas, one of Casey's brothers Jacob had seen around the caravan, emerged a moment later, ducking his head down next to his horse's neck to avoid the brush.

When he straightened up again, Jacob darted out of hiding and swung the pipe, meaning to catch the rider under the chin but instead only managing a glancing blow off his shoulder.

Thomas grunted and twisted in the saddle, but didn't fall.

Before he had a chance to recover, Jacob spun back around the other way and swung for Thomas's ribs. He connected with a solid blow that caused the rider to sag to one side.

The horse tried to bolt, but Jacob caught its reins and steadied it.

Thomas was trying to right himself in the saddle. Jacob didn't give him the chance. Before the rider could sit up straight, Jacob swung again for his chin, and that time connected with the solid crack of metal on bone.

Thomas twisted off the saddle, landing heavily in the grass. The horse ran into the middle of what had once been the street, leaving Jacob face to face with Casey's brother. He advanced on the man and quickly stripped the rider's revolver from his holster. Jacob jammed it into the waistband at the small of his back, pulled the wire cutters from his back pocket, and flipped Thomas over onto his stomach.

The rider muttered something—a threat, a plea, Jacob didn't know and didn't care at this point—and tried to pull away, but Jacob held him firm. Jacob grabbed the man's right wrist and pulled it up. Then he grabbed one of Thomas's fingers, pried it apart from the others, and lopped it off with the wire cutters.

Thomas began to scream. The noise was horrible, such pain, such terrible, terrible pain.

Jacob backed away, horrified at what he'd just done. Thomas was rolling around in the grass, holding his bleeding hand, wailing uncontrollably in pain. At first the noise scared Jacob. A lifetime of conditioning had taught him that noise equaled death, especially out here in the wasteland, but as he looked around and saw moldering corpses lumbering out of one hiding spot after another, he realized he'd gotten exactly what he wanted.

He ran to Thomas's horse, removed the saddlebags and the rifle he found there, and then mounted his own horse and took off at a gallop.

He met up with Kelly and the others a few blocks away.

"What the hell is going on?" she asked.

Jacob looked back. He could see a few of Casey's riders in complete disarray, men shouting and twisting their horses around as more and more zombies flooded into the area. There'd been more riders than he suspected.

More zombies, too.

"Jacob," Kelly said. "What the hell is going on?"

"A distraction," he said. He nodded to the west. "Let's get out of here."

36

They rode hard across open fields and more slowly through densely wooded countryside until they reached a wide, slow-moving river.

The trip took them most of the day, and for Jacob it had been an exhausting ride. The others had moved out in front to survey the river and started discussing something, but Jacob couldn't hear them. He felt cold, even though he was wet with sweat. It was hard to focus. His head was a soupy mess. He tried to focus on what the others were doing, but found it hard even to stay upright in the saddle.

The world started to swirl around him and he blacked out.

The next thing he knew Kelly was next to him, her hand on his shoulder. "Hey," she said. "How you doing?"

"Huh?"

"Jacob, it's those dog bites on your arms. I don't think you're doing so good."

He looked down and saw the bandages on his arms were red and hanging loose from his wrists. The cuts all over his forearms were red and black and oozing white pus in places. His arms had started to swell. The undergrowth they'd traveled through back in Malden, he thought. It had stripped the bandages from his arms, exposing wounds that smelled like decay. That and all the fighting back at the ranch house.

"You need some real medical attention, Jake," Nick said.

"What river is this?" he asked.

They said something, but he didn't catch it. He fought against it, but couldn't keep his eyes open.

He blacked out again.

37

When he woke next they were riding under a hot sun across an open field. He looked around and saw green trees crowding the horizon and an enormous flock of what looked like ducks flying off a nearby pond.

In his head, he meant to say: *Where are we?*

All that he could manage though was a feeble groan and a hoarse-sounding cough.

Somebody—Nick or Kelly he couldn't tell—put a hand on his arm and said something he didn't quite catch.

He looked down, and saw a yellow nylon rope looped around his waist. Tracing it, he saw it came up around his shoulders and back down to the saddle, holding him in place.

They tied me down, he thought, his head lolling on his shoulders. Sweet Christ, they had to tie me to the saddle.

38

He was in and out for a long time. At least two days, maybe longer. He would wake only long enough to see some strange highway sign or empty field or railroad bridge going by, and then he was out again.

But then at last he opened his eyes and he was staring right into a horse's ass.

He blinked and looked around. He was at the bottom of a short but steep hill with shaggy thorn bushes and short trees all around him. Kelly was at the top of the hill, framed by a window of vegetation, staring dumbfounded at something beyond Jacob's view. Nick and Chelsea were halfway up the hill. It was Nick's horse giving him the view.

"What's wrong?" Nick asked. "Why'd we stop?"

She was shaking her head. "You guys have got to see this."

"What is it?"

All she could do was shake her head.

Nick helped Chelsea to the top of the hill and together they stood abreast with Kelly, all of them in awe.

"What is it?" Jacob managed to say.

Kelly glanced back, then turned her horse and came down to meet him.

"Jacob," she said. "How are you?"

He shook his head. It was hard to focus. Nothing seemed to work quite right. He glanced down at his arms and tried to see what was going on with his wounds, but he couldn't even make those out.

"Come with me," she said. "You have to see this."

He started to protest, but she was already leading him up the hill. Jacob leaned forward to keep his balance in the saddle, and nearly blacked out from the pain.

"Look," Kelly said. "Look at that."

Jacob opened his eyes. It took a moment for the blur to recede to the edges of his vision, but once they did he understood the amazement that had come over the others. Even with his brain addled by fever, he understood. Below them, in the midst of a vast plain of what had once been farmland, was the wrecked remains of a gigantic aerofluyt, looking like a skyscraper fallen on its side. A huge gash had been torn in its roof, and there were holes in the sides where birds flew in lazy circles. A debris field a thousand feet in diameter surrounded it, and vines and shrubs had started to grow where the hull met the ground, but even in its wrecked form, Jacob could still see the majesty of it.

At least until he blacked out again.

39

When he woke next, he was in a bed with sparkling white sheets. He sat up blearily and looked around. Fresh bandages dressed his arms. He touched them. The wounds still hurt, but not as much. His skin was cool, too. The swelling seemed to have gone down quite a bit. And when the sheets fell away from his chest he realized his skin was clean and he was clad in a fresh pair of light blue boxer shorts.

"What the hell?" he said.

His head was clearer now. He could still feel a residual hangover from the fever, but at least he could think straight.

Or at least he thought he could.

He was in a small, but clean room, lined with book-shelves and a dresser and an open closet on the far wall. Next to him on the bedside table was a picture of a man and woman in strange clothes, and in front of them a young boy of perhaps six and a baby girl of perhaps a year.

He studied the picture a second, and then climbed out of bed.

"Hello?" he called.

Nick appeared in the doorway a moment later. "Hey, buddy, how you feeling?"

"Better. A lot better."

"Thank God. That's good to hear. Chelsea's showing Kelly around right now, but when she gets back . . . Man, Jake, we were so worried about you."

"How long have I been out?"

"About three days. I thought you'd be out a whole lot longer, but Kelly was able to patch you right up with the steroids and antibiotics they found in the sick bay. You look about a million times better than when we brought you inside."

Jacob nodded. "What is this place?"

"This is the aerofluyt," Nick answered. "Can you believe it? Four days ago we were still headed south along US 167 and we see this field of wild soybeans growing up around all these junked cars. Chelsea asks us to stop. She says she recognizes the area. We thought she meant from being carried around with the caravans, but it turns out she remembered it from when she and her older brother were wandering around after this thing crashed. It took a little bit, but she was able to lead us pretty much right to this place."

Jacob managed a nod. "Do they have any water around here?"

"Yeah," Nick said. "Believe it or not, almost everything still works. The water runs. It tastes great, by the way. The toilets flush." He waved a hand over a plate of black glass on the wall next to the door and the room filled with a soft white light. "Even the electric lights."

Jacob looked at the lights in amazement. The last time he'd seen anything like this, a room lit with electricity, he'd been three years old. He barely remembered it.

It was glorious.

"Jake, my man, we have to make contact with Chelsea's people. They are decades ahead of us technologically. As if, you know, we couldn't tell that already from seeing one of these things glide through the sky, but . . . you know the electric cars she told us about? She wasn't kidding. Hell, even the medicines they've got onboard justify making contact. You should have heard Kelly talking. She said even if Dr. Williams was treating you himself back at Arbella, you'd probably be dead. But there you are, three days later and you're up and walking. Jake, you see this, right? I mean, we've got to make contact. Think of the good we could do for Arbella."

Before Jake could answer, Kelly called to them from another room.

"In here," Nick answered. "He's awake!"

Kelly and Chelsea came running. They both looked amazing, like completely different people. Chelsea especially. There was actually an attractive young woman under all that accumulated grime and grit.

Only then did he realize he was standing in the middle of the room wearing nothing but his boxer shorts.

"Oh, crap," he said. He looked around for a blanket or a pair of pants or something, but saw nothing.

"Don't be such a prude," Kelly said. "Who do you think took those clothes off you in the first place?"

"Oh," he said. But it still didn't do anything for his embarrassment.

"This was my parents' room," Chelsea said. "Some of my dad's clothes are still in that closet over there. I bet they'd fit you."

"Yes, get dressed," Kelly said. "Jacob, I can't wait to show you this place. It's amazing."

"That's what I hear."

He found a pair of blue pants with an expandable waistband and a gray, V-neck shirt that had WALKER printed on the right breast. For shoes he found a pair of white slippers that looked as flimsy as paper, but offered a surprising amount of cushioning when he walked.

A few minutes later, he stepped into a simple living room dominated by a kitchenette, a small table mounded over with notebooks and science journals and a couch with a black glass mirror mounted into the wall in front of it.

He went over to the mirror, but couldn't really see a good reflection of himself.

"That's a video monitor," Chelsea said. "I checked, though. It doesn't work."

"But everything else onboard does," Kelly said excitedly. "Jacob, I can't believe it. The technology that these people have at their fingertips. It's . . . it's . . ." She broke off there, unable to get the words out.

"I know," Jacob said. "Nick told me. Thanks for patching me up."

"Yeah," Kelly said. "That was close. That alone is reason we have to make contact with these people. Jacob, please, let's not pass this chance by."

"Nick said that, too."

Kelly rushed across the room to the little kitchen table. She picked up one of the books she'd evidently been studying and stuck it in Jacob's hand. "Here, look at this. There's another reason. Do you see that?"

Jacob squinted at the page. What he saw written there was like his worst dream, chemistry formulas piled on top of math so strange it made his head spin.

He handed it back to her. "Please. I've still got a bit of a headache."

"Oh, God," she said, and set the book down. "If you'd actually bothered to stay awake during chemistry you might have the sense to realize you're standing in the presence of genius."

"Genius," he said. "Well, that explains why I have no idea what I'm looking at, doesn't it?"

She huffed at him, exasperated.

"It's the basis of morphic field theory," she said. "This is basically the bible for zombie behavior. It explains so much.

I know I scoffed at it before, but the proof is all there. It all makes sense. And there's so much more, too, it's . . . it's genius."

"My dad wrote that," Chelsea said.

"Your dad was a genius, Chelsea," Kelly said. "I wish I could have met him. I'm sorry he's gone."

Chelsea smiled wanly. "Thanks."

Kelly turned to Jacob. "Her parents, and most of the others, died on impact. This part of the ship, the top twenty levels or so, are relatively intact, as is the engine room, but a lot of the lower decks, which is apparently where most of the passenger quarters were, are all gone."

"Oh," Jacob said. Nobody spoke for a long moment. Then, finally, Jacob said what was on all their minds. "Chelsea, if you don't mind me asking. How did you survive, you and your brother both? What happened?"

"I don't know why we crashed," she said. "As to how we survived, I guess we were just lucky. We were in scuba diving class at the time."

"I'm sorry?" Jacob said.

"Scuba diving class," she repeated. "You know, the tank, the mask, a regulator?"

He shook his head and looked to Kelly for clarification, who only shrugged.

"Scuba diving?" Chelsea said. "Self-contained underwater breathing apparatus? It's a mechanical system that supplies air to divers underwater. It's not new. It was an old technology even before the War."

"I'm sorry," Kelly said. "I've never heard of it."

"Well, you always dive in pairs. Chris and I were sixty feet underwater when the crash happened. We got thrown all the way to the other side of the pool, but nothing much more than that. When we surfaced, we found the ship like this. And everybody dead. After that, we just wandered. Until, you know, the Farris Clan found us in that soybean field."

"Wow," Nick said. "You're lucky to be alive."

She shrugged. "I didn't think so. At least not until recently."

"What about those members of the crew who weren't down in the passenger area?" Jacob asked. "The ones up here working on the top levels. I mean, if you guys survived, others must have, too."

"No, I think they all died on impact."

"Yes, but what happened to them after?"

"They turned," she said.

"Yes," Jacob said, "but after . . . what happened?"

"Chris got me to the bridge. He'd been in an engineering class the year before and he kind of knew how to work things up there. He turned on the morphic field generator and that drew all the dead down to the lower levels. Once the sensors said we had them all, he simply closed off the hatches below a certain level and locked them out."

"Pretty impressive," Nick said. "Hard to believe he turned out to be such a dick."

Chelsea nodded.

"What about a rescue party?" Jacob asked. "Why didn't your people try to look for the downed aerofluyt?"

"Oh, they did," she said. "We were already outside the ship when that happened though. We saw them flying toward the wreck, but we couldn't get back to them."

"Why not?"

"Well, the place was crawling with zombies. We were on the run."

Nick shook his head. "You really are lucky to be alive. I wonder why they didn't try to salvage this ship, though. There's so much here worth saving."

"I guess they couldn't risk it."

"Why not?" Jacob asked.

"Well, because of the zombies."

"But they would have drifted away after a few days," Nick said.

"No, no, wait a minute," Jacob said, holding up a hand to stop Nick. He turned to Chelsea. "Are you telling me there are still zombies onboard this ship?"

"Yes," Chelsea said. "But they're trapped."

"How many?"

"I don't know. There were one thousand eight hundred and fifty-three people onboard this aerofluyt when it crashed, so I guess, if they're all still viable, about eighteen hundred."

"Oh, crap," Jacob said.

"Relax," Kelly said. "Jacob, I've been all over this vessel. I've explored nearly every part you can still get to. I haven't seen a single zombie."

"Yeah, but they're still here."

"Yes, but they're contained."

It was his turn to feel exasperated. He turned to Nick. "What about weapons? Did you find any?"

"Yeah," Nick said. "They've got a pretty well-stocked arsenal. I've got rifles set aside for each of us."

"Anything good?"

"Oh, yeah. Ruger 10/22 Tacticals. All of 'em in mint condition."

"Nice. Ammunition?"

"Sure, that, too. About four hundred rounds each. The good stuff, too. Twenty-two long range, subsonic."

"What did you do with the horses?"

"They're in the loading bay."

"The loading bay?" Jacob asked.

"Yeah," Kelly said. "That's how we got in. That part of the hull broke open during the crash. The hydroponics lab was pretty close to that and all the plants from there have grown into the loading bay. We figured that'd be the perfect place to keep the horses. They're out of sight and they've got enough food to get 'em good and fat. You should have seen them go after the strawberries."

"But the loading bay is open? We can get in and out real quick, if we need to?"

"Sure, I guess."

"All right. I need to see the bridge."

"Jacob, chill out. I told you, I've been all over this place. There are no zombies above the crash line. Plus, you still need to rest."

"I believe you," he said. "And I'll rest later. But that's not what's bothering me. If Chelsea recognized this place, don't you think her brother will, too? Who knows how much of a lead we have on Casey and the rest of them. But as soon as Walker picks up the trail, they're going to be headed this way."

He looked at them each in turn, and he realized that the thought had slipped by them all.

"Jacob," Nick said, "I don't think you need to worry. We stayed away from the roads and moved across open country for two days. They'd have no way of knowing where we went to."

"I don't believe that for a second," he said. "You heard what they said when they first took us prisoner. They started tracking us even before we entered Sikeston. We can't afford to think they've given up, because I guarantee you they haven't."

None of them had a response for that.

"Nick, go and get those weapons. Everybody needs to gear up for the road. I want to be out of here as fast as we can."

"But, Jacob," Kelly said. "This place, it's like a treasure trove. There's so much here, so much we can learn from."

"None of which will do us any good if we're dead," he said, and realized as soon as the words left his mouth that he'd been too harsh with her. "I'm sorry, Kelly. I didn't mean to snap at you. I get how important a find like this is. Believe me, I get it. But we can't stay here. Not right now. When we get back to Arbella, we can organize another expedition to come here and mine whatever we can from this place, but staying alive is priority one right now."

But something else was bothering her. She looked troubled. "So . . . we're going back to Arbella?" she asked.

The question surprised him. "Well, yeah."

"But what about making contact with Chelsea's people? The Templenauts."

"Kelly, I really think we need to head back home. We do that, and we can deal with Mother Jane and the Family. Once that's done, we can organize a proper expedition to go and make contact. It'll happen, I promise."

"Well, hold up a second," Nick said. "Jake, what she's saying actually makes sense to me. I mean, if Casey's as good at tracking us as you say, won't he be waiting for us to double back? You said yourself we'd have a hard time losing him. He's gonna expect us to try and go home. He'd never expect us to keep running to the coast."

"To the coast?" Jacob said. The thought of going that far, all the way across Arkansas, and then across Texas, it seemed impossible. "I don't know, you guys."

"Jacob, please," Kelly said. "Please say yes. We can change this world we live in. We can. I believe that. Please say you believe it, too."

Jacob looked at her, and for just a moment let himself see the seventeen-year-old girl she'd once been, the girl he had known and thought he'd spend the rest of his life with. It was crazy, what she was asking of him. But in the end he knew he could never tell her no, and finally, he nodded.

She leaned forward and kissed him. "Thank you, Jacob! Thank you so much."

He nodded again. "Just take me to the bridge first."

"All right," she said. "It's this way."

40

Most everything still worked, but the rest of the ship certainly hadn't faired very well. There was trash everywhere they stepped. Some of the debris Jacob could recognize, or at least guess its purpose, but some of it was so strange he had absolutely no clue as to what it was for. As he stepped over it, he found himself imagining what it must have been like during the impact. Everything that wasn't nailed down must have surged forward in a wave, crashing to the deck as metal groaned and snapped. It must have happened suddenly, too, for there were bodies trapped in some of the debris. None of them appeared to be moving, though, and he wondered if they'd been so badly crushed by the impact that they'd been unable to come back, or if perhaps they had come back, and since expired for lack of food. Hard to say, because they all looked badly decomposed. Some, in fact, were little more than skeletons, and he found himself wishing that it had been quick for them. The idea of dying like that, trapped under a flood of debris, over a period of days, was horrible.

He forced himself to focus instead on the ship's construction. The hallways were long and narrow, and their footsteps echoed into the depths. The walls were bare metal, painted an industrial white in most places, but peeling and rusting wherever water had managed to collect. The rust and the trash were the only signs of weakness, though. Everywhere he looked he saw indications of just how well the ship was made, even beneath the rubble. Everything looked designed for where it was. There'd been no cobbling together of odds and ends, no cannibalization that he could see. The level of advancement was simply awe-inspiring, like something from the world that had once been, only cleaner, and even more advanced.

They passed open areas and closed-off laboratories with long names, most of which Jacob could only guess at pronouncing. He could see why Kelly loved it here so much. She was born to the wrong people, no doubt about it.

They reached the bridge a few minutes later. It was a large, rectangular room with the workstations sunken below the main deck and divided into four sections by an elevated walkway. The walkway also ran around the edges of the bridge, near the windows, which offered a full three-hundred-sixty-degree view of the surrounding countryside.

He went to the main windows that looked out over the front of the aerofluyt. Birds had started to nest at the base of the window, but they didn't seem at all interested in him as he stepped up to the glass. He was high above the top of the wreck, which itself was a good twenty stories above the ground. It was dizzying, and he discovered, much to his displeasure, that he was afraid of heights.

But he forced himself to look.

Below him, stretching out to a line of trees far in the distance, was empty farmland. He scanned it in every direction, but there was very little to see. Just a lot of empty land, gone to riot, and a dark and broken skyline to the south.

"Nick, do you have any idea where we are?"

"You mean like on the map?"

"Yeah."

"About midway between Jacksonville and North Little Rock would be my guess. Those buildings to the south are downtown Little Rock."

"Jacob," Kelly said. "Why did you want to come up here so bad? What were you hoping to find?"

"I'm hoping this thing can be our eyes and ears," he said. "Chelsea, you told us your brother used the morphic field generator to lure all the zombies inside the ship down to the lower decks."

"That's right."

"And after that you guys used the ship's sensors to make sure all the zombies were belowdecks?"

She nodded. "We had to so that we would know when to power down the morphic field generator. I remember Chris saying that if it overloaded it would blow up the ship."

"Do those sensors just scan the inside of the ship, or can they be used to scan the outside as well?"

"I would imagine they could do both. I wouldn't know how to work them, though. Chris did all that."

"Where are they at? The controls, I mean."

Before she could show him, Nick spoke up from the window. "Hey, Jake, I don't think you're gonna have to worry about those scanners."

Jacob, Kelly, and Chelsea ran to the window and looked out. Nick pointed to a line of riders emerging from the trees at the far edge of the field. One by one the riders came to a stop and looked up. They were too far away for Jacob to see their faces, but he knew the awe they must be experiencing upon seeing the wreck for the first time.

"Looks like you were right, Jake."

Jacob shook his head. "I hate being right."

41

Jacob watched the riders coming on and felt empty inside. Out there on the plain, leading his riders, was Casey, son of Mother Jane and a latter-day Ahab hell-bent on revenge. There's no reasoning with him, Jacob thought, no bargaining. He was going to have his revenge on Jacob, even if he had to chase him into the midst of the Great Texas Herd to get it.

What could you do with an enemy like that?

Could you even hope to turn his wrath?

"Anybody got any ideas?" Nick asked. "They're gonna be here in about ten minutes."

"We've got rifles now," Kelly said. "Plenty of ammunition, too. I don't see but like seventy riders. Maybe we can shoot them as they try to come through the loading bay. The entrance is only about ten feet wide. They'd only be able to come in one or two at a time."

Nick considered that. He looked at the guns he'd found, a whole armory full of Ruger 10/22 tactical rifles. Beautiful guns passed down from a bygone age.

"Jacob," he said, "what do you think?"

Jacob turned away from the window. "A standup fight will never work. There's too many of them."

"Too many of them?" Nick said. "But we can funnel them. They'd walk into a meat grinder."

"The first few, maybe. After that, Casey will regroup. He'll find another way in."

"So what do we do?" Kelly asked. "Run away?"

"There isn't time," Jacob said.

"Jake," Nick said. "I hate that look you get. You're scaring me."

"We need to level the playing field," Jacob answered, ignoring Nick. "Chelsea, where are the controls to the morphic field generator?"

"Jacob . . ." Kelly said.

"Jake," Nick said. "What are you doing?"

"The controls," he said again, more firmly. "Where are they?"

Chelsea took them to a workstation near the front of the bridge. She went down the line until she found the right one and pointed. "That one," she said.

Jacob looked over the control board. It was mind-numbingly complex. So many dials, so many buttons and levers and gauges.

He turned to Chelsea and said, "What are we supposed to do here?"

She looked as lost as he was. "I don't know," she said. "I only watched Chris do it that one time, and that was years ago."

"Well, think, damn it. What did he do? Remember it. Walk yourself through it."

Chelsea studied the controls.

She reached out for a button that read INITIATE STARTUP SEQUENCE and pushed it down.

The workstation lit up like a ball field at night.

Alert signals beeped at her.

"I . . . I don't remember that," she said.

"Keep on," Jacob said. "Keep going."

Chelsea pushed a few more buttons, and at last the familiar, deep bass hum of the morphic field generator began to rattle in their chests.

Kelly turned and had to catch herself. "That's it," she said. "It's working. I can feel it."

"Yeah, me, too," Nick said.

"Looks like you did it, Chelsea," Jacob said. "Is there anything else?"

"No, I don't think so. From what I remember if it's allowed to overload it'll explode."

"How long will that take to happen?"

"I don't know. A day, maybe two. It all depends on how good of a shape the components are in."

"Hey," Nick said. "What kind of explosion are we talking about? I mean, is it just gonna sparkle and fizz out, or are we talking about something more?"

"Most of this ship is built around the morphic field generator," Kelly said. "I think it's safe to say we're talking about something pretty big."

"Hopefully," Jacob said. "Either way, I want to slip out of here as quickly as we can. With any luck, Casey and his Family will be in here looking for us when this thing blows."

42

It was slow going down to the loading bay. The deeper they went into the bowels of the aerofluyt, the more damage they saw. In some places the decks were so badly crushed as to be impassable. The architecture that had been so impressive abovedecks was horribly twisted down here and choked with debris.

"How did you guys even get through here the first time?" Jacob asked, throwing aside a section of bent and twisted handrail that had come from the stairs somewhere above them.

"It wasn't easy," Kelly said.

"Yeah, especially since I had to carry your fat ass all the way," Nick said.

Jacob smiled and gave him a nod of thanks.

"It gets easier as we get closer to the loading bay," Kelly said. "I'm guessing the ship crashed at an angle like this." She held her arm out straight and then angled her hand down about ten degrees. Then she pointed to the bottom of her arm, about midway between her wrist and elbow. "We're trying to get here."

"Great," Jacob said. "Half an arm to go."

But it did get a little easier the farther back they went, and by the time they reached the loading bay, there was little more than clutter to deal with.

They emerged onto an observation deck about twenty feet above the main floor of the loading bay. They got down on their bellies and crept up to the edge of the platform, looking down at the cavernous compartment. It was a jumbled mess of big armored vehicles with ten wheels and smaller, light trucks. There was a great profusion of parts and barrels and forklifts and even a few vehicles that looked like they might be flying shuttles. And of course there were a handful of Casey's riders leading their horses outside, where another fifteen riders were standing watch over the Family's contingent of horses.

"Those are our horses, Jacob," Kelly said.

"Yeah." Jacob frowned, wondering what to do next. He should have anticipated this. He'd been foolish to think Casey and his riders wouldn't immediately find their horses and seize them. They were a bunch of ignorant, debased rednecks, but that didn't mean they were stupid. Casey had already proven that to him back at Malden. He should have known better.

"So what do we do now?" Chelsea asked.

"We have to get outside," Jacob said.

"But Casey's men are out there," she said.

"Not all of them. I saw maybe twenty riders. When we saw them from the bridge, they had closer to seventy."

"That means most of them are probably already inside, looking for us," Nick said.

"Yeah," Jacob said. "My thoughts exactly."

"So where do we go?" Kelly asked.

"We need another way out. Did you guys see anything on the way in?"

"I didn't see anything," Kelly said. "There's bound to be other ways out, though."

"Yeah," Jacob said. "And other ways in."

He was about to push back from the edge of the platform when he noticed movement on one of the platforms below them. It was an observation deck, similar to the one they were on, only one floor down. One rider was advancing down the hallway that led to the platform, a rifle at the ready, like he was expecting to take somebody by surprise there.

Jacob watched the man swing his rifle around the corner, sweeping the platform.

When he didn't see anything, he motioned at someone behind him in the hall.

"This is a trap," Jacob said.

Kelly looked at him in surprise.

"Nick," he said. "Weapons up. We're on the clock."

He jumped to his feet and moved to the wall behind them, his rifle held at port arms across his chest. He motioned for the others to line up behind Nick on the opposite side of the entrance to the hallway that led back into the ship.

"What's going on?" Nick said.

Jacob went to sign language. *They'll send a single man out to clear the platform. More will be behind him, in the hallway. I'll get the man out here; you fire at the ones in the hallway.*

Nick nodded. He gripped his rifle, ready to move.

Just a few moments later, they heard footsteps coming down the hallway. Jacob gripped his rifle and glanced over at Nick.

"Ready?" he mouthed.

Nick nodded back.

When the rider stepped into view, Jacob grabbed him by the shirt and heaved him over the railing. The man never even saw it coming. Behind him, Nick leaned around the corner and fired three rounds. Jacob raised his own rifle and caught a glimpse of a man ducking back behind a corner. A second man writhed on the floor, dying from Nick's rifle fire. Jacob didn't give the first man a chance to regroup and fire back. He charged into the hallway, jumping over the dying man, and fired around the corner, hitting the rider hiding there in the gut.

He stepped forward and knocked the rifle from the man's hands. The man rolled over, holding his gut in agony. Jacob shot him in the nose, the man's face swelling and distorting as the gases from such a close-range rifle shot expanded inside his shattered skull.

He scanned the rest of the hallway, but it looked empty.

For now.

He motioned for the others to follow him. The stairs leading down to the main floor of the loading bay were just to his left, and he could hear the Family gathering at the ground level. It was a trap, just as Jacob had feared.

From where he stood, he could see a thin slice of the ground level, right at the base of the stairs. Casey was there, motioning for the others to hurry up the stairs. One of the riders spotted him and trained his rifle in Jacob's direction.

Jacob ducked back behind a corner just as a shot rang out.

"So much for silent running," he said as the shot zinged off the metal walls just around the corner. "We need to hustle."

"But where?" Kelly asked. "I don't know where to go."

He motioned toward the front of the ship. "Back that way," he said.

"But all the debris . . ."

"Maybe it'll make it easier to lose them," he said. "Hurry."

Casey and his men were already coming up the stairs.

Jacob motioned for the others to keep going, while he stayed back to cover their retreat. As soon as he saw the first of the riders coming up the stairs, he fired, emptying his entire magazine. He thought he saw one of the men go down, but couldn't be sure.

Besides, there were more coming up the stairs every second.

He ran after Kelly and the others. Ahead of them the hallway met another flight of stairs. Kelly and the others stopped at the head of the stairs and motioned for him to indicate which way they needed to go.

There were more hallways leading to the left and to the right. The one to the right looked like a short one, leading to three rooms, all with the doors closed. To the left, the hallway seemed to go on a long ways. He could see a number of other hallways leading off from the main one, but where they led was anybody's guess.

"Jake, they're coming up from here, too," Nick said.

Jacob leaned over the railing, expecting to see more of the Family scrambling up the stairs, but instead saw a flood of slow-moving dead things staggering up the stairs.

"Oh, no," he said.

"What is it?" Kelly said. She looked over the railing, and her eyes went wide. "But how?"

"I guess all those alarms we heard when we turned on the morphic field generator."

"You mean we opened the doorways to the lower decks?"

He nodded.

She looked ill. "Oh, God."

"Okay," Jacob said. "We know they're going to be coming up and heading to the rear of the ship, right? Toward the morphic field generator?"

"Yes," Chelsea said. "That's right."

"So we go up and forward."

"But how will we get off this ship?" Kelly asked.

"We have to get away from Casey and the Family first. We do that, then we'll worry about getting off—"

Something whistled by his ear and zinged off the wall behind him.

"What the . . . ?"

Another thud against the wall.

He turned and saw Casey running toward him, a half-dozen riders coming up behind him. He had Sheriff Taylor's suppressed M4, and he was firing as he charged.

"That way!" Jacob said, and pushed them down the left side corridor.

They turned right at the first intersecting hallway, and then left at the next one after that. Jacob stopped them just around the corner and listened. He could hear gunfire and men shouting.

So they had run into the zombies from belowdecks, he thought.

Good to know.

"Listen," he said. "I think our only chance is going to be that loading bay. That's the only definite way out we know." He pointed deeper into the ship. "Let's go that way, and then turn left. We'll start making our way to the rear as soon as we can."

The ship was a maddening network of intersecting hallways that offered lots of chances to change direction, but nowhere to hide. As soon as they rounded a corner and stepped into a new hallway they walked into a new line of sight that extended almost the entire length of the ship. Their only chance was to move fast.

They were running at a quick trot when three dead men lumbered into the hallway ahead of them. "Whoa!" Jacob said. He pointed to the right. "That way. Go!"

One of the zombies lurched forward. He was wearing bloodstained blue overalls, his face torn away in strips, as though another zombie had ripped his cheeks and lips away with its teeth. One eye bulged from a lidless socket, a chalky white orb against a field of decaying flesh. And it was fast, much faster than the other two. Jacob barely had time to register just how fast before the thing was on him, its gnarled hands groping at his face.

He swung his rifle at the bulging eye and managed to deflect the zombie, but didn't do any damage.

The zombie fell a few steps to one side, then turned and lunged for him again. It was on him before he could back away. He managed to get his rifle up and used it to block the thing's hands, but it kept coming. Jacob kicked it in the legs, making it stagger, but it wouldn't fall. It kept coming for him, slashing at his face with blackened fingers. Then the zombie caught his fingers in Jacob's hair and pulled him into the wall, pinning him there. It brought its face in close, teeth bared, breath putrid with rot. Jacob had no other option. It was now or never. He jammed the rifle up to the thing's throat and fired. The bullet entered just below its chin and blasted a wet chunk of bone and scalp off the back of the zombie's head and all over the ceiling.

It collapsed to the floor in a heap, but Jacob wasn't off the hook yet. From somewhere down the hall he heard Casey and his men shouting, and running his way.

The other two zombies rounded the corner and lumbered after him. He didn't waste the ammunition on them. Instead, he ran after Kelly and the others. He could hear the sound of a struggle up ahead. He went up to the next opening and turned the corner, rifle up and ready to fire. Two zombies were crossing the office space from the next hallway over. One had definitely been a woman. The other he couldn't be sure of. He backed out of the opening and found himself face to face with a tall zombie in blue scrubs, like the ones he wore. The man was tall with slumping shoulders and black hair that was caked into stiff wires with blood. It reached for Jacob's face, but it was slower than the first one he'd dealt with and he was able to grab its flabby arm and throw him into the room with the two other zombies.

He turned just as one of Casey's riders fell into the main corridor ahead of him, a zombie all over him, tearing at his throat and scratching his face. Another zombie staggered into the corridor, right behind the first. Both fell on the man like rabid dogs, snarling and tearing, teeth snapping at the man's face.

Jacob shot both zombies in quick order. They fell off the rider, leaving him on his back, bleeding and moaning, but still alive.

"Please . . ." the man said.

Jacob almost left the man to suffer until he died, but something inside him wouldn't let that happen, even if he was part of the Family. Jacob got a bead on the man's forehead. The rider let his hand drop. He closed his eyes and braced himself for the shot.

That's when Jacob pulled the trigger.

In the silence that followed the shot Jacob heard the sound of shoes scraping across the floor. The first two zombies had come from there, and Jacob wasn't about to get ambushed by more. He raised his rifle and rushed around the corner, leveling the sights on the man he saw there.

And almost fired.

He quickly moved the barrel away from Nick, his hand still in the air in front of him.

Jacob let out a sigh of relief. "Oh, God, I almost shot you."

Nick looked as stunned as he was. "I'm glad you didn't."

Jacob laughed and put a hand on his shoulder. "You and me both, buddy." Behind Nick, Kelly and Chelsea were both breathing hard, but hanging tough. "Everybody ready to head to the loading bay?"

"Do you know where it is?" Kelly said. "I got turned around."

Nick pointed down one of the corridors. "The rider came from that way."

"You sure?" Jacob said.

"It's that way," Nick said.

"All right."

They moved out at a trot, Jacob in front, Nick bringing up the rear. They saw zombies in almost every corridor, but none of the riders. From the sound of the gunfire, Casey and his men were a good ways off. But then, sound did weird things inside structures like this. It was hard to gauge exactly where the sound was coming from.

The loading bay was empty. On the far side of the bay, a huge gash ran up the hull, as though a giant had come through with a can opener and torn it apart. Outside the crack, in a sliver of sunlight, they could make out a pair of riders standing guard over a field of restless horses.

Jacob went to one knee, hoping to see a little more of what was outside the ship, but when he did, he heard something ping off the metal wall behind him.

He looked up, then back down the corridor.

Casey and the others were closing in on them at a full sprint.

"Oh, crap," Jacob said. He gauged the distance between their position and the opening in the hull. There was no way they'd all make it. Casey and his men would reach the spot Jacob and the others currently held, and they would have an easy time picking off all four of them. They'd be like fish in a barrel. Jacob let out a breath and made up his mind.

He reached into his back pocket and took out the one thing he'd managed to keep with him through everything they'd experienced. The baggie Maggie Hester had given him the night before their expedition met for the first time.

"Nick," he said. "Take this."

Nick looked at the plastic baggie in his hand. "What's this?"

"Inside that baggie is an address. It's in Little Rock. Can't be far from here."

"Jacob, what are you doing?" Kelly said.

He ignored her question. To Nick, he said, "There's an address on the piece of paper inside that baggie. You guys go there. I will meet you there."

"Wait a minute," Nick said. "What are you doing?"

"I'm gonna cover you. You take out those guards, you get some horses, and you head due south. Make that address, and I will find you there. I swear it."

"Oh, Jacob, no," Kelly said. "That's stupid. Come on, let's make a run for it."

"You better go," he said. "You're burning daylight."

And with that he turned and started firing down the corridor. Casey and the others dove for the nearest cover, but at least fifteen of them were caught out in the open, with nowhere to go. Jacob shot into their group until his magazine ran dry, then he ejected it, slapped in a new one, and started firing again.

He glanced over his shoulder just long enough to see Nick and the others sprint toward the gash in the hull.

Nick ducked into the bright sliver of daylight and fired four or five times, Jacob couldn't be sure. But evidently he'd found his mark, for he and the girls slipped through the tear and were out of sight a moment later.

Good, he thought. At least they're safe.

He raised his rifle to fire on Casey's group again, but a voice from behind made him stop.

"Don't do it, boy. I'll bust your skull like a melon."

Jacob turned his head just enough to see one of the riders, a huge, meaty man he knew only as Anderson, with a shotgun pointed at the back of his head.

"Go on," Anderson said. "Put the gun down."

Jacob's chin fell to his chest and he let out a breath. "Damn," he said.

He started to put the gun down, but just as he took his hand away, he heard a mechanical whirring noise and the clopping of heavy feet.

"What the . . . ?" Anderson said.

Jacob glanced around again, and couldn't believe his eyes. A man in some kind of space suit was plodding into the loading bay, coming right for them. The suit was impossibly bulky, with a heavy nylon webbing bib in front that looked to be part body armor, part utility belt. There was a large pistol in a holster at his side, but the man didn't use it. Instead, he reached for Anderson like a zombie would, grabbed the man's arm, and with a mechanical groan, ripped it from his body.

Anderson went down screaming.

The man in the space suit fell on top of him, his knees making a loud crunch as they impacted the ground. He lowered his face down to Anderson, as though to feed, but the helmet he wore prevented him from taking the bite he so obviously wanted. Anderson, who writhed in agony but couldn't shake the grip the space-suited man had on him, tried to beat on his attacker with his one remaining arm, but all he managed to do was hit the heavy shielded collar that rose up all around the man's helmet.

Unable to take a bite out of Anderson, the space-suited man stood back up, put both hands on the sides of Anderson's head, and squeezed until the skull gave way with a sickening crunch.

Then he stood. Anderson's blood was all over his helmet's copper-coated glass facemask, but for just a moment, Jacob could see through the facemask to the man inside. His neck looked broken, and one side of his head was caked over with blood. When he moved, he made a sound like the whirring of servos and gears, and in the back of Jacob's mind it occurred to him that the suit was some kind of battlefield gear, meant to amplify a man's strength and resiliency.

Jacob fired at the zombie in the space suit, but the bullets just ricocheted off the helmet. The zombie started toward him. Jacob fired at the zombie's chest, and watched in horror as the bullets bounced harmlessly off the space suit. He ran for the nearest corridor, making it there just as Casey and his men entered the loading bay. They fired at Jacob, their bullets chewing up the wall just inches from his head. It spurred him to run faster and he sprinted back into the recesses of the ship. The last thing he heard as he put the loading bay behind him was the sound of Casey's men attacking the zombie in the space suit.

And from the sounds of it, they weren't doing any better than he'd done.

He didn't stick around to hear how it played out, though. He rounded a corner, saw four zombies coming at him, and turned right into the next corridor. A slender woman in a bloody white lab coat lumbered toward him, her mouth greasy with blood, her hair caked to the sides of her face.

Jacob took a step back as he struggled to get his gun on target. The woman was almost on top of him before he got a shot off.

He had stepped into some kind of lab. There were three more zombies on the far side of the room moving toward him. Orange emergency lights on the walls of the lab made the zombies look like gray ghosts. They slouched toward him, moaning, reaching for him. He could run, he thought, but just as quickly put that out of his mind. That would only take him right back into the waiting crosshairs of Casey and his riders. Instead, he ran right for the zombies closing in on him, twisting one way and then the other, threading between them even as they lashed out at him.

There were more zombies out in the hallway, blocking

him from turning right so that he could double back to the loading bay. A woman in a black skirt and red top fell on him, her arms wrapping around his neck like a drunken lover. He grabbed her by her hair and spun her around. She was shrieking at him, arms flailing all over the place in a moot attempt to latch on to him again. Jacob pushed her forward, using her as a shield to plow through the zombies that were closing in around him.

He hit the top of another stairwell and had to stop. There was a zombie coming up the stairs, and the stairs were too narrow for him to be able to run around it.

The woman whose hair he held in his fist leaned forward, and as she did, her rotted skin separated from her skull with a sucking sound, like someone trying to pull a boot out of the mud.

The zombie staggered down the first two stairs, then turned on him. In his hand he held her hair and a huge chunk of her scalp. Disgusted, he threw it to the floor.

The dead woman charged him, and Jacob kicked her in the face with the heel of his boot, sending her sprawling down the stairs and into the other zombie that had been blocking the way. Both tumbled down to the next landing, and Jacob, recognizing the opportunity, ran for it.

Both climbed back to their feet as he ran by, but he didn't bother to put them down. He kept running down the stairs, and as he did, the sound of some huge machine rapidly turning began to grow louder and louder.

He followed the noise until he came to a door labeled ENGINE ROOM MAINTAINENCE—EXTERIOR ACCESS PERMITTED ONLY WHEN GROUNDED.

A way out, he thought. Maybe, if he was lucky.

He tried the door but it was locked.

Back in Arbella, shortly after taking the job of first deputy, he and Steve Harrigan had made a call to Mitchel Foster's home. The man was going through advanced Alzheimer's disease, and neighbors had raised the hue and cry that he'd taken his wife, Gloria, hostage. They said he'd stood on the porch with a knife to her throat, saying he'd never let anybody break into his home like she'd done. He'd fought at the Battle of the Barricades, for God's sake. Wasn't nobody gonna break into his house now. And so he'd pulled his wife inside and sat for the next hour with her on his lap, the knife pressed into her flesh, no idea who he was, no idea who she was, no idea what anything was, only that he was a terrified man living in a world out to get him.

Jacob had leaned in through an open window and tried to talk him down, but it hadn't worked. It was like trying to talk to someone when you don't understand the language they speak. At last he'd been forced to give the order to kick down the door. Harrigan, forty years Jacob's senior, had stepped up without hesitation and kicked the door open. Then they'd both rushed inside and wrestled the knife away from Mitchel Foster, Harrigan holding Foster in a choke hold while Jacob peeled the man's fingers back from the knife hilt one at a time. The whole thing was over in seconds, and the adrenaline high felt great, but it was the ease with which Harrigan had kicked in the door that impressed Jacob the most. He wondered if he'd be able to do the same, if the need ever arose.

Well, it was here. He looked left, looked right, and saw the corridor was empty. He took a step back, gave the door a good hard kick, and was both surprised and proud when it flew open.

Just like Steve Harrigan did it.

He stepped onto a metal floor made of a heavy gauge mesh. He could see right through it to some kind of access corridor. But he barely noticed that, for the room he stepped into was the strangest he had ever seen. It was a tube, perhaps three stories high, with gigantic turbine fans at either end. The fans were the same diameter as the tube itself, and though they seemed to be turning at a greatly reduced speed, the noise they produced was so loud, so powerful, that it made it hard for him to walk straight.

Snakelike metal tubes, mounted on the walls and on the ceiling, ran the length of the room, which had to be three hundred feet long at least, and down toward the end of the room was a sign that read EXTERIOR ACCESS PORTAL.

He clapped his hands over his ears and lurched down the tube-shaped room until he reached the access portal. On the door was the same warning he'd seen at the entrance: EXTERIOR ACCESS PERMITTED ONLY WHEN GROUNDED. He waved a hand over the black glass panel next to the door and it shot open with a solid, well-constructed thud.

Beyond was blue sky and green grass.

He was a good twenty feet above ground level, and he had little choice but to jump. He sat on the edge of the doorway and then lowered himself down so that he was hanging by his hands, minimizing the distance he had to drop. The ground below had been chewed up by the crash, and he dropped down onto a hill of upturned dirt that padded his fall but still hurt like hell.

He stood up slowly and dusted himself off, grateful to be alive. The sudden quiet and the sunlight on his face felt good. He turned around and faced the enormous wreck towering above him. Such a marvel, even in its desolation. It was a wonder to him that such things could be in the world. Just a few weeks ago, his world had been a shell from which he'd been eager to break free. But now, as he stood on the precipice of a future he couldn't even hope to understand, he felt small, and mean, and scared to his core.

Reeling, he turned away.

And froze.

Circling in the sky behind the wreck were hundreds of black ravens.

43

Jacob clutched his rifle with both hands and headed to the rear of the crash site, careful to stay in the shadow of the aerofluyt. When he reached the end of the wreck, he got down on his belly and crawled forward to see what he could see.

Mother Jane was in her lawn chair, sitting under an awning, cooling herself with a fan. Two of Casey's riders stood guard over her, but they both looked bored and tired. Jacob scanned the rest of the crash site, but there was no one else. Perhaps they were all inside, looking for him. Or fighting that zombie in the space suit. Or perhaps they were riding hard to the south, chasing after Nick and the others. Either way, Mother Jane was sitting there, wide open, and if he had any chance at all at breaking the Family's back, it was this right here.

He sighted his rifle on the guard to Mother Jane's right. There was a wagon a few feet behind the rider that could be used for cover. Best to take him out first. The other one didn't have cover anywhere near him, making a follow-up shot on him all the easier.

Jacob took his time with the first shot, putting it square in the man's chest. The guard looked young, maybe twenty at the most, but Jacob didn't let that bother him. The man was old enough to have chosen how he wanted to live his life. If he chose to be a slaver, then a bullet out of nowhere was good enough for him. Jacob squeezed the trigger and when the guard shuddered and sank to his knees, Jacob immediately swiveled the sights onto the second guard and fired twice at him.

The second guard folded to the ground immediately, dead right there.

The ravens took to the air, squawking furiously.

Once they'd all flown, he turned his attention on the first guard. He was still on his knees. He held his rifle loosely in his right hand. Jacob sighted on him again and fired. The man's shoulders shook, but he still didn't go down.

"Crap," Jacob said. He fired three more times, and each time the man's body jittered and danced, but he didn't fall. "Goddamn. Come on, go down."

Jacob advanced on Mother Jane's position. She was on her feet, a pistol in her hand, yelling for somebody to shoot that son of a bitch. She pointed her weapon at him, but before she could fire, he got off a hip shot that hit her in the elbow.

She screamed out in pain as the pistol went flying.

"You!" she said. She was holding her bleeding arm across her chest, her breath coming hard and fast. "Boy, you better . . . you know what's good for you, you put that gun down right now."

He laughed at her.

The young guard was still on his knees. He still held his rifle in his right hand, though it looked ready to fall. He had blood coming out his mouth and more of it spattered across his face. He was trying to speak, but all he managed to get out was a long, stuttering groan.

"Die already," Jacob said, and fired a round into the man's ear.

The other guard was already dead. Jacob could see him lying face up in the grass, one arm bent over his eyes like he was asleep.

"You . . . you put that gun down," Mother Jane said. She was breathing hard, her right arm immobile.

"Shut up, bitch," Jacob said. He stood over her, and felt a red-hot rage cloud his mind. This was the woman who had made him a slave, who was responsible for the deaths of his friends and the worst degradation he had ever experienced. Remembering it made his whole body shake with anger.

But instead of the fear he expected an old woman to show, she only sneered at him.

He punched her in the face with his rifle. "Choke on that," he said.

She went down, her one good hand coming up to cup her mouth and catch the teeth Jacob had knocked loose.

He turned back to the dead man with an arm over his eyes. The man was trying to climb to his feet, but couldn't quite manage it. The ravens were eager to finish him, but Jacob couldn't afford to have a zombie wandering around, not while he still had business to settle with Mother Jane. He walked over to the man and shot him at point-blank range.

With both guards dead, he turned his attention on Mother Jane.

She was staggering toward her weapon, blood oozing in ropes from her face.

Jacob grabbed her by the back of her shirt and threw her into the grass. He pointed his rifle at her face and let the moment settle, just so she knew where she stood. "You attacked us without provocation," he said. "You had no right to do what you did."

Her face was a flower of blood. She was missing teeth and her lips were smashed and swollen. She spit blood into the grass and smiled at him. "I don't need no right to do nothing," she said. "You make your own right in this world. Ain't you learned that by now? I made you a slave because that's what you deserve to be. You and all the rest. Nothing more than tracts and bridemeat. Go on and shoot me, if that's what you think you've gotta do. But know this. My Casey is a better man than you. He's your master, and you belong to him. And he's gonna hunt you down to the ends of the earth to take back what's his. There ain't no place you can hide from him."

Jacob pointed the rifle at her face. His anger was in full bloom. Every fiber of his being hummed with rage. He squeezed the trigger, hungry for the kick to follow, hungry to see her die.

"That's it, slave," she said. "Go on, do it! Do what you're told."

But he didn't fire. He lowered the weapon.

"You ain't even got the guts to pull the trigger, do you?"

Jacob barely heard her. In an instant, his rage was gone. When he'd thrown her to the ground he'd torn her blouse open. It was hanging in two strips from her shoulders, her bra wet with sweat and dark with years of worn-in grime. And from her neck hung a silver, heart-shaped locket.

He stared at it, frozen by it.

"You lookin' at my titties, boy? You're a sick little fuck, ain't you?"

"Where did you get that?" Jacob asked, pointing at the locket.

She put a hand over it, and from the look on her face, Jacob could tell she thought she'd found a weakness in him.

"You like that, do you?"

She smiled wickedly. Jacob kicked her in the chest, knocking her onto her back. She rolled over, groaning, spitting blood and wheezing through her shattered nose.

"Where did you get that? You tell me right now!"

Though she was in pain, she laughed at him. "Wouldn't you like to know," she said. She grinned wide, all her remaining teeth stained red with blood.

He pushed her down onto her back again, grabbed the locket, and yanked it from her neck. He was afraid to open it because he knew what he would see. It was Jasmine Simmons's locket, and when he opened it and saw the cameo of her mother there, his stomach turned over. He felt lightheaded and a little sick, and he knew there were a million questions that needed answering, but for all that, the only thing he could think of was Amanda Grieder falling to her knees in the town square, her breath misting in the frozen air as she screamed at him: "You made a mistake. You didn't even find the locket. How can you kill him if you didn't even find the locket?"

Jacob turned his attention back to Mother Jane. "Where did you get this?"

"I don't answer slaves," she said, and spit at his feet.

He turned his rifle around and shot her in the left leg.

She screamed as she fell over onto her side, writhing uncontrollably. He stood over her as she tried to pull herself toward her pistol. "Where did you get this?" he demanded. "Where?"

"Fuck you," she said.

He grabbed her foot and pulled her back, away from the pistol. Then he dug his thumb into the hole that had once been her knee and twisted.

Her screams echoed off the sides of the wreck.

"Where did you get this?"

She stared at him with wild, terrified eyes, but she had the inner strength to deny him even still. He got down on his knees next to her and rested the barrel of his gun on her cheek.

"Where did you get this locket?" he asked. "You're going

to die here in a few minutes. But whether you die from a gunshot, quick and easy, or whether I have to cut off a piece of you one at a time, depends on your answer. Last chance for the quick and easy option. Where did you get this?"

She tried to spit at him again, but he managed to turn her face to the grass before she could get it out.

"In pieces it is," he said.

The younger of the two guards had a Buck hunting knife on his belt. Jacob pulled it from the man's scabbard and walked back to Mother Jane. She was watching him, her body shaking, but her expression was still one of maddening defiance.

"Tough old hen, aren't you?" he said. "Get on the ground."

He pushed her head down into the grass, then sawed into her right ear until he'd cut all the way through.

He held it out for her to see.

"I'm not playing with you anymore. Do you hear me? Where did you get this locket?"

Whether he'd finally gotten past her pain tolerance, or whether she'd finally realized how far he was ready to go, he couldn't tell. And he didn't care. He wanted an answer, and he was going to get it.

"Tell me!" he shouted.

"Out of your backpacks," she said.

"Mine?" he said. "What?"

"Your backpacks. The ones Casey took off you when he captured you."

Tears had turned her bloody face to a red river. It had spilled down her front like a baby's bib, coloring her bra and the remnants of her blouse.

Jacob leaned over her and said, "Whose backpack? Describe it. What else was in it?"

"I don't know," she said. "Drawings and shit."

"Drawings?"

"Yeah, drawings. A bunch of young girls sleeping. Maps and shit. I don't know."

"Maps?" Jacob said.

"Yeah, maps." She rolled over and curled into a ball, the pain seizing her like a fist, squeezing her until she couldn't even pretend defiance.

He backed away from her, horrified, both at his own actions and at the implications of what she'd said.

He grabbed her by the throat and pushed her onto her back.

He looked into her eyes, searching for some indication that she was lying, that she was the devil attempting to throw discord into that which was in harmony. But the pain on her face was real.

It was the truth.

He backed away from her. She stared up at him, her face a mask of pain and blood and now, even a touch of beggary. She knew the end was upon her, and she wanted absolution. She wanted mercy.

Jacob searched inside himself for that quality of mercy which is not strained, and he couldn't find it. He was not that strong. If he was honest with himself, he was simply a man on the edge of survival, clutching at existence like it was the edge of a cliff. When he turned his mind inward, he saw an animal without mercy, without remorse.

He leveled his rifle at Mother Jane's belly and he fired until he'd emptied his magazine. He watched her body twitch and shake, and he felt nothing but disgust. He stared at the corpse for a long moment, hating her, but his mind still turning backflips over what she'd said. Finally, he dragged her out from under the awning so that the sun fell upon her. He ejected the magazine from his rifle and slapped in a new one. Only then did he walk away.

Somewhere in his mind he had held a vision of her getting devoured by her own ravens. He thought there'd be justice in that. But as he walked away, and heard the ravens descend upon her risen and zombified corpse, he felt no need to look back.

The real hurt was still to come.

part five

THE EMPTY TOWNS

44

The next morning Jacob sat astride a stolen horse, looking at a moldering one-story home waist deep in the weeds, and asked himself if he really wanted to know the truth.

He looked up and down the empty street, taking in the skeletal remains of the houses, some of them with trees growing through the windows, some of them with roofs long since gone, and it occurred to him that he could simply throw the locket into the tall grass and go inside.

He could keep silent.

He could set his mouth in a smile of grim determination and pretend that out here in the wasteland, things were different.

After all, hadn't he himself become a thief? Hadn't he killed his fellow man in abominable ways? Hadn't he even thrilled at the brutal, soul-destroying torture and murder of an old woman who desperately deserved it? Hadn't he done all these things and claimed that the end of his own survival somehow justified the means?

That was really the question that needed answering.

What was justice? Was it a pure Aristotelian form, a thing

that existed unto itself as an absolute standard somehow removed from the muddy particulars of day-to-day life?

Or was it a bendable thing?

Could a man believe in a thing, in the Code that was at the heart of who he had been raised to be, and yet somehow shuffle off that coil for the mere convenience of survival?

Was such a bargain possible?

And if those sins—be they sins—be forgiven, what other sins might he set aside?

Jacob looked at the locket in his hand and just didn't know. He couldn't answer the questions that plagued him. They seemed to form a knot so large and so dense he had no power to untie them. When he looked inward and tried to figure out the answer, the best he could come up with was a vague sort of emptiness where his certainty had once been.

Feeling sick to his stomach, he climbed down from the saddle and trudged up the porch, the steps creaking beneath his weight.

The voices he heard inside the little home went suddenly silent.

He knocked twice on the door, then twice more.

"It's me," he said. "It's Jacob."

Kelly opened the door, and the fear and worry on her face blossomed into joy. She threw her arms around his neck and squeezed him hard. "Oh, Jacob," she said. "Oh, God, I'm so glad you're here."

She held the hug for a long moment, and then leaned back to arm's length and studied his face.

"Jacob, are you okay?"

He nodded, and stepped past her.

"Jacob?"

The house was deep in shadow, but he could see all right. Much of the ceiling plaster had fallen to the floor and turned to mud with the rainwater that had gotten in over the years. Tree limbs grew in through the empty windows. Everywhere he looked there were signs of animals encroaching on the remains of human habitation. Owl pellets crowded one corner. Birds and raccoons had pulled the couch cushions apart and repurposed the stuffing. And everywhere he turned he smelled the odor of rotting wood.

But the really important things, many of them anyway, were still there.

The photos on the walls.

The handwritten notes on yellowed, curling paper tacked to the remains of a bulletin board. Even among the ruins, signs of everyday life remained. Jacob saw those things, and walked farther into the house.

"Hey, Jake, you okay, man?" Nick said. "You had us worried."

Jacob turned. His old friend was sitting at the kitchen table, Chelsea behind him with her hand on his shoulder. Nick's rifle was on the table. Ever since they were kids Nick had been able to pull off that effortless smile. He could look so cool, so totally relaxed, even here at the end of the world.

Jacob crossed to the table and picked up the rifle. He examined it, thinking about the lifetime they'd shared together, and then handed it to Kelly, who took it with a stunned and frightened look on her face.

"Jacob . . . ?" she said.

Nick stood. "Hey, man, what's up?"

"Sit down," Jacob said. The bark of command filled his voice.

Nick looked around the room. "You talking to me, Jake?"

"Yes."

"What's wrong?"

"Sit down," he said.

"All right," Nick said. With a glance back at Chelsea, he sat at the table. "What's up, Jake? Come on, man, you're scaring me." He tried the grin again.

Jacob took out the locket and showed it to Kelly.

Before she could ask what it was, he threw it on the table next to Nick.

Nick stiffened. He reached for the locket, and then pulled his hand away like the thing was a venomous snake. He glanced at Kelly, and then at Jacob. But he said nothing.

"What is that?" Jacob asked.

Nick looked at him and, for a moment, his face was a mask, inscrutable. But then the old confidence that had for so long, and so quietly, reminded Jacob of the ass kicking he'd taken at Nick's hand all those years ago, suddenly cracked. Jacob saw through it all in an instant. He knew, absolutely knew beyond a shadow of a doubt, that Nick was the man Jasmine Simmons had seen in the dark in the corner of her bedroom.

Nick seemed to know it, too.

"What do you want me to say, Jake?"

Jacob said nothing. He raised his rifle and pointed it at Nick's forehead.

"Whoa, hold on!" Kelly said. "Jacob, what are you doing?"

Jacob took his hand off the trigger and pointed at the locket on the table. "Look at that, Kelly."

"What?"

"Look at it!" he shouted.

"Okay," she said. "Okay, I'll look at it."

She picked it up from the table and opened it. At first she seemed ready to glance at it and dismiss it and turn her attention back to Jacob, but then spotted the cameo inside the locket, and a horrible knowledge passed over her face.

"This is the locket Jasmine Simmons lost," she said.

Jacob put his finger back on the trigger.

"Nick?" she said. She held out the locket. "What is this? What's he talking about?"

Nick didn't answer. Calm as could be, he stared up the length of the rifle barrel at Jacob, waiting for him to speak.

"Oh, my God," Chelsea said. "What are you doing? Put the gun down."

"Do you want to tell her about it, Nick?" Jacob said. "Do you want to tell her about the young girls? There's a dozen just like her back at Arbella. Maybe more than that? Some that didn't respond the way you wanted. Wouldn't pose for your drawings. But you had a way around that, didn't you? Burglary was incidental, wasn't it? The real reason you did it was to get that little peek you desperately wanted. That's it, isn't it, Nick? You're a fucking predator, aren't you?"

Nick didn't say a word.

"Put the gun down!" Chelsea said. "Holy hell, what is this?"

"He's a thief," Jacob said.

"So what?" Chelsea said. "So are you. So am I. So is everyone in this room. You're holding a stolen gun, for God's sake. Put the gun down. Come on, everybody. Show a little common sense."

Jacob took a deep breath. "We have a law," he said. "It's called the Code. It is the moral fabric that we live by. It is who we are."

"Is it?" Nick said. "Is it really? Look at us. We are on the edge of the map here. We have traveled outside of our moral sphere. The Code teaches us that we have survived because we support each other, no matter what. Isn't that true? Didn't I lift you out of the herd? Didn't I carry you when you couldn't even walk? Haven't I earned the right to say I support my brother?"

"Yes," Jacob said. "And that's what makes it worse. We had a contract, you and I. We took an oath. We swore to each other that we'd always have one another's back." He kept his weapon trained on Nick's face. "But the locket is still right there. The truth is still right there."

"What truth?" Chelsea said. "Good God, put that gun down."

"Our Code is who we are," Jacob said. "It doesn't exist only in Arbella. It is who we are. Our word to each other follows us around wherever we go. It is woven into the truth of who we are. Wherever we go, we carry Arbella with us."

"Platitudes," Nick said. "This is the fucking wasteland. Out here, we make our own laws. We decide what is right and what is wrong. We live by our wits, and by our fists. Haven't you been paying attention, Jacob? This is the Wild West. The law here is what we make it."

It was his first misstep. Even up to that point, Jacob had doubted his ability to carry through with the punishment the Code meted out for all thieves, but upon hearing Mother Jane's words spoken from his best friend's mouth, his self-doubt thawed and resolved itself into conviction. Jacob glanced back at Kelly, and saw her face, tear-stained, but just as resolute as his. She nodded yes to the question that hung unspoken between them.

He turned back to Nick and adjusted his grip on the trigger.

"Wait!" Chelsea screamed. "What are you doing?"

Kelly moved forward and pulled the young girl away. Chelsea put up a hard fight, but Kelly pulled her to the side and squeezed her arms over her chest, holding her down and muttering in her ear to calm her.

It didn't work.

Chelsea screamed at him the whole time, and as she railed, Jacob heard not her, but Amanda Grieder screaming for her husband's innocence.

He leveled the rifle at point-blank range.

"Nick, you violated the Code."

"Bullshit," Nick said.

"You committed burglary in the night."

"And what have you done? What right do you have to exact justice on me? How fucking dare you exact anything on me?"

"You stood by and watched me put an innocent man to death."

To that, Nick had nothing to say.

"You even congratulated me on a job well done. You fucking bastard." Jacob couldn't hold it back any longer. The tears were rolling down his face. "How could you do this to me? Nick, Goddamn it, I loved you like a brother. How could you do this?"

"I love you, too, man," Nick said. He was holding back the tears by a mighty effort. "Justice shouldn't ever be personal. They told us that. Remember that? You can't do this if it's personal. The Code tells you that."

Jacob could barely hold the rifle steady.

Kelly was crying, too. She stared at Nick, tears streaming down her face, and she shook her head in bitter pain.

"You bastard," she said. "Goddamn you."

Nick had seemed on the edge of a rally, but with that, he sagged. He looked at Jacob, and the effortless courage he'd always shown, the cool, calm confidence that defined him, was gone. He looked up at Jacob and all that was left was a pitiful man in the depths of shame and empty words.

"You don't have to do this," Nick said. "You don't."

Jacob raised the rifle. "I do. I will. I'm sorry, Nick."

He pulled the trigger, and Nick's head snapped back on his shoulders like his wires had been cut. Jacob watched him for a long moment, his mind utterly empty, until finally he let the barrel fall to the floor.

Only later, and then only dimly, did he become aware of Chelsea's sobs filling the room.

45

It was Kelly who ended up doing the hard work.

Jacob took the body into the backyard and dug a grave. Then he put his friend in it and filled the hole back up with earth. Afterwards, he took one of the chairs from the kitchen and sat on the porch and watched the sunset come and go.

Meanwhile, Kelly was inside with Chelsea, trying to explain it all to her. Jacob listened for a time, nodding to himself as she recited the lessons they'd first received as children about the Code. Every word she said was right. She told Chelsea about how the Code was a contract that one simply didn't slough off because it made life hard, or because it required you to make hard choices. The Code sustained them, and it made life in a world that wanted to sink its teeth into your throat possible.

Jacob listened to her, the same words he'd heard all his life, and he wondered how he could believe in something that demanded he kill the best friend he'd ever had. How could something that was meant to hold him together tear him up so badly inside?

He thought about that for a long time.

And he was still thinking about it later that night when the aerofluyt's morphic field generator finally went critical, and a dark gray mushroom cloud rose into the sky above the ruins of North Little Rock, Arkansas.

46

"Are we in danger?" Jacob asked.

They'd gone to the front porch to watch the sky. The horizon was bleeding orange across the roofs of the buildings to the north, and the mushroom cloud was still rising.

"Is there gonna be like fallout or something?"

"We're fine here," Kelly said. "The morphic field generator utilizes non-ionizing electromagnetic radiation. No fallout, but it'll give anybody anywhere close to the blast site a nasty sunburn."

"Like how close?" Jacob asked.

Kelly shrugged. "I don't know. The hot zone is probably something like ten miles. Anything inside of that range is probably toast. There's probably going to be a warm zone outside of that, say another fifteen miles."

"We're about forty miles away, I think," Jacob said.

"Yeah, about that. We're probably okay."

"Probably?"

She grunted in frustration. "Like I would know? Jacob, I have no idea. I'm just guessing."

He nodded.

Over at the far corner of the porch Chelsea had a blanket wrapped over her shoulders. The night air was damp and chilly, but Jacob suspected she wasn't using it for warmth. She'd stopped crying a while ago, but her face was still red and puffy and her eyes rheumy. She hadn't spoken since her talk with Kelly earlier that evening, and Jacob got a strong feeling they weren't going to be hearing anything out of her for a while. He'd underestimated her feelings for Nick. He could see that plain as day. Eventually, they'd have to come to an understanding about what had happened. But right now, watching her, Jacob had no idea how that was going to happen. He was no closer to sorting it out in his own head, much less being able to put it into words so that she could understand. He felt lost.

And then Kelly put a hand on his arm and squeezed so tightly he cried out.

"Shhh, Jacob."

She was staring across the street, where a zombie had just limped out of the weeds. The dead woman was dragging a ruined leg behind her, making slow but steady progress to the north, toward the explosion still glowing on the horizon.

She hadn't seen them, but they weren't out of danger. Jacob scanned the rest of the street. In the dark it was difficult to discern substance from shadow, but there was movement all around them.

"More of them over there," Kelly said, pointing to Jacob's right.

"Crap," he muttered. Now that he was looking for them, he could see dozens of zombies threading their way through the abandoned cars and strewn rubble of the dead city. "Where are they all coming from?"

"You ran the morphic field generator for nearly two days," Chelsea said bitterly. She wasn't even trying to keep her voice down. "What did you think would happen? You've probably drawn every zombie for five hundred miles."

Jacob and Kelly traded a worried glance. She was right, of course. In the back of his mind Jacob knew he was courting disaster by overloading the morphic field generator, but he hadn't anticipated it taking so long to go critical. Based on what Kelly had told him, he'd thought five or six hours at the most. But Chelsea was right. With the home fires burning for two days straight, they might as well have sent a personal invitation to every zombie within five hundred miles. Things were about to get hot.

"We need to get inside," Jacob said.

"Yeah," Kelly said. She crossed the porch and put a hand on Chelsea's shoulder. "Come on. Come with me."

But before any of them could get inside there was a loud crash from the backyard.

"The horses," Jacob said. "Shit, the horses."

He ran through the house, scooping up his rifle as he went out the back door. He jumped off the porch just as a zombie stepped into the yard. The wooden privacy fence that had once enclosed Maggie Hester's backyard had long since fallen down. Tall shrubs and weeds had taken its place, and zombies were coming through it from every side. The horses were terrified. They reared and kicked and ran every which way. Jacob tried to secure them, but they wouldn't calm.

One of the horses found a hole in the underbrush and dashed through. The others followed close behind, and within seconds they were gone and a tightening circle of the undead surrounded Jacob. A dead woman got too close and he punched her in the side of the head with his rifle. Another put her hand on his back. He spun around, grabbed her arm, and flung her to the ground.

"Get inside!" Chelsea said.

He took one last glance around the backyard. The dead were closing in from every side.

"Jacob!" Kelly yelled.

The dead were coming through the front door and through

the windows. He ran up the steps and charged through the back door. He closed it just as four of the undead fell against it, but he knew it wouldn't keep them out for long. Already they were coming through the back windows, the urgent moaning that Jacob thought of as their feeding call so loud now that he could feel it in his chest.

Chelsea had retreated to a back corner of the living room. She was trying to extract her rifle from her saddlebags but couldn't seem to make it budge. A dead man whose clothes had nearly rotted off his body was an arm's length from her. He slashed at her with a withered hand, but Chelsea didn't panic. She lifted the saddle with both hands and shoved it in the zombie's face. The man pitched over backwards, landing on his side at Jacob's feet. Before the man could get up, Jacob jammed his heel into his face. A living man would have blacked out from the blow, but the zombie barely registered it. He reached for Jacob's leg and tried to claw his way through Jacob's pants.

There was no choice but to shoot.

Jacob spun his gun around and fired into the dead man's face. The zombie's head smacked into the wooden floor and he went still.

"We need to get out front," Jacob said. "We need to run."

Kelly had Jacob's pistol in her hand, her head on a swivel as she watched the zombies pouring in through every window. "How?" she said. "They're everywhere."

He was only a few feet from the two empty windows that looked out on the backyard. Zombies were climbing through both of them. More were breaking in through the kitchen. Jacob could not have taken it all in, yet somehow he did. He watched Kelly turn her pistol on its side and fire at a woman clawing her way through the back door. He saw Chelsea punch at three zombies that were trying to pull her down, then fire her rifle for two perfect head shots. Both zombies folded to the ground. Something invisible sliced through the air in front of his face and he wheeled around. Kelly was there with his pistol, the muzzle trained on him. He glanced over his shoulder and saw that she'd landed a perfect kill shot on the zombie behind him.

"Thanks," he said. There were zombies coming in from every direction. They needed to get out the front door and into the street. He shot three zombies near the front door and then grabbed Kelly by the shoulder.

"Go!" he said. "Go on, hurry!"

She ran out the front door, Chelsea right by her side. Jacob covered them, firing into a group of zombies that were right on their tails. Two of them went down. His third shot hit one of the zombies in the shoulder and knocked it to the ground. Watching it get back up again was all the motivation Jacob needed.

He ran after Kelly and Chelsea. Zombies were coming at them from both ends of the street. They'd been headed north, toward the explosion, but the sound of gunfire had turned their course and now they were closing in. They'd even pulled down one of the horses. A tight knot of them were feeding on the animal, tearing into it, elbow deep in its guts. But when they saw Jacob and the others, they slowly rose from the kill, teetered for a moment, then advanced.

"Where do we go?" Chelsea asked him.

They were three houses down from the end of the block. He'd come from that way and he remembered seeing businesses to the south, gas stations and a grocery store and a strip mall. They might be able to get on a roof somewhere, lay low and let the river of the dead pass them by.

"Go that way!" he said.

There were at least twenty zombies between them and the intersection, and more were coming into view with each passing moment. Jacob ejected his magazine and slapped in a new one. Six of the dead came around a rusting car and headed straight for them. He took aim and fired. He burned through half the magazine in just a few seconds. Four of the zombies went down, but more quickly took their place.

They wouldn't stop coming. Everywhere he turned, there were more of them. They flooded the street, their moaning echoing off the houses.

When they reached the intersection, Jacob directed them south. The strip mall and gas stations he'd seen on the way in were four blocks away. In between were about thirty zombies, maybe more. Most of the ones farther off were heading toward the house they'd just fled, following the noise, but the ones closer by had already spotted them, and they were coming on, moaning at a fever pitch.

Jacob's plan was to get to the gas station. Now that the sun was coming up, he could see a black metal ladder on the back of the building. If they made that, they could climb to the roof and lay low.

"You see that ladder up there?" Jacob called back to Kelly. "That's where we're going."

"I see it," she said.

They sprinted for the gas station, Jacob ranging out front to intercept any of the dead that crossed their path.

He put down two of them and was about to shoot a dead woman in a blue dress when he felt something hot stab him in the leg. He staggered and then fell. Rolling over he looked at his leg and saw a gash across his calf.

"What happened?" Kelly asked.

"I think I got shot," he said.

She and Chelsea were about twenty yards away. They veered toward him but stopped almost immediately. Zombies were charging into the street from the west. They went straight for Kelly and Chelsea. The two women fired into the advancing crowd, but they failed to land any head shots and within seconds the zombies had effectively cut them off from Jacob.

He raised his rifle to fire at the zombies, but before he

could pop off a shot, a small puff of dirt appeared in front of his feet.

Then another, just inches from his hip.

He looked up. Through the crowd of zombies he saw Kelly and Chelsea surrounded by zombies, and beyond them, riders.

Jacob's blood went cold. It was Casey and Chris Walker and three other men, and they looked horrible, their faces burned and peeling. Caught by the blast, Jacob thought.

They were a hundred feet away, but riding their horses hard for Kelly and Chelsea. Casey had Sheriff Taylor's M4 and he was firing it one-handed at Jacob. The shots were silent, and the zombies didn't even know he was there until he was right on top of them. He and the other riders fired into the zombie herd, putting them down one after another, until they were looming over Kelly and Chelsea.

"Drop the guns," he ordered them.

Chelsea, terrified by her former master, immediately threw her rifle to the ground.

Kelly dropped her pistol a moment later.

"Jacob," Casey called out. "You best drop your rifle. It's you I want. You and me, we got a score to settle."

Zombies were closing in around them. He glanced behind him and saw three running—actually running—toward him from the gas station. He was still too far away. He'd never be able to make it there, not with Casey and the others on horseback. They'd run him down in seconds.

Unless he leveled the playing field.

He couldn't get a clear shot of Casey. Kelly was in the way. But the horse Casey rode was a big target, and putting the man on the ground would change things.

"Jacob," Casey said. "You put that gun down right now, you hear? I'll kill 'em if you don't."

Jacob sighted in on Casey's horse and fired.

The animal lurched under its rider, teetered, and then fell to the ground, dumping Casey into the weeds.

He jumped to his feet screaming. "Get that mother-fucker!" he said to his riders. "Get him!"

The riders spurred their horses and charged.

Jacob sprayed bullets at them, firing the Ruger as fast as he could. He managed to hit two of the horses, sending their riders to the ground. The third rider circled around him, but the zombies were on top of the rider at that point and he was forced to fire at a dead woman who was clawing at his hip.

Jacob didn't give him a chance to recover. He fired at the man, hitting him twice in the leg and once high up on his chest. The man reeled in his saddle, struggling to bring his mount under control, but his wounds were too severe and all he could manage was to sag across the back of his horse's neck.

Meanwhile, Casey was trying to get back on a horse. The zombies had spooked them though, and all of the animals were rearing, eyes rolling wildly, kicking and bucking.

Casey grabbed Chris Walker by the arm and pulled him down. "Get off that horse!"

Chris went sprawling to the ground.

A zombie grabbed at Jacob. He caught the thing's arm, twisted it behind the zombie's back, and shoved it into one of the riders he'd grounded just moments before. The zombie bumbled into the man, confused at first, and then tore into him greedily.

More zombies surrounded the other rider Jacob had un-horsed. They clawed at his face, grabbed his clothes, and finally succeeded in pulling him to the ground.

Jacob jumped behind the carcass of one of the horses he'd shot and tried to find Casey amidst all the confusion. Casey was trying to get the horse under control, but he couldn't manage the frightened animal and hold on to his rifle at the same time. The horse spun away from him, and for a moment Jacob had a clear shot.

He wasn't fast enough though. Casey ran for Chris Walker and pushed him toward Kelly and Chelsea.

"Get them up on that roof!" he said.

Jacob emptied the rest of his magazine in a vain attempt to put a round in Casey's head, but all he managed to hit were the zombies closing in around them. He scanned the scene, taking it all in. Chris Walker was pushing the girls toward the gas station, and it looked like they were going to make it. Zombies had already fallen on the other riders and were tearing them apart. Casey was standing in the open, swinging Sheriff Taylor's rifle at every zombie who got within striking distance. And still more of the undead were pouring into the street, attracted by all the noise.

Jacob ejected the spent magazine from his gun, and was about to load the only one he had left when Casey scooped up Kelly's pistol and turned it on him. Jacob ducked down behind the dead horse just as Casey emptied the gun into the animal's back. When Jacob heard the pistol click empty, he jumped to his feet and ran for the strip mall across the street, threading his way through the zombies that tried to pull him down.

He rounded the corner and dropped to the ground. He glanced around the corner and saw Casey loading another magazine into the M4.

But once it was loaded, he dropped to the ground and waited.

The zombies in the area came to a stop as well.

There was nothing for them to key on once silence fell over the area. They stood stock-still, motionless, as though waiting for something to pull them along.

Jacob ducked back behind the corner. He was looking at a back alley full of trash. Over the years the wind had carried countless amounts of debris into the alley. He looked over it all, hoping for inspiration.

He found it in a two-liter plastic bottle of Dr Pepper.

If Casey could fight silent, so could he.

He slipped the bottle of Dr Pepper over his Ruger's barrel and found it fit pretty well. It wouldn't hold by itself, but it was pretty close.

He took the duct tape from his pocket and wrapped it tightly around the mouth of the bottle so that it formed a seal around the barrel. It didn't look pretty, but it was a serviceable suppressor.

He went over to a gap in the buildings and scanned the street. The zombies were everywhere. Kelly was on the roof of the gas station, watching Chris Walker as he paced back and forth, watching the street.

There was no sign of Casey though.

Jacob knew he had to move. He needed to get across the street. Casey had seen him run. He knew where he was. If he stayed put, he'd be an easy target, and Jacob wasn't ready to die just yet.

He moved in a crouch, weapon at the ready. He was as silent as he could be, but there were so many zombies a few were bound to see him. Those that did turned his way and began to moan. Jacob fired on them only when they got too close. He had just thirty rounds left and he had to make them count.

With the plastic bottle suppressor his weapon was almost completely silent, just the sound of the gun's action cycling to indicate it had been fired at all. Those zombies who weren't already looking his way never even knew he was there. He made it across the street without attracting Chris Walker's attention and slipped into the tall weeds that had grown up along the edge of the street. Once there, he went down on his belly and low crawled toward the ladder on the far side of the gas station.

He was about to run for the ladder when he caught movement out of the corner of his eye. In the gap between a metal shed and a leaning section of a wooden privacy fence, on his belly, was Casey. He was set up like a sniper in the tall grass, watching the ladder, waiting for Jacob.

"Got you," Jacob said.

He crawled forward, getting as close as he could. There was a good sixty feet of open ground between them. The M4, with its heavier ammunition, would have no problem making a kill shot at that distance. The .22 would have a harder time of it. His best bet, he figured, was to flush Casey from his hiding spot and force his hand. Make him make a mistake.

Jacob sighted in and fired three times, hitting Casey with at least one of the shots. The rider screamed and rolled over. He pulled himself to his feet and fell against the side of the shed. The bullet had hit him high up on his thigh and he was having trouble supporting himself. But he was a fighter. Even as the wound continued to leak out, Casey scanned his surroundings, trying to figure out where the shots were coming from.

Jacob fired at him again, but Casey had moved just as Jacob was pulling the trigger and the rounds plinked harmlessly into the side of the shed.

Casey tried to guess where Jacob was. He backed deeper into the gap, thinking it would put him out of sight, but instead it opened up a clean shot for Jacob. Jacob sighted in and fired six times before the Ruger jammed. Jacob ejected the magazine and tried to clear the malfunction, but the action was jammed up so tightly he couldn't work it.

Back pressure from the makeshift suppressor was Jacob's guess.

But Casey was lying still in the grass. Jacob watched him for a moment, just to make sure, but the rider was down and out. Malfunction or not, he'd beaten the son of a bitch.

Jacob bolted for the ladder. Even though their weapons never made a sound, all the commotion had attracted the zombies, and they were closing in around the gas station, their moaning getting louder and louder.

He hit the ladder at a run and scaled up it. He was over the top before Chris Walker knew he was there.

"Hold it," Jacob said, leveling his rifle at Chris. The gun was useless, but the other man didn't know it. "Put the gun down."

Chris's surprise slowly melted into anger, but he tossed the weapon aside.

"That's it. Now step away from it."

Chris raised his hands and backed toward the edge of the building.

"Kelly," Jacob said. "Grab that please."

"You bet." She picked up the weapon and trained it on Chris. "Where's Casey?"

"Back there," Jacob said. "In the weeds by that shed over there."

"Did you kill him?" Chris asked.

"Yep."

Jacob wasn't sure how to describe the look that passed over Chris Walker's face. Relief, anger, resentment: a little of all those things, maybe. He lowered his hands a little and the air seemed to bleed out of him. He looked down at his feet, completely dejected and broken.

Chelsea had been watching him since they'd disarmed him, and Jacob could see the anger swelling up in the girl. The brother who should have protected her had betrayed her instead and, looking at him now, it all seemed to boil up in her at once. Jacob could see her hands shaking, her teeth digging into her bottom lip. He watched her rage mount, and he could see her coiling.

"You bastard!" she shouted, running at him. Before he could make a move to avoid her, she shoved him over the side. Chris went flying into a pack of zombies. They fell on him in a mad rush, ripping him apart with their teeth and their fingernails, lashing out at each other like wild dogs as they fought for pieces of him.

Chelsea was leaning over the side, watching them feed. Jacob stood next to her, watching the sobs hitch in her chest.

"Jacob," said Kelly from behind him.

From her tone he knew something was wrong even before he turned around.

Casey was standing there by the ladder.

His face was blackened and blistered from the burn he'd taken when the aerofluyt exploded, and most of his hair was missing. He'd been shot in the leg and twice in the left arm, and yet it didn't seem to slow him down. He had Sheriff Taylor's gun pointed at Kelly. He advanced on her and took the weapon from her hand.

"Get on your knees," he said.

"Kiss my ass," Jacob shot back.

Casey tossed Kelly's gun behind him, then quickly stripped the magazine from the M4 and slammed in a new one. Jacob could see the white smiley face on the bottom of the magazine as Casey charged the bolt and brought up the rifle to center it on Jacob's head.

Taylor's little surprise, Jacob thought, remembering what he'd said about the magazine with the smiley face. Good God, please work. Please, please, please.

"Get on your knees," Casey repeated.

"No way," Jacob told him. "Shoot, if you're gonna do it. But I won't die on my knees."

"You'll go to your knees one way or the other," Casey said. He lowered the muzzle so that it was pointed at Jacob's legs and pulled the trigger. The weapon exploded in his face. Screaming in rage and pain, Casey threw the gun to the ground. He lurched to one side, holding his bleeding face in his hands.

Jacob saw the gun Casey had taken from Kelly and ran toward it. He almost had it when Casey tackled him.

Both men went over the side of the building, and Jacob landed hard on his left arm. He felt it break and the pain was so intense he nearly blacked out. Casey was already on his feet. The man was a tank. He roared and lashed out, half-blind, but still managed to land a crushing haymaker across Jacob's chin. Jacob's legs wobbled beneath him, but he didn't fall. He took a few steps back and turned his hurt arm away from Casey.

Still bellowing in rage, Casey charged him again, wrapping his arms around him as he dragged him to the ground. Attracted by the noise, more zombies closed in around them. Casey got on top of Jacob and twisted his broken arm. Jacob screamed and his vision went purple. When he opened his eyes again, Casey had flipped him over. He was holding Jacob by the hair and he had his legs pinned so he couldn't move. There were three zombies coming toward them, and Casey was holding him still for them.

"Which one of them do you think will take the first bite?" Casey whispered in Jacob's ear.

Jacob thrashed, but couldn't break Casey's hold. He tried to lash out with his right arm, but Casey was just out of reach.

"I listened to all that bullshit you said about your Code, and you know what? For a little bit there, I was impressed. But it's all bullshit, isn't it? Every word. What kind of code allows you to let a pregnant woman die? Can you answer me that?"

The zombies were just a few feet away, closing fast. Jacob struggled, but couldn't get free.

"You ain't got an answer? You gonna go to your death without an answer?"

Jacob lashed out. He tried to push his way to his feet, but Casey leaned forward and held him down.

"I'm gonna watch you die, Jacob."

A gun went off somewhere to Jacob's right. Casey lurched to one side with a loud grunt. Jacob jumped to his feet, ducked his shoulder, and ran into the zombies that were closing on him. Before any of them could react, he knocked them to the ground, then wheeled around and found Casey climbing to his feet.

Jacob swung at his chin. Casey's head snapped back. Jacob swung again and again. Casey tried to raise his arms to block the hail of punches Jacob threw at him, but Jacob overpowered him, and eventually Casey sank to his knees.

"Look who's on their knees now, motherfucker," he said.

Casey looked up at him. His face was a ruined mess, his eyes nearly swollen shut. Jacob glanced up at Kelly and nodded.

She fired twice, hitting Casey in the chest.

The man shook with the impact, and then collapsed to the ground. Jacob stared down at the dead man, and he could feel the anger and the hate and all the rest of it draining away, leaving only emptiness in its place.

"Jacob," Kelly shouted. "Behind you!"

The zombies had regrouped. They circled around him, fifty of them at least. "Throw me the gun," he said.

She tossed it at his feet.

Jacob scooped it up and started firing, trying to clear a hole to get to the ladder, but every time he hit one of the zombies three more took its place. He couldn't move his left arm. He was forced to fire the rifle one-handed, and he wasn't doing very well with it. Jacob was only landing head shots every third or fourth shot, and he was almost out of ammunition.

"Behind you!" Kelly shouted.

Jacob wheeled around just in time to see a zombie's head get blasted into a red mist. When the body fell to the ground Jacob saw three of the gray space suits he'd seen back in the aerofluyt's cargo bay. The three figures made the same hydraulic whirring as they moved, yet they were far more coordinated than the one he'd faced on the aerofluyt. These moved with purpose, their movements powerful, but precisely controlled.

The figures spread out, their suits clanking and sighing as they brought up strange-looking weapons. They fired at the zombies, but their weapons made no noise. They pointed, shot, and another head would explode. In a few quick seconds, they'd cleared most of the field, leaving dozens of headless corpses on the ground at Jacob's feet.

One of the figures advanced on Jacob and he raised his rifle to fire at the figure.

"Jacob, no!" he heard Chelsea shout.

The suited man caught the rifle and turned it away. There was so much power in his grip, and he pulled the gun out of Jacob's hand as easily as if Jacob had given it to him.

The figure seemed to study Jacob's clothes. He examined the shirt and shoes Jacob had gotten from Chelsea's father's closet, and then raised what looked like a white microphone with two little wings up near the head. He ran the device up and down Jacob's right arm. A little green light blinked on it, but it didn't make a sound.

"Wait!" Chelsea yelled.

Jacob glanced over his shoulder and saw Chelsea and Kelly climbing down from the ladder. They ran toward Jacob.

The figure released him and turned to face the girls.

Kelly stopped short, but Chelsea walked right up to the figure in the space suit. "I'm Chelsea Walker," she said. "I'm from Temple."

The helmets and high protective collars made it hard to see the men inside the suits, but Jacob could recognize their surprise. The three suited figures glanced at one another. Chelsea stuck out her right arm. The figure with the microphone-type device ran it over Chelsea's arm, and right away the thing beeped and the light began flashing faster.

The figures glanced at each other again, and the one with the microphone twisted his helmet off. He was an older black man with a gray beard and a dense network of lines at the corners of his eyes. He had earphones in his ears and some kind of flat, black electronic device secured to the side of his throat.

"You're from the *Darwin*, aren't you?" the man asked.

"Yes," Chelsea said. "Yes, that's right."

"Are there any other survivors?" the man asked.

"No," Chelsea said, after what seemed to Jacob to be a thoughtful, measured pause. "No, I'm the only one."

"I'm Lester Brooks, from the *Newton*. We saw the explosion. We've been surveying this area ever since, trying to determine the degree of environmental impact. It's lucky for you the wind was blowing south during the explosion. If it had been blowing north, we'd be up in Jacksonville instead of down here. We'd have never found you."

"I'm glad you did," she said.

"I bet. It's been a long time, Chelsea. Are you ready to go home?"

"Yes," she said. "More than you could ever imagine."

"Who are your friends?"

Again, that thoughtful, measured pause before she answered. "That's Kelly Banis, and that's Jacob Carlton. They're from Arbella."

"Arbella?" Brooks asked. He looked to Kelly, and then to Jacob.

Jacob was in so much pain he could barely stand. He tried to speak, but managed only to mutter.

Kelly said, "It's on the maps as New Madrid."

"Ah," Brooks said. "Yes. Yours is a very successful community. We've been watching you."

"You have?"

"Yes, for several years now. Yours is one of about twenty successful outposts east of the Rocky Mountains, and one of the largest."

"Twenty others?" Kelly asked, stunned.

"Twenty-two, actually," Brooks said. "Most are smaller than Arbella."

"You say you've been watching us? Why haven't you made contact with us? With all the things you can do, we could have learned so much from you."

"You still can, now that you've contacted us. That's our way, Ms. Banis. Our law. We don't force ourselves on others, but once another society reaches out to us, we offer what we know freely. If you and your friend want to come with us, we will share all we know with you."

For Jacob, it was too much. His head had become a soupy mess, and the world around him started to swirl. He grew dizzy and fell over. He woke with his head in Kelly's lap. Chelsea was next to her. Lester Brooks was pressing a series of white tabs onto his face and arms and chest. Jacob could feel electricity move over his skin, prickling at his hair.

Brooks was looking at a flat black device that looked like a small TV. "Left arm is broken in four places. Two broken ribs. Internal bleeding. Brain swelling. Massive infection from the injuries on his arms." He put the device down. "Your friend is in some serious pain. We'll need to get his fever down right away."

"You can help him?" Kelly asked.

"Oh, yes. He'll be in bed for a while, but we can patch him, no problem." He touched the device on his throat. "Brooks 390, requesting extraction. We've picked up three packages. Have a medic and a quarantine team standing by for our arrival."

A few moments later a dust cloud appeared on the road. Jacob rallied enough to sit up and stare in amazement at the gigantic ten-wheeled armored vehicle that rolled through the ruins, crushing the zombies in its path before finally pulling up next to them.

Brooks opened the back door to the vehicle and helped them inside one after another. When Jacob was seated and buckled in, Brooks said, "We'll get that arm fixed up for you in a bit."

Jacob nodded. "Thanks."

"Hang on," Brooks told them. "It gets a little bumpy out here."

He closed the door and the vehicle took off.

Jacob leaned his head against the window and watched the ruins of Little Rock slip into the distance. The armored vehicle trundled through the abandoned city, causing Jacob to sway in his seat. In places, the streets were black rivers seething with bodies. In others, ivy climbed the sides of buildings, creating green canyons through the past glory of man.

And what of glory?

It made him think of Sheriff Taylor, the man who had meant so much to him, and so much to Arbella, gone now, dead and rotting in the sun on some nameless street in a small town a million miles away.

He thought, too, of Bree. She'd been so young and so devastatingly gorgeous, yet the only image of her he could hold in his mind was of her slipping to the grass under a hail of bullets. She had, in his memory at least, seemed almost grateful to receive them.

But mostly he thought of Nick.

He watched a solitary zombie lumber down the road, reaching for their vehicle even though it was much too far away to put its hands on them, and he thought of the time he'd had with his dearest friend. He felt heartsick at all that had happened. He had loved Nick as a brother. For all the tension that had run under the surface of their friendship since that fight twenty years earlier, they had been the best of friends, and Jacob couldn't shake the memory of the tears running down Nick's face right before he pulled the trigger. What had he cried for? Was it out of remorse? Or for what had happened to their friendship? Or was it simply for his own life?

Jacob looked across the darkened cabin of the armored transport. Chelsea had her eyes closed, a blanket pulled up under her chin. It didn't look to Jacob like she was sleeping, more like she was trying to forcibly push the memory of the last seven years from her mind.

Beyond her, Kelly was looking out the window, and the tears were rolling down her cheeks.

Jacob looked away. Though this journey of theirs was really just beginning, in so many ways, it marked the end of the man he'd thought himself to be.

Four Tales from the First Days of the Living Dead

State of the Union

I know when I'm being lied to. It's not hard to figure out, even when you're a stranger in a country halfway around the world and you don't speak the language. Bullshit smells the same, no matter how it sounds. And that's what our Chinese hosts were trying to shovel down our throats.

Bullshit.

Pure unadulterated bullshit.

Our group went down for dinner at eight p.m. We stepped off the elevator, but barely made it into the hotel's lobby before a couple of blue-shirted cops started yelling at us to go back upstairs.

"What's this all about?" asked Brad Owens. He was our leader, a Young Democrat from Columbia University. Tall, slender, and dignified, Brad stood an easy six inches taller than the cops, but it didn't seem to impress them at all.

"You go back upstairs," one of the cops said. "Go now."

"But I want to know what's going on," Brad insisted. He pointed to the reception hall. "They're supposed to be throwing us a party."

"No party for you. Party over. You go now. Go upstairs."

While Brad was busy arguing with the Chinese cops, I was looking through the glass doors of our hotel. Outside, Beijing was in the middle of a riot. I heard screams overlapping screams. I saw people running for their lives, others throwing rocks. A small crowd knocked down an injured man right outside the front doors and swarmed over top of him, like they were trying to pull him apart.

"But why do we have to go upstairs?" Brad asked.

The concierge came over. He looked utterly frazzled, and more than a little distracted, but he kept his tone level and his smile bright when he talked to us.

"Please," he said with a slight bow. His accent was good, even if the syntax was off. "Please, you and your friends to go upstairs please. We have the flu outside."

"The flu?" Brad said.

I looked out across the Beijing skyline and saw buildings on fire in the distance.

"People don't riot because of the flu," said Jim Bowman, our Young Republican representative.

The concierge's smile wavered for a moment. "You to go upstairs to your rooms now," he said, and then muttered something to the cops in Chinese.

The next moment we were being hustled upstairs and forced back into our rooms.

I tried the door, but it was locked from the outside.

I beat on it with my fists and got no reply.

I looked out the peephole and saw the cops pacing the hallway. They looked scared and anxious and I didn't like it. One of them kept swallowing, his Adam's apple pumping up and down in his throat, looking to his partner for some clue as to what they were supposed to do.

I gave up on the door and sat down on the foot of the bed and tried to get online. Nothing worked. E-mail; Livejournal; Twitter; Facebook; even Google was down. I put my iPad down and tried my iPhone. Same thing. I had been sending e-mails all that day. I had even sent my latest article to my editor at *The Crimson* right before I took my shower and got dressed for dinner. But now, nothing. Just a network connection error message.

That's when it really hit me. Not only was I a stranger in a strange land, but the Chinese government had somehow managed to shut down the Internet. My one umbilical cord back to the real world had just been cut.

It hadn't seemed real, standing down in the lobby and watching Beijing tear itself apart, but once I found out the Internet was down . . . well, that was the clincher.

We were being lied to.

And like the old Bob Dylan song goes: "You don't need a weatherman to know which way the wind blows."

Okay, so what do you need to know?

Introductions first, I guess.

My name is Mark Wellerman—though I suppose you already know that, my name being what it is. These days, I run a small farm in Georgia. It's not much, but I grow all my own food, raise my own livestock, make my own bullets. I can take care of myself. That's a far cry from the plans I had growing up, but don't think for a minute that I'm a failure. Like I said, this farm makes all the food a man could ever need, and there is no fortune greater than that.

Believe me. I know that better than anyone.

I'm twenty-four now, but I was twenty-two when this story I'm about to tell you happened. I was a senior at Harvard, majoring in journalism. I had the world by the balls, every door ahead standing wide open. And that's how I landed in Beijing that summer. I was one of two dozen college students from across the United States selected to take part in an exchange program to China called Our Best, Your Best.

Our group was called the Young Americans. We were supposed to represent the best and brightest of America's up-and-coming generation. We were a cross-section of this once great country, our own mini melting pot. We had Brad Owens, our Young Democrat from Columbia; Jim Bowman, a Young Republican from the University of Texas at Austin; and Sandra Palmer, a junior Tea Party Patriot from the University of Nebraska; all three of them were intent on becoming president one day. But we had a lot more than politics going for us. We had a cop from a junior college in Texas, a West Point cadet, a teacher's assistant working on her master's degree at Florida State, a UAW assembly lineman from Michigan doing an online graduate degree in pension fund management, computer programmers, rich kids, poor kids . . . we had it all. Hell, we even had a guy who was attending UC Berkley illegally, but got to go with us anyway because of the DREAM Act. Between the twenty-four of us, we were America.

For better or for worse.

Most of the trip up to that last night in the hotel was mindless arguing, everybody talking and nobody listening. I had plenty to write about, but it still wore me down. I remember feeling irritable every time Brad or Jim or Sandra opened their mouths. The bickering just seemed so pointless.

But all that changed later that night. I hadn't taken off my clothes. I was standing at my window, looking across downtown Beijing twenty stories below, every now and then catching the wail of a siren or the muffled sound of a nearby scream, when the Chinese cops burst through the door. One of them went for me, the other for my luggage. As I watched, the cop tossed my iPhone, my iPad, even my headphones into the trash. Then he crammed some clothes into my backpack and threw it at me.

"But, my phone . . ." I said.

He said something in Chinese and pointed to his partner, who pushed me outside.

Everyone else was already standing there, trying to get somebody to tell them what was going on. Jim Bowman was yelling, and it wasn't hard to see why. The cops had pulled him and Sandra out of bed without even giving Sandra a chance to put on her pants. She was standing behind him, tugging her jeans over her hips and looking embarrassed as hell.

Those of us who could speak a little Chinese tried to get answers out of the cops, but they weren't talking. They hustled us downstairs and out the back door.

As soon as the doors to the parking lot opened, we could hear the sound of screams and gunshots and sirens in the distance. I saw what looked like military helicopters sprinting overhead. I watched them race over the heart of the city, and when I looked back down to street level, I saw a group of burned and bleeding people limping toward us. One of them was so badly burned I couldn't tell if it was a man or a woman. The poor devil was black as charcoal, and still trailing wisps of smoke. The others behind were less burned, but each of them were terribly wounded and their clothes dark with coagulated blood.

One of the girls in our group let out a scream and the cops hurried her onto the bus. Then, while the rest of us watched in horror, one of the cops went over to the crowd and shot those wounded people one by one with deliberate head shots. I couldn't believe it. The cop never even gave them a chance to run away. He just shot them. And weirder still, not a single one of that crowd bothered to so much as flinch, even with a rifle pointed at their faces. It was like they didn't know what was happening.

The next moment, we were on the bus. Our driver, a thin, terrified-looking man in shabby clothes, turned the bus toward the street with a lurch and built up speed. The shooting we'd just witnessed had left us all stunned and silent. Cowed, I guess you'd say. We sat in our seats, staring out the windows at the destruction and the insane crowds banging on the sides of the bus, and I don't think any of us even thought to ask where we were being taken.

Just like I don't think any of us thought to use the word *zombie*.

At least at that point.

From our hotel they drove us to the Beijing West Railway Station. Let me say this first and foremost on the behalf of the Chinese.

They took care of us.

They never once forgot that we were their guests. They could have left us in that hotel to die along with everyone else. I'm pretty sure, if this was the US, that's probably what would have happened. But the Chinese had a sense of obligation that was so strong, so ingrained, that even in the face of a zombie apocalypse, they took real pains to get us out of harm's way. They had no idea the hell they were condemning us to, and I cannot fault them for what came afterwards.

They tried to be good hosts.

They really did.

The railway station was a mad, screaming hive of humanity. Hundreds of thousands of people were surging toward the platforms, trying to board the trains. We lost Virginia Wilder, our professor from Florida, and Wade Mallum, our UAW representative, somewhere in that mad scramble to the trains. I don't know how it happened, but I saw Jim and Sandra running away from where Virginia and Wade went down.

"Those crazy yellow bastards are eating each other," Sandra said.

"What?" I said. I had only known Sandra for a few weeks at that point, but I was already well aware of her ability to say things that defied the logic used by sane people.

"They got Virginia and Wade," Jim said. "We couldn't save them."

"What do you mean?"

"They were deadweight slowing us down." He was winded, but he managed to turn to Sandra and smile. "We're okay."

I just stared at him, dumbfounded. Amid the deafening roar of hundreds of thousands of panicking people, after watching two of our group get trampled and possibly eaten, he had the audacity to call them deadweight.

But I didn't get the chance to call him on his words, for at that moment our escorts managed to zipper open a path through the crowd and get us onto a train. It was a fairly new, fairly clean commuter car. No frills, no special compartments. Just three rows of seats on either side of a center aisle, like a small jet airliner.

And we had the car to ourselves.

I dropped down into a window seat and looked out across the crowded platform. I found it hard to believe we'd ended up the only ones in our car. As we pulled away from the platform, I saw people screaming for a chance to get on. Mothers held up their babies, begging us to take them. Hundreds jumped onto the outside of the train and held on as long as they could. It was a sorry, sad sight, and as Jim and Sandra and Brad began to scream at each other about whose fault all this was, I slipped farther down into my seat and pressed my hands over my ears and tried to block out the screams of all those poor people falling away behind us.

We did not make it very far.

As soon as we cleared the gates I saw people surging

against the sides of the train. I heard their bodies thudding against metal and felt the train lurch as they collapsed onto tracks and were run over.

I looked to one side and saw our entire group with their faces pressed against the windows, none of them speaking, but all of them wearing stunned, horrified expressions on their faces.

"My God," I heard someone say. "Look at all of them. There's so many."

And there were, too.

Hundreds of thousands of them.

I looked out the window and all I could see were faces closing in around us. They were pressing against the train, swarming over the top of it.

Suddenly, the train lurched and came to a violent, shuddering halt. All of us were thrown from our seats. For a moment, I felt like I was getting pushed forward, like I was on the crest of a wave. And then, just as suddenly, I hit the deck and banged my head against the bottom of a seat.

I blacked out for a second.

When I came to, I was groggy, disoriented. I stood up and looked around. My hair felt wet. I touched it and came away with blood on my fingers. Sandra Palmer had her hand over her forehead, a runner of blood oozing out from between her fingers. Her mouth was twisted, like she was about to scream, or cry, but couldn't decide which. Brad Owens had landed in a heap against the forward door. Jim Bowman was right next to him. His arm looked broken.

"They've knocked us off the rails," somebody said.

"Impossible," someone else said.

"Take a look if you don't believe me."

Several of us went to the window, and I could tell at a glance he was right. From where I stood I could see the half-dozen cars ahead of us, and the lead car was jackknifed across the tracks.

"How is that possible?" the girl next to me asked.

I shook my head. But I knew. I think we all knew. We'd run over so many bodies the wheels had just skipped the tracks.

And now, an army hundreds of thousands strong was surging against our train car, banging on the side panels. The combined roar of their moans and screams and their fists pounding on the sides of the train was deafening. The girl next to me, a culinary arts major from SMU, was in tears.

For a moment I wanted to take her in my arms and hold her. But before I got the chance, Jake Arguello, our Texas cop, started hollering from the rear of the car.

"They're breaking in the door back here!"

Billy Gantz, our West Point cadet, rushed that way. "I'll help you."

I watched the two of them punch and kick a Chinese woman who had managed to squeeze through the busted door. She fell back into the writhing mass of hands and faces and they slammed what was left of the door against the surging crowd.

Jake put his back against the door to brace it.

"I've got it!" he yelled. "Get something to help me hold it."

A metal handrail had snapped and fallen to the ground. Billy scooped it up and jammed it into the well of the doorway on the opposite side. Once it was in place, it looked like a curtain rod between the two doors. It was an elegantly simple solution. The harder the crowd pressed from one side, the more pressure it put against the doors on the opposite side, where the crowd was also pushing inward.

Billy rushed into the door well and pulled Jake back into the car. We gathered around to look at him, then recoiled. His back had been shredded by the fingernails of the crowd. He was bleeding badly, and screaming from the pain.

"Those fuckin' yellow bastards," Sandra said. "We gotta stop 'em."

"No!" Brad said. "They're cold. They're hungry. They're tired and poor. We should let them in."

"What?" said Jim. "Are you fucking insane?"

Brad raised his chin. "No, I'm not. We will be judged on how we handle ourselves here. Those people are scared. I think we have a moral obligation to share our resources."

"I'm not sharing anything with them."

Brad was standing at the opposite end of the car, still nursing his bruised shoulder. He scanned the rest of us to see who had spoken and saw Tynice Jackson staring back at him. She'd been Brad's biggest cheerleader throughout the first part of our trip, defending him every time Jim and Sandra railed against his leadership, but now she stood defiant, arms akimbo.

Brad steepled his fingers together in front of his belt. "Tynice," he said patiently, "we're going through a rough patch right now. We need to approach this logically."

"Logically?" said Jim. "Dude, they tried to kill our cop. How much more logical do you need to be than that?"

"This isn't a job for law enforcement," Brad said.

"Well, it's pretty much *become* a job for law enforcement," Tynice shot back, "because you won't do anything about it. Get over here and help. As long as you're standing way over there out of harm's way you got no business to talk."

I was frantically writing it all down, thankful I had stayed awake during my shorthand class, when Jake started to convulse.

"Something's happening!" said Billy. "He's foaming at the mouth."

And he was right, too. I watched Jake shaking on the floor. He was bleeding from the corners of his eyes and from his nose. He was trembling like we'd just pulled him from a frozen pond.

"What's happening to him?" Sandra said. "Those bastards did something to him, didn't they?"

Nobody answered her.

Wayne Scott, a second-year med student at Johns Hopkins, rushed over to Jake's side and looked into his eyes. The foam at Jake's mouth was turning pink from blood.

"His pupils are dilating," Wayne said. "He's going into cardiac arrest."

"Help him," somebody said.

"I can't. I'd need a . . ."

Wayne trailed off mid-sentence. Jake's convulsions had suddenly stopped, and now he looked like a tire rapidly going flat. A faint, rattling gasp rose up from Jake's throat and then he went still, his bloodshot eyes staring off toward the ceiling, the only movement a runner of blood leaking down his cheek from one nostril.

"Is he . . . ?" Jim said.

Wayne looked up at him and nodded. "It happened so fast," he muttered. "I couldn't do anything."

None of us spoke for a long moment. We all stood there, looking at our dead friend. I saw the same dawning terror on all their faces. What were we going to do? Who was going to bail us out?

I honestly had no idea, and I'm pretty sure none of the others did either.

Outside, the roar of the crowd continued. Their moaning was awful. I tried not to listen to it, to block it out somehow, but that was impossible to do. The sound was making my skin crawl, and all I wanted to do was go to the corner and throw up.

"Something's happening," Wayne said.

I stood on my tiptoes to get a look at what he was doing. He was still kneeling at Jake's side, but his expression had changed to one of disgust, and he was rocking back on his haunches away from Jake.

Jake's dead gaze had been turned up towards the ceiling, looking at nothing, but now it was locked on Wayne.

"I thought you said he was dead," Jim said.

But before Wayne could answer, Jake sat up. He looked at the circle of horrified faces staring down at him, and then lunged for Wayne. Wayne tried to push him away, but Jake was already on top of him, clawing at his face and biting at Wayne's fingers as Wayne tried to turn Jake's chin away.

None of us moved. I think we were all too shocked. I watched one of Wayne's fingers stray too close to Jake's mouth and then Jake bit it off. Blood gushed from the wound. Wayne opened his mouth to scream, but at that instant Jake locked his teeth onto Wayne's throat and silenced him.

Only then did the rest of us react.

Billy, our West Point cadet, rushed in and pulled Jake off of Wayne. He threw Jake to one side, and was about to check on Wayne, when Jake got back to his feet. He reached for Billy and started moaning.

"Get the fuck back, man," Billy said.

Jake kept coming.

"I'm serious, dude, take a step back."

Jake swiped at him with his bloody fingernails. Billy sidestepped the blow easily and swept Jake's legs out from under him, dropping him to the ground.

Before Jake could get up again, Billy grabbed another piece of handrail that had fallen from the ceiling. Gripping it like a police baton, he took up a position between Jake and the rest of us.

"Come on, man, don't come any closer."

Jake's eyes were dead and vacant. If he heard a word Billy said, there was no recognition of it in his expression.

His hands came up again, clutching at Billy.

"Shit," Billy said, and swung the piece of handrail at Jake, hitting him across the flat of his jaw.

Metal hit bone with a sickening crunch and Jake collapsed onto the back of a chair. Anybody else would have stayed that way, or maybe even slid to the floor, unconscious. But Jake showed no sign of pain. He straightened himself back up immediately, his face a smashed and bleeding mess, and staggered toward Billy a second time.

Billy took a step back, shaking his head in disbelief.

"Do something," Brad said. His cool, calm veneer was gone. The look on his face was positively frantic.

I saw movement from the floor, behind Brad. It was Wayne. He had been convulsing, the same as Jake had done, but now he was rising to his feet. When he turned to face the rest of us, I saw a large flap of skin hanging from his throat like a bloody napkin.

One of the others pulled Brad out of the way, and the next instant, Billy was standing between Wayne and Jake, the two of them closing in on him from either side.

But Billy kept his cool. Holding the handrail like a spear, he jammed it into Jake's chest, impaling him with it.

A raspy gargle escaped his lips, but the enormous shaft of metal sticking through his chest didn't slow him down at all.

"What the hell?" Billy said.

"They're zombies," said the girl from SMU. "Oh, my God."

The word was like a peal of thunder in our midst. Jake's imperviousness to pain; Wayne's injuries; the moaning crowd outside; the burned people we'd seen the police shooting back at the hotel; it all made sense now. All through school, most of us had listened to those idiots who talked so gleefully about the coming zombie apocalypse and laughed at them.

But none of us were laughing now.

And Billy wasn't wasting any time, either. He kicked at one of the wall speakers until it broke loose from its mounts.

Then he scooped it up, lifted it two-handed over his head, and brought it down on top of Jake's head.

That dropped him.

Jake collapsed in a heap and didn't move anymore.

By that point Wayne was almost on top of Billy, but Billy was able to step to one side at the last instant, kick the back of Wayne's knees, and drop him to the floor so that he could finish him with another two-handed blow to the back of the head.

When it was done, Billy stood over the bodies of our two friends, his chest heaving like a bellows, and looked at Brad, Jim, and Sandra.

"Well," he said, "what now?"

Over the next three days, Billy, our representative from West Point, emerged as our greatest resource. He worked tirelessly. I don't think I saw him stop once.

Our first problem was what to do with the bodies of Jake and Wayne. We couldn't leave them inside, we all knew that, but it didn't seem like there was any way to get rid of them.

It was Billy who proposed pushing them out the half-windows up near the overhead luggage racks. They were high enough up on the side of the train that the zombies outside couldn't force their way in. The only trouble was, no one wanted to touch the bodies. Finally, Brad ordered Billy to do it, and the rest of us watched as he dragged the bodies of Jake and Wayne up to the window and shoved them out.

The zombies grabbed the bodies before they'd even cleared the window and began to rip them to pieces.

But none of us had the stomach to watch that.

We all turned away and pretended it wasn't happening.

Later that afternoon, it became obvious we were going to have to do something about going to the bathroom. Pissing was no trouble for the guys. They could just go over to the door well and piss down the short flight of stairs. But the girls, and whoever had to take a dump, couldn't. Putting your back to the door where all those zombies were trying to break in was like taunting them. They pressed even harder to get in.

Plus, there was the issue of privacy.

Brad put Billy to work removing the seats from the floor. He used a dime to unscrew them, and once he had them loose, he hoisted them over to the head of the car and arranged them like a horseshoe, like cubicle walls, so that people could do their business behind a sort of screen. The smell was bad, but it was the best we could do under the circumstances.

As night came on and we started to tire, Billy worked at prying loose the seat cushions on the few remaining chairs so that we could have pillows for our heads. I used mine as a writing desk, where I continued to scribble notes about what was said and done.

Later still, it started to rain.

Billy got excited, though at first none of us knew why. Then he pulled down the plastic covers from the overhead lights and slid one of them out of a luggage rack window, forming a sort of gutter to catch the rain. It trickled down inside the car, where Billy caught it in an empty water bottle.

"We're gonna need water," he said to Brad. "You guys help me."

"Good idea," Brad said, and though I could tell it plagued Jim and Sandra to admit it, they thought so, too.

Brad, Jim, and Sandra ordered the rest of us to partner up and do as Billy was doing, and within a few minutes, we'd filled every container we could find.

When we were done, Brad said, "Do you think that's enough?"

"For a few days, maybe," said Billy. "Who knows? We'll

have to start conserving and rationing. And if anyone's got any food, that's gonna be an issue as well."

Once again, it was as if a peal of thunder had gone through our group. I don't know if any of the others had already considered the food issue, but I certainly hadn't. I looked around the car and saw a few others pulling their backpacks close to their chests.

The zombies went on moaning outside, and inside, Billy kept on working.

Sometime during the early morning, the zombies managed to knock down part of the door. The sudden rise in volume woke everyone, except for Billy, who had evidently never gone to sleep.

In the dark it was hard to see what was happening, but after my eyes adjusted, I saw Billy hacking away at the hands reaching through the door.

"Bring me that chair," Billy said to Sandra and Jim. With his chin he was gesturing at the cushionless frame of a chair at their feet. "Hurry! I need to brace this door."

Jim grabbed the guy next to him and pushed him toward the door. "Take it to him!"

"Why me?" the guy said.

"Hurry!"

Jim could be commanding when he yelled, and the guy obeyed almost out of reflex. He picked the chair up and brought it back to Billy. He stopped well short of the doorway, though, and held it out to Billy like he was trying to feed a rope to someone clinging to the side of a cliff. Billy managed to get ahold of it and jam it down into the door well, and between the chair and the handrail he and Jake had installed the day before, the doors were secure again.

"That'll hold them for now," he said. "But we're going to need something else to make sure it holds."

Brad nodded.

"Okay," Billy said. "You do that. Get somebody to help you."

Billy looked around for a volunteer, but nobody would look him in the eyes.

In disgust, he shook his head and went off to do it himself.

Around noon the next day, Tynice went into a diabetic seizure.

"Somebody needs to get her a candy bar or something," Brad said. "Who's got a candy bar?"

He looked around the room, his gaze finally settling on Russell Bailey, a computer programmer from UT Austin.

"Russell, I saw a Hershey bar in your bag."

Russell pulled his backpack tight against his chest. "I'm not giving her my food."

"Russell, you have to. She needs it."

"Well, I need it, too. We're gonna run out of food soon, and what am I gonna do then?"

"Russell," Brad said, "this is for the good of the group. You have a lot and she doesn't have any. You need to give her some of yours."

"Bullshit," he said. "It's not my fault she didn't bring what she needed. I have food in my bag because I had the foresight to put it there. If she didn't do the same, why is that my problem?"

"Because it's the right thing to do."

"Give her some of yours, then."

"Russell, that's not helpful."

Then Brad motioned to Billy. "Get his food. Distribute it around."

"Don't," Russell said, pleading with Billy. "Please don't."

"Give me the bag, Russell," Billy said.

Russell shook his head, and Billy, wearing a look of grim determination, moved in to take it from him.

Over the next four days, we lost six people. Tynice and Gustavo both went into diabetic shock and died. The other four, weakened by a lack of food and no water, gradually shut down, and when we woke to the sunrise on the morning of the fifth day, they were dead. Once again Billy had to crush their heads to keep them from coming back, and then pushed the bodies out the window. Again we all looked away as the ever-growing crowd of zombies outside ate their corpses.

It rained later that day and we were able to get more water, but the food shortage was becoming critical. We were down to a dozen people, all of whom were starving, and a small package of beef jerky to go around.

"Well, we need to divide this up," said Jim. "Here, I'll do it."

"No, you won't," said Brad. "We decide together."

"Oh, that's great," said the girl from SMU. "And while the two of you argue about it, the rest of us starve. Just hand a piece to everybody."

Brad and Jim and Sandra went off to another corner of the train car and talked about it. When they came back, they each had a big piece of jerky. They handed some of the smaller pieces around and told us to divide it up.

"But there's not enough here for any of us," said Billy.

"Times are hard," Brad said. "I know. I understand. But we'll just have to tighten our belts."

I got a piece and went off to one side to eat it. I hadn't had anything in more than a day, and tore into it eagerly.

A moment later, Brad and Jim and Sandra went over to Billy and whispered to him. He looked upset, but he didn't yell. He just took his piece of jerky and tore it into three parts and gave each of them a piece. Then he went over to the far side of the car and sat down. He looked utterly exhausted and used up, but he didn't protest.

Then they came to me. Brad asked me to give up what I had left for them.

He said as the leaders they needed to stay sharp.

They couldn't afford to go hungry.

"Can't do it," I said. "I'm the press. I'm an observer. You can't do anything that keeps me from that role."

They reluctantly agreed and went off to get what was left of the jerky from the others.

The next morning, Billy was dead.

None of us had the energy to move. We were all starving, most of us were sick. And—always—there was the constant roar of the moaning crowd just outside, reminding us that we were not long for this world.

"What are we gonna do?" asked the girl from SMU.

"I think it's plain what we have to do," said Brad. He looked at Jim and Sandra, and though they didn't want to agree with a Democrat just out of principle, they still nodded their heads in assent.

"I don't understand," the girl said. "What? What are we gonna do?"

"We have to eat," Brad said.

The girl looked at him, dumbfounded, not understanding. "Eat what?"

Brad, with his mouth set in a harsh, grimacing frown, pointed at the body of the soldier who had done so much for all of us.

* * *

Two weeks later, there were only four of us left—Brad, Jim, Sandra, and myself.

Sandra was not doing well.

Actually, none of us were doing well, but she was feeling really bad. We hadn't been able to cook any of the friends we'd eaten, and the shock of consuming all that raw human flesh was doing terrible things to our systems.

Sandra was doubled over on her side, holding her gut with both hands and moaning like one of the zombies outside.

Jim was sitting next to her, stroking her hair.

"I'm dying," she said.

"You're not going to die," Jim said. "You're just sick. This'll pass."

She looked up at him, and there was pain and fear in her eyes, but also acceptance. That acceptance was the hardest thing for me to see, for I had seen it before, on the others that we'd already eaten. And when people started to get that look in their eyes, it was a self-fulfilling prophecy.

It was only a matter of time.

"I'm dying, Jim. I know it."

He didn't say anything, for I think he knew it, too.

"Promise me," she said. Her voice was weak, raspy.

"Anything," he said, still stroking her hair.

For a moment, as she strained to look toward Brad Owens, who was sitting against the opposite wall, the acceptance and fear in her eyes changed to hatred.

"Don't let him eat me. I don't want some liberal bastard eating me. I can't die knowing some liberal sack of shit lived another day because of me."

She wanted to say more, but another wave of pain shot through her gut and she let out a choked scream.

"She's delirious," Jim said to me.

But when he put his hand back on her face and pushed the hair out of her face, she was dead.

"Sandra?" Brad said. "Sandra, no, baby, no!"

He lifted her head and cradled it in his lap, rocking her corpse gently, like a child he was trying to put to sleep.

An hour or so later, Brad came over to him with the piece of metal from one of the seats that we'd been using to carve meat off of our friends.

"It's time," he said.

"Fuck off," Jim said. "You're not touching her."

"Jim," Brad said. "Please don't do this. We have to survive."

"She didn't want a sorry sack of shit like you touching her. No worthless Democrat is going to touch her."

"I've as much right to her corpse as you do."

"Like hell."

I knew what was going to happen even before they lunged at each other. Jim knocked the blade from Brad's hand and the next instant they were rolling around on the ground, their hands at each other's throats.

I took complete notes of what happened during the fight, but I guess that really doesn't matter now. The end result was that they strangled each other. Democrat and Republican, neither would quit until they'd snuffed the life out of the other, and now they were both dead.

So I sat there, the only member of the Young Americans left alive.

And a short while later, I picked up the blade and started eating.

I was rescued by the Chinese Army a week later.

They hadn't planned on finding me there. They hadn't planned on finding anyone alive, I don't think. Someone told me they were looking for the train, that they had spotted it from the air and went in to retrieve it because they needed it to deliver troops across the country. The zombie apocalypse, they told me, had been contained. For the most part. A few pockets of zombies remained, but those were being taken care of. I was lucky to be alive, they told me, but I could tell they didn't think much of me for it. The first soldiers to board the train had taken one look at me, and at the pile of bones surrounding me, and had turned their heads to vomit.

News of what had happened went ahead of me.

The Chinese Army put me on a cargo ship and sent me back to the States. The ship's crew seemed to already know everything about me, and that made mealtimes rough. As soon as I would enter the mess hall, the others would get up to leave. No one, it seemed, could stomach watching me eat.

No one, it seemed, even back in the States, could watch me eat.

Live with that long enough, and it hardens you.

That's why I live here, on this farm in Georgia, where I grow my own food and raise my own livestock.

I live alone, and I like it just fine.

That way, there's nobody to turn up their nose if I like to eat the occasional steak raw. Besides, it's nobody's business but mine.

This is still the goddamned U.S. of A., for Christ's sake.

Jimmy Finder and the Rise of the Templenauts

"Is that your experiment?" Captain Fisher asked.

The infantry captain gestured toward the boy on the other side of the one-way glass. From the look on Fisher's face, it was obvious he didn't think much of the kid. He certainly didn't see humanity's greatest hope in the war against the zombies. What he saw was a mop-haired runt, too skinny, too short, too awkward, about as far from a soldier as one could hope to find.

"His name is Jimmy Finder," Dr. David Knopf replied. "I try not to refer to him as my experiment."

"Finder? You're kidding. That can't be his real name, can it?"

Knopf smiled amiably enough, but inside he was holding on to his patience with both hands. It was always the same with these military men, their smug condescending abuse and smirks of disdain whenever they were confronted with something that challenged the conventional wisdom of the battlefield.

"James is all we were able to learn from him," Knopf admitted. "We started calling him Finder after his abilities became apparent."

Fisher shook his head. "Frankly, doctor, I think this is all a load of crap. You should probably know that from the start."

Knopf's expression carefully masked his frustration. It wouldn't do any good to alienate the military now that they'd finally agreed to let him demonstrate Jimmy's talents in the field. It had only taken twelve long years.

"That's all right, captain. I'm used to skepticism."

"It's a wonder you still bother trying."

You bastard, Knopf thought. Fisher was really trying to bait him. "I believe in what we're doing here, captain. I wouldn't have put twelve years of my life into this project if I didn't. That boy in there is going to save lives and help us turn the corner on this war."

Knopf, afraid he was about to say something he'd regret, turned his attention on Jimmy, and a familiar mix of pity and pride rose up in him. Twelve years earlier, a contingent of Warbots discovered the boy wandering the hills above the nearby town of Mill Valley, Ohio. The provisional government gave him to Knopf's Weapons Research Team with orders that they find out how a two-year-old toddler had managed to survive an entire summer right under the noses of ten thousand zombies. It had taken Knopf three years to discover the answer. It took another nine before anybody in the military's High Command would take him seriously enough to let him prove it. But he did find the truth.

"You really believe that kid in there has psychic powers?"

"That's not exactly what he does," Knopf said. "He's not a psychic. He doesn't predict the future or read minds, none of that gypsy fortune-teller stuff. Think of him as a sort of bloodhound that we've trained to sniff out zombies." Fisher was staring at him, his expression inscrutable. "Look," Knopf went on, "you're familiar with the morphic field the-

ory, right? The idea that zombies move in large groups because their brains are linked by a neuro-electric field in the
reptilian core of their brains. Jimmy can pick up on that morphic field."

"I've heard the theory, doctor. I've also heard a lot of re-
spectable scientists say that it's a bunch of rubbish."

"It's not rubbish, captain. You've probably experienced it
yourself. Ever felt somebody staring at you from across the
room? Or have you ever thought of somebody completely
out of the blue, and then moments later they call you on the
phone? Ever watched a large flock of birds change direction
without running into each other? How about watched a school
of fish? Same thing. It's not rubbish. It's a documented fact.
And it's what allows Jimmy to do what he does. Think of how
helpful that would be on the battlefield. Think of the tactical
advantage you'd have if you knew where your enemy was all
the time."

"Anybody can find a zombie, doctor. Just go outside the
walls and make a lot of noise. You'll find plenty in no time."

The military, Knopf thought. Such fools. They couldn't
even come up with new jokes, much less open their minds to
new possibilities. It was no wonder they were getting their
butts handed to them on the battlefield. And if Captain Fisher
was any indication of the kind of officer the High Command
was turning out, the future looked bleak indeed.

"Yes," Knopf said, "but the trick, as I'm sure they taught
you in your officer training school, is to find the enemy before they find you. Wouldn't you agree?"

"We already have sensors, doctor. The robots can detect
zombies with an eighty-six percent accuracy rate. In my
opinion, that's—"

"Hardly an acceptable margin of error," Knopf said, shaking his head. "Not when lives are on the line. And eighty-six
percent is nothing compared to what Jimmy's capable of.
Wait until we arrive in Mill Valley, captain. Your robots

claim to have cleared the town of every last zombie. What will happen if that boy in there is able to lead us to even one zombie? What will you say then?"

"It'll never happen."

"All I ask is for you to keep an open mind, captain," Knopf said.

"You're asking me to believe in mumbo jumbo, doctor. I prefer to put my faith in robots and bullets."

Knopf glanced over at Jimmy. The boy was tossing in his sleep. Nerves, probably. Or bad dreams. Poor kid. Sleep was usually the only time his mind got any rest, the only time he could turn off his gift.

"Just you wait, captain. Tomorrow, that boy's going to make a believer out of you."

2

"All stop!" Fisher shouted.

The expedition ground to a halt. They'd been walking for hours, and the clattering and clanking and whirring of a full company of robots had made a tremendous racket that even now, in the sudden silence that followed the captain's command, continued to ring in Jimmy Finder's ears.

But the ringing only lasted a moment. Once the racket faded, the pulsing images of the dead flooded back into his brain. The town was definitely not clear. He could sense hundreds of pulses going off all around him, like he was standing in the middle of a huge orchestra made of nothing but big bass drums, all of them pounding out a violent and relentless and tuneless rhythm.

He groaned in misery, wanting only to curl up in his hammock and fall asleep. Going outside like this, with nothing to shield him from all those morphic pulses, was crippling.

Dr. Knopf had tried to teach him a few tricks to get rid of the pain, like focusing on a single thought-presence and letting everything else fall away, but most of the tricks were too hard to do outside of the lab. And right now, he could barely open his eyes his head hurt so badly.

I can't do this, he thought.

James.

Jimmy stiffened in alarm. He looked around, uncertain who was talking to him. He was surrounded by Troopbots. They had no faces, only curved, featureless metal plates that they turned toward their human masters whenever they needed to speak or were spoken to, but none of them were looking at him now. They stood like statues, tall and mute in the settling dust and gloom of evening.

And there were no humans anywhere around him. Dr. Knopf and the soldiers had moved to the shade of the portico of a deserted gas station, talking in hushed tones. Knopf wasn't even looking in his direction.

It is you, isn't it? My God, how long I've waited!

That time the voice was so strong it caused his eyes to fly open wide. The hairs on the back of his neck were standing on end, as though from static electricity. He could feel the blood rush to his head. He was dizzy, his cheeks flushed with an uncomfortable heat. It wasn't just a voice, he realized, but a thought. A thought with weight, with force behind it.

The sensation didn't last long, though. The dizziness faded. A cold sweat replaced the heat on his cheeks. He had a very real, almost tangible sense of the contact fading. The next instant, all trace of the link—yes, that was it; it had been a link he felt, like another mind wrapping its grip around his mind—echoed away, leaving him confused and feeling somehow vulnerable.

Again he looked around.

No one was paying him any attention.

He cocked his head to one side, trying to make sense of what he had just felt. Dr. Knopf had always said his power was of a class known as remote viewing. He could sense zombies, locate them with a degree of precision the machines couldn't even begin to approach, but only that. He had never heard voices before. Thought-speech was out of the range of his abilities, much as people were unable to hear the high-pitched tones of a dog whistle. And for that Jimmy was supposed to be thankful. Dr. Knopf had told him so, and his own short excursions outside the lab had backed that up. It was hard enough holding on to his sanity while sensing the morphic fields that emanated from the dead. If he could hear the thoughts of the living as well . . .

But then, what was happening to him? Was this something new?

The expedition had stopped on a hill road above the little town of Mill Valley. Jimmy walked through the perfectly ordered rows of Troopbots and continued on until he was well out in front of the rest of the expedition. From here, he could look down on the whole expanse of the ruined town. The mind-voice was coming from somewhere down there, under the rubble.

Cautiously, one small bit at a time, he opened his mind and searched the ruins. This always hurt, even in the controlled circumstances of the laboratory, but he was curious.

Gritting his teeth, he sent out a thought:

Who are you? How do you know my name?

Jimmy waited, his mind open and unguarded.

Who are you?

But there was nothing. Not even the morphic pulsing of a zombie's brain. The evening gloom settling over the town was like a burial shroud, silent and unfathomably deep. Was it any wonder it frightened him so?

3

Why won't you answer me!

The mind-voice slashed like a knife through Jimmy's sleep. He flinched awake, eyes shooting open in panic. His breaths were coming in fast, shallow gulps, his body soaked with sweat.

Please stop! Oh, God, please stop. You're hurting me!

He sent the thought out in desperation. His head felt like it was about to split open, like there was a crazy little man inside there going to town with a hatchet on his brain.

I need help. I need help now!

Jimmy gasped. The pain was coming in waves now. He gritted his teeth against it, tensing the muscles in his temples, and surprisingly, that helped a little. The pain started to ebb away.

Who are you?

But there was no need to ask the question, for now that the pain was no longer tearing him apart, Jimmy knew.

The mind-voice belonged to his father.

Yes, James! It's me! Oh, thank God you've come!

They told me you were dead.

Jimmy dropped out of the hammock he'd slung between the gas pumps of the abandoned gas station and staggered numbly toward the moonlit road, where the robots stood in silent, perfectly ordered rows.

They told me you were dead.

Do I sound dead to you? James, come to me. I need help.

Nodding slowly, transfixed by the mind-voice pulling him toward the town, Jimmy began to walk.

4

The silence hanging over the town was massive. Jimmy could feel it like a presence, vast and powerful, full of menace.

Many people had died here. In the four days since the army retook the town the birds and the rats had descended on the corpses that were still heaped in the gutters and had begun to feast. The carrion feeders watched him silently as he passed, their eyes gleaming yellow and full of hate, their bodies wet with gore. So many dead, Jimmy thought. Such a terrible waste. Instinctively, he found himself emptying his mind, measuring his breathing, the way Dr. Knopf had taught him, so that he could stay calm when facing the horror of a badly decomposed zombie.

But not even Dr. Knopf's calming lessons prepared him for the horror of this place. The fighting here must have been intense. Besides the bodies and the carrion feeders, hardly a wall was free of bullet holes. A few of the buildings had been reduced to rubble. Many more were burned to blackened skeletons.

And no matter where he looked, no matter what road he took, the silence was everywhere.

Daddy, which way?

Daddy.

That word stopped him, and he couldn't help but smile. It sounded funny to him. He'd spent his entire life an orphan, the subject of countless stupid tests, trying to justify what he did for people who seemed only interested in mocking him and treating him like a freak—and now here he was calling for his daddy

The military men already thought of him as a runt, he knew that. What would they think of him now? They'd call him pathetic. Or worse. But what did they know? They weren't orphans. They hadn't walked in his shoes, cried his tears, felt the kind of heartsick loneliness that carried him off to sleep each night. Screw them. So what if he walked around the world calling for his daddy? What did they know about it?

Feeling mean, feeling bitter, Jimmy wandered the ruins, searching for a way down under the town. He sent out his mind-voice constantly, trying to get his father to answer. But he never felt anything more than a curious tickling sensation at the base of his skull. Even as he opened up more and more, out of desperation, there was nothing but the town's foreboding silence.

And then, he found it. A way down.

He had turned down an alleyway because he sensed it was the right way to go, and that same feeling had led him to a half-hidden flight of stairs. They terminated in a rusted metal doorway marked:

MILL VALLEY WATER AUTHORITY
AUTHORIZED PERSONNEL ONLY

This was it.

The hint of a smile appeared at the corner of his mouth. Trust your instincts, Knopf had told him. Well, he had trusted his instincts, and they led right where he wanted to go.

Then Jimmy wriggled the knob.

Locked, damn it.

He rammed it with his shoulder and only managed to hurt himself.

Out of frustration, he picked up a piece of rebar from the sidewalk and banged on the knob until it snapped off.

The hinges groaned as the door fell open.

Leaning forward, he peered into the darkness, gagging on

the noisome stench of sewage coming up from the levels below. Jimmy opened his mind, intending to find his father's mind-voice, but instead was hit by something else.

Do not go down there.

"What?" Jimmy said. As before, he looked around, because this voice was different from his father's. It seemed to be someone talking to him. But he was alone. A sheet of newspaper, carried by a breeze, drifted down the empty street. Nothing else moved.

"Who's talking?" Jimmy asked.

If you go down there you will die.

"Tell me who you are," Jimmy insisted.

This is Comm Six. State your designation.

"My designation? What the . . . I'm Jimmy."

He shook his head, trying to make sense of the sensation the voice was causing in his ears. It wasn't a voice. Not exactly. It was a mind-voice, like his father's, but very different. Where his father's voice was a spike trying to hammer its way into his brain, this voice was like insects buzzing around in his head. And yet it was just as clear, just as insistent, as his father's. Only it was . . . soothing somehow. Not at all harsh.

What's a Comm Six?

I am Comm Six.

Yeah, but what does that mean? Who are you? How come you can talk to me?

I am a Combot. I directed the robots that fought to retake this town. I was damaged. I was left behind.

I've never heard of a Combot. And you don't sound like any robot I've ever heard of.

I am not like other robots. I am a Combot. I am sentient.

Sentient? What's that mean?

It means that I am aware of my own presence. I know there is a me and a you and that we are different from each other. I can think.

Can't other robots do that, like Warbots?

Not like I do. Warbots have adaptive programming. They have built-in algorithms that allow them to interpret their environment within a narrow variety of preprogrammed ways. I do not have those limitations. My thinking is based on nonlinear models, more like your own.

I've never heard of robots being able to do stuff like that.

I was an experiment.

Jimmy laughed. "Uh-huh. You and me both."

Why do you laugh? You are in danger. Do not go into the sewers. There are many zombies down there still.

I don't sense any. Usually I can sense the zombies. That's what I do.

Perhaps the lead residue is blocking you.

I don't get blocked. My sensors aren't like yours. And besides, my dad's down there.

A pause.

There are only zombies down below.

Yeah?

Yes.

Well, I guess we'll see about that, won't we?

5

The ground shook beneath the Warbot's weight. To Knopf it looked like some grossly deformed Tyrannosaurus Rex, a tank on two monstrously thick mechanical legs. It advanced down the rubble-strewn ruins of Oak Street and stopped in front of Fisher, bowing its enormous head down to eye level with the captain in a whir of servos and pneumatic sighs.

"We have searched the town, sir. The sensors do not register the boy or his ankle monitor."

"Yeah, well, he didn't go somewhere else. He's here."

A pause.

"What are your orders, sir?"

"Find him."

"We have scanned everywhere, sir."

"You haven't scanned where he's at. Scan again. I'll tell you when to stop."

"Yes, sir."

The Warbot left to resume its search.

"Trouble?" Knopf asked to the young captain's back.

"It's all the lead dust," Fisher said, turning on him. The captain adjusted the surgical mask he wore, clearly frustrated with it. Mill Valley's smelting factory had been destroyed during the fight to retake the town and it scattered lead particulates and aerosolized bits of brick all over everything. The masks *were* uncomfortable, tending as they did to trap sweat at the corners of the mouth, making the wearer feel like they were constantly drooling, but they were absolutely necessary. No one wanted to breathe in that stuff. Especially because the robots kicked so much of it up into the air. "It's playing havoc with the robots, everything from their sensors to their servos. It's no wonder we lost so many robots in the fight."

"Or that you misstated the presence of zombies here."

"You have no basis to support that comment, doctor."

Fair enough, Knopf thought, and nodded.

They had already looked over a good part of the town, and even now, the Troopbots were sifting through buildings and overgrown lots, continuing the search. But even with the robots tirelessly performing their duties, Knopf couldn't help but feel frustrated. He'd grown used to Jimmy's precise directions, his ability to describe exactly where a zombie was hidden, and the waiting and the uncertainty of doing it the military's way was maddening.

Before Jimmy, everyone believed the zombies were nothing more than dead-meat husks. Beyond a few weak electrical impulses in the reptilian core of their brains, which generated the morphic fields that allowed them to find each other and to move around, searching for living brains, the zombies were thought to have no neurological function whatsoever. Certainly they retained no sense of self, no memories, no desires. They possessed only an insatiable need to feed on living tissue. Most scientists stopped short, however, of accepting Knopf's ideas of morphic fields. That was, until Jimmy came along.

Knopf remembered asking him once how he did it, what it felt like to sense a dead man's mind.

"It hurts," Jimmy had said. "Beyond that, it's hard to describe."

But then, several months later, on a foggy morning in early May, the two of them had taken a walk outside the lab, and through the dense screen of fog they'd seen sentries up on the walls, picking their way with flashlights, the beams muted but distinct in the sodden air.

Jimmy had stopped and stared.

Knopf continued walking for a few steps, and then turned back to see what was wrong.

"That right there," Jimmy said, pointing at the flashlight beams bobbing on the wall. "That's what it looks like in my head."

"When you sense the zombies, you mean?"

"Yeah. It looks like that. Like flashlight beams in the fog. Only the light feels like a current, you know? Like the way you can feel water moving over your skin. Or how you can sense static electricity when it makes the hairs stand up on your arms."

The description had impressed Knopf. Little moments like that had brought them closer together, and if he wasn't exactly a father to Jimmy, he imagined he at least qualified as a benevolent uncle.

"If the boy's around here, we'll find him," Fisher said.

Knopf realized he'd been drifting. He glanced at Fisher, a vacant look on his face.

"Doctor? Did you hear me? I said we'll find him."

Knopf nodded.

"Why do you suppose he ran off?"

"I don't know," Knopf answered truthfully. "It hurts his head terribly to be out of the laboratory like this. There's so much mind-noise."

The captain rolled his eyes. "Well, if he can't handle the heat, sounds like he needs to get out of the kitchen."

Knopf looked at him in surprise. It was a cruel thing to say, even for Fisher. But what did Fisher know, anyway? He was too young to remember a world before the zombies. All his adult life had been spent in the army. Fisher knew soldiering and little else. It may have made him an impressive man, commanding and resourceful beyond his years, but it hadn't taught him compassion.

Knopf, though, remembered the world as it had been. He remembered eating a meal without having to glance over his shoulder. He remembered not having to sleep in shifts, a weapon always at the ready. He remembered his wife, and his little boy. Knopf remembered being human, something he doubted Fisher could lay any claim to.

But perhaps more important, Fisher wasn't a father. He couldn't speak to the world of a child. Sure, he had been a child, but he hadn't also been a parent. What did he know of the pain, the fear, the joy that came with raising a child? As a soldier he claimed to be fighting the most important war humanity had ever fought, a war for the survival of the species. And yet, he had no direct emotional stake in its survival. It was just an academic proposition for him. Human lives were simply numbers for him, pieces to be moved around a game board, little different from the robots under his command.

Knopf had essentially raised Jimmy. The boy had been

handed off to him less than a month after Knopf's own son had died at the hands of the zombie horde, and Knopf, wounded to his core, had at first held the screaming toddler at a disdainful and resentful distance. He had looked at the scrawny, screaming brat, and all he'd been able to think about was himself, standing in the middle of a road at the crest of a hill, looking down on the base housing where he'd lived with his wife and child, zombies streaming out of the bungalow, blood covering their faces and chests like bibs, and the resentment had grown to an intense hatred.

But that hatred softened by degrees.

For several years, Jimmy had been unable to do anything but cower in a corner, screaming and yelling anytime anybody got remotely close to him. Only gradually, through repeated effort and a thousand small acts of kindness, had Knopf managed to lure the boy out of the shadows. It was longer still before the boy would sleep anywhere but under the cot in Knopf's office. And across the gulf of those years, the two of them had healed each other. They'd learn to trust one another. Neither was emotionally seaworthy, not yet anyway, but together, they were getting close.

And now this. The boy missing . . .

6

Jimmy stopped at the top of a rickety metal staircase, waiting for his eyes to adjust to the darkness. Farther on ahead he could see what looked like a glowing blue slime coating the handrails and parts of the walls. The glow was faint, but it provided enough light to give him a sense of the curved, tiled tunnel around him.

The stairs shook and groaned beneath his weight, moving with every step, and he was almost to the bottom when the metal suddenly snapped and gave way, dropping him into the muck on the bottom level.

He barely managed to roll out of the way as the structure crashed down around him.

Afterwards, surrounded by tangled pieces of rusting metal, he sat there blinking up at the ruined staircase, looking like the exoskeleton of some giant, malformed insect up there.

Grunting, he sat up.

The room in which he found himself was a horror. There were rotting bodies everywhere. Arms and legs and ropes of intestines hung from rusted piles of equipment, and the place smelled powerfully bad, worse even than the zombies Dr. Knopf occasionally brought into the lab for Jimmy to practice with.

Something moved beside him, and Jimmy turned, only to find himself nose to nose with a zombie. Its face was dripping with blood and sewage, eyes opaque, like cataracts, yet at the same time intensely alive with hunger and violence. The skin around its mouth was ripped and shredded, exposing its blood-blackened teeth so that it almost seemed to be grinning at him.

Jimmy screamed, backpedaling as fast as he could go.

The zombie stayed where it was. It sniffed the air. It opened its mouth, almost as though to taste what it smelled, but instead let out an aching moan.

The next instant it scrambled after him.

Still scrambling, Jimmy tripped and landed in a mass of arms and legs. He jumped to his feet, only to realize a moment later that the arms wrapping around him belonged to a Docbot, the cord tightening around his knees the shoulder sling from the Docbot's medpac.

The zombie was coming closer, clawing its way over the wreckage of robots and dead bodies. Jimmy looked around for a way out, but there was none. He was standing at the apex of a curving tunnel, both directions extending off into darkness that could hide anything.

But he did have the medpac. Those things were heavy. Jimmy had seen them used back at the lab. Carrying one was like lugging around a bag of bricks, and they'd make a good weapon.

He tugged at the shoulder strap until the pack came loose from the muck.

By that point the zombie was almost on him. Jimmy stumbled backwards, and at the same time swung the pack with both hands, smashing it against the zombie's jaw with the satisfying crunch of broken bone.

The zombie went sprawling backwards into the sewage and rotting bodies, landing in a twisted heap.

Jimmy didn't wait to see if it would get back up. He turned to run.

No!

Jimmy slowed, but didn't stop. That was Comm Six's voice.

I have to get out of here.

No! There is no time to run. Hide. Right now.

Where?

Under the robot. Now. Before the zombie gets up.

Jimmy dropped to the floor, crawling under the wrecked bodies and robots, and pulled the Docbot whose medpac he had just used over on top of him.

Be very still.

It was good advice. During the many experiments Dr. Knopf had put him through, Jimmy had learned that the zombies' morphic field acuity was imperfect at best. Certainly not as strong or as finely tuned as his. If a person remained very still, and was able to clear his thoughts, a passing zombie would think them no different from a lamp post, or a mailbox, or any of the other inanimate objects that populated the world.

Through a hole in the Docbot's damaged skull, Jimmy watched the zombie slowly scan the ruined figures at its feet. Flies swarmed around its head. Filthy water dripped from its beard. It turned its mangled face left, then right, and then walked off down the darkness of the receding tunnel.

Jimmy listened as the sounds of its splashing grew faint, then he slowly climbed out from under the Docbot.

You must find a way out. There are many zombies down here. You must leave.

Jimmy shook his head.

I can't. My father's down here.

You will not leave?

I can't.

Your decision is unwise. But if you must stay, you should have a weapon.

Jimmy huffed at that one. *Thanks, that's great advice. I'll remember to bring one next time I'm crawling through a zombie-infested sewer.*

I can lead you to a weapon.

Jimmy stopped. *You can?*

One hundred and sixteen feet to your left you will find a small room. One of the soldiers who died retaking this town is still there. He is a zombie now, but his corpse still carries a weapon. Go now. Move quickly.

He made his way down to the room Comm Six had told him about, noticing as he went how the luminescent scum on the walls seemed to be thickest at the waterline.

Where's this light coming from?

When the army realized they would have to fight down here they seeded the sewer water with bioluminescent algae. It cleans the water and glows with the light you see. Eventually, the water in these sewers will be clean enough for human use.

Oh. That's kind of cool.

The room you need is on your left. Careful now. The zombie will attack when he sees you.

Jimmy stepped into the room. There were several pieces of metal tubing at his feet, old rusted pipes that had fallen from the ceiling. He picked one of them up, tested its heft, and decided it would work.

The zombie Comm Six had warned him about was on the far side of the room.

As Jimmy watched, it pawed at the wall, scratching uselessly at the mold-covered stone wall, its fingernails long since ripped from the tips of its fingers.

Then Jimmy noticed that the thing had no legs.

From the waist down there was nothing but ropes of viscera and blackened shards of bone protruding from the torso.

His stomach rose into his throat, and he coughed.

The sound got the zombie's attention. It turned its head sharply, and an urgent, hungry moan rose up from its rotting throat.

Move quickly. Do not let it make noise.

The zombie pulled itself toward Jimmy with its ruined fingers, its moaning growing more insistent, more desperate.

"Right," Jimmy muttered.

He stepped into the room with the metal pipe in both hands, raised high above his head. The zombie held its broken fingers up toward him, trying to grab him.

But Jimmy was quicker.

He sidestepped the zombie's hand and brought the pipe down as hard as he could.

Jimmy had never killed a zombie before, and he was surprised, and sickened, by how easy it was. Three quick strokes and the back of the thing's head was pulverized into a ruined mess of blood, hair, and bone.

It took a moment for his mind to break through the adrenaline rush.

I did it. Oh, God, I think I'm gonna puke.

The weapon is against the far wall.

"Huh?"

The weapon. Take it now.

Feeling dizzy, lightheaded, Jimmy scanned the far wall. The weapon was in a leather gun belt wrapped around the zombie's severed hips and legs.

You must move quickly. The zombies have heard you. They are approaching.

He had to peel the gun belt off the corpse's bloody hips. It made a sucking sound as he pulled it free.

This is so gross. I don't know if I can—

Hurry.

He worked the buckle open, then wrapped it around his own waist and pulled it as tight as it would go. Jimmy moved his hips back and forth. The gun belt was still loose, but it didn't fall off, and that was something at least.

Okay, I've got the gun. Which way do I go now?

Nothing.

Jimmy opened his mind a little more.

Comm Six, you there? Which way do I go?

But the Combot's voice was gone. There was nothing but the echoes of water dripping from the ceiling somewhere down the tunnel. And from farther on, barely audible, came the faint moaning of the living dead.

Well, he thought, pulling the pistol, here goes nothing.

And he stepped out into the tunnel.

7

With only the faint blue light from the algae growing on the walls to guide him, Jimmy headed deeper into the sewers. The water was up to his knees and every step made a splash that echoed a long way down the tunnels. He tried to reach out with his mind and sense the zombies that Comm Six had told him were down here, but in his mind he saw nothing but a gray depthless fog. For the first time in his life, he realized, his mind was a quiet place.

It might have felt good, if he wasn't so scared. And so unsure of himself. What are you doing down here? he asked himself. Dr. Knopf had told him bunches of times that his parents were dead. He'd accepted that a long time ago. And didn't he have his own memories from the night the dead overran this town? They were vague, cloudy memories, but they were there.

He remembered a room with dark-colored carpet and walls of wood paneling. He remembered a striped couch and a big chair that his infantile mind understood as DADDY'S CHAIR.

He remembered his mom, the source of kindness and nourishment and safety. She smelled like comfort, like goodness. At least, that was the way she smelled in his memories. But the next instant, she'd gone wild with fear.

And he remembered his father, not his father's face, but the anger in the man's voice. Daddy, the protector, the violent one, driving his shoulder into the door, yelling at his mother to take the boy and *go, go, go!*

The room filled with smoke, seeping under the door, crawling in through the windows.

The memory broke apart with the first tinges of smoke. From there, all he remembered were broken images, crazy things. More screaming, and zombies reaching for him everywhere he turned. He remembered getting separated from his parents, his mother's cries echoing away into nothingness in the smoke that was filling the house where they lived.

And then, when he realized he was alone, that his parents were gone, some kind of light had turned on inside his head.

Through the smoke, through the screams, he could sort of see the bad people trying to hurt him. They glowed in the smoke, shimmering like flashlight beams, except that the light carried with it a bad . . . was it a smell? That was the only way his mind had been able to frame the sensation. Their minds smelled bad. The light that came from them was bad. They wanted to hurt him. He'd taken that knowledge and he had . . .

What?

He didn't know what he'd done from there.

He had gone walking, he supposed.

The next thing he could remember for sure was sleeping on the cot in Dr. Knopf's office, crying himself to sleep. Sometimes, Dr. Knopf would read from a book about a big rabbit and a little rabbit and the big rabbit saying this is how much I love you. He remembered sometimes Dr. Knopf would cry when he read the book, and how the man's tears and the choking sob in his voice had scared him for some reason he couldn't quite understand. And he remembered grabbing Dr. Knopf's leg in a stranglehold whenever the military men came by to ask questions and laugh at the answers they got.

Ah, ýes, Dr. Knopf.

There was the other problem of Jimmy's life.

For several years now he'd understood what he meant to the High Command. He was an experiment, an asset. They talked about him the same way they talked about programming groups for Warbots. Or pallets of ammunition. Or the shifting lines in the sand that divided the living from the dead.

Only Dr. Knopf thought of him as Jimmy.

And that was what made things so hard.

Dr. Knopf was as close to a parent as Jimmy had ever really known, but he wasn't the ideal parent that Jimmy always imagined his real parents would have been. He was distant. He could be cold. Sometimes, he could be harsh, even cruel when Jimmy failed to cooperate. Dr. Knopf was the one who made the rules, and Jimmy hated him for that. He had many memories of the two of them screaming at each other, Jimmy calling Knopf the meanest man he'd ever met, and Knopf, so angry his fists trembled with rage, making harsh, declarative statements that made Jimmy shrink into himself. Things like, "I don't care what you think. I just care that you do what I say." Or, "Nobody asked your opinion. Just do what I tell you. Why can't you get that through your head?" Or, "I'm sorry. I love . . . I just want you to be happy, Jimmy. Please, do this for me. This one last test. Finish this, and we can get some dinner. I'll do the macaroni and cheese you like so much. . . ."

It was the occasional kindness that made things so confusing. There were times when Knopf actually felt like a father to him. And he was sure Knopf felt the same. Why then did they always pull away from each other in the end? Why did the rare moments of closeness always end with the look of love fading from Knopf's face, and a terribly remote sadness invariably taking its place? The man was haunted by his memories. Jimmy knew that. But why did memory have to make things so hard?

There were so many questions, and so few answers.

But still you haven't asked the right question.

Jimmy stopped.

"Daddy?"

Yes, James.

What question? What did I forget to ask?

How, James. How come you can sense the dead? Didn't you ever think to ask? When the military men were laughing at you, didn't it seem strange that you knew you were right?

Yeah, I guess. Well, no, not really. I always felt like I was wrong.

Because they weren't inside your head. They didn't know what you knew. But I do, James. And you know how I know?

Jimmy shook his head, unable to articulate the thought aloud.

I know because I have the power, too. It turned on the night the zombies came to Mill Valley, didn't it?

"Yes," Jimmy said, breathlessly. *Turned on* was exactly how he had come to think of that night, like somebody had just flipped a light switch inside his head.

The same thing happened for me, James. My power to sense the zombies, it flipped on that very night.

You mean like a light switch.

Yes, exactly like that.

Daddy?

Yes?

Why isn't it working now? The sight, I mean. Usually I can sense the zombies. I could sense them before I came down here.

I don't know. It doesn't work down here for me, either. That's how I got trapped. Now hurry, James. I need help.

But Jimmy didn't move. Ahead of him was some kind of catwalk, another metal platform like the kind that had collapsed under his weight back at the entrance to the sewers.

What's wrong? Why aren't you coming to me?

Jimmy turned and looked behind him. The blue light from the algae didn't carry far. Twenty or thirty feet down and his visibility was gone, swallowed by the darkness. But something was down there. He could hear it splashing, and moaning.

James?

He could see silhouettes down there now, bunches of them, coming toward him.

Daddy, I think I'm in trouble.

8

Jimmy pulled his pistol just as the first zombie lumbered into view.

As she came closer, the faint blue glow from the algae lit her ghastly features. It was a woman, or had been once. Her shoulder-length hair was matted now with blood and clods of mud. Her neck seemed unable to hold up the weight of her head, making her hair hang like a curtain in front of her face. The skin on her arms and neck was oozing with abscesses and open cuts that no longer bled. The clothes had been torn from her chest, and when she moved, black ribs showed where the flesh had been eaten away. She raised her gnarled hands and began to moan.

There were more behind her.

A lot more.

Jimmy raised the huge pistol, holding it with the two-handed grip all children inside the walls were taught. He squeezed off a round, and the blast clapped over his ears like an enormous pair of hands, leaving him momentarily deaf, and stunned.

He didn't even realize the lead zombie had closed the distance between them until she put her filthy hands on him.

But that was enough to get him moving.

He ran for the platform he'd seen a few moments before,

but stopped at the railing. The stairs leading down to the aqueduct must have collapsed during the fighting, for they lay in a broken, rusted heap twenty feet below him.

Where more zombies had gathered, attracted by his gunshot.

The dead went into a frenzy when he appeared on the landing.

Oh, God, oh, God, oh, God, Daddy, what do I do?

The woman with the black ribs was clutching the air between them. He could smell the rotten-meat stench she carried with her. Even over the open sewage he could smell her. Another three steps and she'd be on him.

"No," he said, kicking at her. His heart was pounding painfully in his chest. "Stay back!"

But zombies, of course, don't ever stay back, and Jimmy was forced to back up until he was pressed against the railing.

It was then he knew what he had to do.

He jumped.

9

Dr. Knopf stood in front of what was left of the Huntington Movie Theater, wiping the sweat from the back of his neck. Not even ten o'clock yet and already the sun was punishing him. He had never handled fieldwork well, and now that he was getting on into middle age, he had even less patience for it.

But he had to deal with it. At least this one last time. Jimmy was out here, somewhere, and he had to find him.

But which way?

To his left, the street was piled high with the rubble of collapsed buildings. To his right, the street was a silent canyon between windowless buildings. It would be easier to go that way, but just because it was easy was no guarantee that Jimmy had gone that way. The boy had survived here as a toddler because of his gift, going not where the going was easiest, but where his senses told him it was safest. Avoid the zombies. That would have been his only concern.

So which way was that?

"Well, how about it, Dr. Knopf? Any ideas?"

Knopf shifted his attention away from the crumbling buildings and looked at the young captain. Fisher's uniform was still crisp, his tie knot still regulation perfect. Despite all the walking they'd done in this godawful heat, his gig line was straight as an arrow. The man didn't seem to know how to sweat.

"He could be anywhere," Knopf said. "I suggest doing another sensor sweep."

"We've done eight sensor sweeps already, doctor. Are you sure the boy even went into town? Perhaps he ran back to the compound."

God save me from idiots in uniform, Knopf thought. Yes, they'd done their sensor sweeps, but Fisher himself had admitted that the high concentrations of lead in the ground were playing havoc with their equipment. It was probably doing the same thing to Jimmy, though to what degree there was no way of knowing. He'd have to do further research. The only remedy was to keep running the sensor sweeps, keep tracking over the same ground. Eventually, they'd hit pay dirt.

"He's here, captain. I'm sure of that."

"Hmm," Fisher said. "You have a special bond with the boy, I suppose."

Knopf looked at him sharply. He didn't like the way that sounded, the nasty implication in the captain's tone. "What exactly is that supposed to mean, captain?"

Fisher raised his eyebrows, as though to feign ignorance.

"Only that you raised him. It would be natural, I suppose, for you to learn how he thinks."

Knopf didn't answer that.

"You were given charge of the boy shortly after your own wife and son were killed. Isn't that right, doctor? It would make sense that you'd invest extra effort to keep the boy close. Perhaps he filled some psychological hole in your head?"

"That's pretty damn bold of you, captain."

"Perhaps. Perhaps not. You forget, doctor, that I have an assignment as well. You are trying to get me to believe in magic. My job, if you'll pardon my French, is to make sure you aren't full of shit."

And then it hit Knopf what was really going on here, what the captain was actually accusing him of.

"Captain, are you suggesting that I faked more than a decade's worth of research just so that child could take the place of my own son? Is that really what you're suggesting?"

Fisher shrugged. "You tell me," he said.

"You're a bastard, captain. A certifiable bastard."

"Maybe. But that still doesn't answer my question."

Knopf nearly hit him in the nose. He might have, too, if at that moment the street to his right hadn't erupted with yelling and gunfire.

Knopf ducked his head, backing away from the commotion.

"What the . . . ?" Fisher said. He was standing with arms akimbo, peering into the clouds of dust pouring down the street.

The next instant two troopers hurried out of the fog. A steadily retreating line of Troopbots was right behind them, firing into the dust.

One of the troopers, a soldier named Collins, hurried toward Fisher. "Zombies, sir! A whole mess of 'em!"

"What the hell happened?"

"We were going building to building, searching the rubble. A couple of our Troopbots found a door down to the sewer system and when they opened it, they uncovered a whole nest of them things."

"How many?"

"Hard to tell, sir. Forty, maybe fifty. They overran our Troopbots."

They could hear moaning now. A few of the approaching zombies were visible through the screen of dust, but from the volume of the moans it was obvious there were many more behind them.

"So much for the eighty-six percent accuracy of your sensors, captain?" said Knopf. "Guess you can never trust a zombie to play fair."

"Don't start with me, doctor."

The next instant he was on the radio, calling for the Warbots to converge on his location.

Knopf felt their approach before he heard them, the tread of their Tyrannosaurus-size legs sending shudders through the pavement.

When the Warbots entered the intersection, they turned immediately to the advancing horde of zombies. Their limited AI capability allowed them to process the scene and reach immediate conclusions about what had to be done. Without waiting for orders, they strode to the leading edge of the street, took up side-by-side positions, and opened fire into the approaching horde, mowing down the zombies beneath a hail of automatic weapons fire.

To Knopf, it seemed the shooting went on forever, and when the dust finally settled, the rattle of the guns still rang in his ears.

But the street was still. Nothing moved.

One of the Warbots turned to Captain Fisher. "What are your orders, sir?"

Fisher looked mad enough to spit. He glared at Knopf before turning back to his robots.

"Another sensor sweep," he growled. "Find that kid."

10

As he went over the edge, Jimmy saw a crowd of zombies lunging for him. Their ruined faces and bloody hands loomed large in his sight, and for a terrifying moment he thought he was going to be shredded alive before he hit the water. But when he landed in the sewer channel he kept his head under the water and started thrashing for the far side of the channel.

The water was black as ink and he couldn't see where he was going. He pushed and pulled his way through a forest of legs even as their hands groped at his back.

One of them managed to get a grip on the collar of his shirt.

Jimmy twisted away, breaking the zombie's fingers, but still it held on. He swatted at their hands and kicked whenever he could, and somehow managed to reach the stone ledge on the far side of the channel.

They stayed on him, though.

He saw a rotten wooden pallet leaning against the wall under the ledge and climbed on top of it. The ledge was another five feet or so above that, and he jumped for it, hooking his elbows over the edge so he had enough support to pull himself up. He kicked at the smooth cement wall below him, his toes sliding on the algae that grew there while hands groped at his shoes.

"Get away!" he yelled, pumping his legs with everything he had. "Get . . . away!"

And then he was up and over the edge, his full weight resting on the ledge. Jimmy rolled over onto his back and sobbed, his chest heaving.

What was he going to do? There was no place to go.

He rolled over on his side and stared down at the hungry crowd. Their hands were just a few inches below the ledge, their moans reaching a frenzied intensity. He knew he should keep moving, but the panic and adrenaline that had helped him climb had left him numb, and all he could do now was stare with glassy eyes at the hands clutching for him.

You must get up. You must leave.

Jimmy blinked. The Combot again.

How am I supposed to do that? There's nowhere to go.

Stand up. I will help.

What're you gonna do?

Stand up.

With a strange disconnected feeling, almost like he was dreaming this, Jimmy rose to his feet. The ceiling was arched and this close to the wall he had to bend over slightly to keep from banging his head. It made him feel like a diver looking over the edge of a cliff. Staring straight down into the ravenous horde brought a wave of nausea over him, and he groaned.

What now?

You must move to your left. Eighty feet down that tunnel you will find a large platform. Go there.

That's your plan? What am I supposed to do when I get there?

There is a functioning Warbot there. It will protect you. Go now. You must move quickly.

The Combot wasn't kidding, Jimmy thought. One of the zombies in the front had fallen against the wall, pushed

down by the weight of the horde behind it, and its fellows
were now ramping up its back. A zombie in some kind of
uniform was pulling itself up onto the ledge. The zombie's
lower jaw was almost completely gone, like it had been torn
off. Or shot off. Maggots swarmed in the rotting flesh where
its chin and cheeks had been.

"No," Jimmy muttered, shaking his head.

You must move quickly.

Slowly, inching carefully along the narrow concrete ledge,
hands grasping at his feet, Jimmy made his way to a corner up
ahead. The zombies matched him step for step, their moans
echoing horribly off the walls and quickening his pulse.

*How am I supposed to get down from here? They're fol-
lowing me.*

Round the corner. You will see.

And when he reached the corner, he did see. Immediately
below him was a railing that went across the channel. It wasn't
high enough to keep the zombies at bay forever, but it was high
enough to give him a chance at escape.

Yes, he thought, that's how I'm gonna do it.

He jumped into the water.

The zombies stuck their hands through the railing, but he
was already out of reach and running for the platform.

Right where you said it'd be.

They are coming. You must move quickly.

Jimmy looked back over his shoulder and saw, once again,
that the Combot was correct. Already the zombies had tipped
the railing forward and were scrambling over it. He had maybe
a thirty-foot lead on them.

He closed the last few feet to the platform and rounded
the corner. A sudden, intensely white light flooded his vision, momentarily blinding him.

"You are human," a robotic voice said.

It took a moment for the purple blotches to clear from
Jimmy's sight. When they did, he saw a badly damaged War-

bot trying to stand on its Tyrannosaurus legs—but something was wrong. One of its legs wouldn't work. Its status lights blinked and flickered. It stumbled forward, and then sagged to the ground, the spotlight on its shoulder lighting up the carnage at its feet.

The ground was covered with rotting corpses.

Fear gripped him anew. He had gambled on the Combot's instructions, and this was where it had led him. To an abandoned sewer platform, and no way out.

"Zombies," the Warbot said, raising a .50 caliber machine gun. "Human, you must take cover at the rear of the platform. Move quickly."

Jimmy heard moaning behind him. That was all it took. He ran forward, scrambling over badly decomposed bodies, too frightened to allow the gore into which his fingers were sinking to slow him down.

The shooting started a moment later.

Jimmy reached the back wall, turned, and saw a zombie's head and shoulders atomized by a three-round burst from the Warbot's guns. But every zombie shot as it rounded the corner was replaced by more, and soon the Warbot's gun was blazing in one continuous stream.

But it wasn't enough. The dead kept coming, pouring around the corner faster than the Warbot's gun could put them down. Jimmy, who was so exhausted he could barely move, pushed himself up against the back wall of the platform. There was some kind of vehicle abandoned there, like a rail truck, only on rubber wheels. Its windshield had come loose and broken into two pieces. Jimmy pulled the bigger of the two over him and tried to shrink into the gore of ruined bodies below him.

But it was only a matter of time.

There were just too many of them.

Jimmy's gaze found one zombie that was staring straight at him as it climbed over the pile of torn-up corpses. Its gaze never wavered. It had zeroed in on him and meant to have him.

Jimmy braced himself for the attack.

The zombie fell on top of him, moaning, pawing at the glass with its bloody hands. Jimmy screamed back at the thing, pushing back with everything he had.

And then the zombie's head exploded. One moment it was pounding on the glass, smearing it with blood and sewage, and the next the glass was splashed with bits of bone and brain and clumps of bloody hair. The zombie's headless corpse sagged against the glass as Jimmy gaped in shocked silence.

The sound of gunfire was gone.

So too were the moans.

"Human," the Warbot said. "Human?"

Jimmy had to tilt the glass like a ramp to roll the corpse away, and once it was off him, he could see the gun smoke lingering in the foul sewer air.

"Human, they are gone. Please acknowledge."

"I hear you," Jimmy said.

He stood up and looked around. The far wall was dripping with fresh gore, and there were bodies piled high near the corner. How many? Forty? More than that?

Jimmy couldn't tell.

He turned to the Warbot.

"Thanks," he said, because it was the only thing that came close to how he was feeling at the moment.

"I cannot move. You must go. Gunfire will travel far in these tunnels. More zombies will come."

"How many?"

"Unknown. You must go."

He watched the Warbot as its status lights blinked and dimmed once again. The machine could not die, but if it had an equivalent, it was doing it now. Its lights were going out.

It was then that a thought occurred to Jimmy. Something he had overheard once in the weapons lab.

"Don't Warbots usually work in teams?" he asked. "Where's your partner?"

But the Warbot didn't answer. Its status lights continued to fade, and as Jimmy watched, they went dark permanently.

There was nothing else to do but leave.

11

Jimmy found the second Warbot a few minutes later.

He had returned to the main channel and was following it farther into the sewer system. There were more platforms here, lots of them, and other channels leading off in other directions.

He had entered some kind of hub, he realized, the main part of the sewer system.

What did you do? The zombies are all gone.

For once, his father's mind-voice didn't knife into his head. It was almost pleasant, in fact. Jimmy wasn't sure if it was the tone of surprised gratitude that softened it, or if he was just getting used to their thoughts passing back and forth, but either way the pain was gone. Jimmy let his mind reach out to his father.

Daddy, where are you?

I'm close, Jimmy. Keep coming. Around the next corner to your left.

The fighting, Jimmy saw, must have been intense through here. He had seen plenty of rotting bodies along the way, and even more wrecked Troopbots, but the carnage was especially bad through here. In some places he actually had to climb over the twisted, severed limbs of dead people and the faceless heads of downed robots rusting in the sewer water. And everywhere he turned there were bullet holes in the walls and the ceiling.

Then he rounded the corner and the smell of rot nearly knocked him over.

What lay before him was a gallery of horrors. The room must have been some kind of staging area for large equipment before the fighting, for there were oversized sleds loaded down with machinery and portable pumps and generators scattered around the room. But those were only the backdrop for the carnage Jimmy saw. Corpses were piled three and four deep. Most were so badly decomposed they were unrecognizable, their bodies swollen and discolored and swarming with flies and writhing worms. Others had been eaten, and what remained of their faces was twisted by pain that was frozen there like a picture. One man lay on his back atop a generator, his arms hanging limply off either side, his mouth open in an eternal scream, his torso ripped apart and emptied of its viscera so that he looked like the gaping belly of a canoe. Jimmy saw a dismembered foot here, an upturned hand there, the fingers curled up and inward like the legs of a dying crab.

And standing in the middle of it all, a grotesque king presiding over his court, was his father.

Jimmy's mouth fell open.

The man could barely stand. His right arm had been chewed off just below the elbow, stringy lengths of sinew and shredded flesh hanging from the blackened wound. His neck too was open. Worms fed on the ruins of his throat. The green T-shirt he wore was stained with dried blood, and all Jimmy could read was the word *Nationals* in what had once been white lettering. And his face! Bits of skull showed through the holes in his forehead. His lips were gone, revealing the full horror of his bloodstained teeth. He leered at Jimmy. Almost like he was grinning at him.

Jimmy turned his head, the bile rising in his throat.

Jimmy, look at me.

Slowly, uncertain for a moment that he would even be able to keep his feet, Jimmy straightened up. He faced the train wreck that had once been his father and, running the back of his hand across his face, wiped the spit from his lips.

You lied to me.

For a reason. I had to get you here.

But you lied to me.

You don't need to be frightened of me.

Jimmy backed away, shaking his head.

That was when Jimmy saw the other Warbot. At first it had blended in with the other machinery, one more piece of metal streaked with human gore.

Then it rose to its full height.

Eighteen feet of rusting metal on Tyrannosaurus legs.

It stood so tall it had to stoop to avoid scraping the ceiling. It had fully automatic machine-gun cannons for arms and it turned them in Jimmy's direction.

"I am human," Jimmy said, reciting the mantra that Dr. Knopf had taught him when dealing with robotic sentries. "Confirm my status as human."

The Warbot's status lights flickered wildly, but it made no sound. The guns remained trained on Jimmy.

"Confirm!" Jimmy said.

It's not the robot it used to be. Watch, Jimmy. Let me show you.

The Warbot stooped forward then and swung one of its machine-gun arms under his father. As Jimmy watched, his fear mounting, the robot raised the zombie version of his father into the air and placed him on its shoulders.

Jimmy took a step back.

Do you understand?

Yes. You control that robot.

Yes! That's exactly right. It has a limited intelligence. AI, they call it. It isn't a smart machine, but it's smart enough to be used. Do you see?

No.

Jimmy, look at me.

Jimmy did. He stared up at his father, who rode the Warbot like some demented child playing horsey on his daddy's shoulders, and he was frightened.

This is bad. This is very bad.

No! That's wrong. Jimmy, this is right. Don't you see?

See what?

I control this robot. I can control zombies, too. Anything that has a mind, or had a mind, is like a pawn waiting to be moved. Don't you see the potential? All it takes is a mind that can move those pawns. A mind like mine. A mind like yours.

I want to go home.

You are home, damn it!

The robot took three long strides forward and knelt down, bringing Jimmy's father closer to eye level. Jimmy tried to back away, but his heel caught on a Troopbot's severed arm and he pitched over backwards, landing on his butt.

Don't back away from me!

But Jimmy wasn't moving anymore. For the first time, he could see the wall behind the Warbot. There was a flight of stairs there, and on the wall at the back of the first landing was a red EXIT sign.

A way out.

Don't you see what I'm offering you? Don't you understand what this means? I can make you a king, boy. I've seen into your memories. I've seen how they've used you. Do you want it to stop? Don't you want to give it all back to them? I can help you do that. As father and son, the way it was meant to be.

Slowly, Jimmy stood up.

Answer me.

Glancing across the floor between where he stood and the stairs began, Jimmy picked out the route he was going to take. Dr. Knopf had tried to teach him a trick once to hone his psychic locator skills. Visualize each move, Knopf had told him, picture it in advance. See yourself making it. That way, when you make it for real—

Knopf is the man who raised you, the scientist?

Yes.

The one who experimented on—

Jimmy blocked the rest of it, slamming the door on his father's mind-voice. He heard his father grunt in surprise, and Jimmy ran. He darted around the Warbot's right side, ducking to miss the robot's heavy cannon arm as it rotated toward him, and then he was past it, running for the stairs.

But he didn't move so fast he missed his steps. He picked his way through bodies and machine parts carefully, planting his feet exactly as he had pictured them in his head. He couldn't afford to miss a step. Not now. Not with his father and that Warbot behind him. If he tripped, slipped, they'd be on him. The heavy cannon would knock him to the floor and hold him there. And he had no idea what his father would do after that.

Jimmy was still blocking him with his mind. He had his teeth clenched so tightly his jaw was trembling, his breaths coming fast and noisily through his nose, but he didn't dare let up. His father was no doubt screaming into his brain, and if one of those mind-voice screams got through, Jimmy knew it would be enough to cripple him with pain. He'd never be able to get up.

He hit the stairs at a full sprint and ran up them three at a time. When he reached the landing, he turned and saw his father astride the Warbot, the two of them crashing forward.

They were close, almost on him.

Jimmy kept running up the stairs. He had to scale three flights to reach the promised EXIT door. Once there, he grabbed the handle, and twisted.

It was locked.

"No," he said.

Below him, the Warbot was trying to climb the stairs, even though it was far too big to fit into the narrow confines. But it could force its way up, and that it was doing, banging its huge cannon arms against the railing, smashing through the floor with its enormous metal shoulders. The ground beneath Jimmy's feet was moving, trembling from the impacts.

He tried the door again, yanking on it with everything he had, and it still wouldn't budge.

"Please, no," he said, his voice almost a whimper.

He looked down. The Warbot was slowly crashing its way up through the floor, but that wasn't the worst of it. Through a gap in the split-level stairs Jimmy caught a glimpse of his father's zombified face. It was a hideous, dead face, yellowed with disease and dark with scabs and open, rotting wounds. The right side of his mouth had been damaged somehow, so that the corner of his lips hung slack in an ironic grin.

The eyes, though, those were most certainly not grinning. They were lit by a mad, malignant hatred. There was violence in those eyes that frightened Jimmy down to his bones.

But he still had to get through the door. How?

The gun. Use the gun.

The Combot's voice.

The gun?

Jimmy looked down at his waistband. Sure enough, the pistol was still there, right where he'd stuck it after his narrow escape back at the ledge.

How do I . . . ?

Shoot the knob. Move quickly.

Jimmy took a step back. He drew the weapon and steadied its front sight on the knob. Below him, the Warbot was fast approaching. It was on the next landing down. Jimmy had a few seconds, maybe less. He swallowed hard as he tried to center the front sight on the knob and pulled the trigger.

The gun nearly jumped out of his hands as he staggered backwards, the sound of the shot deafening.

Shaking his head, he looked down at the lock. The knob was hanging at an odd angle from the plane of the door, a big gaping hole just to the left of it. He reached for it, and the knob came away in his hand.

The door fell open.

Run. You must run.

The Combot again.

Where?

I will guide you. Run now. Move as fast as you can.

He lunged through the doorway and into the lobby of a large, shabby building. This, he gathered, had been the home office of the water authority. There were desks everywhere, most of them pushed haphazardly out of the way. Trash lay thick on the floor. A few pieces of furniture had been jammed up against the front door of the building, which meant a few people must have made a final stand here.

But the furniture had been toppled, and the front door behind the pile was hanging from the bottom hinge.

Jimmy ran that way, scaling over the furniture. He was almost through the door when the ground shook and he lost his footing. He landed on top of a desk, facing the length of floor he'd just traversed.

A heaving mound formed in the middle of the floor, the cement there popping and groaning from the Warbot's efforts to push itself upwards from the other side. There was a crash, and the mound cracked and popped. A second crash came immediately after, and the next thing Jimmy knew, the Warbot was busting through the floor, sending bits of tile and chairs and desks flying off in every direction.

The Warbot climbed out of the hole, Jimmy's father still hanging on to its neck, still staring at him with those same hate-filled eyes.

"No," Jimmy said.

Run. Now.

But Jimmy didn't need to be told. He was already sprinting into the street.

12

A bullet skipped off the pavement at Dr. Knopf's feet, hitting the wall behind him. He ducked, and with his hands over his head, turned in every direction, trying to find someplace to run. The air was full of dust, the noise deafening. He felt disoriented, and in his confusion, stepped right into the middle of the fighting.

After their first successful skirmish in front of the movie theater, some of the Troopbots had surrounded another water authority access point to the sewers, their weapons at the ready, and opened the door. It had been like knocking the top off an ant pile. One minute they were expecting a simple mop-up operation of a few remaining zombies, and the next, they were getting overrun, trampled underfoot, ripped to pieces. Knopf had been standing less than thirty feet from one of their Docbots when a wave of zombies knocked it to the ground and pulled it apart like a man being drawn and quartered. They'd been overrun so quickly there was hardly a chance for Knopf to question the strangeness of what he saw. But Captain Fisher was a good soldier, a capable leader. He regrouped his forces, pulling his troops back in ordered rows while at the same time bringing his Warbots forward, where the bigger guns could do some damage. But the battle was decided almost from the beginning. Fisher's expeditionary force was small, intended more for light escort duty than a stand-up fight, and the best he could hope for at this point was to keep his escape route to the rear open. By keeping his lines moving, they at least stood a chance of escaping to a better defensive position.

That was how it looked to Knopf, anyway.

But there was something else, something disturbing. Knopf had spent years studying the zombies in every way possible. Know thy enemy, as Sun Tzu had said. He'd used that knowledge to design and perfect the weapons systems his shop built for the military. But in all his studies, all his observations, he'd always worked under the philosophy that the zombie was a mindless, relentless opponent with no sense of strategy and no skills. Their only strengths were their numbers, a complete lack of fear, and the ability to fight without sleep, without pain, and without ever quitting. They advanced headlong, regardless of the odds, with no sense of winning or losing.

That didn't seem to be the case here, though. Knopf had accidentally wandered into the middle of the fighting, and while he was ducking and dodging bullets like some kind of fool, he watched a large number of zombies break away from the main horde and circle around the ruins of a hardware store, so that they could come up from behind their robot opponents in a fairly well-executed flanking maneuver.

Knopf was shocked. Doing something like that took strategy, it took forethought, it took goal-oriented behavior. None of the game theory equations he'd put into the robots' programming could deal with behavior like that. It wasn't playing by the rules. And yet the action was undeniable. It was a wide street, with a park off to his left. There had been plenty of room for all those zombies to continue their advance. By all rights, they should have massed into the open areas, where Fisher's strategy would have turned the street into a meat grinder.

But they had deliberately turned off. They had taken themselves out of the fight in a clearly premeditated way, almost as though . . .

Another bullet hit the pavement at his feet and glanced off with a loud, high-pitched whine. Knopf blinked at the little white cloud of dust that drifted away from the impact point.

"What are you doing?" someone yelled. "Get out of the street!"

Knopf looked up. Zombies and robots were swarming all around him. The ordered lines had broken down, and everywhere he turned Troopbots were being ripped apart.

"Knopf, you idiot, get out of the street!"

Captain Fisher was running at him, a pistol in his hand. He looked angry, white flecks of spit flying from his lips, the white scar across his chin almost completely obscured by the dirt and mud and blood on his face.

"Get out of the street!"

The next instant Fisher was on him, grabbing him by the sleeve, pulling him towards the corner of a red brick building. Then he slammed him against the wall.

"What the hell are you doing?" he demanded.

"Those zombies are using strategy, captain. Something's guiding them—"

But Fisher wasn't listening. His attention was already back on the street, eyes darting from one corner of the battle to the other.

"We're pulling out," he yelled. "I'm ordering us out of this town. Get yourself ready to move out."

"Wait," Knopf said. "What? No, you can't."

"I can, doctor, and I am. We are leaving!"

"But Jimmy . . . he's still out there somewhere. We have to find him."

"Like hell we do. He ran off. He's dead."

"You don't know that!"

"I know this experiment of yours has failed, doctor," Fisher said. He emphasized his point by jamming a finger into Knopf's chest. "You're done. You and this whole ridiculous experiment—you're done! This is over. My only concern right now is to salvage what's left of my command. Now get yourself ready. We are leaving."

And with that he stormed off, yelling for his human soldiers to fall back.

13

Jimmy hit the street running.

Behind him, the front of the building he'd just escaped exploded, the force of it knocking him onto his hands and knees. He glanced back in time to see the Warbot erupting into the street, crouching like a bird, furniture and bits of rubble tumbling out all around its feet.

From atop the thing's shoulders, with the cold, hard light of insanity in his eyes, Jimmy's father leered at him.

"Oh, God," Jimmy said.

He pulled to his feet and started to run again.

But he only made it a few feet before he stopped. Ahead of him, zombies staggered out of alleyways and out of buildings. At first there were only five, then eight, then more. He turned to his left and saw the side street there filling up with more of the living dead.

It dawned on him then what was happening. The zombies closing in on him . . . the things his father had said down in the sewers . . . the fact that all the town's zombies had retreated into the sewers, as though waiting for something . . . his father was controlling them, steering them towards this spot. Jimmy could feel the force of his father's thoughts moving around him like the current in a river, but gaining in strength. Now that he was out of the sewers he was growing more powerful every second.

What am I supposed to do?

Jimmy stretched his thoughts, trying to connect with the Combot.

And then, a connection.

Help me, Comm Six. Where do I go?

There is a building to your right. Run through there. Hurry.

Jimmy turned. The building was made of red brick, the windows empty and dark. He sprinted towards it just as the Warbot reached for him, its enormous machine-gun arms missing him by inches. Jimmy jumped through one of the empty display windows and hurried through the shop toward the back.

Go out the back door. When you reach the alley, turn right. I will guide you.

Jimmy did as he was told. The shop was crowded with trash and bits of the tile and insulation where the roof had collapsed, but he threaded his way through it and out the back door.

He found himself in a narrow alley between low buildings. Looking to his left he saw zombies turning the corner. To his right, the way looked clear.

Go. Hurry.

His father's Warbot had already started smashing its way through the shop and Jimmy knew he only had a few precious seconds. He ran for the end of the alleyway, rounded the corner, and kept on running.

The next corner is Tanner Street. Turn left there. You will see a movie theater at the end of the street. But you must hurry. The humans are leaving.

Leaving? What? No. Stop them.

I cannot. But you can.

Me? How?

With your mind. Reach out. Find one of the humans and enter his mind. Hurry. The Warbot is coming. Do it as you run.

Jimmy rounded the corner onto Tanner Street. He could hear his father's Warbot back there, wrecking everything in sight.

Focusing his mind, he tried to picture Dr. Knopf, to remember the sound of his voice, the shape of his face.

Dr. Knopf.

Something clicked for Jimmy then. He could feel the connection when it happened, like toy blocks snapping together. Dr. Knopf was confused and frightened by the contact. Jimmy could sense his fear, and feel him trying to pull his mind back and break the contact. He could picture Knopf standing perfectly still, his back rigid, Adam's apple pumping up and down like a cylinder, much as Jimmy had done when his father first made contact with him.

Dr. Knopf, I need help.

Jimmy, you're alive! Where are you?

There was no time to explain. Instead, Jimmy pushed his thoughts into Dr. Knopf's mind, showing him everything he had seen and heard since coming to Mill Valley. He wasn't even sure if it would work, but he sensed it would, and so he pushed.

Doctor?

Silence.

Dr. Knopf, I need you!

Oh, you poor boy. Jimmy, I'm so sorry. I had no idea.

Help me!

Zombies were moving through the smoke ahead of him. Now that he was free of the sewers he could sense them.

They were facing away from him, and Jimmy sprinted right for them. With luck, he'd get past them before they knew he was there.

But then, all at once, the dead stopped their attack on the

retreating Troopbots and turned to face Jimmy. Several of them lunged forward, reaching for him.

It happened so fast Jimmy barely had time to adjust.

He veered to his left, shooting a gap between them just as his father's Warbot reached down to scoop him up. Instead of pinning Jimmy, it flattened one of the zombies.

Jimmy didn't slow down. He ran right into the thick of where the battle had been. He was in no-man's-land now, midway between the retreating Troopbots on the one side and the zombies and his father's Warbot on the other.

Jimmy looked back just as the Warbot crashed through the zombie horde, trampling some and throwing others out of the way. Still carrying his father atop its shoulders, the Warbot stepped slowly into the intersection. They were close now, less than twenty feet between them, the Warbot towering over Jimmy. His father's badly decomposed face was incapable of expression, but Jimmy could still sense the madness, the betrayal, the rage emanating from the man's mind.

Jimmy met his stare without blinking, and at the same time realized he was feeling exactly the same thing, betrayal and rage. The thought scared him, and for a moment, Jimmy felt his resolve waver. This was his father, after all. The man had done nothing but hurt him. And yet, angry as Jimmy was, a part of him wanted to love the man . . . needed the man's approbation. But the scariest thought of all, the one Jimmy couldn't get around, was that maybe they weren't so very different, father and son. Maybe there was nothing but a fine line between them. Maybe Jimmy was just a gentle shove away from being exactly like him.

"No," Jimmy said suddenly. "I won't join you. I won't."

Maybe there was just a fine line between them, but the line was there. He looked up at the horror that his father had become and he was suddenly, absolutely, irrevocably sure.

That zombie up there was not what he wanted to be. Jimmy was more than that.

"Go on and do it, if you can," he told his father.

The Warbot straightened then. Jimmy could see it gathering itself for the final, crushing blow, like stomping out a bug, and he tensed to leap out of the way. But as the Warbot's leg rose in the air, Jimmy saw a flash of movement off to his left. A second Warbot, this one bearing the insignia of Fisher's expeditionary force, smashed into his father's Warbot and both robots went tumbling into the side of a building, knocking down the brick wall there.

The expeditionary robot stood up first. It backed away from the collapsed storefront, and right before it started firing, Jimmy caught a glimpse of his father's Warbot inside, its enormous Tyrannosaurus legs bent up in front of it like a man who has fallen into a low, deep couch.

And then the shooting started.

The expeditionary Warbot fired both its .50 caliber machine guns, the bullets glancing off the other Warbot's armor plating, but doing little harm. His father's Warbot pulled itself loose from the wall and charged its opponent, and when they hit, it felt like the ground was splitting open beneath Jimmy's feet.

Their great weight tore up the pavement. Every step sent bits of rock and vast quantities of dust into the air, and within moments, Jimmy couldn't tell the difference between the two. He could only marvel at the destruction they caused. They threw each other into the air and into the sides of buildings. The zombies swarming around their legs were crushed like bugs. Both robots were firing their machine guns continuously now, and the noise grew so loud Jimmy fell to the ground behind a pile of rubble, his hands clapped over his ears.

Jimmy had no idea how long the fight went on, but gradually, the guns fell silent.

And when the sound stopped altogether, and Jimmy looked over the pile of rubble he'd hid behind, he saw one of the Warbots tangled up in a collapsed wall, wrapped in metal cables, one of its cannon arms missing. It tried to step out of the wall, but one of its legs wasn't working, and all it managed to do was fall face-first onto the pavement.

The other Warbot was in two large pieces, electrical cables and wires oozing out of its severed parts like guts. Neither machine was going to be getting up again. Jimmy could see that plain enough. And when he searched them with his mind, he could tell the one was dead, and the other, the one facedown on the street, was shutting down.

But there was something else.

Jimmy turned. A lone figure was limping toward him through the dust and smoke.

"Don't come any closer," Jimmy said. "I'm done with you."

His father's face was dark with blood and dust, except for the eyes, which were milky white and vacant. He raised his one good hand to Jimmy, the fingers clutching, and inched his way forward.

You can't have me! Do you hear? I'm not yours.

Jimmy scooped up a heavy chunk of asphalt and threw it at his father. It hit him in the shoulder, but he showed no reaction.

He kept coming.

Just then Jimmy felt a hand on his back. He knew who it was without having to look around.

"Step away, Jimmy," said Dr. Knopf. "I've got this."

Dr. Knopf raised a pistol and pointed it at Jimmy's father. But before he could pull the trigger, Jimmy touched his arm, guiding the weapon away.

"No," Jimmy said. "It's for me to do."

Dr. Knopf looked at the pistol, and then at Jimmy.

"Let me have it."

Knopf handed it to him without saying another word. Jimmy looked down at the pistol, so many things weighing on his mind, and then pointed it at his father.

"I'm sorry," he said. "But we're not the same. Not at all." And then he pulled the trigger.

14

Later, after the last of the zombies had been put down and the dust and smoke had cleared, Jimmy walked into the middle of the street and looked around. There was a darkened movie theater just ahead of him. He felt drawn to it.

"Jimmy?" Knopf said, coming up beside him. "You okay?"

Jimmy nodded.

"You put a lot into my mind. I guess we have a lot to talk about, don't we?"

"Yeah, I guess so."

Both of them were silent for a time, watching the movie theater.

"There's something I have to do," Jimmy said.

"What's that?"

"The Combot." Jimmy pointed to the movie theater. "Comm Six . . . it's in there."

"You're sure?"

Jimmy nodded. He was sure.

Knopf looked around uncomfortably. He seemed uncertain, doubtful. "I don't . . ." he said. "Stand back for a second, okay? Let me send in a Troopbot first."

Jimmy looked at him, but said nothing.

Knopf grabbed the first Troopbot he saw and pointed it towards the movie theater. After he'd explained what he wanted done, the robot marched inside, weapon at the ready.

Jimmy and Knopf waited, listening.

Several human soldiers stood nearby, looking on curiously.

About a minute later, a single gunshot sounded from somewhere deep in the recesses of the theater.

"One female zombie neutralized," the Troopbot announced over the walkie-talkie.

Knopf motioned to one of the human soldiers, who nodded back and went inside the theater to check it out.

When he came back out, he was holding something in his right hand.

He walked up to Knopf and handed it to him. A photograph. Black-and-white. Dirty with grime and creased where it had been crumpled and wrinkled over the years. It showed a little boy, about two, smiling, still a lot of the baby he once was in his chubby face, playing with a toy truck on a kitchen floor.

"That was pinned to the zombie's shirt," the soldier said, nodding at the photograph. "There was nothing else in there."

"Thank you," Knopf said.

He stared at the picture, lost in his memories of a boy he had once hated, but had grown to love as though he was his own son.

"What is it?" Jimmy asked.

Knopf handed him the photograph. "It's you," he said.

"Me?" Jimmy swallowed, his attention shifting from Knopf to the entrance to the movie theater. "But, Comm Six . . ."

"I'm afraid so," Knopf said. "I'm sorry, Jimmy."

Jimmy nodded, his mouth pressed into a thin, tight line. Then he slid the picture into his pocket.

"Dr. Knopf, I'm done. I want you to know that. I'm done. I don't want to do this anymore. No more experiments."

Knopf put his arm around Jimmy's shoulder. His touch was warm, kind, accepting.

"Come on," he said. "Let me take you home."

"I'm not going back to the lab."

"No," Knopf said. "I know that. I'm taking you home."

Resurrecting Mindy

The big Christmas tree in front of the Dayton Mall had fallen down sometime during the last year. Kevin's gaze drifted over the faded tinsel and mud-encrusted ornaments and wondered when that had happened. Probably during the rains back in early September. Those were bad. A lot of the area had flooded, and the winds that came with the rains must have done that damage to the tree as well.

Of course, he really didn't know for sure.

And, really, when it came right to it, he didn't care.

The only time he ever came back here anymore was at Christmastime. The world had ended three years before, just before Christmas, and the inside of the Dayton Mall still had a lot of decorations hanging from the common areas and inside the shop windows. Every year right around this time he made the trek back to the mall and scavenged whatever he could carry to decorate wherever he was living at the moment. These days, it had become a ritual, just like keeping up his calendar, and keeping his hair trimmed, and making sure his food stores were well stocked. The rituals, in fact, were about the only things that kept his morale up anymore.

And God knows there was enough to feel depressed about.

There was a sort of soul-sucking loneliness that came with being the last man left alive.

It made him wonder if there was any reason to keep going. After all, did it matter *when* he died? Tomorrow, or thirty years from now, the results would be the same. After he was finished, humanity was finished. Wasn't he just postponing the inevitable?

Could be. But he wasn't quite ready to throw in the towel just yet.

For now, he had a mission.

Kevin got down on his belly so he could squeeze between the front tandems of an eighteen-wheeler. From there, he watched the parking lot, figuring out a safe route over to the doors.

It actually didn't look like it'd be very difficult this year. The zombie hordes that had swarmed the area in years past had thinned quite a bit. He didn't know if the majority of them had moved on or decayed away to the point they couldn't move anymore. Maybe they'd started to eat each other. Who the hell knew?

He supposed it didn't really matter.

Fewer zombies meant it was easier to stay alive, and that was all that mattered.

There were fewer than fifty of them out there walking the parking lot now, and it didn't take long for a wide gap to open up in the crowd. Kevin tensed, ready to run. Another few seconds and it would be wide enough for him to go.

And that's when he saw her.

Mindy Matheson.

Holy shit, he thought. He stared at her for a long moment, watching her curious, clumsy movements. That really was her. That's Mindy Matheson.

And she's faking it.

* * *

It had been a while since he'd seen a faker.

Most didn't last long. Right after the outbreak, Kevin and some of the other survivors he'd hung out with back then had seen one or two a week. The fakers tried to make themselves look like zombies. They smelled like zombies, moved like zombies, had flies swarming around their eyes and mouths like zombies. But they weren't zombies, and sooner or later, they messed up. They slipped out of character for just a second.

And that was all it took.

One tiny slip, one momentary distraction, and the zombies they moved with swarmed them.

Usually, at least as far as Kevin was concerned, it wasn't much of a loss.

The only reason a person ever decided to fake it was because they had given up on their humanity. Surviving among the ruins of what the world had once been was hard. It sucked, in fact. In order to survive, in order to stay sane, you had to work at it. Every day was a fight. Every breath was bought with tears and sweat and loneliness. And sometimes, living free didn't seem much of a payback.

The fakers couldn't hack it. The world they'd lived in, believed in, trusted, had collapsed. Many had made weapons, built strongholds, fought bravely, but in the end, their spirit of resistance had collapsed. Everything had collapsed, leaving them alone, scared, miserably vacant of purpose. They looked at the world and saw ruins; they saw emptiness; they saw a pointless future without faith, without hope, without meaning. They accepted that this was the end, and that going on with this world didn't matter anymore.

But they didn't have the courage to end it all either.

They were the real walking dead, not the zombies, and Kevin had never felt anything but disgust for them.

Until now, of course.

He and Mindy Matheson, they'd dated right after high school. She'd never said two words to him during school. Neither one of them had been all that popular, but it had been a big school, and she had her friends and he had his. But afterwards, when they found they were working at the Home Depot together, neither one of them with the foggiest notion of what they were going to do with their lives, they sort of fell together.

For about eight months.

They didn't end on an obvious note. No cheating, no fighting, nothing like that. They just drifted apart. At the time he'd figured they just weren't right for each other. That explained why they hadn't noticed each other back in school. What happened while they were working together was just the natural gravity of two lonely people. And so, just as their orbits brought them together, those same orbits carried them apart. She grew distant, he grew irritable. She stopped calling, he stopped caring. Soon they were basically strangers again. The brief interlude was forgotten, and the two of them went back to their lives of uncertainty and quiet desperation.

He found it funny that the world had changed so much, and yet he and Mindy had changed so little. It made him laugh, the way the two of them were still living their half-lives, midway between life and death.

But he laughed louder than he wanted to, and she had heard him. He saw her cock her head to one side. She turned toward the truck where he was hiding, her shifting, searching gaze the only thing that separated her from the wandering corpses nearby.

Kevin whistled faintly, just loud enough for her to hear.

She staggered forward.

For a moment, he thought of running away from there. What did he think he was doing anyway? What could he do?

It wasn't like they were going to run off together or anything. Not now. To fake it for any length of time at all, she would have had to go native in a mighty convincing kind of way.

And that she certainly had.

Kevin looked her up and down, from the stringy, matted mess that was her hair to her bare and blackened feet, and tried not to grimace at the stench that came off her. Her face was filthy, her lips cracked and flaking. Her clothes were so stained and ratty he couldn't even tell what color they had once been. Flies swarmed about her face.

But she was standing right in front of him now, watching him. She swayed drunkenly, her mouth hanging open slightly. He wanted to hate her, but her eyes were overly bright, pregnant with the suggestion of pain, and despite his loathing, he felt his heart breaking out of pity.

He could, after all, still see the girl under all that grime and slathered gore. She had gotten skinny in a ghastly kind of way, but the curves, or at least the hint of them, were still in the right places. And she still had that cute little upturned nose that used to drive him wild when she smiled.

"Hi, Mindy," he said.

She just stared at him, no expression on her face.

"Hey, you know why they put fences around grave-yards?" he asked her. Kevin waited a beat. "Because people are just dying to get in."

Again, he waited.

Her expression didn't change. She just stood there, swaying.

"You heard that one, huh?"

She might have nodded, but if so, it was faint, and he couldn't be sure.

"How about this one? A guy finds out he only has twelve hours to live. He goes home to his wife, determined to live it up for his last night on earth. So they have sex, and it's great. An hour later, they do it again, and it's even better. And then, a few hours after that, he tells her he thinks they can go at it a third time. 'Easy for you to say,' she tells him. 'You don't have to wake up in the morning.' "

He beat his index fingers on the truck tire in front of him like he was firing off a rim shot. *Ba dum bum*. He smiled at her, and then the smile faded. Why in the hell was he doing this? There was no reaching this girl.

And was he really so lonely that he was talking to a faker?

But then he saw a flicker at the corner of her mouth, the faintest trace of a smile, and that brought a huge grin to his face.

"Are you doing okay, Mindy?"

The smile disappeared. He saw what looked like a tear forming in her eyes.

He almost reached up for her hand then, and had one of the real zombies not let out a moan at that very moment, he might have thrown her over his shoulder and carried her away from there.

But a few more real zombies had spotted him. Several were moaning now, staggering toward him. He'd been careless, and now it was time to go.

"I'm staying in an apartment at Woodlawn and Spruce," he said.

A zombie dropped to the pavement and started crawling under the truck toward him.

"I gotta go," he said. "Remember, it's the Bent Tree Apartments. Woodlawn and Spruce, number 318."

More zombies had gotten under the truck now. The lead one held up a mangled, handless arm, the blackened, jagged tips of its ulna and radius extending from rotten flesh.

"Gotta go," he said.

* * *

Several days later, with Christmas right around the corner, Kevin was putting up ornaments on a fake tree. There was a Hallmark in the Dayton Mall and he'd made good use of the Snoopy ornaments piled on the floor. Growing up, his mom had waited out front of the local Hallmark in order to scoop up whatever was new that year. At the time, he'd thought it was a stupid tradition. But they're collector's items, she'd said. Or they will be. Which, to his way of looking at it, hadn't made it any less stupid.

But now, hanging the Snoopy with the little typewriter and Snoopy as a World War I ace ornaments on his tree, he sensed a surge of painful memories trying to surface.

Christ, he thought. He didn't need this. Not now.

He heard moaning coming through an open window and he jumped to his feet to take a look. There was no point in it, really. The zombies keyed off of what they saw and heard. Those were about the only two senses that seemed to work, and as long as he stayed out of sight and kept quiet, his little hiding spot up in this third floor apartment was as safe as any spot on Earth.

But he crossed to the window anyway because checking out the zombies was a way to stay busy, and staying busy kept him from his memories.

And that's when he saw Mindy Matheson for the second time.

Her group had wandered from the mall over to here, probably in search of the pack of wild dogs Kevin had heard baying in the night the last few days. This zombie herd wasn't especially large. He counted about thirty, though there were almost certainly a few more somewhere out of sight. They wouldn't be much of a threat when he needed to go out, but even still, there were enough of them that they would probably be sticking around for a few days at least. They hunted collectively, he'd discovered, so the bigger groups tended to stay in one place longer.

Just as well, Kevin thought. It would give him a chance to talk with Mindy again.

He slid out the window and into the chilly evening air. It looked like it would probably rain later. There was a ledge just below his window that led over to another building's roof. From there, he climbed onto a billboard that looked down on the intersection, where Mindy and the others were wandering around, moaning.

He kept a can of spray paint up here, just in case.

He gave it a shake and wrote:

HEY MINDY! I'M IN 318 OVER TO YOUR RIGHT.
COME ON UP.

He'd gathered quite a crowd. At a glance, he noticed that he'd underestimated the size of the group by at least half, probably more. Their mangled, upturned faces and ruined hands were all pointed at him, their moans taking on an urgent, pulsing quality that he had come to think of as their feeding call. He saw quite a few of them down there.

But Mindy wasn't with them. She was drifting away from the group, stepping back toward a screen of shrubs at the far side of the intersection while the others surged forward.

"Good girl," he muttered.

Moving quickly, he went back to his apartment. The zombies wouldn't be able to follow, and besides, he had some quick cleaning up to do.

She wouldn't sit down.

He offered her a place on his couch, at his table, on the floor. She just shook her head every time he offered.

Kevin tried small talk, but she wouldn't answer any of his questions, and after a while, he began to feel foolish and stupid, like he was wasting both their time. He jammed his hands into his pockets and looked around the room for some glimmer of inspiration.

Nothing.

"So," he said. "You know what they call a fast-moving zombie?" He waited a beat, hoping for another of her half smiles. "A zoombie."

She just stared at him, and the cold, lifeless emptiness there sent a chill through him.

"How about a hockey-playing zombie?" he said, forcing a grin. "A zombonie. What do you think, huh? I got a million of them. How about this? A zombie, an Irish priest, and a rabbi walk into a bar—"

"This was a mistake," she said. "Coming here. I'm sorry."

She spoke quietly, her voice cracked and hoarse, as though she'd almost forgotten how to use it.

"I'm going, Kevin."

"What? No."

He took a step toward her, but stopped when the smell hit him.

He tried not to let his surprise and his disgust show on his face, though it probably did anyway.

"Please, Mindy, don't. It's Christmas."

She didn't answer. But she didn't turn to leave either.

"I've got some food. Are you hungry?"

She nodded immediately.

He went into the little kitchenette and slid a cube of Spam out of a can. He cut it into four big slices, then handed her the plate.

"I'm sorry I don't have—"

Mindy snatched it from his hands.

She ate with her fingers, jamming the meat into her mouth, barely chewing. Several times she nearly choked. Bits and pieces fell from the corners of her mouth.

She stopped eating only once, long enough to look at him over her plate.

"Don't look at me while I eat," she said, her words about as close to a snarl as any he'd ever heard a girl make. And then, more quietly, sounding damaged: "Please. Don't look at me."

He nodded. "Sure. Okay."

Kevin went to the cupboards and took down some more cans. He had Vienna sausages, some fruit cocktail, applesauce, a jar of sauerkraut. Better take this stuff out of the can, he thought, remembering the way she'd jammed her fingers into the pile of Spam. Last thing he wanted was for her to cut up her fingers on the can's sharp edges.

He went to work putting the meal onto paper plates and then setting the plates onto the table.

When he turned around, she was standing right behind him, and it startled him. He jumped.

She was staring at his neck, and the look in her eyes, the way she wet her lips with every pulse of his carotid artery, disturbed him.

"Shit," he said, trying hard—and, he thought, uselessly—to hide his unease. "You scared me."

Her gaze drifted down to the food on the table.

"Go ahead," he said. "I have tea and water, whichever you'd prefer."

She fell on the food without answering, without bothering to sit in the chair he pulled over for her, so he got her a cup of water and set it down next to her plates.

She had asked him not to watch her eat, which was okay with Kevin. The wet, slurping noises she made were enough for him to know he didn't want to watch. He went over to his couch and looked at some of the magazines he'd left there. A bunch of old *Playboys* he'd found at the used bookstore over by the mall. He gathered them up and hurriedly stuffed them under the couch, but not before catching a glimpse of the sleepy-eyed plastic blonde on the cover of the top magazine.

So much had changed, he thought sadly. So much had been lost. The good and the bad.

Eventually, Mindy's eating noises stopped.

Kevin walked over to the kitchen. Mindy was still at the table, looking around at the cupboards with a bovinelike vacuity.

"Are you still hungry?" he asked. "I have more. You can have anything I have."

She shook her head.

"More water, maybe? I can make you that tea I promised."

Again she shook her head.

A joke about Little Johnny, a bucket of nails, and a zombie hooker came to mind, but for once his internal filter was working and he cut it off before it had a chance to get out.

Instead, he let the silence linger.

She had turned to face him, and now she was swaying drunkenly, the same way she'd done in the mall parking lot. It occurred to him that she had probably internalized so much zombie behavior that, even now, when she was completely safe, she was unable to turn it off.

But the silence was murder. He had never dealt well with uncomfortable silences. It was the main reason he told so many bad jokes. Better to fill up the void with inane nonsense than let a painful silence grow.

He said, "Listen, there's no need for you to go back out there. You're welcome to stay as long as you'd like. I've got some Sterno. We could heat up some water, let you take a hot bath maybe. . . ."

All at once the tears started. One minute she was watching him, quietly and vacantly, and the next she was crying.

Big, muddy-colored tears ran down her cheeks.

"Ah, shit," he said. "Mindy, I . . . I'm sorry. What did I say . . . I—"

"I shouldn't have come," she said. "This was a mistake."

She moved hurriedly to the door. Every impulse in him told him to go after her, hold the door closed, take her in his arms.

But he didn't do it.

He just watched her go without a word

Mindy shuffled through the rain, her mind a blank.

Or at least she tried to make it a blank.

Right now, that wasn't working out so well.

It was cold—windy and rainy and cold. Her clothes were little more than rags; they offered no protection whatsoever. For too long now she'd wandered, mindless, emotionless, denying all pain and shame, a true ascetic. The rain tore at her skin like icy razors and chilled her to the bone, but she did not tremble, nor did she cry. She let her arms swing limply by her side, her fingertips grazing the ice that formed on her clothes, as she kept pace with the horde of dead things brushing against her.

Thought was the enemy, not the dead. With thought came fear, and pain, and a memory of all that was gone. If she thought too long—if she thought at all—the dead would see it in her eyes, and she wouldn't last long after that.

But the mind was like a flood. It could be contained for a while, even a long while, but it could never be truly silenced. Sooner or later, the mind would turn to the low ground and dwell there.

And right now her mind was turning toward shame.

But it wasn't the shame of what had happened to her that bothered her so.

It was that damn Kevin O'Brien.

When she was by herself, she felt no shame for what she was doing. Why should she? She was surviving. And she was doing it in the face of a universe that didn't give a rat's

ss for what happened to her. Or the rest of humanity, for
hat matter. She was surviving, damn it.

Then she thought of Kevin.

He, too, was surviving.

And he hadn't given up anything. He hadn't debased him-
elf like this. He hadn't sacrificed every last scrap of his
elf-respect just to draw another breath.

She hated him. She hated him because he was still human.
And because his charity reminded her that she was not.

Not anymore.

So she turned off her mind and wandered. Damn him.
Damn the world. Damn life. There was nothing of the world
eft for her anymore. Nothing but emptiness and the slow, re-
entless crawl of time.

One foot in front of the other.

Forever after.

The billboard came as a surprise to her.

For a moment, just a fraction of a second, she stopped.

And she stared.

She hadn't realized where she was. But up there, up above
he mindless crowd, was a message written just for her.

> HEY MINDY, IT'S COLD. COME ON UP.
> I'VE GOT A WARM BED.

A memory floated up into her mind, unbidden. The two
f them, finishing off their shift, her letting him walk her out
o the parking lot. He had a joint in his pocket and she didn't
ave anywhere to go. They went around back to the loading
lock and passed it back and forth, talking about random
hit, nothing either of them really cared about.

He was nice. A little dorky, but all right.

She could tell he was getting interested. It was in the way
he cracked his lame jokes when he should have let the quie
grow, the way his fingers twitched when they touched whenever she took the joint from him.

She could have shut it down right then. He was the scarec
type. He'd back off and nothing more would ever become of it

But she wasn't going to be doing anything else that night
or any other night for that matter, and they both knew it.

She went back to his place.

Sitting on his couch, her hand on his thigh, he actually
asked if he could kiss her. That had never happened to he
before. Most guys went straight for her tits. Or put a hand o
the back of her head and guided her down to their open fly
At best it was a wrestling match to see how long she coul
keep her pants on.

"You don't have to ask," she'd said, and eased in close to
him.

Before she knew it, they were some sort of couple.

But he wasn't wasting that kind of time now. The apoca
lypse, it seemed, had made him a little bolder.

COME ON UP. I'VE GOT A WARM BED.

Yeah, right, she thought, I bet you do.

But she'd been careless. She'd thought too long, droppec
out of character.

One of the dead ones a few feet to her right had turnec
her way, and now his dead, vacant stare was locked on her
She tried to clear her mind, to stumble forward, but the zom
bie's gaze never wavered.

He raised his hands like he was trying to take something
from her and staggered after her, a moan rising above the
wind and the cutting rain.

She pushed his hands away and looked around.

This wasn't going to work. Every moment she lingered

more and more of them turned her way. She scanned the crowd, and in the dark the only way out seemed to lead around the corner, where she had taken the stairwell once before up to his apartment.

A limp hand fell on her shoulder and that was enough.

She ran for the stairs.

She stopped in front of 318.

Had she really sunk so low? Getting torn apart by the walking dead almost seemed a joy compared to coming to him like a penitent. She'd thought she was done with guilt, with shame. But it hurt now more than ever.

Utterly demoralized, she knocked.

He couldn't sleep.

In the dark he rose and put on his boxers and went to the kitchen to light a candle.

Enough light filled the room that he could see her sleeping in his bed. The rain had washed away a good amount of dirt and grime from her body and hair, but her breath had still been enough to turn his stomach. And even in his sleep he couldn't quite hide his disgust. He had dreamt of a zombie forcing her face into the soft part of his neck, and when he awoke, he'd found her, pressing her cracked and ulcerous lips into the well beneath his chin.

Flinching awake, he'd recoiled from her, almost falling out of the bed before realizing that it was only a dream.

Now, fully awake, he watched her sleep and tried to hate her.

But he couldn't. He was feeling guilty.

Who in the hell was he to judge her, anyway? She was desperate. She was lonely. She was scared. Wasn't he all of that, and more?

In fact, the only thing he had on her was the appearance of normalcy.

But that was only appearances. The truth was he was drowning. His life was an act. His jokes, the Christmas decorations, his calendar keeping: All of it was a terrible, useless, stupid joke. He drifted from one empty apartment to the next, from one false front to the next, like a ghost blown on the wind, and he called it a life.

Were they any different, he and Mindy?

He couldn't answer, not truthfully anyway; and eventually, he blew out the candle and crept back to bed and reluctantly put an arm around her as he drifted off to sleep.

When he awoke the next morning, he was alone, the only sign she had been there a muddy stain on the sheets.

He sat on the side of the bed, asking himself why he ever bothered.

She had left him, again, and this time it was because she knew he was the one who was faking. He was the hypocrite. He was the disgusting one.

And she had found him out.

Mindy stopped in the doorway as she left Kevin's apartment building and scanned the street.

There were no dead in sight, but that didn't mean they weren't there. She'd seen it happen a few times over the last year. She'd be shuffling along with the others, absolutely nothing going on inside her head, and suddenly there'd be a scream. Another careless person had wandered into their midst, completely surprised by the sudden appearance of a zombie horde that, in reality, hadn't been trying to sneak up on anybody. Most of the group's kills were made that way, completely by accident, people caught by their own carelessness.

Without realizing it she had assumed the awkward shuffle

f the dead. Her bare feet, no longer sensitive to heat or ice
r even broken glass, slid across the cracked and weedy
avement as though on autopilot.

She tried to turn off her mind as well, but she found that
much harder.

She kept thinking of Kevin.

What, exactly, had happened last night?

Not *what*. Not really. She knew *what* had happened. That
ad actually been quite pleasant. Better than she remem-
ered it, anyway.

No, what she really wanted to know was *why*. And why
ow? She'd seen others before him. She knew they weren't
he only ones. She suspected—and she believed this without
eservation—that there were more normal people out there
han she'd seen. There had to be. The world couldn't simply
e empty. That wasn't possible.

But none of the others had managed to arouse her pity.
he'd watched them die, and in some cases rise again, and
he'd felt nothing.

And then . . . Kevin.

He'd told her his stupid jokes. He'd offered her a place to
tay, all the food he had, even a warm bath. In the few days
ince she'd first seen him she hadn't been able to stop think-
ng about him. Before him, walking around being dead was
o trouble at all. She could go days at a time without a single
hought passing through her mind. The world was one un-
nding parade of nothingness.

And then he came along, and she couldn't take three
teps without falling out of character, without thinking of
he life they'd once shared.

That's what it was, she told herself. He was a window to
he world that used to be, a shipwreck from her past that had
ysteriously surfaced to haunt her mind. There was nothing
ore to it than that. He was nothing but a ghost, and she was
erely lonely.

But a voice at the back of her mind kept prodding, questioning.

What if this was more than just two people feeling lonely and desperate at the end of the world?

What if this was . . . love?

Maybe, she thought. It was Christmas Day, after all. Christmas had a way of warming even the coldest heart.

Wasn't that the secret to Scrooge's redemption? She'd never paid much attention to books in school, but she thought she remembered that much. For Scrooge, it hadn't been fear of the grave, but fear that the heart would no longer love again that made it possible for him to accept the spirit of Christmas into his life.

She stopped then, a sudden alarm causing her pulse to quicken.

She had fallen out of character again. She'd stopped walking like the dead. Like her mind, her feet had started to wander. If she'd happened upon one of the dead while walking like that, they'd have torn her to ribbons.

But, for now, she was alone on the street.

Turning, she happened to see her reflection in a shop window. And at first, that one quick glance threatened to send her over the edge of reason. She looked horrible. In a word, she looked dead. And she played the part well. Her hair was stiff with mud and probably blood, too. Her face, which hadn't been that bad back in the day, was discolored with God knows what; attractive, it seemed, only to flies. Her body was a bony jangle of sticks. She looked like a crack whore, though she imagined that even the crack whores of the world gone by had more self-respect than she did at that moment.

She had nothing.

But then her gaze shifted beyond her reflection in the

window, to the Sexy Elf costume in the display. For a moment she experienced an odd sense of displacement. It was her face, her gaunt, exhausted face, but her body was draped in the red velvety finery of the elf costume. Her fingers reached for, and could almost feel, the cotton candy fringe at the edge of the playfully short skirt.

She smiled.

Kevin O'Brien, you wonderful bastard. I'm gonna blow your mind.

It was Christmas morning.

He had hoped to wake up late and spend the day with her, hopefully draw her out little by little. The two of them had been pretty good, he thought, back in the day. And they were certainly good last night. When they were good, it seemed, they were really good. He'd hoped it could be that way again.

But she'd left him sometime in the night.

His attempts to draw her into his world weren't fair, he supposed. Why would she want to join him anyway? Hadn't she found him out? She knew he was faking it. He knew he was faking it.

And he was tired of faking it.

The choice, once he'd given it voice, was surprisingly easy to make. The only hard part had been accepting *that* as an option. But once he opened his mind to it, it actually made a lot of sense.

He went to the billboard and spray-painted a message for her.

Then he went down to the street and climbed on top of a brick wall and waited for one of the dead to come along.

He thought he'd be scared, but for the first time in a long time, he felt relaxed, at ease with himself and the world in which he lived. You can settle in quite comfortably to even the most horrific of circumstances, he thought, given enough exposure to it. All horrors lose their immediacy, their nastiness, sooner or later. The nerves can only be slashed and cut and shredded so many times before they deaden to the pain.

No, he was far beyond horror now. What he was feeling now was far worse than that. In the time before he found her again, his world had been filled with zombies. The horror they represented was a shallow, fast-moving river that beat him down and cut him on its jagged rocks.

What he was feeling now, though, made horror seem small.

Here, in this world that suddenly included Mindy in it, the waters ran far slower, but they were deep, endlessly deep, and what lurked down there was something he could not fight.

For what lurked down there was love.

A zombie was at the base of the wall, its hands clumsily scratching at the bricks just below Kevin. Kevin stared into the thing's eyes and saw the emptiness he'd fought against for so long, but had never truly understood. That would all change now. He had tried to get Mindy to live in his world, and that had failed. So now, he would live in hers.

And only love could allow him to do that.

He jammed his left hand down into the zombie's face. It shook its head, as though to shoo away an insect, and then realized what was in front of it.

The zombie grabbed Kevin's forearm and clamped its teeth down on his wrist.

"Mother fu—"

Kevin pulled his hand away, holding his wounded wrist in his right hand while blood oozed between his fingers. It hurt so badly he nearly rolled off the top of the wall. Already he could feel the virus creeping through his bloodstream, racing for his heart. It felt like somebody was jamming a red-hot copper wire up his veins.

He didn't have much time. Maybe thirty minutes, but probably less.

Kevin rolled off the wall and trotted back to his apartment. Once inside, he washed the wound with hot water and wrapped it in a towel. It was already starting to smell like death. His head was soupy and walking to the chair in the center of the room was hard.

But he made it.

He dropped down into the chair and turned it to face the door and waited for the pain to stop.

This felt absolutely glorious.

Mindy had spent the day cleaning herself up, scouring off the stain of more than a year of living down among the dead. Now, her hair was washed and brushed. Her legs were shaved, her skin soft and fragrant from cocoa butter, still a little pink from her hot bath. The Sexy Elf costume showed a lot of leg, and a lot of bruises and cuts, but those would heal. If her heart could heal, her legs certainly would.

She felt better than she had felt in a very long time. She couldn't remember a time she'd felt this good, even before the world died. Mindy Matheson had come back from the dead, and love had done it for her.

And it was glorious.

Now, she picked her way carefully through the rubble-strewn streets. The dead were out—the dead were always out—but there weren't many of them around at the moment.

Then she saw the sign, and she smiled.

IT'S ALL FOR YOU, MINDY MATHESON.
I LOVE YOU.
I WANT TO BE WITH YOU FOREVER.

She couldn't hold herself back any longer. She sprinted up the stairs and down the hall to his door.

Slightly out of breath, she knocked on the door.

No response.

Maybe he was out getting stuff, she thought. More candles, maybe. Or, God help her, even a bottle of wine. Wouldn't that be great? And heaven help him if he got her drunk. She'd make his toes curl for sure.

With a huge grin on her face she turned the knob and swung the door in slowly.

"Kevin?"

Bury My Heart
at Marvin Gardens

Jon rolls double fours. He lifts his marker, the old shoe, his favorite, from GO and drops it onto . . .

. . . Vermont Avenue, where the zombies are drifting thick as fog through the cracked and weedy streets, picking their way through the rusting hulks of abandoned cars, searching, always searching, for food. The mother catches sight of one in particular, broken arms swinging limply at his sides, ribs showing through tatters of decomposing flesh, flies swarming about its head, and she's worried. She's seen these before, the wounded ones. The ones that can get around more or less on their own power are predictable. They come straight for you, attack without strategy. But the wounded ones, like this one, are far more dangerous. They hide. They wait. They become part of this desiccated world, one of its hidden dangers. She knows if she loses sight of it, it will surface again when she least expects it.

She sets the wheelbarrow down quietly and finds her daughter's hand. She gives the girl's hand a squeeze, just to let her know everything is going to be okay. She doesn't believe this, but she knows she has to be strong, for the child's sake, and so she squeezes encouragement.

The little girl meets her mother's gaze and smiles. It's a pretty smile, lots of healthy teeth. She's a pretty girl, too good for this world.

The mother surveys their surroundings and shudders. Everywhere she looks she sees a world in ruins. So many buildings have been reduced to rubble. But where the walls still stand, she sees exposed lath and standing garbage and doorways without doors. Not a window has gone unbroken. A sign that reads PEDESTRIAN CROSSING has been bent over and nearly flattened by an out-of-control vehicle, which still rests within the ruins of a dress shop, busted glass all around it, catching the oranges and scarlet reds of morning light like an explosion frozen in time. Inside the car is a corpse, motionless and decomposed, but probably only dormant. Given a reason, it could walk again.

In the wheelbarrow is the body of the woman's dead husband. The woman, on the night the man died, went to great trouble jamming an ice pick up the dead man's nose to make sure he wouldn't come back as one of them. It was an agreement between them, something she never wanted to think about, let alone do, but did anyway when the time came because she loved the man with a love so deep it made her ache inside. She still aches. She aches all the time. Even when she's numb, she aches. She's told the daughter none of this and has no intention of doing so. She's told the girl only of the dead man's enigmatic wish to have his heart buried at Marvin Gardens; though now, as she looks around at the wasted landscape that is Atlantic City, and watches as the dead man with the broken arms and the flies swarming about his head wanders off, she wonders why.

Why this place?

* * *

Jon buys Vermont Avenue. At $100, it's a no-brainer. The cheap properties on the first leg of the square are good buys. Purchase cheap, build hotels, gouge your opponent later. They are investments in the future. It is the strategy of a man who thinks long thoughts, who goes deep into the future of things.

That's Jon, the studied approach. The logical approach.

I am different. I am the wild scramble opponent, the one who buys, buys, buys, and worries about building hotels later, once I see what I've got to work with.

We have never decided who is right, Jon and I.

He rolls a puny two-one combo, but it is enough to skip over Jail and land him at . . .

. . . St. Charles Place, where the weeds grow up through the sidewalks and the streets have buckled and blistered in the endless cycle of seasons since the world gave way to zombies.

There are no apartments here, no casinos, no hotels. This is an urban wasteland of vacant lots and mounds of trash and the occasional dog sniffing out a rat among the piles of lumber and brick dotting the landscape.

Nothing of any substance grows here.

Only grass and weeds.

And the woman carrying the wheelbarrow and the mysteries of good men dead and the little girl with her hand clasped tightly around her belt can only stare around in wonder and confusion and bootless anger at the injustice of it all.

Why here? she asks the corpse in front of her.

Why, for the love of God, here?

* * *

The game is just part of the reason I've asked Jon over here. I'm a little worried about my kids. They fight with each other constantly. Jon, he's a wizard at things like this. The man has a way of getting to the heart of things. He's made it his life's work, understanding people, and especially kids.

It's nothing serious, I tell him, nothing bad. They don't do drugs. They don't try to hurt themselves. Nothing like that.

"They're just little kids," I say. "I know that. But damn it, they fight like two little beta fish. Put 'em next to each other and the next thing you know they're trying to claw each other's eyes out."

"Exactly," Jon says, and meets my questioning gaze and won't look away.

"Huh?" I say.

"Exactly," he repeats. "It's nothing like that."

I shake my head. I know he's parroting what I've just said, like any good psychologist, but I don't understand.

"It's nothing like that," he repeats. "Not at all. They're good girls. They're your girls, part of you. They love you, and you love them."

"Yes . . . ?" I agree, but with the hope that he'll explain more.

"Remember that. Even when you're mad. Even when you feel like you're not getting through. They are part of you and you are part of them. You may not think you're getting through, but you're imprinting yourself on them. Years from now, they won't remember why they fought, or even that they fought at all, but they will remember you. It's pretty simple, when you boil it down to what really matters."

I don't have an immediate response. It's true, every word. Everything he's said is right on the money. But it's a hard thing to remember when you're mad.

"It's your turn," I say.

* * *

On Illinois Avenue the mother has to move quickly.

Screams, the sound of fighting, fill the air.

She pushes the wheelbarrow between two ruined cars and pulls her child underneath the lead vehicle. From their hiding spot, they can see the street, smell the tinge of death on the morning breeze.

Soon the screams of rage and desperation turn to panic.

Whoever they are about to meet is close.

Very close.

A young woman, her left arm limp at her side and blood running down her body, runs into the street. Three men, zombies, stagger out of an alley behind her. These men have fresh blood running from their mouths and the mother knows they have just fed. They'll be strong. But they'll also be focused on the young woman.

The mother's heart is a good one, and it's telling her to go help the woman.

But she's smart, and her head is telling her to stay down, stay quiet, keep the child quiet. She has responsibilities, and they extend far beyond this moment.

The child whimpers as the zombies fall upon the woman.

The young woman's screams seem louder than any human could possibly make, and they go on and on and on. The mother can only put her face in the dust and hold her baby and tell herself that there must be a reason, there has to be a reason.

Or else nothing in life makes sense.

And it has to make sense.

It has to.

Jon buys Illinois Avenue for $240, looks at me, and smiles.

"You bastard," I say. He has just secured two-thirds of the board.

He raises his eyebrow, like Spock, only it's not a casual sign of surprise that the universe is not as logical as it should be, but a smug, self-satisfied gesture that denotes imminent victory.

He knows he has me.

"You bastard," I say.

"Your turn," he says.

Jon has me over a barrel. He has both Boardwalk and Park Place, and I have surprisingly little. Not for the first time I wonder about the fickleness of luck.

"Damn it," I say. "I surrender."

He nods. He's not above enjoying a victory.

"A pity, though," he says.

"What?"

He nods at the board. "Nobody got Marvin Gardens. I've always wondered about that place."

The mother has studied this place, she knows the history of Illinois Avenue, because this isn't the first time she's wondered about her husband's fascination with Atlantic City. She knows how the city started as a dream, a conversation among wealthy investors and railroad tycoons on a lonely, windswept beach, and how it ended as a nightmare.

Like the rest of the world.

Like her own life.

She knows that the city died long before the rest of the world fell beneath the relentless tread of the walking dead. The zombies are really only an afterthought to this place. They are the symbols of a world that has moved on, but they are redundant here. This place needs no reminder of the glory of the past, or of the wasteland that is the modern age.

She looks down at the body in the wheelbarrow, the man

whose eyes had shown such surprise, such fear, such un-knowable depth, at the time of his passing, and which were now closed against all time, and she wondered what was in his mind when he asked to be buried at Marvin Gardens.

Did he see the old-world splendor that R. B. Osborne saw back in 1852 when he glibly described his vision to his in-vestors, his pen scribbling out the names of the streets to be—Oriental Avenue, States Avenue, Tennessee Avenue, New York Avenue, Pennsylvania Avenue. Or did he see the world of Charles B. Darrow, who stole the game of Monopoly from Lizzie Magie, daughter of the prophet of the single tax theory?

It is hard to tell, for her husband, who was so kind, so in-telligent, so impossibly giving, was also—sometimes frus-tratingly so—an enigma to her.

She looks at the only map of the city she has, an old Mo-nopoly game board, and doesn't understand. She wonders if she ever will.

Why this place?

Why would he want his heart buried at Marvin Gardens?

The crowd of zombies seems to materialize out of nowhere. One moment, the mother is putting on her brave face for her daughter, telling her how they are going to bury Daddy in his favorite place, and the next she is ducking for cover, pulling her daughter close to her breast.

She'd been forced to leave the wheelbarrow out in the open, and that made her mad. It seemed like a failure some-how, like leaving him was a weakness on her part, something she didn't do right. But the zombies don't like dead flesh. They rarely touch a corpse, even a fresh one, and so it's a chance she feels she can take.

The zombies pass the wheelbarrow by. They hardly seem to notice it. One by one, they shuffle past it, dragging their feet, pulling their weight endlessly through a world without meaning, without purpose, without even the hint of redemption. Even the grave is an empty promise for these dead ones.

Then one of the zombies stumbles—and howls in pain.

Mother and daughter raise their heads above the tall weeds where they've taken shelter, searching for the injured one.

Zombies don't make noises like that.

They damage themselves all the time, tearing hands and arms reaching through shattered windows, shredding bare feet on busted glass, and then they get up and walk away. Soundlessly. No emotion, no pain, no nothing.

But this one . . . he is standing up, holding his bleeding wrist in his other hand.

One by one, the dead turn their heads slowly in his direction.

Faker, the mother thought, and pushed her daughter's head back down into the tall weeds. She has seen these fakers before. They live by pretending they are one of the dead, by walking among the dead. They live, if it can be called living, by abandoning all sense of self, by surrendering completely to the emptiness and pointlessness that is death in life, death on two feet. They live by giving up.

Her husband hated these people.

She looks down at his corpse, the runner of dried blood eking from his left nostril where she drove in the ice pick to keep him from coming back as a zombie, and she sees a man who lived his life like every moment mattered, who understood the importance of his life, even if he didn't fully grasp its meaning. His life stood for something, and his death was painful, and too soon, for the truly good are always gone too soon.

She looks again to the street. Already the zombies are closing in around the faker, moaning, clutching at the air in anticipation of the kill to come, and she feels nothing but disgust. Her husband never would have given up like that. Never.

She watches the man sink to his knees. She watches him drop his head to his chest rather than lash out with the last breath he has. The mother cradles the child's head in her hands, covering her eyes. But she herself does not look away, because what's going on out there reminds her so much of how strong her husband was, and how much is gone from the world.

She doesn't like it, doesn't want to admit it, but the faker's silent acceptance of death makes her feel a powerful sense of pride in her husband.

He had been a man worth having.

Our second game has gone down smoothly, like a fine whisky.

As usual, Jon has picked up a lot of properties through his slow and studied method. But it has cost him. He has property, but little development, and he has next to no cash held in reserve.

I, on the other hand, am sitting pretty. Fat on cash.

I have three houses on Pacific Avenue, and when he lands there and counts his cash, he has no choice but to concede.

"Too bad I didn't land on Marvin Gardens," he says.

I look up as I clear the board.

"I like Marvin Gardens," he says, catching the look in my eye. "It's special."

I wait for more, but it doesn't come.

After a pause, I finish clearing the board.

The mother knows what's coming, even before she passes the jail. She can hear the zombies banging their fists against the chain-link fence. She can hear the musical clanging it makes, even over the awful moaning of the dead.

She doesn't look at them as she passes down the alley-way. They are sticking their shredded fingers through the diamond-patterned wire, surging against it, pressing against it with the combined weight of their dead bodies, but she ignores them. All she does is move her daughter to her other side, putting herself between the little girl and the hungry dead.

The little girl is brave. She doesn't shrink or break down, the way some adults the mother has seen have done. This makes her proud.

But the thing that really strokes her pride is the way the little girl hitches her backpack up onto her shoulders, looks up, and smiles.

So young, and so brave.

It's then that the zombies break through the fence. It had seemed so secure just seconds ago, but now it's leaning over into the alley like a drawbridge caught on the way down, and the dead are pouring over it, filling up the alley behind her.

And now, in front of her, too.

The mother has no choice. She gently lowers the wheel-barrow down. Even in death she can't imagine dropping him. Then, before the child can speak a word, she scoops her up into her arms and runs away, leaving the body of the man she loves in the middle of the alley.

He'll be safe.

The dead don't attack the dead. Even the newly dead seem to not exist for them. Only the living, only those with pain in their heads and love still in their hearts seem like food to them.

The mother finds a bakery with a large oven and puts her daughter in it. Deer hide their yearlings in the tall grass, she remembers from the years she lived in the Texas Hill country. Perhaps it will work now.

And some atavistic impulse seems present in the daughter as well, for she understands without words. She doesn't ask questions, but instead sinks into the darkness at the back of the oven. From the depths, her brown eyes seem to shine like jewels under halogen vapor lights. She is so vulnerable, so beautiful, so incredibly trusting.

The mother hopes she knows what she's doing.

"I'll be right back," she says. "I'm going to get Daddy."

She slips off her own backpack and removes a collapsible police baton she got from a friend during the early days of the outbreak. She snaps it open and circles back around the City Jail so she can re-enter from the other side.

When she steps back into the alley, she sees a small group of zombies gathered around her husband's corpse.

They seem uncertain, but interested, as though they just might fall upon the body. When one of them lifts her husband's hand and tries to put it in his mouth, the woman rushes in like a fury and swings at every face and hand that tries to close upon her. It's a fast job, a messy job, and she hardly registers the dull crack of flesh-covered bone, the give of skulls as they cave beneath the baton.

And when it's done, she jams the baton down on the pavement and collapses it with a sharp smack.

She looks around. Nothing else moves.

Then she picks up the wheelbarrow that holds her husband's body and carts him out of the alley.

We're thirty minutes into our third game and I have Jon handily by the throat. Pacific, North Carolina, and Pennsylvania are dull properties, never seeming to gather much action, but they are the only properties I have left without hotels and so I start to develop them.

Jon, realizing he's beat, concedes.

* * *

The woman is looking down North Carolina Avenue, into the heart of the city. It is a vast ruin of empty buildings and darkened windows. This could be a war zone, abandoned to the scavengers. It looks that bad. Roofs have fallen. Bricks are strewn about as though thrown by an explosion. But this isn't some military scar. This city, this collection of empty buildings, is the product of decay, a complex rune speaking of all things past.

Dark clouds are rolling in off the sea, turning the sky to a washed-out gray. The wind carries sand down the cracked and buckled street, lifting it like curtains dancing on the wind, and the city seems so lonely, almost sublime in its desolation. Again she wonders why his last wish has brought her here. What could he have possibly seen in this world?

He was a kind man, a caring man who knew that there is a presence moving in the background of our lives. That presence is hard to fathom, especially now, especially since her husband's death, but it is there. She can feel it. Her husband never doubted it. And because of that conviction she knows there must be a reason.

"Momma, you're all gross."

The woman looks down at her daughter, her voice surprising her out of her thoughts.

"What?"

The girl points at the spattered gore on the woman's jeans, the clumps of blood and brain left from when she fought the zombies off her husband's corpse.

She wipes her palm across her shirt, clearing away the dirt and sweat and grime before taking her daughter's hand and giving it another reassuring squeeze. "We're gonna be okay," she says, and in her soul she tries to believe it, because she has to. She needs this one truth to be real.

She takes out the game board she's been using as a map, her gaze darting back and forth between the cartoon board and the sea of ruin before her, and she's confused. Marvin Gardens must be here somewhere. According to the board, it should be right here.

We've started our fourth game. Most people think Monopoly takes forever to play, but with just two players, and a deep understanding of its finer points, you can finish off a game in less than twenty minutes and still stay soundly within the rules.

This one is going fast, and Jon's luck is getting on my nerves. He takes Boardwalk, and Park Place. He looks at me, sees me scowling, and laughs.

To lighten my mood, he asks about my writing. "More zombies?"

"Yep. And death cults, too."

"Cool."

I like discussing horror with Jon. He gets it. After reading a rough draft of my first novel he told me zombies were the perfect means to reinvent the world and all its problems. They're entirely metaphorical, more so than any other monster in fiction, and because of that, they can represent any societal issue or any personal crisis.

As I said, he gets it.

But meanwhile there is still a game to be played, and I've just landed on Ventnor Avenue, where he has four houses.

"Stop smiling," I say, and concede.

Game five is our tiebreaker. We race around the board, and I get Ventnor and Atlantic Avenues, and then Water Works. Only Marvin Gardens remains unclaimed.

Jon looks worried.

* * *

The woman stands in the shadows of a movie theater entrance, watching a death cult make its way down the street. These people she understands even less than the fakers. At least the fakers are a known quantity. Their motivation is simple. Death terrifies them so much that they're willing to embrace it in order to hold it at bay. She can understand fear. And she can understand—even though it disgusts her—why some people are willing to give up on their lives in order to keep them.

But these people, these death cults, they are a mystery.

She has heard of them in other cities. They believe that the zombies are a means to set the soul free. The zombies are prophets, they claim, and they welcome the act of getting slaughtered as though it were communion.

This cult is made up of a dozen people, walking two abreast down the street. They seem eerily content and unworried. They are happy to die.

Zombies stagger out of doorways, peel themselves away from the insides of abandoned cars, and close in on the cult.

Screams come with the killing, but they are not screams of pain. When the woman realizes this she is truly and utterly horrified. These people are in love with their own slaughter, and for them it is some kind of grotesque joy. It is spiritual. It seems vile to her, obscene somehow.

"Come on," the woman says to her daughter. She takes up the wheelbarrow again and slips away.

Jon takes his fourth railroad, but looks disappointed.

"What's wrong?" I ask. He's pulling ahead, and the tiebreaker that I thought was mine seems to be tilting in his direction.

"I want Marvin Gardens," he says. "I keep missing it."

"You said that before. What's so special about it?"

"It's the only place on the board that isn't a real location in Atlantic City."

"Really?" I look at the board. I didn't know this. I've loved this game since I was a little boy, and I never knew. "I wonder why they'd put it there if it isn't really there."

"Well, it's a mystery, isn't it?"

The woman and child have made it to the Boardwalk. The long pier extends far out into the Atlantic, which has grown irritable from the weather.

"Momma?" the girl says. "Where do we go now?"

The woman has no idea. None of this makes sense. Why would he make this request of her, and why can't she find Marvin Gardens?

Acting almost on autopilot, she pushes the wheelbarrow out to the end of the pier, and stops before a bronze plaque featuring a raised relief of Charles B. Darrow, inventor of the game of Monopoly. Briefly she considers asking Darrow where she might find Marvin Gardens, but doesn't want to scare the little girl. No need to make her think Momma's lost her mind.

A strong wind gusts off the water and shoves her roughly to one side. She staggers, and the wheelbarrow topples over, spilling out its precious cargo onto the pier.

The woman looks down at her husband sprawled there and she finally breaks down. She sits down beside him. She's so tired. She has no way of lifting him back into the wheelbarrow. Not now. Not like this. She doesn't know what to do.

She hears footsteps on the planks behind her.

The woman jumps to her feet and wheels to face the intruder, pulling her daughter behind her.

But it's an old man, not a zombie. She relaxes, but only a little. There are other dangers in the world besides the walking dead. But the man makes no move to attack. He actually looks kind. He's dressed in a full-length black coat, the collar pulled up tightly against a scarred cheek. The brim of a floppy old hat shields gray, weathered eyes.

"Let me help you," he says.

Together, they right the wheelbarrow.

There is another gust of wind and then the rain starts to fall. "We need to get under shelter," he says. He's holding his hat down on his head as he nods toward a nearby arcade. The inside is dark, but dry. "In there," he says.

She reaches for the wheelbarrow, but he puts a hand on her wrist.

"No," he says, "leave him here."

She wants to object. At first it seems like a gross disrespect of the man she loved—and still loves—with all her being. But as the rain turns to silvery sheets curling on the wind, it suddenly seems right to her, and the three of them run for the cover of the arcade.

The little girl knows the routine. They won't be going anywhere for a while, so she removes her backpack and sits on the ground and makes herself busy with the few belongings they've been able to carry with them.

"Thank you," the woman says to the man.

He nods, says nothing. The man removes his coat and hat and shakes the water from them.

"Can you help us?" the woman says. "We're trying to find Marvin Gardens."

The man looks up from his clothes and a strange smile tugs at the corners of his mouth. "There is no Marvin Gardens," he says. "Not here, anyway. Not in Atlantic City."

This floors the woman. Her first instinct is to get angry. She's been lied to, made a fool of. Why would her husband do this to her? Why would he send her on an errand like this, wandering a blasted land with only a stupid board game for a map? It doesn't make sense.

"Bubbles!"

The woman shakes her head, clearing her thoughts. Dozens

of tiny bubbles are rising from the floor, filling the air around her head. She looks down and sees her daughter clapping her hands and giggling wildly as her little bubble-making machine whirs.

One bubble in particular drifts past the woman's nose. She focuses on it, and its beauty startles her. The way it shimmers and catches the light like a diamond. It is geometric perfection. It is a delicate thing, like a flower, or a life; and it is, she realizes, the most perfect, the most beautiful thing she's ever seen.

It explodes suddenly—even over the pounding rain she swears she hears a faint, muffled pop. It's gone.

She stares at the empty air where it once floated, but she isn't seeing the air. She's actually looking inward, and backward, across the years. Images of her husband crowd her mind, and though she doesn't realize she's doing it, she's smiling, for he lives there, whole and perfect, a part of her soul that will never die.

But what of this crazy quest he's sent her on? What of that?

He knew there was no Marvin Gardens here. He had to have known. Her husband was crazy smart that way. This was deliberate. Not a cruel trick. He wasn't that kind of man.

There is a lesson here. Something she is meant to understand.

But what?

And then she thinks of the bubble, how it was beautiful, and then gone. And she thinks of this world, how it, too, was once a thing of beauty.

It dawns on her all at once, understanding swelling inside her chest like a balloon until she can barely breathe, barely contain it. He gave her an impossible quest, not because he expected her to fail, but because he knew she would succeed. She would come to this point. The old world is gone, and though the new world, the world without him, is a little emptier, it is still a place for beauty, and a place to raise the little girl who is so much like her daddy.

She looks out across the rain-swept pier, to where her husband's body faces the open ocean, unknowable in its vastness, and she thinks again of bubbles.

And smiles.